DETECTIVE OMNIBUS: 7 TO SOLVE

Adam Carter

Copyright 2018, © Adam Carter. All rights reserved. No content may be reproduced without permission of the author.

Originally published as Detective's Ex (2014), The Murder of Snowman Joe (2015), One-Way Ticket to Murder (2016), The Murder of Loyalty (2015) and The Woman Who Cried Diamonds (2016).

Cover Design by James, GoOnWrite.com

Visit: https://www.facebook.com/OperationWetFish for news, illustrations, previews and short stories.

For Paul

Also available by the same author:

Dinosaur World books:
- Excavating a Dinosaur World
- Dinosaur Fall-Girl
- Dinosaur Plague Doctor
- Ike Scarman & the Dinosaur Slavers of Ceres
- Dinosaur Prison World
- The Dinosaur That Wasn't
- Awfully Wedded Strife
- Tales of a Dinosaur Prison World
- Deities of a Dinosaur World
- Return to the Dinosaur Prison World
- Nikolina Finch & the Dinosaur Utopia
- Of Stags, Hens & Dinosaurs
- Dinosaur World Gladiator
- The Wounding Tooth
- Dinosaur World Massacre
- Dino-Racers
- Dinosaur World Unscripted
- Christmas on a Dinosaur World
- Utara the Savage

Sheriff Grizzly:
- Book 1: Sheriff Grizzly
- Book 2: The Horse Thief Honey
- Book 3: The Coyote Colt Kid
- Book 4: Joins the Circus
- Book 5: The Haunting of Athelstan Swift
- Book 6: The Santa Claws Showdown
- Book 7: The Kangaroo Claim Jumpers of Crumbling Gulch
- Book 8: Gets a Reality Check
- Book 9: Bets Against the Card Shark
- Book 10: The Hairy Walrus of Truespire Peak
- Book 11: The End
- Book 12: In the Afterlife

Knights of Torbalia gamebooks:
- The Return of the Stolen Jewel
- Into the Massacre
- March of the Demon Trees
- The Thief of Tarley Manor
- The Class War
- The Haunting of Past Wraiths
- The Hunt for the Adulterous Bard
- A Peacock in the Den of Foxes
- Attack of the Demon Trees

Jupiter's Glory:
- Book 1: The Dinosaur World
- Book 2: The Pirates and the Priests
- Book 3: The Obsidian Slavers
- Book 4: Just Passing Through

Miscellaneous gamebooks:
- Lost Treasures of a Dinosaur World (300 paragraphs)
- The Underworld Horror (300 paragraphs)
- Sheriff Grizzly: The Good, the Bad & the Grizzly
- Sheriff Grizzly: The Wild West Dungeon Adventure
- The Christmas Adventure of Sam and Klutz
- Operation WetFish: Vengeful Justice
- Jupiter's Glory: Oppression of the Press
- Dinosaur World: The Forest of Fiends

Hero Cast trilogy:
- Book 1: The Villainous Heroes
- Book 2: The Heroic Villains
- Book 3: The Forge of Heroes

Detective books:
- Who Slew Santa?
- The Curse of the Genie's Detective
- The Prostitute Butcher
- The Santa Worshippers

Dinosaur Frontier:
- Book 1: The Lightning Angel
- Book 2: Lightning Strikes Twice
- Book 3: The Law of Ceres

Operation WetFish, Vampire Detective:
- Book 1: The Power of Life and Death
- Book 2: Chasing Innocence
- Book 3: The Hunt for Charles Baronaire
- Book 4: Christmas on the Kerb
- Book 5: A Necessary Evil
- Book 6: No Comment
- Book 7: Fear and Ecstasy
- Book 8: Call of the Siren
- Book 9: Happy Families
- Book 10: A Step in the Right Direction
- Book 11: What Money Can't Buy
- Book 12: 'Tis the Season
- Book 13: The Power Trip
- Book 14: Trust and Betrayal
- Book 15: A Gathering of Minds
- Book 16: The Pain of Life
- Book 17: The Happy Place
- Book 18: The Terrible Truth of Barry Stockwell

Miscellaneous:
- Holding the Nuts
- One Week to Love: Speed Dating of the Gods
- The Trojan Ant
- Gauntlet of Daedalus
- The Faerie Contract
- Token Love
- Sleigh Ride Slaughter to Saturn

Table of contents:

Detective's Ex	9
The Murder of Snowman Joe	89
Murder While You Wait	155
One-Way Ticket to Murder	197
The Murder of Loyalty	229
The Woman Who Cried Diamonds	317
Chasing the Shadow Man	395

DETECTIVE'S EX

CHAPTER ONE

The Victim

Mr Polinski was a kindly old man, large of life both in his frame and his exaggerated moustache. He was always ready with a smile as he bagged up the groceries, always willing to listen to any town gossip but never betraying a secret by imparting too much himself. He liked to listen and he enjoyed talking more than anyone could have believed possible. He had three children – two boys and a girl – waiting for him back home, although he would never mention just where home was. He was a proud man and a decent human being.

Last week someone walked into his shop and put three bullets in him.

Everyone knew Mr Polinski and no one had a bad word to say about him. He ran one of those places I like to call "hard-working shops". You know the kind; they're all over the place. They sell every essential from bread and milk to fruit and veg; their shelves are stacked full of cans and boxes and bottles and packets. And they never close, just run a neon sign outside flashing deep into the night saying "Open 'til late" in a desperate cry to entice any wayward moths who for whatever reason are returning home so late.

I didn't see the attack of course, but I was among the crowd of people gathered outside the shop that day as they carted off Mr Polinski's body, covered with a drape so we couldn't see the mess someone had made of him. People about me were muttering, telling one another how wrong this was, shielding their little ones from having to see too much yet not thinking to just not have brought them to a crime scene to begin with. I blocked out all that noise, the murmurs which I knew wouldn't do any good. Instead I was trying to listen to what the police were saying, although it wasn't much. They had a big enough job trying to keep the crowd back and I figured they had probably been trained not to gossip at murder scenes anyway.

Then I caught sight of Detective Carl Robbins stepping through the police cordon. Carl, a tall man coming up to his fortieth birthday, was almost lost in the thick coat he was wearing, and while no one could have blamed him for that at this time of year it almost seemed too convenient, that he could pull the lapel up as he pleased in order to avoid looking at the crowd. It did nothing to disguise from me his crop of untidy hair, nor his sincere, yet always far too-serious-eyes. I called to him through the crowd, having worked my way to the front. A constable held out a hand to stop me passing the cordon, but I hadn't really intended on just running into the crime scene and ruining any chance Mr Polinski had for justice.

Carl looked over to me and for the briefest of instants it looked as though he was going to ignore me entirely, pretend I didn't even exist. But then he trotted over to me, keeping both his head and voice low. "Lauren? Lauren, what are you doing here?"

"They're saying Mr Polinski's dead," I said, not having had confirmation at the time. I didn't of course know about the three bullets, but the rumour was that someone had tried to rob the place and Mr Polinski had put up a fight. That sounded just like him and I didn't doubt it for a moment.

"You didn't just watch him get carted out?" Carl asked.

"Aren't you supposed to examine the crime scene before they remove the body?"

"And who says I haven't already done that? Maybe I like crowds of people watching me re-enter crime scenes."

I never cared for his dry humour when we were together, and I certainly wasn't going to put up with it when someone had just been shot to death. If he had even smiled when he had said any of that it might have made a little difference, but the truth was Carl Robbins seemed incapable of such a thing. I remember taking him to a comedy club one time and his expression didn't change the entire night. He'd enjoyed it, he said, but who can tell with Carl? I won't go into the reasons we split up six months ago, but suffice to say that was only one of the ways in which he was simply infuriating.

"Carl," I said in as flat a tone as I could manage considering what had happened, "just tell me what's going on."

"Tell you what's going on? No, why would I tell you what's going on?" He walked off shaking his head, and a part of me was glad because it meant I couldn't punch him in the face. The constable who had been holding me back offered a sheepish shrug and I felt like kicking him in the shin just to make me feel better. I didn't, obviously, because then I would have been arrested.

My back pocket buzzed and I stepped away from the constable to retrieve my phone. There was a message from Carl. "Mancini's restaurant. 19:00. I'm buying."

Well it actually said "Im buying" but I decided to let him off the apostrophe.

Mancini's restaurant was not a restaurant. It wasn't even called Mancini's; we only ever called it that because the guy who ran the place always seemed to wear shorts, so we could see the man's knees. Actually, when writing that down it doesn't sound anywhere near as funny as saying it out loud, but it was one of the things Carl and I both found amusing during our time together. Never one to stretch his wallet, Carl used to insist on this being what qualified for our night out. In reality it was called "Fry and Dry" and it doesn't take a genius to work out that in the main they served fish. And chips, open or closed.

I arrived shortly before seven that evening, not wanting to miss Carl, and found him just stepping out with two unwrapped parcels. He handed me one, a welcome warmth flooding through my hands, but I was more focused on Carl. He had started walking away from me and I kept pace, wondering what he was playing at.

"I shouldn't be talking about my cases," he explained without any real emotion as he stuck in his tiny wooden chip-fork and started eating, "so I'd appreciate it if we don't stand around where we could be overheard."

That made sense, and since it was him giving me the information I felt I couldn't argue over a point like that. We set into a stroll then, and I fought for something to say, something to break the ice between us. It had been a while since I'd even seen him, after all, and there was actually a part of me that did wonder what he had been doing with himself since we'd broken up. There was a large part of me which didn't give a whit, but I knew I would have to suppress that a while longer.

"So," I said without thinking, "you still seeing that blonde?"

He didn't even look my way as he methodically cut up his fish with his chip-fork. "Nope."

"She dump you too, then?"

"Oh that's right," he said without inflection, "we came here to snipe, didn't we?"

I stared into my chips but could not bring myself to apologise. Carl had made me angry even when we were together, but now we were apart it was infuriating even being with him.

"What happened to Mr Polinski?" I asked.

That was when Carl told me about the three slugs the attacker put in him. That was also the moment I entirely went off my chips.

"Mr Polinski was just a kind old man," I said, not even realising I was saying it aloud. "Who'd want to kill him? I take it this was a robbery?"

"Nothing was taken."

"So the gunman panicked?"

"In my experience when off-licence robberies go sour, the gunman doesn't stop to shoot the owner three times. When people are panicked, Lauren, they run."

I wasn't sure what he was trying to tell me, although I was hardly stupid enough to miss his implications. "You're saying whoever shot Mr Polinski intended to kill him before they even went into the shop?"

"I didn't say that. But if that's what you're seeing in this I can hardly fault your observations."

I knew what Carl was doing, but he didn't have to meet with me at all so I had no right to tell him how to talk to me. Even when we were together he would be secretive about his assignments, as though I had a direct route to the media and was desperately searching for a reason to get him fired. It was actually one of the things we split up over. That he was telling me anything at all was confusing, and I could not for the life of me work out what his angle was.

"So why are you telling me any of this?" I decided to ask him straight.

"Haven't told you anything," he said with a shrug. "The police are on the lookout for a gunman involved in a robbery gone wrong."

"You are? But you just told me ..."

He fixed solid eyes on me which made me feel about half a foot shorter. He had done that sometimes when we were together. It was one of the reasons we split up.

Actually, thinking back, there were a lot of reasons we split up.

"You may not see this on the television shows," Carl continued as though he didn't think I was especially stupid, "but detectives are like most employees. We do what we're told. And I'm told we're looking for a gunman involved in a robbery gone wrong, so that's what I'm looking for."

It clicked in my mind and I could only imagine how stupid he truly thought I was. Someone above him wanted this matter swept under the carpet; perhaps someone above him was even involved somehow. I put the possibility to him in the most delicate manner I could manage.

"What?" he asked with a genuinely furrowed brow. "No, of course no one above me is in on it. What are you ...?" He took a deep breath to calm himself and continued. "You really that stupid that you want me to spell it out for you?"

I gritted my teeth. I won't bother suggesting his constantly calling me stupid was in any way responsible for us splitting up. I think the main reason was that he was a jerk, and that about covers it all.

"We're understaffed and overrun," Carl continued. "You heard about that bank robbery last month, right?"

I had vaguely read about it in the local paper, but had not paid much attention. There had been an armed robbery and a customer had been killed.

I must have mentioned some of that aloud because Carl nodded. "That's the one. We're tied down to that and don't have time to look into this as well."

"Do you think they could be connected?"

"No. I don't need ballistics to tell me the guns used were completely different. Besides, the bank was amateur while this is too precise."

"So you *are* saying it was an intentional hit?"

Carl rubbed at his eyes with thumb and forefinger. "I'm not saying anything, Lauren. But this case will be a whole lot easier if we're looking for one man and a discarded firearm. If it was planned it means there may well be a gang involved, and that would mean more bodies being assigned to the case. The public don't know squat, so it's more convenient for all concerned if this is just a one-man job. And I doubt Polinski will be complaining much."

"Mr Polinski," I corrected without even thinking. "He always liked to be called Mr Polinski."

Carl looked at me strangely. "I don't think he cares any more, Lauren."

"So explain one thing to me," I said with narrowing eyes, "and please feel free to assume I'm an idiot."

He shrugged. That wasn't going to be difficult for him.

"What do you intend for me to do about it? Run my own investigation and solve the murder myself?"

"What? No. Why would you even ...? I want you to go to the media and tell them this was an organised killing. I want you to get more officers assigned to this case so I don't have to do everything myself."

"So you want me to ease your workload?"

"Well, yeah."

I could not believe the audacity of the man. When he had seen me in the crowd he must have thought he had struck the jackpot. Good old Lauren Corrigan, willing to bail him out of yet another scrape. I can only imagine the expression tearing across my face in that moment, because Carl looked more frightened of me than I had ever seen him look before.

"Thanks for dinner, Carl," I said, shoving my fish back at him. "Don't call me again."

Thinking back, I probably left him quite happy, seeing as he now had two dinners. Carl always was a pig. The very thought only infuriated me further.

I arrived back home probably half an hour later. It wasn't that we were half an hour from my home, but that I ended up trying to walk my anger off. Carl had never been the greatest human being in the world and could have lectured on insensitivity, but he had always been good at his job. He took it so seriously I often wondered whether he'd thought about marrying it. It was no wonder then that he had come to me because his job wasn't going too well, and not because he knew I wanted to see him. Not that I wanted to see him, I don't want you getting that impression. But I'm rambling, which is something I'm prone to when I'm angry.

Getting back to an empty flat had not bothered me at all in the previous six months, although for some reason the silence preyed on my nerves that night. As I hunted through the fridge for something to throw in the microwave I couldn't help but feel the oppression of the flat bearing down upon me. I convinced myself it was because of what had happened to Mr Polinski, that there was a part of me afraid that whoever shot him would come after me. But I knew that wasn't it. I knew my trepidation had more to do with Carl than anything else. Carl, who wanted me to do his dirty work just so he could have a few more bodies put onto his case. His cause, when I stopped to consider it, was admirable; it was just his reasoning I had a problem with. If Carl desperately wanted to bring the killer to justice, that would be something I could get behind, but that wasn't his motivation at all. Carl loved his job, lived for his job, and it killed him to think that he wasn't capable of seeing the case through. His superiors may have wanted a body in custody to satisfy the media and to make their numbers crunch, but Carl Robbins wanted the right body. It was one of the only good aspects to his character, until you stopped to remember that he didn't want the right body for any reason other than his own personal egotism.

There was some lasagne leftover in the fridge I probably should have eaten a few days before, but I gave it three minutes and it came out fine. Taking it to my living room, I turned on the television just for a little white noise and found the news. The news was, as always, filled with the morbid stories folk seem to love. Potential wars, missing teenagers, killers on the loose, and to round it all off a little mention of the football.

But then that was life. You lived, you died. They were the only two certainties: there wasn't even a certainty you were going to be born between the two.

Mr Polinski kept resurfacing in my mind. Mr Polinski who had never hurt anyone in his life. Mr Polinski who hadn't deserved to be shot three times in his own shop. I felt perhaps Carl was right after all: perhaps I should have just contacted the media and got him the attention he needed to have more people assigned to the case. It would help track Mr Polinski's killer, but it wouldn't bring the man back. It wouldn't do anything for Mr Polinski actually; in fact the only person it would help would be Carl.

So I determined not to call the media.

But I also wasn't about to let the murderer run around free as a gaol bird that wasn't in gaol. If I wasn't going to phone the media, however, I could not see any way in which I was going to help the poor man. By this time of course I already knew precisely what I intended to do; I was just trying to convince myself I hadn't reached that conclusion. During my time with Carl I had picked up on a lot of things regarding his work: tactics, skills, terminology. Carl loved his job and never shut up about it, so it wasn't as though I even learned it all on purpose. There were times when we were together that I felt I knew more about being a detective than some of the people he actually worked with.

The news descended into the weather and a stupidly attractive redhead told me there were dark clouds moving in that night. By this time I was already far away. If I solved the case myself, that would be helping Mr Polinski and would really annoy Carl in the process. If the police weren't that bothered in finding the killer, I would do so myself.

A small smile crept its way across my face as I realised this was the one thing Carl would hate me for. It wasn't the first time I'd done something intentionally to wind him up, but certainly this was going to be the greatest.

In all fairness to Carl, my sadistic streak was also one of the major reasons we split up in the first place.

CHAPTER TWO

The Landlord

There was no chance I was ever going to get a look at the crime scene, but I reasoned I should have been able to pump some answers from Carl the next time I met up with him. If he could meet me solely to get me working for him I certainly saw no reason I could not turn the tables. In the meantime my investigation needed to get underway, so the first thing I did was find out where Mr Polinski lived. For some reason I had always assumed he lived above the shop: after all, it always seemed to be open so I figured it would not have made financial sense for him to have spent much of his time anywhere else. The phone book however told me a different story. I didn't know his first name, but Polinski isn't exactly a surname one can hide well, and so it was that I found myself early next morning knocking on the door of his landlord. I should briefly mention how I obtained the name and address of his landlord, which was relatively easy. I just asked Mr Polinski's next-door neighbour and it turned out she had lived in the street for over twenty years and knew the landlord well.

Mr Polinski's landlord was named Albert Wentworth and judging from what I could see of his house the landlord business was doing rather well for him. It wasn't as though Wentworth owned a three-storey mansion with massive animals sculpted out of the hedges of his front lawn, but he clearly had a lot more money than I ever would. His driveway held two cars, while a garage promised the possibility of a third. The house itself was detached, with ivy climbing aesthetically past the windows. My flat could have fit into his house twice over with room to spare, and that was with a conservative estimate; I didn't want to depress myself too much after all.

Attached to the door was one of those old-fashioned knockers and as I slammed down the iron ring it sent a dull metallic thump through the entire house. It was impractical to have such a thing, when a doorbell worked so much better, and my first impression of Wentworth was that he was a man who liked his wealth to be seen. I had met people like him before, and they had always annoyed me. I had visions of him coming to the door in a suit, and had no idea how I was going to handle this situation if that happened.

Something shadowy appeared behind the glass and I braced myself as the door opened. The man standing before me was aged somewhere in his seventies, with wispy white hair brushed meticulously to the side. He stood straight and proud, refusing to surrender to the stick upon which he supported his weight, as though he thought it was him doing the stick a favour by giving it a job. His eyes were narrowed, his chin slightly raised as he appraised me, and there was a distinct tang of spices to his porch which very much reminded me of a certain shop currently cordoned off by the police.

"Yes?" he asked imperiously.

"Mr Wentworth? My names Lauren Corrigan. I ..." Suddenly I experienced a horrible, sinking feeling that the police had yet to even contact this man. After all, he wasn't next of kin, which meant I could well have been the one to break the news to him.

I must have trailed off longer than I had intended because he asked with narrowed eyes, "You with the papers? You think I really want to talk to the papers about this?"

So he had heard what had happened, which was something of a relief. "I'm not with the papers, Mr Wentworth. I was a friend of Mr Polinski."

"A friend?"

"Well, he had a lot of friends. I saw him almost every day."

"You mean you were one of his customers?" He was being incredibly short with me. I didn't know whether it was because he was an uptight man, whether his age was a factor or whether he was just grieving. It didn't much matter: the point was he was entirely correct.

"Mr Polinski was a good man," I said without actually answering his question. "I'm just trying to find out what happened to him."

"He was shot. Police told me that much."

"But why?"

"Attempted robbery."

"It wasn't."

He stared at me as though expecting me to say something more. I could tell in that moment Wentworth was a man of few words and that he always expected other people to fill the silence. "You know or you guessing?" he asked.

"If I was guessing I wouldn't be disturbing you, sir."

He adopted an air of being incredibly put out, but I could see that was all it was. He needed to make a show in order to justify to himself his involvement. Over his life he had clearly built up an impression to others that he did not care for anything, and that had consumed his entire being until the point that, years later, he had even begun to believe it himself. He would agree to talk with me, but he would feign annoyance at the very idea of doing so. Or at least that was my impression of him after having only met him two minutes earlier.

"You'd best come in," he said, and trundled away from the door. Stepping quickly into his home, I wiped my feet on his welcome rug as though it was a touchstone stealing all the bad vibes as I entered his domain. It was at this point that I stopped and asked myself what I thought I was doing trying to solve this murder. I wasn't a police officer, wasn't even trained as one. Yet suddenly I thought I could do their job a whole lot better than them. What if I got in the way of the proper investigation? Carl had told me he didn't have the manpower to deal with the case properly, but that didn't mean he wasn't investigating it at all. Even if they were willing to put it down to a chance shooting, they still needed to find someone to pin the blame to. Carl may have been told to hang it on anyone he could find, but knowing Carl he would also be looking for the real culprit. I could be tipping off all the suspects, or worse yet implicate myself by having had contact with all the people Carl would also be talking with.

But I was in Mr Wentworth's home by that point and had given him my name, so I had already doomed myself. While I was there I decided I might as well try to find out all I could.

Wentworth proved a cordial host, offering me tea from a pot he had freshly brewed for himself. As I sat in a chair far more comfortable than anything I would ever be able to afford I looked about his living room. It was not incredibly large, but what he had accomplished with it was impressive. There were two bookcases against one wall, filled with what appeared to be old tomes and encyclopaedia, while a writing bureau was nestled in the corner.

There were paintings on the walls, all original, none of them from artists I recognised. His furniture was minimalist, although what he did have was expensive, including the chandelier which hung in the very centre of the room. It was glass of course, not crystal, but drew the eye immediately. The room, likely the entire house, was designed to appear to be something it was not. Albert Wentworth was a man who found satisfaction in people believing he was wealthier than he was, and I had no problem with that. It was his house and I was intruding upon him; it was good enough that he had invited me in at all. But then if he didn't invite people in, no one would ever see the character he wanted them to see.

"Can I interest you in a digestive, Miss Corrigan?"

I smiled as I returned my gaze to him. Some people would have felt irked that I had spent so long looking about their living room, but Wentworth glowed with delight. "Thank you," I said as I took the proffered biscuit from the rose-etched plate. "You have a lovely house, Mr Wentworth."

"One tries one's best," he replied as he poured the tea and splashed in some milk. "Sugar?"

"No thank you," I replied sweetly, but nor do I drink my tea with milk and wondered what his reaction would be were I to point such out. He was in such high spirits as he handed me my tea that one could have been forgiven for forgetting that one of his tenants had just been brutally killed. I also noticed he wasn't being so short with me now I was stroking his ego.

"Mr Polinski was murdered." I didn't know what else to say, how to broach the subject Wentworth did not seem to have any intention of approaching. It may have been blunt, but at least I wasn't hiding anything.

"And who'd want to murder a nice man like Mr Polinski?"

"I don't know. I didn't know him too well. He had a family. I suppose the police are telling them."

"I would suppose they are."

"Do you know where he was from?"

"Do you?"

He knew I didn't; otherwise I wouldn't have been asking. "I could never tell from his accent," I said, "but his name sounds Russian."

"Turkey."

"He was from Turkey?"

A slight nod. "It does sound Russian, now that you mention it. But he told me he was from Turkey and I believed him."

I felt bad even sounding as though I was questioning such a thing. The man was dead: it didn't much matter where he was from. Unless of course it did. Maybe it mattered to his killer. Maybe it mattered a great deal.

"If you don't mind my asking, Miss Corrigan," Wentworth continued while my mind was busy assessing all the various possibilities with which it was getting nowhere anyway, "why are you here asking me these questions? Am I to expect the police next?"

"I'm sorry, Mr Wentworth, I realise I must be scaring you witless just turning up like this. I guess I just wanted to make sure the police got the right guy. Did you ever have any problems with Mr Polinski?" I knew I had no right to be asking this man anything but ploughed right on ahead and hoped he would answer some of my questions before booting me out on my backside.

He did not seem to mind answering anything, and I wasn't sure whether that was a good thing. "Mr Polinski was the perfect tenant, Miss Corrigan. He paid his rent on time, never complained about anything. The boiler broke one time and he was very apologetic that he had to contact me to get it sorted. He was that kind of man. Never wanted to bother anyone with what he considered little matters."

That fit with everything I knew about him. When I had spoken to Mr Polinski's neighbour earlier I had asked a couple of questions then. There did not seem to be any bad blood between Mr Polinski and anyone in the street. But it was clear someone had it in for him, otherwise they wouldn't have shot him.

"You said," Wentworth said slowly, almost carefully in fact, "that you were certain Mr Polinski's death wasn't the result of an attempted robbery."

There was no question involved in his statement, but nor did there need to be one. Wentworth was a guarded man, but being careful did not necessarily mean he was guilty of anything. I had a sudden sinking feeling that he was being so guarded because he thought I had something to do with the murder; that for some reason I was coming after him next. I could think of no way in which to ask him such a thing without putting him even more on edge so decided to just go with some of the facts.

"I have a ... friend in the police investigation." Detective Robbins was many things, but I'm not sure I could ever really have considered him a friend, even when we were living together. "It doesn't look like a robbery. He was shot too many times, no money was taken. There are too many reasons why this looks like a specific attack on the man."

"Ah, so your evidence is circumspect."

Actually it was, and I tried to work out whether he looked pleased or even relieved by this news. Or was he relieved purely because he was beginning to see that I was working with the police and not the people who had killed Mr Polinski? Or was he not looking relieved at all and I was just looking far too much into things?

I was beginning to see why I never would have made for a very good detective.

"Did Mr Polinski have any friends?" I asked.

"I thought you were his friend."

"I meant friends outside of his customers."

Wentworth thought a moment. "I didn't really know him, to be honest. I only met him a few times. But I can't say he ever mentioned any friends. He has family back home."

"Have any of them ever visited him?"

"I wouldn't know. Important thing, family. I get the impression if Polinski was involved in something illegal, perhaps his family would be better off staying where they are."

I blinked. "What do you mean?"

"Well, from what you've told me you think someone targeted Polinski on purpose, yes? I don't know about you, but I can't name anyone I've ever known who even owns a gun, much less anyone who's prepared to use one. If someone shot Polinski he must have had a reason. And if someone shot him, that shooter must have been connected enough with the wrong people to even be able to get a gun."

"So what are you suggesting Mr Polinski may have been involved in?"

"I have no idea, and I'm not suggesting anything. But what do either of us really know about him? Maybe he was dealing drugs under the counter or something."

"I've seen him demand ID from middle-aged people trying to buy cigarettes."

Wentworth shrugged. "Like I said, I really didn't know the man all that well. Maybe neither of us did."

It was a fair point, and I found any argument I might have given would have sounded false. I liked Mr Polinski, but that didn't mean for one moment I knew anything about him. However, I could find no common ground in the man I had known with the man whose image Wentworth was painting. The clever thing at that point would have been to take a step back and allow the police to do their job. At the very least Carl would investigate and uncover a portion of the truth. Maybe Carl's suggestion was a good one: maybe I should have gone directly to the media and get them to create enough of a noise to get the police to solve the case properly.

If there's one thing I had never been in my life, it was clever.

"Thank you for your time, Mr Wentworth," I said as I rose. "And the tea."

"Not at all. Would you like for me not to tell the police you dropped by if they come to talk to me?"

"I'm not hiding anything from the police, sir. But I would advise you having a hard think about what you might know. Even the most inconsequential thing may well be of use."

"You sure you're not the police yourself?"

I smiled, knowing the gesture was insincere. "It just rubs off on me."

Wentworth was not saying all he knew, although as I left his house and walked back to where I had left my car I knew there was nothing more I could really say to him. I did not know his connection to the killing, or even if there was one at all, but I was certain Wentworth was hiding something. I wondered whether Carl would be able to get it out of him, or whether I might have just screwed up the whole investigation by tipping off the prime suspect.

Pulling away from that nice house, it struck me that I had nowhere else to turn. My investigation had died before it had ever truly begun.

CHAPTER THREE

The Spanner

I spent the remainder of the day trying to work out how I could do anything which might actually help Mr Polinski. Returning to his house and questioning his neighbours further was one option, but I could not see how I was going to get much from them. The one I had spoken to had likely given me an answer which would have been repeated by them all. Mr Polinksi was a pillar of society and no one would have a bad word against him. If Wentworth was right and there was a chance Mr Polinksi was involved in something illegal, he was hardly going to let his neighbours know about it. I still could not reconcile the two images of the man, however, and by the evening a part of me was thinking that perhaps it was best I had no idea how to proceed. I could in fact be doing Mr Polinski more harm than good, and he was such a nice man I could not live with myself were I to do that to him.

That evening I tried to keep myself as busy as I possibly could. I'd never been a great TV watcher, had never been able to sit still in one place long enough, and found myself pottering about the flat doing whatever chores I had been putting off all week. Several times I was sorely tempted to phone Carl, just to see how the investigation was going, although always stopped myself. If he wanted to talk to me he would call, and if he had found out about my going to see Wentworth then he would definitely call. That I had not done the one thing he had suggested, go to the media, told me I still felt there was a chance I could do some good by my own investigation. It was a silly thought, yet one I could not seem to let go. I was not trained in this, and it didn't matter whether I had stumbled upon Carl's junior detective kit; I was simply not able to do what Carl could.

Phoning the media was still something I could do, certainly, but I would see to that tomorrow. I would sleep on things first and reach a decision come the morning.

I had just decided to rearrange my kitchen cupboards purely for something to keep my mind occupied when the doorbell sounded. I frowned, checking the clock on the kitchen wall. It was approaching ten in the evening and I could not think of anyone who might be stopping by at such an hour. That it was Carl was more than likely, and if it was Carl it meant he would be on at me about whether I'd called the papers yet. That was an argument I could have done without and I contemplated just ignoring the bell.

It sounded again, and if possible seemed more insistent this time. I knew it was exactly the same sound as before, that a doorbell could not grow angry any more than the door itself could sprout legs; but my imagination had been running wild since I had learned of Mr Polinski's death and I knew I would have to rein things in. Carl was at the door and he wanted to ask me a simple question. That was all it was. I could open it, he could ask, I could reply, and he would leave. Maybe he would even let slip a few more details about the case. If he did that, I could even gain enough material by which to continue my own investigation. At which point I could forget all about rearranging my kitchen.

Moving quickly to the door, I pulled it open, a smile ready upon my face, an emotional guard up as always around Carl, but there I froze. The person before me was not Carl. In fact the person at my door was as much Carl Robbins and Toto was the Wicked Witch of the West.

She was tall, although by her slouch it was difficult to determine for certain. She was also slim and wore clothes to make herself look thinner than she was. She was aged somewhere in her late-thirties, early-forties, although with such liberal application of make-up it was difficult to be certain. Her face was rounded, with small, slit-like eyes. It was as though God had experimented with the possibility of creating a human snake in defiance of everything that had happened in the Garden of Eden. Her cheeks were too pink, her lips a full-bodied red which was far too striking in the darkness of the doorway. Her hair was long and frizzy, exploding about her head and culminating at her shoulders as though it formed the mane of a lion. Her attire was tight, while about her shoulders was draped some form of animal-skin scarf which did not appear all that dead. The woman assessed me with almost demeaning eyes and did not seem all that impressed with the results.

Despite myself, I became immediately self-conscious and raised my chin perhaps a little haughtily. After all, it wasn't me knocking on her door at ten o'clock at night.

"Can I help you?" I asked with far more disdain than I had intended.

"Vodka," she purred, suddenly in my flat without having actually pushed past me. "Straight."

I watched as she wandered into the living room and gazed about as though she was a prospective buyer. I was left holding the door, staring and wondering not only who this woman was but who the hell she thought she was. Then I realised I was still being the doorwoman and slammed it shut before marching back into my own living room.

"Who are you supposed to be?" I barked. "And I don't have any vodka, Miss Slinky-McSlink."

She regarded me with curious, even amused eyes. "No vodka? My dear, how do you live?"

I did not grace that particular comment with an answer.

The woman had slipped into an armchair without having been asked, and I half expected her to strike up a cigarette held in one of those long, thin black things ladies of elegance always used to use. I could not imagine this creature was sincere in anything she was doing, and I found she was laying the Russian accent on a bit too thick to be real. I had a sudden reminder of what I had discussed with Wentworth: that Mr Polinski had a Russian-sounding name. That this woman was somehow connected with the case was obvious even to me, although whether it was a connection in a good way remained to be seen.

"I have whisky," I said as calmly as possible, telling myself my fists were not clenching at my side so tightly my fingernails were drawing blood.

"Whisky," the woman said with nose-twitching disdain, turning her head as though she was to spit that vile substance from her tongue. "The drink of devils, Miss Corrigan. The sweet, brown turgid waters of the sewer. Vodka is the purity of life. There is no deception in so clear a drink."

"Arsenic."

"I beg your pardon?"

"Arsenic is clear as well. Arsenic in vodka would kill just as invisibly as arsenic in whisky."

"But at least I would die in ecstasy."

She had a strange comprehension of ecstasy, but it was hardly my place to say how a woman got her kicks. "Well the point's moot anyway," I said, "since I don't have any vodka. And, come to think of it, I'm fresh out of arsenic too."

"Then your whisky will do fine, Miss Corrigan."

I fixed the drink she didn't want and made myself one. We both took it neat for no particular reason, and I took a seat opposite her, eyeing her as calmly as I could while I tried to figure out just what she wanted. "You have me at a disadvantage," I said.

"You are referring to my hidden gun?"

"Uh, no, I meant I don't know your ... You've brought a gun into my flat?"

"No, dear." She even laughed in that outrageous accent and I suddenly wished I actually had some arsenic after all. "It is the joker in me." She extended a hand, palm up, fingers down, as though she expected me to kiss it. "Rowena Silvers."

As a compromise between kissing and slapping the hand, I gripped it in a firm shake. Miss Silvers looked at her hand as I released it as though it had caught the plague and I began to consider that this woman wasn't quite the act I had taken her to be. There was a chance, perhaps not an amazing one, but a chance nonetheless that she was one hundred per cent authentic.

Which would mean she was either a stuck-up cow or a loon. Possibly both.

"This might be a dumb question," I asked, "but who are you?"

"Tsk, Miss Corrigan. Dumb is having no ability to speak. Stupid is what you mean."

I knew what she was doing and I wasn't rising to the bait. "And you are?"

Silvers gently shook her whisky beneath her nose, inhaling the aroma while she smiled my way like a cat contemplating the lock of a birdcage. "You are unnerved by me, Miss Corrigan."

"I'd probably be less on edge if you stressed a v now and then and called me comrade."

"I could miss few words if make you feel better."

"Now you're just being annoying."

"No, I being – how do you say? – pedantic." Her smile deepened. "That is way you expect foreigners to talk, dah? We ask how to say word before saying it anyway."

"Just tell me who you are or I phone the cops right now."

I pulled my phone from my pocket and thumbed through to Carl's number. The only chance I had of actually phoning him was if she did indeed pull a gun on me, although she understood the threat well enough: I was through playing games.

"You will not phone the police," Silvers purred, relaxing in her chair and crossing her shapely legs. She even sipped at the whisky, although I could tell by her grimace that she didn't much like it. I took a strange level of satisfaction in that discovery.

"I won't?" I asked. "Sort of thought I might myself."

"The police are not doing much about Anthony, Miss Corrigan."

"Anthony?"

She stared at me with only the faintest hint of amusement. "Mr Polinski?"

"Oh." I had always assumed Mr Polinski must have had a first name, but I had not really put that much thought into what it might have been. I did not want Silvers to realise this, although my hesitation must have already shown her everything she needed to know, even if my face hadn't.

"The great detective," she said, raising her glass.

"I never said I was a detective," I snapped. I don't know why, but this woman was getting under my skin. She had turned up at my front door, invited herself in, ordered a drink and so far hadn't even told me who she was. In fact I had only her word to go on that Anthony was even genuine. Maybe she had simply made it up, pulled it out of the air. I had no idea, and it would have helped some if she just got around to telling me who she was.

Perhaps she wanted me to guess.

"You think the police aren't doing anything," I said, "so you've come to me. How did you know I was looking into it?"

"I saw you talking with the detective. You seemed to care."

"So you want me to find the killer instead."

She shrugged. "I think you have a better chance, Miss Corrigan. Whoever killed Anthony was a professional. The police are not going to catch him. But they will not be watching you, so perhaps you have a chance."

"And maybe I'll get myself shot along the way as well."

"Perhaps. But you are already looking into the murder, so perhaps I am here only to offer a helping hand."

"You have information for me?"

"I don't know."

I took a deep breath. "All right, let's come at this again. Who are you? I mean, who are you to Mr Polinski?"

A sly smile took her face once more. "It is a poor detective who cannot see that."

I refrained from telling her once more that I never claimed to be a detective. "You're his wife?"

She tutted. "Anthony's family are all back home. Nyet." Her eyes flashed to show she was mocking me again.

"His bit on the side then," I said, and her eyes lost some of their flash so I pushed as hard as I could. "His wonton, his paramour, his strumpet ..."

"I understand the term, yes."

"... his trollp, his hoochie, his fancy woman ..."

"I think I ..."

"... his scrubber, his quean, his courtesan ..."

"Miss Corrigan!"

I stopped, my point well made. Rowena Silvers was seething, her fingers clutching the glass so tightly it was clear she wanted nothing more in that moment than to smash it over my head. I considered pushing her further but figured I had made my point well enough.

"You have a wide vocabulary," Silvers said slowly, "for a subject you consider so disreputable."

It was almost an accusation, so I felt she could do with another dose. "I got a few left, doxy, so you might want to think about getting to the point of your visit."

She did not relax, and I could see I had at last got to her. However, she had indeed come to me for a reason and she was about to storm out before she got around to telling it to me.

"Anthony did not know bad people, Miss Corrigan. He did not deal in bad people's things. He was a quiet man who liked to know things, but that was his job. His friendliness brought him customers and his customers brought him money."

"His friendliness brought him hussies as well," I said and received a glower. I hid my victorious smile with my own glass. "Sorry. Last one, I promise."

"Anthony," Silvers continued with an air of someone who wanted to wrap things up as quickly as she possibly could, "did not mix with undesirables. No one would have wanted him dead."

"Well someone sure did."

"No one," she repeated emphatically, her eyes almost trembling.

It was at this point I realised what a complete cow I was being. If what Silvers had told me was true, and I had no reason to doubt her word, she and Mr Polinski had been lovers. Regardless of the morality of such a thing, regardless of my own personal feelings, the two had been lovers. And by the very definition of the word it likely meant Silvers had loved him. She had come to me knowing the police were doing precious little to find his killer and all I was giving her was cheap whisky and abuse. She was trying to be strong, perhaps playing up on the whole mysterious Russian woman line because it helped her to cope with what had happened. The woman was grieving and she was angry and more than likely she was also terrified that whoever had killed Mr Polinski was coming after her next. In fact, until someone figured out who had killed him and why we had no idea who might be the next target.

I think she must have seen some of this realisation in my face, because her eyes hardened and she sat up just that little bit straighter. She did not want sympathy from me, not after everything I had said to her. I couldn't blame her for that and resolved not to make any further mention of her being Mr Polinski's other woman. If nothing else I was dishonouring his memory with my childish behaviour.

Knowing she would not want an apology, I pressed on with what mattered to both our hearts. "I haven't been able to find any enemies either," I said. "I'm thinking you have something else you wanted to tell me though."

"Yes." She was making no pretence any longer of even drinking the whisky, and to be honest I couldn't blame her. The bottle had been a present from Carl last Christmas and I reckon he'd only bought it for me because he knows I loathe the stuff. "There is someone you should talk to, someone who might know something."

"Who?"

"Anthony has always run his shop himself. He makes ... made little money, just enough to tide himself over. I was always telling him he should hire a shop-hand, but he always tells me it is too expensive. He was a tight man, my Anthony, but a hard-worker. I had the feeling no one would ever meet his standard and it would be more stressful for him to hire than to not hire."

Some of that fit in with what I knew about the man, but then again his face for his customers was going to be vastly different to the face he showed his friends.

"And then suddenly," Silvers continued, "this boy appears. I'm not good with ages, especially with boys. He might have been late teens, early into his twenties. No older than that though."

"Who was he?"

"Nathan. That was all I get out of Anthony. I asked who this boy was, what he was doing here, and Anthony tells me he is here to help look after the shop. I ask Anthony why do you have someone to look after the shop when you have always refused before? And he tells me not to ask."

"Did he usually confide everything in you?"

"My Anthony kept no secrets from me. I was his secret, as you so love to point out. You do not keep secrets from the mistress."

Mistress; there was one I hadn't thought of.

"So who was he?" I asked. "This Nathan. Did you ever find out anything about him?"

"No. He was simply there one day. He stayed in the shop working for about two weeks. And then Anthony is killed."

"And where's this boy now?"

"I do not know. He has vanished."

"So you think this Nathan was the one who shot him?"

"I do not know. I am not a detective."

Nor was I, but I didn't state the obvious. "Is there anywhere you think he may have gone?"

"If I knew that," she said almost angrily, "I would not be sitting here drinking this awful whisky with a woman whose hobby is to look up naughty words in the thesaurus."

I barely registered her reaction, for my mind was already working ahead. I could not understand why Mr Polinski would have taken a violent youth under his wing. Perhaps he thought he was doing the community a favour, perhaps he was being coerced by this Nathan. But why would Nathan wait two weeks to shoot him? And why would he shoot him and not rob the shop while he was there? Just because this youth had entered the scene, it didn't stand to reason he would shoot Mr Polinski for no reason.

Who was he?

"Do you know what he looked like?" I asked.

Silvers shrugged. "I saw him twice, maybe three times. I do not know; I am no good with faces. He had gel in his hair, I remember the shine. Otherwise I do not remember much."

"Do you remember his skin colour?"

"White, I think."

It was rubbish as descriptions went, but I didn't want to push her; not after the way I had been treating her. "This is good information," I said, quickly searching for some paper and a pen. I scrawled down my phone number. "I want you to contact me if you think of anything else, or if you happen to see this Nathan again."

"Why would I see him again? He is coming to kill me you think?"

"Maybe he didn't kill Mr Polinski at all. Maybe he ran away after the shooting because he was scared."

"Maybe pigs like crispy bacon."

I did not like to point out that they probably did: pigs would eat anything. "Leave this with me, Miss Silvers," I said in as reassuring a tone as I could manage. "I'll find out what happened to your Anthony, I promise."

It was a promise I had extreme doubts of fulfilling, but one to which I would fight to keep regardless.

With a lead at last, at least I had something to go on.

CHAPTER FOUR

The Detective

Since there was nothing immediate I could do about things, I slept on the information Silvers had given me. By the morning I had something of a plan, although not an especially good one. Mr Polinski's shop still seemed the best place to search for clues, although I could not think how many this Nathan would have left. I spent much of the night trying to work out whether I had seen the youth myself; if he was working in the shop there was every chance we had been there at the same time. Not having expected seeing him I certainly had never looked for him; and I was sure if I had seen someone even stacking shelves I would have asked Mr Polinski about it. Why he would employ someone and not put them to work did not make a whole lot of sense to me, yet that was nothing new with this case. I even began to wonder whether Silvers had made up this Nathan to hide her own guilt, but that was ridiculous. I had never seen Silvers before and she would have no reason to approach me with lies and expose herself. An alternative was that Mr Polinski had been lying to Silvers. Perhaps what she had told me was true, insofar as she knew things. Perhaps it was Mr Polinski who had been lying to us all the entire time.

Anthony. I had to remind myself that Mr Polinski had a first name, just like everyone else. If I had not even known that little about him, I could not comprehend why I thought I was such an authority on him.

Heading out of my flat, I just made it to the street when I saw Carl standing there. At first I thought it was a coincidence, but then I noticed he had his irked face on and that always meant he was in his snooping mode. And Carl in his snooping mode had been known to hang around street corners for hours.

"Hey, Carl," I said as I walked past him towards where I was parked. "Was just off out, so if you want something make it quick."

"We need to talk."

"Sure. Just talk quickly."

I had my door open by this point and was slipping behind the wheel. Carl was around the car and sliding in from the other side before I could stop him. I sat silently, knowing he would get around to telling me what he wanted eventually.

"You're not going to drive?" he asked.

"Where would you like me to drive to?"

"I don't know. Wherever you were headed should be fine, Lauren."

So that was his game. He had somehow discovered I was muscling in on his turf and he didn't like it. Carl had never liked me doing things he did, always because he was afraid I was going to end up doing them better. That wouldn't stop him subjecting me to them so he could show me how good he was at them. We had a strange relationship, me and Carl, and it's a wonder it lasted as long as it had.

"If you have something to say, Carl, then it'd be doing us both a favour to just come out and say it."

"Fine." He angled himself so he could face me, which meant his arm was bent against the seat, making him look very uncomfortable. I had half a mind to floor the accelerator just so I could see him fall everywhere. But I wasn't a teenager so I didn't. "You're investigating the murder," he said, not even asking it as a question.

"Yes." I didn't see any sense in lying to him.

"Why?"

"Because you said you wanted help."

"Not from you."

I looked at him then and my eyes must have been filled with venom because he visibly quailed.

"I didn't mean it like that," he said, but still did not back down. "I just ... Lauren, this is a dangerous business."

"I don't see why. This isn't TV, Carl. Detectives don't get shot at every two minutes."

"Why didn't you just go to the media like I asked?"

"Maybe because you asked." He seemed to genuinely not understand what I was saying and I felt disgusted I had ever let this man touch me. "Carl, you always have to control everything, don't you? Well you don't control me and I don't even see why you think you can. I don't know whether you noticed, but we're not together any more. I'm not sure we were together even when we were together." I realised I was rambling, which, I've already said, is something I do when I'm angry. It only made me angrier, and I knew given half a chance it would only make my rambling worse. I needed to get to the point and maybe Carl would even listen this time. "I have to do this for Mr Polinski," I said, trying to summarise in my own head my reasons. "I have to bring him some peace."

Carl listened to my words and slowly nodded. "Polinski's dead, Lauren. I think we went over this already. He's not shuffling around the astral plane waiting for someone to avenge his soul. He's dead, he doesn't care about any of this any more. I get that you want to do something good for him, I really do. But you're not a detective and you're only going to get yourself hurt."

"You don't care about me getting hurt," I laughed. "You just don't want me in your way."

"I don't want you in my way, you're right," he said in a flat tone which always told me he was angry. "But don't tell me I don't care about you. And yes, I know we're not together. You always thought I was callous and cruel, you always treated me like I was some bogeyman trying to scare you. I protect people, Lauren, it's what the police do. So yes, I always tried to protect you."

"You slap around your authority," I snapped. "That's why you're in the police, Carl, and don't give me any bull about being there to help people. You love nothing better than to pull out your badge and flash it around. Make everyone see who Mr Bigshot is. Best thrill in your life is when you make people afraid of you."

"Fine, so I'm such a bad guy. Let's talk about you now."

"No, let's not."

"Oh no, we might as well get all this out in the open. No sense in doing things by half, Lauren. I have to be in control of everything, you say? Well at least I don't have to be right about everything."

"I do not have to be right about everything."

"So I'm wrong about that as well?"

I opened my mouth but no words came out. I realised whatever I said at that moment would be misconstrued so I didn't see much point.

"You always corrected me on everything I did," he continued.

"Well you should have done them right then."

"You kept telling me how to do my job better."

"So why come home and go on about it?"

"Normal couples tell each other how their day went."

"Normal couples don't care about all the details."

"Normal couples care."

I was seething by this point. Once again he had managed to twist my words to make it sound as though I was the one in the wrong. It was a tactic of his I had almost forgotten and it wasn't something I had missed.

"Why are you doing this?" he asked, slightly calmer now.

"What?"

"Polinski. Why are you looking into it? Because I asked you not to. That's what you said."

"I ..." I realised that had indeed been what I had said.

"So you're trying to prove me wrong again?" he asked. "Lauren, we don't always have to fight. We don't have to be at one another's throats every time we see each other."

"Or we could just stop seeing each other."

"Believe me, it was an accident I bumped into you yesterday."

"An accident you thought you could use to your advantage by getting me to do your dirty work."

"I'm trying to solve a murder."

"So am I."

"Well you shouldn't." He sat back in his chair and I could see how angry he was now. It alleviated some of my own aggression, knowing how far I had pushed him. I told myself I hadn't meant to push him that far, that I hadn't meant to push him at all; but it was a lie. We both knew I had fully intended for him to get as angry as he had, and we both knew what Carl was saying was true.

I would not have admitted that to him for all the vodka in Russia.

That particular choice of words made me decide the only way the two of us were going to get along on this was if we stopped talking about ourselves and started talking about the case.

"I'm here whether you want me or not," I told him, "so we may as well pool what we have."

"I could arrest you for obstructing the course of justice."

I laughed in his face.

"Fine," he said testily. "What do you have?"

"Really?" I asked, raising my eyebrows. "I tell you everything I've found out and you run off with it."

"I'm officially and legally investigating this crime, Lauren. If you know something, you're obliged to tell me."

He had me there. "I spoke with a woman named Rowena Silvers. She said she was Polinski's bit on the side."

"Really?"

"You don't know about her?"

"His neighbours didn't mention her."

"I think he liked to maintain an image."

Carl shrugged. "What did she say?"

I briefly filled him in on what I knew about Nathan. The vague description, the even vaguer reason for his being at the shop. Carl listened throughout, and when I was done said, "She may have been lying."

"Maybe. But even if she was, she's a living human being who might know something about what happened."

"I'll try to pick her up."

"Then you'll need some vodka."

"I meant pick her up to talk to her."

"You'll probably still need some vodka."

I could see by his expression he was not certain whether I was joking with him, and I smiled to break the ice. "Look, Carl, we shouldn't fight."

"I don't know, we're so good at it."

I laughed without even meaning to, and suddenly there in that car I remembered why it was I'd put up with Carl Robbins as long as I had. For all his faults he was a good man trying to do the right thing. And on occasion he could even make me laugh.

"So, where were you headed anyway?" he asked.

"The shop."

"Then you'll bump into Lewis."

"Who's Lewis?"

"Detective Lewis. He just got assigned to the case. Maybe someone above me is taking this seriously after all."

"Is it usual practice to have two detectives assigned to the same case?"

"Maybe they don't think I'm up for it," he replied without making any attempt to answer the question.

"Don't ever think that, Carl." For all he used to bore me with tales of his day, for all I used to grow fed up with his every word about his work, Carl was damn good at his job. The suggestion that he did not put one hundred per cent into his work was ludicrous, and it irked me to think that anyone could claim otherwise.

I realised of course I had taken to defending him and it made me smile to think that there was something of our old relationship left. Not love, maybe not even the ability to like one another; but certainly there was still respect.

"Whoever this Lewis is," I told him, "he's not half the detective you are."

"Which means *you'll* be able to control *him*."

I actually even found that amusing.

"There was something I wanted to ask you, Carl. Something you might know."

"Well there's not much point in asking me something I wouldn't know." He said this as a joke, but with Carl nothing was ever a joke. I did not make an issue of it though: he knew full well his jokes annoyed me when he was being pedantic with them and it was an argument not worth dredging up. Not when we were getting along reasonably well at least.

"How easy is it to get a gun?" I asked.

Carl's expression changed immediately. Any trace of humour was gone and he even looked a little afraid. "Lauren, you can't possibly be thinking about getting a ... You're in over your head, aren't you, Lauren?"

"What? No, I don't want to shoot anyone. I don't want a gun at all."

"So why are you asking me for ...?"

"Jesus, Carl, why do you always think the worst of me? It was something Wentworth said about guns. I figured if it was reasonably difficult then it probably means Mr Polinski was innocent."

"Back up: who's Wentworth?"

It was something I had been trying to avoid, although now the man's name had come up there was nothing I could do about it. Lying to Carl was never an option: I've never seen keeping the truth from someone as lying, by the way. So I found I had to explain about Wentworth as well. Surprisingly Carl had never heard of him, which meant he had not bothered to go too deeply into Mr Polinski's background. He didn't know Wentworth, he didn't know Silvers ... It made me wonder just what Carl *had* been doing since the murder.

"You're getting into this very deep," Carl said, and while there was a note of recrimination to his voice I was thankful he did not tell me to stop anything. I think if he started telling me what to do again I was liable to belt him one.

"I'm being careful," I said, although that wasn't true at all. "Carl, I have your number. If it gets too much I'll call, all right?"

"By that point you might have a few holes in you."

"You just told me there was no danger to your job."

He pulled a wry face without even smiling at all. "Just don't take any risks, Lauren. I'll run the name Nathan through whatever contacts I have, but I think the description sucks."

"Hey, I just gather the information. It's up to the police to decide how to deal with it. That's what you said you want, right? Me handing over all the information I have."

"I'm just ..." He did not finish the sentence. He knew telling me one more time he was just trying to protect me would not go down too well. "Just look after yourself, Lauren," was what he settled for. "I wouldn't want anything to happen to you."

"Yeah, think how much work another murder would cause you."

I spoke glibly and instantly regretted it. Our differences did not matter, because here we were on the same side. In theory there was nothing we should have been arguing about, but our problem was always reality.

Carl stepped out of my car and I fastened my seat-belt, wishing I had said something differently, wishing I wasn't so guarded around him all the time. We had always sniped at one another, but just because we were both doing it didn't make it right. As I pulled away I glanced in my mirror to see Carl standing at the kerb. He looked pensive, almost afraid, and I realised then how much he still cared for me. It wasn't just that he was trying to protect me, it wasn't that he was doing his job to the best of his ability. For all he hid his emotions, Carl still cared. And I couldn't with all good conscience claim I didn't still care myself.

CHAPTER FIVE

The Other Detective

Mr Polinski's shop was closed. Mr Polinski's shop was never closed.

Standing before it, staring through the windows at the empty shop, I felt a hollow feeling of how wrong the situation was. The shop had always been a vibrant hub of the community, a place of gossip and laughter. Now all I could feel was emptiness and darkness. I could see the rows of fresh fruit which would soon be spoiling, and the bread which would in a few days start to go mouldy. Mr Polinski was always very particular about stocking up on fresh produce. He did not like for his customers to ever have a bad experience. I knew the thing which would have upset him most about his death would be in letting down so many customers. It seemed sacrilege to his memory to not open the shop on his behalf, but Carl was right. Mr Polinksi was beyond caring what happened in life.

"Miss Corrigan?"

I turned at my name. There was a man approaching slowly. I had never seen him before, and appraised him quickly in case he was carrying a gun or something. He was aged somewhere in his thirties, with short dark hair and a kind face. He was dressed in what he likely thought was smart casual but which I would have termed scruffy urchin. He reached into an inside pocket and I tensed, although what he produced was a badge.

"Detective Lewis," I said, realising I probably should have expected that.

"Call me Alex," he said in a friendly tone which made me want to continue calling him Detective Lewis. I did not immediately dislike the man, that wasn't it at all. I just tend to be put on my guard when strangers are friendly to me. "Carl said you'd likely be dropping by."

I did not know whether that meant Carl had phoned him in the last ten minutes or whether he had known me so well that he knew I would be running around in circles. Either theory infuriated me, and I almost pitied Detective Lewis if he pushed me hard enough for me to take it out on him.

"You know," he said, "ordinarily I wouldn't be talking to you about the murder. I'm only doing this as a favour to Carl and even then I'm not sure about this."

I suppose I should have been thankful for his honesty, although I had almost expected some sleazy line about putting aside his reservations for such a beautiful woman. Even after having talked to him for only a minute I could tell he was the type of man to say such things. That he hadn't said anything like that should have made me happy, but just made me self-conscious that he didn't find me attractive.

"Did Mr Polinski have anyone working for him?" I asked, not wanting to just hand him information if I could make him think he had given it over voluntarily.

"You mean the kid who vanished?"

"Do you have a name?"

"No. Do you?"

"No." I did not hesitate. Carl would of course tell him the name, but at that moment I wanted Lewis to think I was entirely ignorant. Sometimes with men it's best to let them think they've reached their own solutions to problems. Or at least that was the way it always worked with Carl.

He looked at me carefully. I held his gaze, held my breath without even realising it, and finally he simply shrugged and looked back to the shop. "You want to go inside?"

I had not been inside the shop since the murder and shuddered. There had always been a lively atmosphere in the shop, so much life that it would seem strange walking in there and finding only silence.

Lewis seemed to sense my concerns and unlocked the door. "Entirely up to you," he said and walked inside.

Taking a deep breath, I tried to work out whether Carl had been right in everything he had said. Maybe I didn't want to solve this murder because I cared about Mr Polinski; maybe I really did just want to do this to get on Carl's nerves. Otherwise I would be in that shop looking for clues.

Slowly releasing the breath, I took a step forward and gingerly pushed open the door.

Whatever I had expected, I did not see. I knew the shop was a crime scene and as such that the evidence could not be disturbed. I had visions of the walls being spattered with blood, a body lying off to one side covered by a drape. At the very least I expected a chalk white outline detailing just where Mr Polinski had fallen, or that I would retch at the stench of blood and death hanging in the air. But there was nothing like that. Just a shop empty of people. It was eerie just how much the atmosphere was the same. I expected the beaming face of Mr Polinski to appear from behind the counter at any moment and ask me whether it was a pound of plums I wanted or two.

"You all right?"

My eyes snapped around to where Detective Lewis was leaning against the counter. "You look a little peaky."

"I'm fine," I said. "I think the youth working here was the one who shot Mr Polinski."

"And you're probably right. Unfortunately we won't know until we've been able to ask him; and he's made himself scarce. If we had a name to go on, that would be something at least."

I knew he was baiting me, but I'd never much liked eating worms. Besides, I didn't have a surname and there were far too many Nathans in the world for him to be able to instantly narrow it down.

"You're a regular here, right?" Lewis asked.

"Yes."

"So you'd be able to give a description of this kid?"

"I never saw him."

Lewis digested this. "Which means he likely worked in the back. Storage or whatever. But why would someone pay for an assistant that just hung around out of sight?"

I had already been through all of this with Carl, although Lewis's wording made me stop and think. "Out of sight? Maybe there's something there. Maybe there's ..."

"Shh!"

I don't like being shushed at the best of times. Lewis was frowning, his eyes were narrowed and stalking through the shop, so I figured he was either being weird or he thought he had heard something.

Without a word he began to stealthily move towards the back of the shop. There was a door upon the back wall which I had always assumed led to some form of storage area, and carefully did Lewis place his hand upon it and push.

It was dark in the room beyond the door, but Lewis went in anyway. I followed, keeping as low as he was, and it was far from pitch so my eyes adjusted within seconds. There were rows of shelving space, boxes piled upon the floor, and crates packed away tidily. There was nothing amiss that I could see, although Lewis pressed on regardless of what I might have thought.

We walked the length of the room, which was larger than I had expected. The shelves were packed tight in some areas, but even behind these there was no room for anyone to be hiding. If Lewis honestly thought there was someone lurking back there, he was delusional. I did not say anything, however, for if Lewis was Carl he would have blamed me for losing his quarry if I said even one word. While I waited for Lewis to decide he was chasing shadows I thought about the old "returning to the scene of the crime" thing. Surely he could not expect for Mr Polinski's murderer to just randomly turn up at the shop again, just at the same moment that the two of us arrived.

Something fell several metres from us, the sound reverberating through the dark room. I tensed and I could see Lewis looking earnestly in that direction. I had brought with me nothing along the lines of a weapon, and suddenly wished Mr Polinski sold a line of crowbars or something.

A yell split the gloom and something lunged for me. I probably screamed, although things moved so quickly that I don't remember much of it. I know I must have screamed because afterwards my throat was raw and my heart was hammering. At the time I did not have a clue what was happening, much less how to respond.

The dark shape did not collide with me, but brushed past, and while I could see a flailing arm, nothing connected. I dropped to the floor, only partly through design, and fought against collapsing into a quivering wreck. I knew that such would only get me killed and even though I was terrified I forced myself to concentrate on where I was and what was happening to me. I could not see a face, could not hear anything except the rush of the figure's passing, the faint whiff of cologne almost choking me with its nearness.

A cry sounded through the room but the figure was already past me. I felt something grab me and I fought, shrieking as I subconsciously clawed at the hands grasping me.

"It's me, it's me!" Lewis was saying, and released me, holding his hands up in surrender.

I looked up at him, aware I was sitting on the floor, my senses reeling, my breathing haggard. Anger surged through me, burning through my adrenalin, and as with most people I just snapped at him. "Where the hell were you when I was being attacked?"

"If you're all right, I'm going to go chase the felon."

Suddenly I felt incredibly stupid, and in my fury could not abide the fact Detective Lewis was standing around tending to me when he should have been out running down whoever had just attacked me. "Go, go!"

Lewis ran, and I struggled to my feet and stumbled after him. We made it to the back of the room within seconds and charged out into the light of the outside world. There were old materials dumped out there, broken shelves and the like, while one wall was lined with bins. I could just catch a glimpse of a youth wearing trainers and a dark hoodie vaulting over one of the walls, and saw that Lewis was already in pursuit. I ran after Lewis, for I kept losing sight of my attacker and just hoped Lewis knew where he was headed. But Lewis did this sort of thing for a living, and even if he lost sight of the lad for several moments he would still have a better idea of how to track him than I ever could.

Within the span of a minute I had a terrible stitch in my side but knew I could not afford to stop for even a moment's rest. Lewis barrelled ahead as though he was attempting a record for the fifteen hundred metres, and I was suddenly glad I didn't even own a pair of high-heels.

I saw the youth again then, leaping, grabbing hold of a wall and pulling himself up. Before he had the bins to clamber across, but this time he struggled and I felt for sure we had him. But then he was up and over the wall and Lewis was only seconds behind him. He too strained to pull himself up, but then he also was gone. Pushing my body to its limits, I made the leap myself and felt my body slam into the wall, sending waves of pain through my chest. My fingers clung tenaciously to the wall, however, and I steadfastly refused to let go. Instead I concentrated my efforts as much as I could and pulled hard, as though I was attempting to draw the wall down towards where I was hanging. But it was no good, and the more I strained the more tired I became and the farther Lewis and the youth managed to get from me.

Giving it one final effort, I strained for all I was worth, but it was no use and my fingers slipped. I landed hard upon my backside, my hands raw, my fingers stinging. Breathing heavily, I got back to my feet and walked about the wall, trying to find a way around which might still get me close to where the others had long since fled.

Walking slowly, I listened for any sign of them, although there was no way I was going to catch them now. They were long gone.

Resolved not to surrender, I finally managed to follow the wall all the way around, and found it ended at a crossroads anyway. Even if I had made it over the wall, I would have been delayed so badly that I would not have known which way to head.

"Hey!"

I jumped, literally, and almost struck out, but once more Detective Lewis was holding up his hands to placate my somewhat violent tendencies. I collapsed against the wall which had so easily defeated me, bloated in its victory. My lungs felt as though they were shortly to burst, my throat was raw and I could feel my voice was going to be strained.

Lewis shook his head sadly. "Sorry, he was too quick for me."

"Did you ... get a look?"

"Not really. I think he was a teenager though. He kept his hood up the whole time so I didn't get to even see a skin colour."

I swore, punching the wall which had denied me my easy solution. The wall resisted and fresh pain surged through my hand. I'm sure the wall was even laughing at that moment.

"I've put an alert through for him," Lewis said. "He won't get far. Hopefully he'll be picked up by some local constables or something."

I didn't like to work in hope, but since we'd let the kid vanish there was hardly much else to focus on.

"What was he doing in the shop?" I asked, my breathing returning to normal at last. "I mean, why would someone shoot Mr Polinski, then go straight back there?"

"Maybe he didn't get what he wanted the first time around, I don't know. Look, the truth is he's not going back to the shop again. He'd be an idiot to, now we know he's interested in hanging around that place. I'll get someone watching it just in case, but he's not going back there. And that means we don't have any further leads on where he might be going."

"So what do you suggest?"

"I suggest you go home and think about what you're doing. If I wasn't with you today, who knows what might have happened? He could have had a knife or anything. Looks to me like he jumped you and panicked when he realised I was there as well."

"He didn't seem to panic to me," I said, thinking back and at last being able to properly analyse precisely what had happened. "In fact, he just seemed to want to get away from us. I don't think he even touched me when he jumped out. If he attacked me and got scared when he saw you, he would have made contact with me before running off."

Lewis was looking at me with a helpless expression I found quite odd. "So what else was he doing?"

"I don't know. But the more I think about it, the more I'm certain he wasn't attacking me."

"Of course he was attacking you. He jumped out from behind some shelves and ..."

"You saw where he leaped out from?" I asked with raised eyebrows.

"I ... No, I didn't see him leap at you. But where else would he have been hiding?" He adopted an expression which told me he was about to say something gentle and nice, yet something which would be anything but what I wanted to hear. "Look, maybe you should just leave this to the professionals, yeah?"

That certainly qualified.

"Like you and Carl?" I asked, sounding tarter than I had intended. "You need the help, Detective. At least Carl was man enough to admit that to me."

"We need trained help. There's a difference."

"Well this is only making me more determined to see this through."

He looked away and I could see that was not what he had wanted to hear.

A sudden idea tugged at my annoyance factor and threatened to tip it to spilling point. "Hold on a minute," I said. "You set this up, didn't you? That was supposed to scare me off, make me go home and curl up under the duvet and pretend none of this had ever happened? That kid was working for you wasn't he? It wasn't even Nathan."

"Who's Nathan?"

I realised I had said more than I had intended, and Lewis's face became serious then. I had been withholding evidence from a police officer during an ongoing investigation and if Carl didn't take kindly to that sort of thing I was certain a complete stranger wasn't going to cut me any slack at all.

"Carl didn't tell you the kid's name was Nathan?" I asked without mentioning that it was I who had told Carl to begin with.

Lewis still looked monumentally annoyed, but I could tell he intended to ask Carl about this before berating me any further. It bought me a little time, which I could use to get as far from these detectives as possible. But first I had to know just what I was up against.

"If I phone Carl right now," I said, drawing my mobile and stabbing it at his chest, "what's he going to say about this set-up?"

"There was no set-up."

"Sure. And yesterday I had tea with the Easter Bunny."

"Fine, whatever. Yes, we set you up. Carl doesn't want you getting hurt, I suppose. I was just doing him a favour by agreeing. You happy now?"

He was angry and had every right to be; but then so did I. Lewis had stopped trying to be so nice to me, which was something to be thankful for, although at least with his smarmy, solicitous nature I knew where I stood with him. I had never been able to abide people who pretend to be something they're not. It was one of the good things about my relationship with Carl. Actually, I don't think you could find a more honest person than Carl. That was what really rankled about the whole affair: that Carl could have been involved with setting me up like that.

I stormed off, heading back to my car. All the way I toyed with my phone, wanting to call Carl and demand to know whether he was involved. But any idiot could have seen that he was, and I didn't want to place myself beneath the idiots.

Carl's betrayal stung, but as I got back into my car I decided I was going to get over it. I would solve the murder myself, without Carl's input, and shove his face right in the truth that I could do something he never thought I could. Maybe even do his job better than him.

As I drove off, I realised I had no idea where I was even going. Not for the first time in the investigation, my leads had all run dry.

CHAPTER SIX

The Busybody

Mr Polinski had been a caring, talkative, sometimes charming man. He was this way because he wanted to make sure his customers were happy, because he knew that happy customers were returning customers. In short, Mr Polinski was a good businessman. These thoughts played through my mind as I drove away from Detective Lewis. I don't know how long I cruised around for, possibly an hour. I didn't have a destination, but the constant motion helped me think and the more I thought about things the more I came to understand that whatever the solution was, it was all going to rest with Mr Polinski himself. I may have lost faith in Carl and I may not have trusted Lewis in the first place, but I was not on my own. Mr Polinski would extend his hand and help me from beyond the grave; regardless of what Carl believed about him being past caring for such things.

My thoughts formed a river of possibilities, all churning into one mass and rushing headlong through my mind. Sometimes an idea would crash against the rocks and come apart, sometimes three or four notions would merge and form a stronger current. I'm not trying to be poetic here: I actually was thinking of things in terms of flowing water. It's a trick which has always helped my mind concentrate in the past. If I stop thinking about the thing I desperately want to think about, it suddenly pops into my head when I'm least expecting it.

Good businessmen kept stringent records.

The thought hit me so hard I braked suddenly, my eyes wide, my heart pounding. I don't know what you would term the epiphany: maybe in the context I'm using you would call it the river ending in a massive, powerful waterfall over which I suddenly dropped in a barrel. I don't really care for metaphors and didn't think that far. All

I could concentrate on at that moment was the fact that something important had just flashed into my mind, and I had to run with it.

Mr Polinski would never have employed anyone without keeping a record of it somewhere. Even if he was for some reason keeping everything off the books, he would have kept a record. Maybe not in his shop, but maybe in his house. Maybe not even there: maybe just under a rock somewhere. Regardless of the location, Mr Polinski would have kept records about this Nathan he was employing. And if I could find them I might not be able to discover an address, but I could certainly learn a surname to go with the forename.

Deciding a return to the shop would be a bad move, I tried to remember whether Carl had ever run through the procedures for this sort of crime. Would Mr Polinski's house be watched by the police under these circumstances? I knew Carl would have gone into great detail about such a thing at some point during one of his harangues, but I had only ever paid the minimal amount of attention to him at those times and could not resurrect the relevant information now.

Even if I could have remembered, it would not have done me any good, because the fact was I needed to find this information and I couldn't find it by sitting in my car. Gaining entrance to Mr Polinski's house, however, would not be easy, and I could think of no way I might legally accomplish this. That I was willing to step outside the law in order to bring his killer in was not something which sat well with me, but also something I knew I would have to do. And, as Carl had said, Mr Polinski was beyond caring.

I parked two roads down from his house, just in case the police were watching, and headed in on foot. I ran through all the possibilities in my head of how I was going to approach this, yet none of them made me feel any better. Two methods were fighting for dominance in my thoughts and as I slowed my pace I worked through each of them carefully.

Option one: I could break into the house. Highly illegal, yes, but I reasoned that I might be able to find a window at the back of the house or something which I could pry open. It would not be too difficult if I could find such a thing, and terribly difficult if I couldn't. I'd never broken into anywhere before, and a part of me wished I had indeed bought some form of junior detective kit during my time with Carl: or at least a book which explained the art of lock-picking. The ramifications of breaking and entering were that I could face prosecution. I did not know whether it would ordinarily be a prison sentence, but since I was interfering with a murder investigation I was not about to pretend that this would not become a possibility. Also, if I broke into the house I would have to leave everything the way they had been, which would unfortunately include the locks and windows. If the police had to investigate the break-in, they would lose all their precious time doing that and running after the wrong leads when they should have been out themselves looking for Nathan. Breaking and entering seemed, then, a very bad idea.

Option two: I could knock on the door of the next-door neighbour and pretend to be a detective. If, for some reason, they had a key, no locks would have to be broken. I would then have the run of the house and not have to worry about leaving locks in place. Of course, either way my fingerprints would be all over the house, so I would have to be very careful indeed. Still, it would give the neighbour a legitimate belief of my being there, so I would not have to sneak around like a thief. I had just decided on this course of action when I remembered I had already been to the next-door neighbour and they would recognise me and therefore know I was not a detective.

I slowed my pace a little more, trying to buy myself further time to think. I slowed myself so much that I was hardly moving, and still I knew it would not be enough time to work something out. I could see no way out of this, and the reason for that was because I simply was no good at deception.

So I reasoned that perhaps deception was not the answer after all. Maybe I could get through this without having to lie to anyone.

By this point I had almost reached Mr Polinski's house and I chastised myself for having strolled right up to it: if there were officers watching the house they would assuredly think my behaviour peculiar. Ignoring the house, I opened the gate of his neighbour and marched boldly up to their door. The same kindly old woman answered as before, and she smiled in recognition of me. If I had decided to pretend to be someone I wasn't that would have been the worst possible reaction I could have had from her, but my honesty was rewarded in that I needed her recognition.

For the life of me I couldn't remember the old woman's name.

"I was here before," I said with as beaming a smile I could muster. "I was asking about Mr Polinski?"

"Of course, dear. Has something happened?"

I should point out here that I don't think she called me 'dear'. To be honest, I don't remember much about my talk with her: I was always trying to remember all the pertinent evidence and I could not see that the old woman's words would mean much. I just have this stereotypical view of old women calling younger women 'dear' and for all I know she may well have done so.

"I need to get into the house," I said.

"Well come in, come in."

"Not your house. Mr Polinski's."

"I don't think Mr Polinski would much like that."

"I don't think he's going to complain, either. I need to find some information which might help me solve his murder."

"Oh. The police were after that as well."

"Yes, they tend to be. I, uh, don't suppose you have a spare key to his house, do you?"

"A spare key to Mr Polinski's house?"

"Yes."

"Yes."

"You do?"

"Yes."

"Could you possibly let me in for a while? I just need to find out something."

She looked uncertain and I could see she was not going to agree to this at all. I fought for some incentive I might offer her but if she didn't want the killer found for the sake of the killer being found I was not all that sure what else I could have tried.

"What do you want from his house?" she asked with curious suspicion.

"I don't want to steal anything," I protested perhaps a little too emphatically. "I just need to find something. I won't take anything and I'll try not to even touch too much. Maybe you could help me find it. You could come in with me."

She seemed to like that suggestion even less. "It just doesn't seem right, dear. His family haven't even been through his belongings yet."

"His family lives in Turkey. I doubt they're coming over here. His house and belongings will likely be sold off and the money sent to them." I assumed that was how it would work anyway, and if it wasn't I doubted the old woman would have known to contradict me.

"Still, I think we shouldn't be walking around his house."

The woman was infuriating, although she was also entirely correct. I had no right to force her to give me the key and her loyalty to Mr Polinski was admirable. None of that helped me of course and it did not matter how infuriated I felt; I knew there was nothing I could do about it. And that of course infuriated me further.

"I just need access to his records," I said, knowing there was no point in pushing her any further. If I annoyed her too much she might end up calling the police. "For his shop? There's something I need to check out."

"I don't know, dear. Surely the police have access to his records?"

"I think there was something he may have kept off the books."

She straightened herself in indignation. "Mr Polinski was the most upstanding man of this community. He would never be involved in anything illegal."

"I don't think he would, either," I said, knowing I did not believe that. I no longer had any idea what to think of the man. I had begun this investigation because I wanted to find his killer, but the more people I spoke to, the more confused I was becoming. I had so many conflicting concepts in my mind that a part of me truly feared he was indeed involved in something shady. I could not believe such of him, but then how well had I really known him? I only shopped with him, I didn't know him at all in fact. But this woman's attitude only affirmed what I myself had always thought about him, and I felt a rush of shame to ever call his integrity into question.

"I'm sorry," I said. "I didn't mean to suggest anything. It's just I'm hitting my head against a brick wall over this and I don't think it's the wall that's going to crack."

She softened at this, perhaps because she noticed I was close to tears over the whole thing. "There, there," she said in what she likely supposed was a soothing manner. "We all thought a great deal of Mr Polinski, dear. But I'm still not letting you into his house."

The tears hadn't worked, so I was all out of ideas. The only recourse I had left was to break into the house, and that led me back to all my perturbations with that particular strategy. I would have to go away and have a rethink of the situation. I doubted there was anything I would be able to do, but maybe I could go back to Carl and see whether he had anything. I had been trying to avoid Carl because I didn't want to find out he had been a party to that dirty trick Lewis had played on me, but with nothing else to go on I would have to suck it up and talk to him.

"Thank you for your time," I said, wishing I could remember the old woman's name. "Sorry to have bothered you." I was halfway out of her gate when I decided I would ask something on the off-chance. "Mr Polinksi never mentioned a kid named Nathan did he?"

"Nathan? He didn't much like Nathan."

I blinked, wondering how stupid I could have been not to have asked her as soon as I rang her doorbell. "Who *is* Nathan?"

"I don't know." I could tell by the way she scrunched her face that she did not think much of Nathan at all. "He took him in, gave him a job. I don't know why he did it, said he didn't want to lose his house."

I tried to work that out. "What does Nathan have to do with his house?"

"Nothing. He's never been there, but it's what Mr Polinski said. He didn't want to lose his house so he had to give that scroat a job."

"You didn't like him much, did you?"

"Is he a suspect?"

"Possibly."

"You mean yes."

I nodded. "Do you know where I could find Nathan?"

"No."

"And you don't know his connection with Mr Polinski or Mr Polinski's house?"

"No. But if he's a suspect you could always look him up in the phone book."

"I would," I tried to laugh, "if I knew his surname."

"Oh that's easy, dear. His name is Nathan Wentworth."

CHAPTER SEVEN

The Prime Suspect

It was uncomfortable sitting in the same position for so many hours, but I had parked myself outside of Wentworth's house and had been watching carefully for any comings and goings. I wasn't about to miss something just because my bum hurt. I could not believe how many pieces of this puzzle there were, although certainly were things beginning to make sense now. Albert Wentworth had a son named Nathan. For some reason he had told Mr Polinski that he had to give Nathan a job for a while. Mr Polinski had not agreed with that but had done so anyway under threat of losing his house. I have no idea what powers landlords actually have with regards to such things, but clearly the threat sounded real enough to Mr Polinski to force him to comply. He had almost definitely been told to keep no record of Nathan's employment, which would explain why the youth was never seen in the shop, and even Mr Polinski's record-keeping probably did not mention him. But he complained to his neighbour regardless, perhaps solely so he could have some form of verbal record when all written ones had been forbidden him.

This was all just a theory, but if it was true it meant Mr Polinski was complacent in nothing, and only guilty because he was forced into it. And since there was no crime in giving someone a job it might well have meant Mr Polinski was guilty of nothing at all.

I could not figure out why Nathan was there, however, and that really bugged me. Maybe he was being paid under the counter, but his father lived in a wealthy house and clearly did not need to resort to such tax-dodging. But then perhaps he had gathered such wealth by avoiding tax himself. Perhaps I had stumbled upon a huge tax-dodging scam of which certain celebrities could be proud.

I don't know how long I was sitting there but it was getting dark by the time I saw some activity. A car pulled into the driveway and I stared hard at the driver emerging. It was Wentworth, I could clearly see, and to my joy he opened the passenger door and all but dragged out what appeared to be a youth. Wentworth did not look at all pleased, and the youth stumbled as he was practically thrown towards the house by the old man. They were hidden by a bush very quickly so I did not get a good look at the youth, but I would have bet a year's pay that his name was Nathan.

Charging into the house and demanding answers would have got me nowhere, especially if Nathan still had his gun. Phoning Carl was obviously the cleverest course of action but, since Carl had always tried to make me believe he was far cleverer than me, that was not an option I entertained for very long. I tried to work out why Wentworth was so angry with his son, and came up with the obvious: that he did not agree with Nathan having murdered Mr Polinski. But I still could not work out why he had been murdered. If it wasn't for money, why would someone shoot him? Why would Wentworth insist his son was given employment, only to have that son murder his employer?

It made no sense to me so I decided I needed more information.

Leaving my car, I sneaked across to their vehicle and using it as cover headed further towards the house. Approaching one of the windows, I could hear raised voices although could make out no words. There was no window open so I doubted I would be able to hear anything even if I were to press my ear to the window itself; and then they would see me of course. Frantically trying to work out what I should do, and well aware I was missing all the best bits of the heated conversation, I headed to the door, hoping they had forgotten to lock it in their rush to get inside. No such luck, however, so I did the one thing which I figured might stop them arguing until I could hear them properly. I rang the doorbell and jumped into a bush.

My heart hammering at the somewhat childish prank I had been forced to implement, I peered through the bush, the leaves scratching my eyes and bare skin, and I had to admit that as spur-of-the-moment plans went, this had to have been my worst. The door opened almost immediately, a curious Albert Wentworth peering out from the crack of the door still on its chain. He was afraid, then. Perhaps he thought the police had followed him out here. Again I thought I should probably call them myself, but there was still something strange going on and I was determined to find out just what that was before handing my investigation over to someone else.

My investigation. I had to shake my head at how much I was doing this to get at Carl. Shaking my head caused further itching from the leaves and I almost hated myself in that moment for the realisation that, yes, I was only doing this to annoy Carl and that I had come to that realisation with some murderer's thorns in my eyes.

The door closed and I heard no more arguing, so I made my way out of the bush. It was a difficult process and while I managed to get one leg free, the other was snagged and I fell heavily. Biting my lip to stop myself from so much as gasping too loudly, I rolled onto my back and struggled to pull my foot free. The bush rustled in awkward pleasure as it watched me struggle and if I thought it might do any good to punch the thing I would have done so.

I became aware of sounds behind me and half turned my head to see Wentworth standing at the door, open once more. The youth was ahead of him, moving rapidly and looking very much as though he was making a run for it. Wentworth was no longer shouting at him and instead looked extremely worried. No matter what he thought of his son murdering Mr Polinski, it seemed he was willing to let him escape. I don't have any kids but I guess I would do pretty much the same thing. It must be a nightmare for a parent to have their child turn criminal, and I found I could not hate Wentworth for his complacence.

Giving one final jerk, I managed to free my foot from the bush, and went stumbling down the path. Wentworth saw me and shouted to his son, who took one look at me and burst into a fit of speed such as only the young possess. I did not shout to him, did not waste the energy, and simply ran as fast as I could. By the time I got to the street, Nathan was already halfway down the road and I could envision another chase I was destined to lose.

Only this time I had wheels.

Jumping in my car, I peeled away from the kerb with such haste that the screech likely alerted the entire neighbourhood watch. Nathan was running full-tilt, but thankfully for me he was heading down the road, taking none of the side turnings down which my car would not fit. He did not even seem to realise he was being pursued in a car and as I shot towards him I realised I was going to have to slow down or else risk running him down.

My problem now of course was subduing him. I'd never before tried to pin down a young man, not even one who wasn't wanted for murder, and I knew he would be stronger and faster than me. My best bet would be to hit him with my car after all, but that was not something I would even consider. At that stage of things I was not averse to breaking a bone or two, but hitting someone with a speeding car is a good way to get them killed and that was the last thing I wanted.

And then I had an idea and pulled across so I wouldn't strike him. As I passed him, I slowed to his pace and rolled down the window. "Quick!" I shouted. "Get in!"

His first reaction was shock and fear, but I was throwing open the door for him and he took it, sliding into the seat beside me. I drove, not knowing how to play this, certain he would see through my deception at any moment and pull a gun on me. I tried to appraise him while looking as though I was concentrating on my driving. He was in his early twenties, thin and scared. His dark hair was a mop of untidy fashion and he was dressed in a dark jacket which may have been a hoodie for all I know about these things. He was breathing hard, his adrenalin surging, his fear giving him strength, and he seemed genuinely terrified.

It was not what I had expected.

"Who are you?" he asked at last, the question I had been afraid of ever since he had jumped in my car.

"Lauren." I didn't see any reason to lie to him, but pressed on before he could ask anything else. "The police are looking for you, Nathan. You have to get away."

"I know, I know. I ... My dad brought me home to hide me. The cops were there. Ghillie-style."

I cringed at the fight I had with that bush: the fight I had well and truly lost. "Yeah, have to watch those cops sometimes. Why did your dad bring you home to hide?"

"Because of what happened to old man Polinski. He said I'd be safe at home, but the cops were already staking the place out."

Dropping him off at the police station seemed the best course of action for me, although getting him out the car once we arrived would prove the real problem. "When was the last time you were at the shop?" I asked.

"I haven't been back since the shooting. Dad says to stay away from that place."

So, if Nathan could be believed, it meant Lewis and Carl had indeed set up the whole 'attack' on me. Whoever that kid was they got to jump me in the shop, it had not been Nathan. That rankled more than I could say, although at that moment I had to concentrate only on Nathan. I could not see that he was carrying a weapon of any kind, but I knew he was dangerous and if he had any inkling that I was out to get him he would clobber me and steal my car.

"Do you have somewhere to go?" I asked. "Somewhere safe?" My thoughts turned to leaving him somewhere, watching the place to make sure he didn't scarper, while calling the police and getting them to pick him up.

"No. They're gonna find me wherever I go. I have to get out the country or something, yeah? Go live the rest of my days in Spain."

"They have police in Spain, Nathan."

"Who'd you say you were?"

He was beginning to calm down by this point, and with that calm was coming reason. He was at last beginning to understand he had leaped into the car of a total stranger and that this stranger seemed to know far too much about him for it to have been a coincidence that she had picked him up.

"Lauren, I told you," I said before launching into another question which would hopefully steer his mind away from who I was. If I could make him focus on the trouble he was in, I might stand a fighting chance of getting him somewhere useful before he could figure me out and attack me. "I don't get why your dad got you a job working for Mr Polinski. What was that about?"

"He thought it would give me an alibi. Figured if Polinski could say I'd been working for him the past few months, they couldn't pin me down for the shooting."

I was having a difficult time following all of this. Wentworth told Mr Polinski to take Nathan into his shop so that Nathan could have an alibi for when he shot him? None of this made any sense to me, and I was half tempted to just come out and tell him so.

"What did you think of Mr Polinski?" I asked if only to keep him talking while I tried to work through things.

"Why'd you keep calling him Mr Polinski? Are you a teacher?"

"Do I look like a teacher?"

Nathan shrugged and answered my earlier question. "He was OK for an old guy. He was a laugh sometimes. Had a weird sense of humour, but he was all right. Shame what happened to him."

"Yes. It was." It was strange, but Nathan seemed genuinely sorry Mr Polinski was dead. He looked incredibly guilty about it, but there was something I was missing, and the harder I thought about it the further it was moving from me. I considered trying for another river analogy but I had far too much to concentrate on.

"Mr Polinski was shot three times," I said, keeping my voice as level as I could. "That's overkill."

Nathan snorted. "These people don't mess around, Lauren. Hold on, who *are* you?"

I almost didn't care any more that he had all but figured out he didn't know me. "Wait a ... what people?"

"Whoever shot the old man."

"Didn't you shoot him?"

Nathan looked aghast. "Why would I shoot him? He was good to me. He was hiding me, why would I shoot him?"

"So why was he hiding you in his shop? You just told me you didn't want to be blamed for the shooting."

"Not Polinski, the bank. I ..." His face became an almighty frown. "My dad didn't send you after me, did he?"

"Your dad knows me, it's fine."

"No, you're with them!"

He had opened the door and rolled out before I could stop him. Screeching the car to a halt, I looked behind me to see him struggling to his feet. There was blood down the back of his trousers, but that was to be expected if you leaped from a moving vehicle, and I cursed soundly as I got out of the car to pursue him. But Nathan was far faster than me and had greater incentive to get away; I had not taken more than four steps before I could see him disappearing down an alley and over a fence. I would not catch him and did not fancy a repeat of my last chase of someone his age.

Getting back in my car, I drove just to get away from the area. Nathan had said plenty in the short time he had been in my car; enough to make me rethink the entire situation. All this time I had assumed he had killed Mr Polinski, but that had been purely on the basis that he was the only suspect. Yet Nathan had claimed otherwise. He had also mentioned a bank, which brought back something Carl had mentioned to me, something I had vaguely heard about in the news. Someone had committed an armed robbery in a bank and a man had been shot and killed. It seemed that armed robber was Nathan and that his father was trying to hide him in Mr Polinski's shop because of this. If he worked long enough in the back room, Mr Polinski could claim he had been working there for months. It would not be something which would sit well with Mr Polinski, but something he seemed to have agreed to.

Someone had then entered his shop and shot him three times. Nathan had gone on the run again, probably thinking he would be blamed for this shooting as well. Nathan would have to have been the unluckiest man alive to be hiding from one shooting only to have his protector shot as well. The two had to be connected, therefore, but perhaps Nathan had not murdered Mr Polinski, and from his mannerisms and reactions I was beginning to believe he was telling me the truth. Even innocent of this crime, however, Nathan was still guilty of the bank robbery and the shooting there, but that was not my case. Carl could receive the glory for that one if he liked: I would even phone him about it later, I decided. Right at that moment I had bigger things on my mind.

Someone had shot Mr Polinski, and I was growing convinced it had not been Nathan Wentworth. But if not Nathan, who? Who would have a motive to shoot an old man, and what was the shooter's connection with Nathan?

They were questions to which I did not have any answers at all, and no real means of finding them out. Like it or not, now that I had discovered Nathan was responsible for at least one shooting, I would have to contact Carl and tell him everything I knew. Such a thought was by far the worst I had had all day. And that included the fight I had lost against that damn bush.

CHAPTER EIGHT

The Gangster

Meeting Carl would have been awkward because it would have meant explaining far more than I was willing to. So I decided to park somewhere and phone him, for that way I could hang up just as soon as the conversation grew awkward. I told him about Nathan; his surname and his involvement in the bank robbery. Carl seemed more disturbed than anything and I could tell he was about to tell me all over again that I was getting in too deep. He knew I would not want to hear that, however, and to his credit reined it in.

"I can use this," he said instead. "I'm not involved in the bank investigation but this means I can call in extra resource. Two investigations, one suspect."

"What if Nathan was telling the truth? What if he didn't kill Mr Polinski?"

"You think he didn't?"

"You're actually asking me?"

"Lauren, please don't hate me all the time. Yes, I'm asking your opinion. Just because I don't want you involved in this, doesn't mean you're not getting results."

I hesitated, for that was a compliment. I tried to work out whether it was veiled as something else, whether he was perhaps even trying to make fun of me, but every way I looked at that, it sounded very much like he was telling me I was doing a good job.

"Thanks," I said sincerely.

He grunted, and I could hear what effort it had been to take such a blow to his ego. "Truth is, I'm not getting very far myself. I still can't track down this Rowena Silvers woman you mentioned."

"Maybe she gave me a false name."

"Oh, the name's right. I know where she lives, but she's not home. I've been to her work and she's not there either. No one seems to know where she is, she's just vanished."

"She might have gone into hiding in case she's next to be targeted."

Carl shrugged in that infuriating way which meant he preferred to have all the evidence before forming an assessment.

"Do you think she might have been the one who shot Mr Polinski?" I asked.

"I don't know, I can't find her to ask. What impression did you get of her? Is she capable?"

I thought back. "All women are capable of murdering their lover, Carl."

"Is that a threat?"

"We broke up a long time ago; if I was going to shoot you I would have done it already."

"Nice to know I'm safe then."

I thought more about Silvers. She had been the most insincere woman I had ever met, yet her concern had seemed genuine enough. If she was guilty, she was also a fine actress. That did not mean she hadn't killed him, just that if she had she had certainly fooled me.

A sudden thought came to me. "Maybe whoever shot Mr Polinski has taken her out as well."

"Maybe, I don't know. If I could talk to this Nathan kid I might be able to work it out."

"Depends which Nathan we're talking about."

"Come again?"

I didn't want to get into this with him. The last thing I wanted was for Carl to deny that run-around I'd been forced to endure. Still, I was angry enough at that moment not to care. "That trick you and Lewis played on me. I'm not going to ask if you were in on it, Carl, but I want you to know if you were, that was a dirty blow."

"Lewis?"

"Yeah. Don't act as though he didn't tell you about it, Carl."

"Lauren, I really don't know what you're ..."

"I don't want to hear it," I cut in. It was not entirely true, but the fact was I had more than enough to be worrying about at that moment without having to deal with Carl's denials. "Let's just get back to the case. Nathan. If he was innocent, who else could have had it in for Mr Polinski?"

Carl did not seem happy but knew I was in one of my hang-up moods if he played his hand poorly. He therefore did the only thing he could have under those circumstances and agreed to talk about the case again.

"From what I can find out, Polinski really didn't have any enemies," he said, which was of course nothing I had not already determined myself. "Whoever killed him, I can't see that it was because he had done anything that wrong."

"Hiding Nathan seems to have been his only crime," I agreed. "Hold on, maybe they were after Nathan."

"Nathan? What do you ...?" He paused while he thought that through. "That would make sense. Someone goes after Nathan and finds Polinski instead. But surely they wouldn't have mistaken the old man for Nathan?"

"I don't know. I ..." A shadow fell across my car window then and I looked up with a frown. There was someone standing right next to my passenger door, leaning against my car. "Hold on a minute," I told Carl and leaned across to get a better view. Suddenly the driver's door was yanked open and pain shot through my arm as someone grabbed me. I screamed, struggling, wishing I had my seatbelt on, my phone clattering away into the gutter. I was pulled out onto the street, stumbling and falling, splitting my knee on the kerb. The man from the passenger side was upon me as well by this point and the two men dragged me to my feet.

I got a brief look at them even as my panic set in. They were both tall and broadly built, wearing nondescript white T-shirts and dark jeans. Neither was smiling: in fact they seemed to be commanding entirely blank expressions as they drew me away from my car. I looked about, for it was still vaguely light and there should have been people on the street. But there was no one, or at least no one willing to help.

A car pulled up before us and I knew what was happening. I dug in my heels, trying to stop them, but the two men forced me across to the other car. Flailing with my arms as best I could, I kicked backwards into the shin of one of the men. He grunted, his grip slackened, and I convulsed in the grasp of the other man, my arm becoming as slippery as an eel; and then I was out of his grip.

I ran as fast as I could, but only made it several metres before one of the men tackled me to the floor, his meaty arms encircling my midriff and bringing me down hard. His expression had soured and I could tell he was angry that I had shown him up. I thought he was going to hit me, but he did not need to. Instead he just stood, holding me in the air, kicking and screaming, and threw me into the back seat of the car. The door slammed on me and I suddenly ceased my cries as one of my attackers jumped into the passenger seat beside me and pulled a gun.

I could feel my heart stop in that moment; my eyes must have been as wide as saucers. The man seemed a little annoyed, but not as much as the one who had tackled me. Nor did he say a single word, for he could see I perfectly understood the situation.

Another door slammed and the other man was back in the front passenger seat. Without a word the driver took off, leaving my car open and abandoned, my phone buzzing in the gutter. Every connection I had to the outside world was gone and within just a few moments I was in the hands of the very people Carl had been trying to warn me about all this time.

As fearful of my life as I was, I could not help but feel annoyed that perhaps Carl had been right all along. My only sobering thought was that maybe now I would at last find out just what the hell was going on.

Pain had never really been something I could handle very well, but as I sat in a constricted bundle with ropes bound so tightly they were burning into my flesh, it at least gave me something to concentrate on other than my situation. I did not know where I had been taken, did not in fact recall much of the journey at all. I was forced to keep my head low, my mouth shut, and as we pulled up it was into a confusing, dark mess. I reasoned it was a warehouse, since that was where all these sorts of things happened. Abandoned warehouses were the favourite haunt for drug deals, hostages, discreet killings and a whole number of other nefarious, illegal activities. Just which I had fallen into I could not say, especially since I was still attempting to piece together every aspect of my investigation.

My investigation! Ha! It was at this time that I had to admit to myself that I was in over my head, that I never should have set off on this bizarre mission to begin with. I was not a detective, I'd just happened to live with one for a while. But listening to all the various tricks of the trade did not make me a master of them. It was something I should have admitted a long time ago, and as I sat uncomfortably in the terrible silence, I had so much time to reflect on all the mistakes I had made. Not only with regards to Mr Polinski, but with my life in general. I had done so much I now regretted, but it was a regret outweighed perhaps by all the things I wish I had have done. There were so many things I would have done differently, but it did not matter any more. I was going to die trussed up on a chair in the middle of a dark warehouse and there was nothing I or anyone else could do about it.

A click sounded from somewhere and light exploded around me. I clasped my eyes tightly shut for fear of burning out my corneas or something, although knew I needed to see as much as I possibly could if I was going to stand any chance at all of escaping this mess alive. As I slowly raised my eyes, therefore, it was to see a scene I had hardly expected; and yet one which was no less fearful regardless.

I was in a large room and was surrounded by a series of plush sofas and chairs one might expect to see in the waiting room of the Queen's doctor. The carpet was thick and luxurious, with the most exquisite furniture I have ever seen sinking into its glorious depths. There were paintings adorning the walls: actual original paintings of landscapes and nude men and women cavorting with faeries and stuff. I could tell they were old and faintly even recognised one or two, which frightened me at the prospect of just who I had fallen foul of. Glancing further about I could see the reason light had flooded into the room was because the blinds had been lifted from the windows: blinds so effective that dropping them plunged the room into almost total darkness.

There was also an oval area in the centre of the room sitting on a raised stone platform. Within this oval space there bubbled some form of hot tub, and while there was no one in it I felt a sharp shudder cringe its way down my spine.

There was a man in the room with me, the one who had lifted the blinds. He was one of the men from the car, although now his attire was more expensive. He did not wear a suit, in fact was still dressed in a T-shirt and jeans, although even from a distance I could tell they were of quality material. Whoever these people were, they did not want anyone to find out I had been grabbed by people of wealth.

The man said nothing to me and finished opening all the blinds. By the time he was done, the room was practically aglow. I could vaguely see out of the windows, although did not struggle to do so: I did not want him to get the impression I wanted something.

His task done, the man approached me and I tensed, my eyes boring hard upon him, my will silently daring him to try something. He reached into his jeans and pulled forth a flick-knife, bringing the blade to bear with the air of a man who has done such so many times before. He reached towards me with that blank expression he favoured, and I tried not to watch the knife as it approached. I knew he was going to cut my bonds, I knew he was going to do that because if these people had wanted me dead they would have killed me somewhere else. But when you're trussed up helpless and someone slowly brings a knife towards you, you don't have a whole lot of choice in what to believe.

So I closed my eyes. If he was going to kill me, he was going to do so regardless, and I refused to play these little games with him.

A moment later I could feel my ropes coming away and I was able to breathe again.

Opening my eyes, I could see the man had taken to resting against the side of a comfortable chair. He was watching me intently, playing his knife to extract the dirt from under his nails. He was trying to intimidate me, that much was obvious, but since I was already terrified I didn't see he could really accomplish much.

Rising slowly, I tested my limbs. They ached badly, but I flexed my arms and legs where I stood to restore circulation. When my captor made no move to stop me, I decided I would try for a wander around the room. His eyes followed me, but otherwise he made no move at all.

Wandering briefly towards the hot tub, I lingered only long enough to make sure it was what I thought it was and not something like a bubbling vat of human blood. It was, of course, just a hot tub. From there I headed to the windows and gazed out upon the city. It was a wondrous sight, for I had never before seen London from such an angle. I had been on the wheel thing one time, and I could see it now in the vague distance, so tiny beneath us. I did not know buildings were even made this big in London, yet since I don't live there I had never given it much thought.

I was far from home, then. Whoever had taken me had driven me farther than I had thought. They had taken me far away from anyone who might have any chance at rescuing me, which meant I was on my own. I did not at the time know what they wanted, but whatever it was I was going to have to figure out my own escape.

Carl was not coming for me, no matter how much I wished he was.

The door at the far end of the room opened and I span at the sound, my entire body tensing once more, my fingernails pressing into my clenched palms as I tried to stop myself shaking. A woman entered, although it did not make me feel any better to discover it was possibly a woman behind this whole thing. She was tall, elegant and graceful in her moves, and I would have judged her age somewhere in her fifties, although a lot of money had been spent on making her seem much younger. Her build was slim, but she was far from attractive. Her face was almost a square, her eyes too thin, her cheekbones extremely rigid. Her dark hair was cut short, drooping over her eyes in almost an emo's mop. She was wearing a blue dress which did not cling to her lack of form, yet there was still something alluring about her. The benefits of wealth, I reasoned, that it could make even a worm resemble the apple it infested.

The woman did not smile as she glided into the room and did not so much as acknowledge the man casually playing with his knife. Her eyes locked onto mine and I felt an overwhelming urge not to look away. So I met her gaze, hoped I was projecting defiance and not desperation, and knew I would die either way so thought I would give having a backbone a shot.

"Are you the one in charge here?" I asked with what was hopefully more courage than I felt.

The woman continued to regard me for several moments before saying, "Your name is Lauren Corrigan. You've been hanging around with the wrong crowd, it seems."

"Did you kill Mr Polinski?"

The woman raised her eyebrows. "You don't get to ask questions. Leroy tells me you were seen with the Wentworth boy. When he gave Leroy the slip he decided to come after you."

I glanced across at Leroy, who gave me a short salute with his knife before turning his attention back to his personal grooming.

"What are you going to do with me?" I asked.

"Maybe nothing. It depends what you give me, and how easily you do that. I want the Wentworth boy and you're going to give him to me."

I had spent the last couple of days tracking Nathan down myself and there was no way I was going to be able to find him again. I had a feeling that to tell this woman such a thing would buy me a trip to the river.

"Why do you want Nathan?" I asked. "You're not the police."

She did not seem amused by my suggestion and I could sense there was something she was not telling me. A reason she was keeping her face so stony, as though she feared to crack her carefully-constructed demeanour.

"My name is Katherine Redthorne," she told me, and in that moment I knew she was not going to let me walk out of that place. "Four weeks ago Nathan Wentworth walked into a bank armed with a shotgun and the intention to use it if he had to. Things did not go as he planned and he panicked. And because he panicked he shot someone who was there simply because he was making a withdrawal. A legitimate withdrawal. That man was named David Redthorne. He was my son."

I said nothing. I sympathised with this woman to some extent, although of course the main concern running through my mind was how I was going to get out. She was a mother who had lost her son and clearly had the resources to do something about it. She was rich, and her money had likely not come through legitimate means. That this was a family of gangsters I had stumbled upon was so ludicrous it was almost laughable; but it is somewhat impossible to laugh when you know you're about to be killed by professionals.

It seemed I had at last solved the murder of Mr Polinski. In looking for Nathan, her heavies had shot the wrong man, or questioned him and not liked his answers. I had visions of Mr Polinski standing up to Leroy and Leroy taking exception to the old man's tirade. It was a despicable situation and how I wished I could somehow get the information to Carl.

"So you see," Redthorne continued in a flat tone, "I want Nathan Wentworth. My men have had no luck in finding him since he disappeared from your car, so you're going to tell us precisely where he is."

"All right," I said before I could stop myself, and then had to quickly think of something to add to that. "I didn't know he'd killed anyone. I wouldn't have helped him if I knew that."

"So where is he?"

"I can take you to him."

"Just tell us. You talk, we check it out. If Nathan's there, we let you go. If he's not, you get to try out the hot tub, face-down."

I could not help but glance at the bubbling coffin, and in doing so my eyes met Leroy, who smiled at me and offered a wave.

Looking back to Redthorne, I swallowed nervously and said, "There's a shop three down from Mr Polinski's. It's been empty for about six months. Nathan's been staying there."

Redthorne continued gazing at me for several moments, searching my face for the truth, before finally deciding she had nothing to lose by checking it out. "All right, we'll look. Just tell me what all this talk is of Mr Polinski."

I blinked, in total incomprehension that she could not have known his name. These people held no regard for life at all if they could kill so indiscriminately. It drove home the point that as soon as they found the empty shop empty, I was going to be the next to die.

Redthorne accepted my description of the shop and departed, taking Leroy with her. They did not tie me back up, did not restrict me at all. I had no phone, and there would be no landline in the room. I rushed to the window, but it did not open and even if I could have managed to get it open there was no escape for me that way. So I ransacked the room, not even knowing what I was searching for. After ten minutes I collapsed in total exhaustion and fear. There was nothing in the room which could get me out, nothing by which I might even alert Carl. My eyes fell once more upon the hot tub and I shuddered. Leroy would be back within the hour and as soon as that door opened again, I knew I was going to die.

There was simply no way out at all.

CHAPTER NINE

The Help

Half an hour passed and I knew at any moment Leroy and Redthorne would return and inform me Nathan was not at the location I gave them. I had reasoned they would take an hour to get there and back, but I did not doubt these people could somehow halve that time. Of course, Redthorne could simply call back once she reached the scene, but I had a feeling she would want to watch me die. Perhaps give me one final chance to give her what she wanted. She could be making a call even now, telling her people here that I had lied and that they were to rough me up to tenderise me for her return. That was certainly a possibility, but not one I much liked to entertain.

During that half hour, I had gone over every inch of the room, and that isn't an exaggeration. I had discovered just one door, and this led into a bathroom about as large as my living room back home. Searching this room revealed nothing useful either, and while I entertained a fanciful idea of creating some form of slippery concoction from the various bath creams, it was with regret that I had to determine the bathroom was also useless to me. The only thing in my prison I really chose to steer clear of was the bubbling cauldron which would spell my doom, and that was only because I was afraid of it. There were no phones anywhere in the room, no doors other than the main one, no loose floorboards, nothing. I had a feeling that even should I throw something against the windows with all my might, they would hold. And even if I did manage to break through, it was a long drop to my death. My only way out seemed to be that one door through which Redthorne had departed, and I did not have to try it to know there would be sentries upon the other side. Big sentries with expensive suits and concealed firearms. It was an image which had been impressed upon my mind ever since Redthorne had left, and perhaps I had been watching too many gangster films but it was something which unnerved me in the silence of being alone.

A sound came from the door and I knew my time had run out. I had failed to secure a means of escape from the room and now Leroy was coming in with his knife to see what he could remove from under my fingernails this time. I held a vague hope that it might be Carl coming through that door to rescue me, but there was no chance Carl could have found out where I was. He knew I was in trouble because I had been talking to him when I had been grabbed from my car, but there was no way he could have found out what had happened to me. I had images of him having frantically searched for me the entire time I had been missing, but it did not matter because the chances of it being Carl walking through that door were about the same as it being Mr Polinski.

The door opened and a woman shuffled in, pushing a small cart. "Oh, I'm sorry," she said. "I didn't realise there was anyone here."

I stared at her in complete incomprehension. The woman was short, probably only around twenty, and was dressed in some form of black-and-white uniform. The cart she was pushing contained what appeared to be towels and soap.

"Who are you?" I asked.

"I was just going to clean the room, miss. I can come back."

"Whoa, no!" I said before she could disappear back through the door. The young woman hesitated, a mixture of surprise and confusion on her face. "Wait," I said. "I could ... really do with some fresh towels."

"You could?"

"Yeah, one always needs fresh towels." I tried to smile. The young woman shrugged and entered the room properly, closing the door behind her. She moved off towards the bathroom and I followed, thankful to be away from the ears of any sentries waiting outside.

The maid began to sort out the towels in a fashion which told me she had done this a thousand times before. I stood behind her, my nerves ragged and my heart about to explode with fright. She was paying no attention to me whatsoever and I knew if I waited long enough, she would finish and then be on her way before I had plucked up the courage to say even a single word.

"What's your name?" I asked; the first thing that popped into my head.

She looked at me strangely. "Sara Mullins."

I extended my hand. "Lauren. Pleased to meet you."

She looked at the hand quizzically, her frown denoting not only confusion but also a little humour. At last she accepted the hand and I felt we had bonded in some small way. But I could not rush her, I could not afford to frighten her. Whatever I said had to be well-thought and to the point.

"I need your help." It was a start.

"I don't mind changing them," she said, "but you haven't used the old ones yet."

"Old what?"

"The towels."

"Forget the towels. These people are trying to kill me."

She still seemed amused, but was far too polite to show it. "What people, ma'am?"

"Redthorne."

"Mrs Redthorne's trying to kill you?"

"Yes."

"Oh. That's too bad."

I could not quite figure out whether she was being sarcastic. "You do know she's a gangster?" I asked.

"Mrs Redthorne's a gangster? You mean with the violin case and the Uzi? Or the Al Capone off-centre fedora or the Bogey coat?"

"Humphrey Bogart wasn't a gangster."

"No, ma'am."

I refused to have this argument. "Look, I need to get out of here."

"The door's the best place to try that, ma'am."

"There are men posted at the door and you know it."

She did not contradict me. "Have you tried pretending to be ill, ma'am? Or call them in and hide behind the door?"

Once more I felt she was mocking me. "We could always start fighting," I said a little too tersely. "That always seems to work in the pulps."

"Are those the same pulps that are full of gangsters, ma'am?"

"You really are trying to annoy me, aren't you?"

"Annoy you, ma'am? I'm just here to change the towels."

She went back to her work then, ignoring me entirely. I've never been accused of being stuck-up in any shape or form, and certainly I would never demean anyone's livelihood; but her attitude did strike me as a trifle odd. She was, after all, an employee of Mrs Redthorne, and while it was indeed possible she had gained some form of superiority complex because of that, her entire demeanour was not what I had expected. That I sounded insane only made her attitude worse.

Then I realised something.

"You're changing the towels," I said.

"You asked me to, ma'am."

"Why are you changing the towels? I mean," I added hastily when I was about to receive the same answer, only more flippantly, "you're a cleaner, right? And you're changing the soap and towels."

She looked at me wryly. "Do you want me to answer that, ma'am?"

"This is a hotel, isn't it?"

She slowly shook her head.

"No," I said, "I really do want you to answer that one."

She sighed, not wanting to play this game with me, and I desperately fought for her name again.

"Mullins," she said when I asked as vaguely as I could but which had probably turned out very blunt indeed. "And yes, this is a hotel."

"So you don't work for Redthorne?"

"I work for whoever's booked out the room. And Mrs Redthorne sort of permanently owns this floor, so you do the logic there. Ma'am."

"Why the attitude?" I snapped at last. "I mean, aren't you afraid I'm going to tell Redthorne you were rude to me?"

"I haven't been rude, ma'am. You think you're a prisoner here and that Mrs Redthorne's a gangster. You're also terrified, which means you think she's coming back here with a nice pair of lead shoes for you." She shrugged. "I've seen terrified people in this room before. Strangely, I never see them check out. I used to be polite to them, but now I can't really be bothered. It's not like you're going to file a complaint when you get home or anything."

"Then you just ..."

"Your towels, ma'am." By this point she had finished folding the new ones and had gathered the clean ones she was removing. She offered me the most sardonic smile I've ever seen before heading back for the bathroom door.

I am reasonably certain that was the point I punched her in the face.

Mullins went down hard but strangely soundlessly. Nor did she move when she struck the floor. I froze for several moments, expecting the charge of frantic feet as Redthorne's muscle rushed in to see what was going in. But after ten seconds of silence I realised they simply weren't coming. So I looked down to the crumpled maid. She lay unconscious by the looks of her, blood pouring from her nose down her chin and staining her white top. I had not meant to gain anything by slugging her: just to shut her up and vent some anger. But now that I looked at her I suddenly remembered one more cliché escape attempt. It was not going to work – it would never work in real life – but since I was going to be killed at any moment anyway I decided I didn't have that much to lose.

Working quickly, I stripped the girl to her underwear, shrugged off my own clothes and bound them in the lump of towels. Dressing in the girl's clothes was not easy considering she was several sizes smaller than me, but since there was a possibility it might save my life, it was an inconvenience I was willing to endure.

Taking an extremely deep breath, I gathered up the towels and headed for the door to the corridor outside.

At the time I only really had a vague idea of what I would find outside of that room. My expectation of course was that there would be two burly bouncer-type guards flanking the door, dressed in smart suits and permanent scowls. Either one of those men would have been enough to crush my head with his bare hands, or encircle my entire body with his thick, meaty fingers.

I was of course working myself up into a frenzy and tried to calm myself by thinking good thoughts. I had a sore lack of good thoughts to be ruminating upon at the time, so forced myself into some breathing exercises instead. A slight pang of regret entered my heart about the girl I'd bashed, and I knew if you punched someone hard enough to knock them out, you may well have done them some permanent damage. I should probably have phoned her an ambulance or something, but if I had access to a phone, I think the police would have been my first 999 call of the day.

Realising I was rambling once more, I decided I would have to just open the door and get this over with. Before I could stop myself, I pulled open the door and stepped outside.

The corridor was long and wide, a deep brown carpet of quality material marking the hotel as somewhere expensive to stay. To my surprise there was no one at the door at all, and as I looked both ways I could see no sign of anyone. The door had not even been locked, and my perturbation only grew at this discovery. To have to fight for escape would have been one thing, but to simply be allowed to walk around as though I was a guest there was unsettling. I began walking, trying to find a staircase or something. I knew better than to trust a lift, for once the doors opened there would be nothing I could have done to stop whoever was on the other side. At least with stairs I had the chance to reconnoitre and run away if need be. I had walked for several minutes at an incredibly slow pace before I realised there were two things I should have done. One was note the door number of my cell, the other was that I should have brought the cleaner's trolley with me. Walking around clutching a handful of towels was not the best cover I could think of, and the more I was walking the more I was becoming lost.

A door ahead of me opened and I froze, but immediately forced myself to resume walking. Lowering my eyes, I hastened towards the man heading in my direction, deciding it would be too conspicuous to turn and head the other way. I did not pay any attention to his appearance, did not even see his face, and as we crossed, my heart hammered at the thought that I was so close to discovery.

But then we were past one another and I was able to breathe again. I was sorely tempted to turn my head to see if he was watching me at all, but had not come as far as I had just to ruin things now.

Thirty seconds later, I came upon a stairwell. It was ornately-designed, with greater detail than some cathedrals I'd seen. Thankfully the stairs were padded with lush carpet, which meant no one would be able to hear my footfalls as I crept down to the next level. Of course, I was presently far from the ground floor, but I reasoned if I could just get to a level not owned by Redthorne, I might have been able to reach a phone and call the police.

Reaching the next level down was simple, and my poor heart was beginning to hope that it could have actually been this easy. I reached for the door which would lead me into the corridor for this level and tugged, but while the door rattled, it held firm. I tried again, but the door simply would not budge. Stepping away, resigned, I realised that there was no need for guards because I was stuck. I had no doubt that the entire stairwell was owned by

Redthorne, that none of the doors would open no matter how far I went down.

Closing my eyes and forcing air into my lungs at a steady pace, I tried to look at the situation a little more logically. To have enough money to buy a floor or two of an expensive hotel was entirely possible. To buy a stairwell, however, was ludicrous. Yes, I did not doubt that Redthorne had enough money for it, but everyone else in the hotel would have been just as wealthy and none of them would have liked for an entire stairwell to be taken out of service for no reason. And why was it anyway? What possible use could Redthorne have for a stairwell? Why not just lock the door on her own level if she didn't want me escaping?

The only answer I could think of was horrendous: that Redthorne owned the entire building. If she had that much money she would be far more influential than I had reckoned upon. And if she was that rich I was certainly in deeper trouble than I had feared.

I suppressed a yelp as someone grabbed my arm, my towels spilling all across the floor, my clothes falling from amongst them and on show for my attacker to see. The man released me and looked quizzical, almost amused. "Lauren?"

I almost collapsed in relief. "Detective Lewis! What are you doing here?"

He placed a finger to his lips and I knew it was a stupid thing to have made so much noise. "Investigating Mrs Redthorne and following up on a lead."

"What lead?"

"It appears it was you, actually. Redthorne dropped by Polinski's shop earlier. Or at least an abandoned shop a couple of doors down. I felt it was a mighty coincidence for her to show any interest in that place and figured she might have had something to do with the shooting. I knew where she was based so came here to snoop for some answers. I didn't expect to find you here, but I don't think I have to ask whether it was your doing that she went there."

"I think she shot Mr Polinski," I said. "Her son was in the bank the day Nathan Wentworth robbed it. Nathan shot her son and Mr Polinski was forced to hide the boy. She's been looking for him this whole time and I reckon one of her heavies shot Mr Polinski because he was in the way."

Lewis quietly considered everything I was telling him. "Well that's very thorough, Lauren. You would have made a great detective."

"I learned from the best. Just don't tell Carl I said that."

"Don't worry on that score. I'm not going to ask about the maid's outfit, but if you're through with your roleplaying do you perhaps want to get out of here?"

"The doors are all locked."

Lewis produced a key and accompanied it with a smile. "I appropriated it off a guard. The detail is surprisingly light actually, although I'm hardly complaining."

"Are you here to arrest anyone? How much backup have you brought?"

"No and none. I thought I'd have a look around first, work out what was what. I was trying to find a connection between Redthorne and the murder and it looks as though you've found it. Which means I can report this in and get some proper muscle out here." He looked me over and suddenly I felt very self-conscious in my maid's outfit. "But first I need to get you out of here."

I wished there was time for me to change, but surviving was the priority so as Lewis unlocked the door we strolled through the corridor as though we had every right to be there. Lewis called Carl while we walked, to let him know I was all right, and said Carl would arrange the backup to be dispatched. Feeling more secure about the situation, I allowed Lewis to take the lead. He seemed to know where he was headed and I figured he had scoped out the building before bumping into me.

Along the way he asked me questions about what I had seen, what I had discovered, what my thoughts were on things. It made a refreshing change from Carl, who was always so aloof about my ideas, and I found myself chatting away various theories, bouncing things off Lewis and only strengthening them. I hardly noticed as we approached a strange-looking lift and Lewis summoned it.

"It's a goods' lift," he explained to my bemused expression. "You know, to bring in goods? It's a little off the beaten track so Redthorne doesn't have anyone guarding it. Once we get to the street we'll be fine. We'll leave the area and let the police move in."

I nodded my consent and as the lift arrived we climbed in, and descended in the large clunky contraption. It moved more slowly than an ordinary lift, but as I counted down the floors I felt lighter in spirit and knew at last things were going right for me.

The doors opened and we emerged into some grubby corridors for such a pristine hotel. There were a few people around at this point, although they were all hotel staff and none of them in the employ of Mrs Redthorne. With Lewis taking the lead, we simply strolled right out of the hotel through one of the rear entrances. I could not help but feel that people really did pay no attention to servants, even in this day and age.

If anyone thought it odd that a maid was climbing into a car with a respectably-dressed man, no one commented, and as we pulled away from the hotel I allowed myself to sink into the passenger's seat with a smile lighting my face. Things had become pretty hairy back there for a while, but it was all worth it. I had uncovered a nest of gangsters, had shown Carl how the whole detective thing was done and escaped with my life and almost all of my dignity. And to top it all off I had solved the murder of Anthony Polinski.

"What a day," I exhaled.

"It's not over yet," Lewis said as he drove. "I'm sorry, Lauren, but you've been too good at this. Meeting you at the shop was bad enough, but I had to know what you'd found out. You've amassed quite the file on this case."

I frowned, opening my eyes. That was when I saw the gun he was holding upon me so casually, one hand still upon the wheel. I looked up to him, but he was paying me no attention at all, his face a blank expression.

Perhaps the case was not as sewn up as I had thought.

CHAPTER TEN

The Loose Ends

I was back to sitting in a chair, although at least this time I wasn't tied up. Alexander Lewis had driven very carefully at a steady pace until we arrived at our destination. It surprised me that I knew the place, for I had spent enough of my life there. Carl's house was far from big and there was nothing expensive about it. There couldn't be, considering the lack of money in Carl's life. When I lived with him I helped with the mortgage and since I had left I'd honestly expected for him to have not been able to keep making the payments. As we pulled up, Lewis motioned me out of the car with the gun he was taking pains to conceal from casual observers. I felt I could not perhaps be any more conspicuous dressed as a maid as I was, and hoped enough curtains would twitch that someone might think to call Carl. That Carl was in on this was something I could not even contemplate. We may have had our differences, but Carl and I had never wanted one another dead.

Lewis opened the door with a key and I had a sudden fear of what had happened to Carl. I was frantically trying to piece everything together but none of it made any sense. As I walked into the living room, however, all thoughts of Lewis fled me, for the house was precisely as I remembered it. The furniture was all in the same place, the watercolour print still hung over the fireplace. All the ornaments were there, and I noticed with a small smile that there were still pictures of us on the mantelpiece. Carl and I during happier times. About the only thing missing from the room were the carnations I always bought to give the room a little colour.

I slid into what had always been my favourite side of the settee, eyeing Lewis as he stood purposefully away from me, his gun still levelled upon me. I expected an explanation, or at least I wanted one anyway. To be callously shot after everything I had been through did not seem at all fair to me.

"So what's going on then?" I asked, my voice not cracking.

"You're the faux detective; you tell me."

I wondered whether he was challenging me, whether he actually wanted for me to tell him precisely what he was up to. I had reached a few conclusions already but needed to hear it all from his lips. "You're not a detective," I said, to give him something to be getting on with.

"Of course I'm not a detective."

"And you've never met Carl, have you?"

"No."

That meant he had not killed him, which was more of a relief than I could say. "Carl told me I'd meet a Detective Lewis at the shop."

"That was me. Don't worry, I haven't killed any cops or anything. I called your Detective Carl Robbins and told him I was being assigned to his case."

"And he believed that?"

"The name's legit. There is a Detective Lewis, but he and Carl wouldn't be able to recognise one another by voice. He had no reason to doubt me and welcomed the help."

"I don't get it," I said truthfully. "What were you doing hanging around the shop for anyway? What possible reason could you have had to ...?" My eyes widened. "You killed Mr Polinski."

"Asking or telling?"

"Why'd you do it?"

"You tell me."

"I'm not playing these games!" I realised shouting at him was not the best way for me to get out of the situation alive, so I forced myself to calm down. Fine, I decided. If he had challenged me to work things out for myself then that was precisely what I was going to do. "You killed Mr Polinski," I began, "and then stood back and watched, to find out whether anyone could link you to the murder. You somehow found out I was investigating ..."

"It wasn't hard. You were far from discreet."

"And you wanted to know what I would find out about you. I must have been getting too close for you to meet me at the shop. Why were you there anyway?"

"To scare you off. Believe me, I didn't want you to die, Lauren. I arranged for that kid to jump you in the back room. He was supposed to knock you to the ground, but he got scared, thought he'd be done for assault, so he just spooked you instead before making a run for it.

The rest went fine. We chased him, we lost him, and you were scared. Just not scared enough to leave the case be."

"So I carried on investigating," I continued, "and wound up talking to Nathan and uncovered the whole bank robbery thing." I paused. "You don't have anything to do with Nathan, do you? Killing Mr Polinski wasn't a mistaken identity thing?"

Lewis made a face which suggested I was an imbecile. "There's a slight age difference."

"So when I was nabbed by Redthorne, you realised I would tell them everything to save my life. I might mention your name, describe you to them. They might think you were connected to Nathan's escape ... Actually you were. If you hadn't killed Mr Polinski, Nathan would never have gone on the run and Redthorne would have found him. You were afraid Redthorne would blame you for Nathan's disappearance and come after you for it."

He shifted uncomfortably. "People like Mrs Redthorne are unpredictable. It's always better for them not to even know I exist."

"So you went to the hotel looking for me. Took care of the guards, stole their keys and got me out of there."

"You're welcome."

"And you're a psycho."

"But a clever one."

I had to give him that much at least.

"Go on," he urged, leaning against the wall to get comfortable, his gun never wavering. "This is becoming interesting."

I thought perhaps if I could get him as relaxed as possible, I might have a chance. And the more I talked, the more time I had to live. "There's not much more to tell," I said. "You need to get rid of me because I've seen your face."

"And why have I brought you here?"

That was a good question, and I was not at all certain I liked to think about the answer. "Because you've killed Carl and taken his house?"

"Your Carl's alive and well, and I hope he stays that way. Like I said, I've never met him, which means he can't identify me. Even if he knew I existed, that was. No, you're here because when your body is found here, in Carl's house, the investigation will discover that Carl murdered you. He never got over your break up, you know. So sad. You agreed to talk to him to make amends or something, after having met again over this whole Polinski affair, and he brought you back here and killed you. It's all so very tidy for me, you see. I don't like loose ends."

"I still have one."

"One what?"

"A loose end."

He sighed, making a grand show of being bored when I could tell he was still incredibly intrigued. "Go on then."

"Why did you kill Mr Polinski?"

"Why do you think?"

"It wasn't for money because you didn't take any. It had nothing to do with Nathan. But there was nothing else to him. He was just a kind old man who never did anyone any harm."

"And what else do you know about this kind old man?"

"Nothing. Except he always sent money home to support his family."

"And?"

"And nothing."

"Tell me what he thought of his family."

"He doted on them."

"So why wasn't he living in the same country as them?"

"Because he had to work."

"Other countries have work, Lauren. Polinski's wife is something of a harpy. Bitter and twisted and very, very powerful."

I remembered Rowena Silvers then. So concerned for Mr Polinski, so anxious to find out who killed him.

"Mrs Polinski," Lewis continued, "didn't like it when she found out her husband was having an affair. To be honest, when she contacted me I figured she'd ask me to kill the other woman. But like I said, Mrs Polinski is bitter and twisted."

"She paid you to kill her own husband?"

"And if this whole mess with Nathan Wentworth hadn't've come up, it probably would have all blown over too."

It's difficult to explain what I felt in that moment. On the one hand I was glad it was all out in the open, but the main thing I was feeling was disappointment. Huge disappointment that the very thing which gave Mr Polinski any meaning in life – his family – had been that which had destroyed him. I found myself hoping he had not discovered the truth before he died, otherwise he would have died a broken man.

"This," I said, "hasn't been a good couple of days."

Lewis laughed, but was cut off by the sound of a key turning in the front door. He cursed softly, dropping down and covering me with his gun. "One sound," he whispered, "and I blow your head off."

I very much doubted a bullet could actually blow my head off, but it certainly would have made an untidy mess. I sat silently as we both listened to the steady footfalls through the hallway. They stopped as Carl removed his shoes, for he would never walk through the house with them on, even if it wasn't raining outside. He began to whistle and I could hear him approach the door to the living room. I glanced to Lewis, who stared back at me in warning. His plan had not been to kill Carl, yet if Carl walked in on this scene he would see Lewis's face and the plan would have to change. Lewis fully intended to kill us both now, and there was no way I was going to let him shoot Carl.

Lewis must have seen the resolve in my eyes because he glowered at me, silently giving me one final chance to do the sensible thing. But I was done being sensible. The door began to open as Carl came in, and it was at that moment that I leapt. The room exploded in light and sound as I collided with Lewis, although he threw me from him. I remember barely feeling it, however, for my body had petrified into a strangely numb state. I could see Carl by this point, and he reacted quickly, struggling with the gunman, the two men pushing and slamming each other into walls as they fought for the weapon. I watched all of this from the floor, however, the numbness spreading across my entire body. I raised my hand and felt only a mild curiosity as to why it was stained with sticky crimson fluid.

I don't remember much more of that, only that I found it quite funny for some reason. Carl was by my side, that's something I'll never forget. I reckoned he must have given Lewis a good pounding, otherwise he wouldn't have been able to kneel beside me as he did. I couldn't hear what he was saying, but was aware he had phoned someone frantically. He held my hand, which was nice, and was saying even more things I couldn't hear. And he was crying. I remember that distinctly. He was crying and I felt so sorry for him even as his face faded from my sight. I remember thinking he was far too nice a man to be crying and I hoped that whatever was upsetting him would go away soon.

***

I opened my eyes to stare at a flaky ceiling. There was a curtain around me, and my first thought was that I had fallen asleep in the shower. Then I realised I was lying on a bed, and remembered one or two details. At this point the pain surged through my body and I longed for that earlier numbness. I must have groaned or wailed or sworn very loudly or something, because a hand was suddenly clasping mine and I realised there was something else enclosed in the curtains with me.

"How you feeling?" Carl asked, trying to smile but failing miserably.

"Feeling like I cracked the case," I said, my voice breaking as though in sympathy. "I got shot, didn't I?"

"Bullet went straight through. Missed your lung, so you were lucky."

Lewis was a professional killer. I knew I was somewhat beyond lucky.

"What happened to Lewis?"

"I arrested him," Carl said.

"So you got your man after all."

"Only after you solved the case for me."

"Is that a thank you?"

"It's an admission that I need you."

That sounded rehearsed, but it was sweet of him to mention, so I didn't pull him up over it. "Is everything settled then?" I asked. "With the murder, I mean. You know what happened?"

Carl nodded. "Pretty much everything. Now that we have him, Lewis is being surprisingly open. Even supplied us with his real name. You can fill in some blanks for us when you're up and about, but we have all we need."

"Any word on Nathan?"

"No. Maybe he got away."

"I'm sure you'll find him."

"Not my case. If they want help with their bank robbery they can ask, but I'm sure I'll be too busy."

"I know it was gangster-related, but Nathan still killed a man, Carl."

"And if we catch Nathan, Redthorne will get to him. The only way Nathan Wentworth is going to survive this is if he never stops running."

It was a strange thing for Carl to have said. He had always been so odiously stringent with the rules that it never would have occurred to him to let a criminal go. For any reason.

He seemed to sense what I was thinking because he said, "Maybe there's a lot about me you don't realise has changed."

"Oh?"

"Lauren." He glanced away, and when he looked back it was with strength to his eyes, and at the same time an almost childlike vulnerability. "I thought I'd lost you back there, and suddenly none of this mattered. All my rules, all my laws, all my obsession about control. None of it mattered, Lauren, and I realised ..."

"Are you admitting you were wrong about something?"

"What? No."

"Because that would mean I was right, which is kind of a given whenever we argue."

"Just because I might be wrong, doesn't mean you're necessarily right."

"You sound almost indignant."

"Then maybe there are parts of me that haven't changed at all," he all but huffed.

I managed a weak smile as I found myself drifting back off to sleep. "Yeah, I hope so. I always kind of liked you the way you were."

Mr Polinski had only ever been trying to make a living. It was sad what had happened to him, and no one else could ever quite replace him, but I sure hoped Carl had been right all along. He had said that Mr Polinski was beyond caring about any of this, and that was all I wanted. Because if he was looking down on this world, he would have found out just who had ordered his death; and there's nothing worse than losing faith in the person you love.

THE MURDER OF SNOWMAN JOE

CHAPTER ONE

"Billy! Go wide, go wide!"

Billy Plum had no idea what 'go wide' meant, but assumed he was being told to run as far back as he could. He did not understand why he would want to do that, considering how bad a shot Sally was. They were nine years old and every nine-year-old boy knows how bad girls are at throwing balls, so Billy figured if he did 'go wide' he would only have to come back and retrieve the ball from where he was already standing. He didn't even know why Sally had come along, but that was Brian's fault. Brian was a year older. He had told Billy Sally was coming with them and that was that. Billy did not mind half as much as he made out he did, but she still couldn't throw to save her life.

"Billy!"

"Just throw it."

Billy and Sally were standing about fifteen metres apart, with Brian between them, jumping as though to put off her throw. Sally was looking for an opening and Billy was beginning to wonder whether she would ever get around to throwing the thing. Then, finally, the ball was sailing through the air, over Brian's outstretched hands, and smacked Billy straight in the face.

He fell backwards in the snow and wished he had gone wide after all. Whatever it meant.

"Billy! Billy, are you all right?"

He opened his eyes to find Sally crouched beside him, concern to her eyes. Brian was doing the manly thing of retrieving the ball and Billy wished Sally would just leave him alone. He sat up grumpily, trying to ignore the sting in his face. His face was, of course, about the only thing not covered with several layers. The snowstorm this year had been incredible and in some areas there was over a metre coating the ground. They lived in a small community and, since they had been hit so hard, it meant there was no traffic coming in or going out; and anyone who decided to walk was taking their life into their own hands, especially since the next village was fifty thousand miles away. Or something like that. The only way the snow affected Billy, though, was that it meant the school had closed. Normally that would not have happened, but there were so many families snowed in, it meant even some of the teachers could not make it to work. Besides which, the heating had given out.

Billy, Brian and Sally had spent the morning in the fields, doing whatever they could to keep warm in the snow. The fields were great during the winter. If they tried to enter the fields at any other time of year, they were chased away and their parents were always told. But in the winter no one cared. There were no crops being harvested, nothing being sprayed or weeded or anything like that. With so much snow covering the fields, there was no chance of the farmers doing anything at all with them, and most of the farmers did not mind the children running across their lands.

"Billy, are you all right?"

Billy said something unkind and instantly regretted it. But his nose was hurting and he was trying not to cry, so most of his concentration was on that. Thankfully in this part of the field the snow was only half a metre in most places, but that was still high enough for a nine-year-old to get lost in.

"I got the ball," Brian called, pleased he had managed to locate it.

Billy trudged over to him, running whenever he could. There was a trail they had been following, where the snow was more easily traversable, but they had left it in order to play their game. "We should get back to the trail," Billy said.

"Scared of a little snow, Billy?"

"No," Billy replied defensively. "But I think Sally is."

"I'm not," Sally said. Billy had not realised she was so close behind him. "Come on: Billy's in the middle now."

"How am I in the middle?"

"Brian got the ball you dropped."

"I didn't drop it."

"Well you didn't catch it when I threw it."

Billy thought about that. Technically, Sally was right. But having the ball smack him in the face did not really qualify as dropping it, either. He grumbled something, knowing it was an argument he was not going to win, and Brian and Sally ran to either side, keeping him between them.

Billy had no idea why they had to have invited a girl to begin with.

Brian threw the ball quickly, before Billy was ready, and it sailed over his head. Sally tried to catch it, but at the last moment she cringed and she fumbled the catch. Billy was there in an instant, diving through the snow and finding the ball before she could pick it up. He was freezing now, but he had the ball, which meant Sally was back to being in the middle. He did not know why he was so insistent on that, but it was an odd matter of principle for him.

Tossing the ball high, he watched it arc down into the waiting hands of Brian. A perfect catch. That was the way it should have been.

Brian began jumping around, expending a lot of energy as he pretended to throw the ball, making Sally jump each time for a phantom missile. Billy wondered why he was trying to impress her so much and it was starting to get on his nerves. Deciding for some reason Brian was prolonging throwing the thing, Billy looked about the field. It was a great, flat terrain of whiteness, looking smooth and cold and inviting. There were trees in the distance and he knew there was a brook nearby which he had been told never to play around. There was also something else in the field, however, not too far away. At first he thought it was a person, standing very still and watching them. Then he realised the person was dressed in a white gown, so it had to be a snowman.

It was while he was thinking these things that the ball hit him again in the face.

"That's not funny," he said when he saw Brian was laughing hysterically. Sally looked concerned again, and Billy wished she would just leave him alone. "And I'm fed up with this game."

"So what do you want to do instead?" Brian asked. "There's nothing else around here but snow, so we could throw that I guess."

Billy did not fancy having more things thrown in his face, especially if they were cold, wet and made of ice. "There's a snowman over there. I'm going to go check it out."

"A snowman?" Brian whined. "But they're for kids, Billy."

Billy ignored him. "You coming, Sally?"

"Sure, Billy."

Brian's humour dropped off slightly and he said he would come with them. By that point, Billy was not even that bothered what Brian did.

The snowman, it turned out, was quite big. It was taller than even Brian, and was large, as though the snowman had eaten too many snow pies. He had a carrot for a nose, two buttons for eyes and a row of small stones for a smiling mouth. There was neither hat nor scarf, nor was he wearing any gloves. Indeed, he looked a very sorry fellow, although still seemed to remain happy.

"What a rubbish snowman," Brian said.

"I'd like to see you build one this big," Billy said.

"I wouldn't want to build a stupid snowman." Brian kicked at the mound making up the snowman's shins.

"Stop that," Sally said. "That's not nice."

"It's just a pile of snow, Sally."

"Snowmen have feelings as well, you know."

Brian seemed taken aback. "No they don't. They're just snow."

"They're men too."

Billy did not like to agree with Brian, especially not today, but he had a point.

"Stop kicking him," Sally whined, which of course made Brian kick the thing again. Billy could see the snowman was fairly strong. It did not offer resistance as such, but nor did it flake away. It had likely been standing for several days and parts of it had turned to ice.

Billy could see Sally was growing a little distraught and felt perhaps Brian was going a little too far. "Leave it off, Brian," he said. "Come on, don't upset her."

"What do you care?" Brian asked, kicking again. "Thought you didn't want a girl tagging along anyway."

"What's wrong with you, Brian? You've gone weird all of a sudden."

"Nothing's wrong, Billy. Just kicking a snowman."

Billy knew Brian was being mean; he just didn't know why. It had something to do with Sally, that much was obvious. It probably had something to do with how much attention Sally was paying Billy instead of Brian. Billy had no idea what that mattered to Brian: he certainly didn't even want her attention himself. But Brian was being a jerk and making girls cry was never acceptable.

"Brian, stop it."

"Make me, Billy."

"Just stop making Sally cry."

Brian pushed him. It was not a punch, just a shove, but it was enough to make Billy shove him back. His face was hurting, he was cold, and he didn't like the fact Sally was crying. Brian seemed shocked at first that Billy had fought back. For a single moment Billy felt proud for having stuck up for Sally; then Brian launched himself at him and all Billy felt was the pain of having Brian's fists in his face. He could hear Sally screaming and realised he and Brian were on the floor, rolling around in the snow, landing punches whenever they could, but mainly just clinging to each other as they struggled to stay on top.

What seemed like moments later they were apart and Billy pulled himself back to his feet. He wasn't breathing hard, but his heart was racing and his blood warmed him as it shot through his veins. He reached out for something to steady him as he rose and discovered he was standing next to the snowman. Looking into the cold, happy face, Billy wished he could say he had been fighting over the snowman and not Sally. But he would not have said it aloud because he knew it wasn't true.

With a roar, Brian charged him and there was nothing Billy could do to stop the mad dash. Brian ran into him, encircling his waist with his arms, and the two of them crashed through the snowman, a flurry of snow exploding everywhere, great chunks of ice sluicing down into the freshly fallen snow.

Sally began screaming; properly screaming. Lying in a heap on the floor, Billy and Brian had no idea why. At first Billy thought one of them had been seriously hurt, that maybe one of them had broken a bone or something. But Billy didn't feel as though he had broken anything and he could see his own confusion mirrored upon Brian's face so could not believe he had broken any bones either.

Then he realised Sally wasn't looking at either of them, but at what remained of the snowman. She was screaming because the snowman had been killed. Maybe, Billy thought in that moment, Brian had been right after all. Maybe Sally was just a head case.

Billy opened his mouth to console her. Whatever he would say, it would only be to make her feel better, but all he was thinking was that he could really have done without this. He was already resolved to not bring her out with them next time. It could go back to being just him and Brian, like it always was. There was no need to have some silly girl tag along, screaming at every silly little thing.

Before he could say anything, however, he noticed Brian was also staring at the snowman, and Billy glanced to it, wondering what all the fuss was about. The snowman had come apart. Its head was lying split in two, the mouth of stones lost in the snow, a dull orange stick jutting out to mark where its nose had come to a rest. Within the body of the snowman there was a man, an actual man. He was hunched over, lying now on the ground; his hands were behind his back and securely tied to some form of pole. There had been a man inside the snowman; a real man.

Then Billy saw the man's face, frozen by the cold, the blood clinging to his face like icicles. There was a gaping hole in his temple where pieces of bone jutted out, while his eyes were staring out from a perfectly preserved expression.

And Billy and Brian began to scream as well.

CHAPTER TWO

"Here you go, John."

John Stoker looked at the box with a mixture of amusement, happiness and horror. Amusement because he wondered how many more such boxes they had in the attic; happiness because it pleased his wife to have found it; and horror at the thought of having to deal with it. "You do realise, Brenda, we're going to have to take it all down again at the end. And taking it all down's never as much fun as putting it up to begin with."

John Stoker had always liked Christmas, but had never understood why his wife had to go so overboard with the decorations. Before retirement, Stoker had found his workload lessened this time of year. Christmas was all about domestics: arguments about turkeys, Christmas trees and so forth. There were very few violent robberies or murders at Christmas, which showed even bad people tended to have families who cared about them. Snow was good as well. It was like rain in that criminals did not like to go out in it. Hot, sunny days brought out villains like flying ants, but foul weather kept them huddled at home.

Retirement had been good to the Stokers. Brenda had flourished and, while her hair was turning quickly white and her wrinkles were becoming more pronounced, she veritably beamed with happiness each day. Moving from the city had been the perfect salve for her, and Stoker was pleased to see her so happy. As for Stoker himself, he had finally allowed himself to relax. His short hair was still mainly black, but he had let his thick beard grow out, and that was turning a pleasant shade of grey. Physically, he retained the strength and stamina he had always possessed in his youth, although his stomach had filled out very quickly and he was always meaning to do something about that.

Reaching into the box, he removed a string of plastic bells and wished they had thought of a better way to store them since the things were now so intertwined it was going to take him all afternoon to unravel. Once Christmas was over he knew he would be so fed up with putting away the decorations he would just throw the things in the box as they were and have to untangle them again next year.

Dealing with annoyances seemed to be what Christmas was all about.

"John, there's someone at the door."

Stoker looked up, noticing there was indeed someone making her way down their garden path. The Stoker household was a large bungalow with more than enough room for two people. Their back garden was a haven for wildlife, complete with pond and rockeries, while at the front of their house was a well-tended display of flowers of which Brenda was exceptionally proud. It gave her the opportunity to spend a lot of time outside while being able to gossip with the neighbours even as she tried her best to outdo them. At the moment, of course, everything was covered in snow.

Setting down the line of bells, Stoker went to the front door to open it. The snow was so thick outside the approaching woman would still be several seconds away. As Stoker gave the door a shove, however, it only gave an inch before compacting too much snow directly before it. It was at times like this he wished he had a front door which opened inwards.

"I got it," said the woman on the other side, and he could see the faint outline of someone shovelling snow with her feet. She had come wearing wellington boots, he noticed, which was an entirely sensible thing to do in the snow.

Between the two of them, they finally managed to get the door open and Stoker greeted the woman with a smile. She was aged somewhere in her late thirties and was wrapped with enough layers to insulate a loft. Her short blonde hair was carefully tucked beneath a woolly hat, her ears framed by furry mufflers. About the only thing visible about the woman were her cheeks, burning bright red in the cold, her sharp blue eyes and her ever-warming smile. Stoker had known Felicity Hart for the eight years he and Brenda had been living in the village. He had watched her develop from a young, keen tadpole to a beautiful, inspiring frog. Not that she would have much appreciated the analogy, but making inappropriate metaphors was all a part of his gardener's lifestyle.

"Liz, good morning."

"Morning, John. Ooh, you're getting into the spirit."

Stoker smiled, knowing Brenda had decorated the hallway only that morning. "Come on in. Don't stand on the doorstep all day, it's freezing."

"Not by half."

Stoker stepped aside to allow her inside before closing out the cold once more. Hart was shivering, even through her layers, and Stoker felt a pang of concern. "Brenda, dear. It's Liz. Could you put the kettle on? I think she needs warming up."

He took Hart's coat, but she kept most of her layers. Stoker led her into the living room and sat her by the fire. One of the things Stoker had always wanted was a real fire and living in the bungalow had allowed him to actually realise his dream. There were several pieces of wood already crackling, but he added another just to make Hart feel at home. Home was, after all, where the Hart was. Being a real fire, they had to sit a little farther than they would had it been a replica, but there was nothing like the warmth of a real fire.

Brenda arrived with Hart's tea and asked her how she was. The two women got along well, but did not speak much. It was always a pleasure to see Hart; but this time there was something in her face Brenda clearly did not like, but was too polite to mention. Brenda said she had some things to do in the kitchen and left them to it.

"I'm sorry," Hart said as she sipped her tea, her trembling hands clutching the mug tightly. "I don't mean to intrude, John."

"It's never an intrusion, Liz. But you didn't come just to enjoy my fireplace, did you?"

"No, but I am enjoying it," she said with a genuine smile. It was strange how she could keep such a demeanour, but then Stoker supposed this village was a lot different to where he had worked. He had lived his whole life in a big city and had always wanted to retire to a small community, as cut off from the rest of the country as possible. Barrowville was precisely what he had always dreamed of. Once he had managed to get past the somewhat ominous name, he had discovered it was perfect. With a population of one thousand five hundred and seven and most of its area taken by fields, it was small, quiet and peaceful. For eight years he had lived the life he had never been able to find in the big city.

Felicity Hart was the daughter he could have had had he been born in Barrowville. Instead, the big city had taken his only child and left him with his misery. Hart was a detective working for the local constabulary. With such a small community there was a tiny police department, so Hart fulfilled many duties. Primarily she loved investigating things but, with so little crime in Barrowville, most of her time was taken up with domestics.

Today he had the impression Hart had come to him with something more.

"There's been a murder," she said, the words sounding strange as they left her mouth. He could see she did not quite believe it herself, as though she thought there was some explanation she had missed.

"Had to happen eventually," Stoker said. "This your first?"

"Second," she said, sipping her tea. "My first was a couple of years after you arrived. You remember Holly Tree?"

"Liz, Holly Tree was a horse."

"A horse which was murdered."

"What was murdered today then? A cow?"

"A snowman."

Stoker blinked, wondering whether the cold had addled the woman's mind. "A snowman?"

Hart seemed to be having trouble organising her thoughts, which was understandable considering she had never really had to think about this sort of thing before. "Some kids found a snowman in Old MacDonald's field. Turns out there was a man inside."

"A man inside?"

"He'd been tied to a stake and the stake had been shoved into the ground. Then someone had … well, built a snowman around him to hide the body."

That was actually quite clever, although Stoker did not say such aloud. The ingenuity of criminals always impressed him, especially since most of the ones he had dealt with had either been opportunists or had not known how to properly cover their tracks.

"Have you spoken with Old MacDonald?" Stoker asked.

"He won't want to see me."

"You're the police and you've found a body on his field. He doesn't have much of a choice."

She was staring into her mug. "I know."

Stoker shifted slightly in his chair. He knew Hart must have been going through a terrible time over this. It was the first truly bad crime she had ever had to deal with and if she was not careful she would fall apart. Hart was a well-liked woman about the village, but that would not help her at all when she was talking to people about their possible criminal activities. Standing in the stocks at the summer fete was a far cry from knocking on someone's door and asking them to prove where they were the night before.

And then there was Old MacDonald. His real name was Donald Truman, but the nickname had been around long before Stoker had come to the village – likely before Hart was even born – and it was what everyone called him. Stoker had only met Truman twice and had found him to be an aged, abusive ogre who could have done with bathing a little more often. Still, if the body had been found on his field, Hart needed to talk to him.

"I was kind of hoping," Hart said, as though reading his mind, "you might come with me?" She looked him in the eye then and Stoker wished she hadn't. She had such a sweet innocence to her that Stoker had never been able to say no to her in anything.

"I'm retired," he said. "I'm not allowed to question suspects with you."

"This isn't the city, John. Around here you can help as much as you like. I can conscript you, if you like."

Stoker laughed. No, he would not like to be conscripted. "Why don't you just talk with Truman and tell me what you find out? I can help you sort through the evidence and statements, but I'm not getting involved in the actual investigation."

Hart was back to not looking at him, but this time she was staring into the roaring flames of the fireplace. "I can't do this, John," she said in a small voice.

"Can't do what?"

"This is a murder, an actual murder."

"And it's what you've trained for."

"You didn't see the body, John." She was looking back at him now and her eyes were trembling more fiercely with fear than her body was from the cold. "I've never seen a dead body before, I've …" She closed her eyes and controlled herself. When she opened them again, there was a semblance of calm to her, but not much. "This wasn't just a fight that got out of hand. I've dealt with fights, I've dealt with broken bones and brawls over other people's wives. This was murder, John. Someone killed this guy, bashed his head in, then made the conscious decision to stake him in a field and cover him with snow. They even gave him a carrot nose and a stone smile. I didn't train for this, John, and I don't know what to do." She looked into her mug and barely above a whisper said, "I'm terrified I'm going to screw this up."

Sometimes Stoker wished Hart would not be so honest with him. But she was also correct. He had seen some pretty disturbing crimes in the past, had seen Hart deal with despicable crimes herself, but this was a well-planned murder and that was something she could not handle. If she fought this alone she would fail, and the murderer would walk free.

"I shouldn't get involved," Stoker said. "I really shouldn't."

"But will you? For old time's sake?"

"No, Liz. But I'll do it for you." The words were spoken and could not now be taken back, even if he had wanted to. "Besides which, I owe you for clearing my front porch of snow. If not for you, I'd be stuck in the house."

"Thank you, John," she said, not getting excited. She was still nervous, but not nearly so afraid of her failure. Rising, she set her mug to one side. "Thanks for the tea. I'd best get things together so we can go talk to Truman."

Stoker could think of nothing to say, so did not say anything. He took Hart to the door and helped her on with her coat, telling her he would meet up with her so they could talk to the crotchety old farmer together. Then he had the unpleasant task of informing Brenda.

He found his wife standing at the door to the kitchen. She did not say anything; her expression was bland, but he could see the fear to her face.

"It'll be all right, Brenda," Stoker said. "I'll just help Liz with this one case, then we'll get back to normal. Maybe I'll even untangle that set of plastic bells, eh?"

Brenda turned away and headed back into the kitchen, leaving Stoker alone with his memories and fears. She had every right to worry, had every right to be disappointed in him. There was a reason they had left the city, a reason they had abandoned their old life. Now it seemed it had followed them to Barrowville.

By the end of the investigation, they both knew they could well lose everything all over again.

CHAPTER THREE

There was a massive fence around the house and Stoker knew they would not be getting inside. The fields belonging to Donald Truman were clearly not being used by him during the bad weather and the old man had likely holed himself up in his house like everyone else. Thankfully, the snowfall had decreased to a mild flurry and Stoker was able to walk around without much difficulty. It was a fair-sized house encircled by a high metal fence to deter visitors. About the property there stood a guard of trees, heavy with snow and casting deep shadows across the property. The land about the house was thick with vegetation which led into the nearby woodland. Beneath the snow underfoot there was likely a dirt trail through which Truman could bring his vehicles. The farmer's fields were nowhere in sight, but that was one of the first assumptions Stoker had abandoned when first coming to live in the small, rural community.

As he stood at the fence, peering into Truman's property, Stoker tried to work out how much use the old man might be. He had a reputation as being an abusive recluse, but that did not make him a sick enough man to stake an intruder in his field like a scarecrow. Through the fence he could see a messy storage area, boxes and containers strewn around. There was little snow beyond the fence, as though it was afraid to fall upon Truman's property. Or that he had cleared it with a snow shovel, Stoker corrected himself seriously. He could see several tools now, leaning against a wall, and indeed there were spades among them. He would not get anywhere in solving this case if he began to think in a flowery fashion.

"Anything?" Hart asked, coming to join him. Stoker had gone on ahead to see whether he could get Truman's attention, although so far all he could see was the man's front yard. The house itself stood silent and still. There was no sign of Christmas decorations, but then somehow Stoker had not expected any.

"Nothing," Stoker said. "Did you bring everything you need from the station?"

"All I need is my badge, and even Old MacDonald knows me, so I don't think I'll need even that."

"I should probably have taken a look at the crime scene," Stoker reflected.

"It's still there. So's the body."

"At the crime scene?"

"No, the body's in the morgue. I just meant neither of them is going anywhere."

Stoker could see she was still shaken by what had happened. He was willing to give her a lot of leeway on this assignment, but the fact was she was the officer in charge of the investigation and she needed to suck up her gut and just get on with it.

They had not, however, quite reached the point where he needed to tell her that.

"We need to get Truman's attention somehow," Stoker said. "I don't suppose he has a bell on his fence or something?"

"I've never been out here, actually," Hart said. "Truman likes to keep to himself and that's fine with me."

Stoker heard movement then and hoped it meant someone was coming to the fence. Then he saw two massive forms bounding towards him and he recoiled as the beasts slammed into the metal railings, shuddering the entire thing as it fought to resist them. Stoker had seen a lot of different types of dog when he had been a detective, but Dobermanns had always scared him. They were too big and too fierce to be reasoned with, and as they slammed themselves repeatedly against the bars he could see murder in their eyes. The entire area shuddered at their barking while snow fell from trees in fright.

Even though they were on the other side of the fence, Stoker shivered. "I can see how he keeps nosy visitors away."

"It doesn't mean he kills them, though."

"Maybe the noise will get his attention."

"What do you want?"

The voice was old and craggy and seemed to come from nowhere. Momentary fear shot through Hart's face, although thankfully she did not betray her emotions vocally. They turned to find Truman standing only ten metres behind them. He was aged probably somewhere in his eighties and walked with the aid of a gnarled cane. His clothes were not ragged, but they looked highly patched, as though the man did not earn enough to ever buy new ones. He wore a thin coat, but Stoker could not believe it was enough to protect him from the cold; especially since he was wearing neither gloves nor hat. His face was carved of strong, determined lines, mostly hidden by a thick white beard, the hair atop his head frail and wispy. His eyes were burning with something, but Stoker was not certain it was hatred. From his few earlier encounters with Truman, Stoker felt the man just wanted to be left alone.

"Detective Hart," Hart said, recovering quickly.

"I know who you are. What do you want?"

"Mr Truman," she continued, "have you been to your fields recently?"

"No."

"When was the last time you were in one of them?"

"It's snowing, Miss Hart. Why would I go to my fields?" He made a strange sound which was half grunt, half laugh. There was a twinkle to his eye which indicated questions like these were among the reasons he didn't like talking to people.

"I did notice it was snowing, yes," Hart said. "When was the last time you went to the north field by the river?"

Truman seemed about ready to make another sarcastic comment, but probably realised the best way to get rid of these people was to answer their questions. "About a month ago. Before the really bad snow settled. Just walking around to check my property. Am I under arrest?"

"Some kids were playing in that field yesterday."

"If they hurt themselves they've only got themselves to blame. They trespass on my property, they don't have a leg to stand on."

"The kids are fine, thanks for your concern. But they found something."

"An unexploded World War II bomb?"

"They ... What? No."

"Shame. Always fancied finding one of those."

"They found a body."

"Fox?"

"A human body."

"You mean another trespasser?"

"Mr Truman," Stoker said calmly. "A man has been murdered on your property. Do you know anything about it?"

That instantly sobered him and Stoker could see it also came as a surprise. Truman was a man who did not care for other people, but that was when he had believed the death to be attributed solely to the cold. An actual murder did seem to disturb him, which raised Stoker's opinion of him.

"So my field," Truman said, "is going to be swarming with media? I'm going to have cameras shoved in my face? They'll accuse me because I'm a cranky old hermit? What can I do to help?"

It was not the reason Stoker would have liked, but it would do nicely. Stoker smiled at Hart, silently indicating she could now ask her questions.

"The body was frozen," she said, "but initial reports suggest it's been there for about a week. Have you noticed anything strange in the past week? Anyone building a snowman in your field, perhaps?"

"A snowman? No. But I did chase some kids off my property a while back. Might have been a week ago, I don't remember."

"Are we talking about the same field?"

"No. That was the south field. But they were coming from the direction of the river, so they could have murdered this guy and were on their way out when I caught them."

"Guy? I never said the body was male."

"No," Truman said, pointing at Stoker. "He did."

Stoker thought back and could not remember whether he had. He had not realised Hart had been intentionally not revealing that fact and wished he had asked her beforehand how she wanted to play this.

"Am I a suspect?" Truman asked.

"Everyone's a suspect," Hart said. "How many people did you chase off?"

"Three, I think."

"What did they look like?"

"People."

"Anything more specific?"

"Men."

"Were they white, Asian?"

"White. One had a beard. I really don't remember what they looked like. But they had a dog. Little terrier, brown fur and big eyes. Ran with a limp, but it didn't have a broken foot. Probably hit it on something. The snow wasn't as thick on the ground back then, so the dog wasn't swallowed whole by it. I think the worst of the snowstorm hit that night, because I remember wondering how the terrier was going to get around in the thick snow."

Hart hesitated. "You don't remember the people, but you remember everything about the dog?"

"I like dogs, Miss Hart."

"Do you think you'd be able to recognise the dog again?"

"Sure."

"Then we might call on you again. Thank you for your time."

Truman grunted and moved towards his fence. There would be a gate somewhere, although Stoker had not been able to find it. Perhaps Truman hid the thing to deter all but the most intrusive prowlers.

As they strolled back through the snow, Stoker tried to piece together everything they had learned. It was not an incredible amount, but the investigation had only just begun, so everything was relevant at that moment. Stoker had always loved the beginning of investigations because every small thing could mean something. It was as the investigation drew on that it always became more complicated; and that was when things could go sour.

"Thanks for jumping in at last," Hart said. "I was floundering there."

"It's your case, Liz. Besides, you were doing fine."

Hart said nothing to that. She clearly did not believe him, but that was her prerogative.

"So," she said, "what did you think of him?"

"He's innocent."

"How can you tell?"

"Because he wasn't guilty." Stoker realised Hart really had not seen that. She had spent her entire career being able to read people, but her fear of Truman was overshadowing her sense of reason. "Truman doesn't like people," Stoker explained. "He doesn't want attention. You saw how he reacted when he thought the media might come down on him. If he was going to kill a trespasser, I can't see him staking the guy inside a snowman. He'd know it would thaw eventually."

"Maybe it was a cover."

"You don't believe that."

"No. I don't. But I don't have any other suspects."

"There are the three men he saw. And their dog."

"Great."

"It's a place to start." Stoker had never understood despondency following an initial interview. They had gained far more from

Truman than some of the other people Stoker had questioned in his time. The thing which was getting to him most was the whole snowman thing. The current storm was a bad one, but every snowstorm ended. The body was bound to have come to light eventually.

"I just hope we don't have to talk to him again," Hart said, shuddering.

"Truman?" Stoker looked her over and was surprised by her level of disdain, even hostility. "He's harmless."

"How do you figure that?"

"For one thing, he has angry dogs. That's a sure sign of a man who doesn't want to be bothered. That and the fence. He's also savvy, which is a sad thing really."

"How do you mean?"

"He knows as soon as the media get wind of the murder, they'll focus on him. Weird old guy who doesn't talk to people? They'll plaster his face all over the papers and demand his arrest. Maybe you'll even have to bring him in just to please public opinion. This could ruin his life, you know."

"That wouldn't happen here."

"It's happens everywhere. Barrowville's a small community, Liz. It adds a good backdrop for the papers to work their story. And the name will give the journalists a field-day with their headlines."

He could see she was thinking about it and was glad she seemed to be accepting what he was saying.

"So we investigate these people he saw. He said they were men, but he also said they were kids. He didn't seem to remember anything about them except a beard, but I'm assuming they were in their late teens, early twenties."

"They could have been anything. To a man in his eighties, 'kids' could mean anything below forty."

Hart grew only more despondent over this. "So we round up every male in the village and question them all?"

"I don't know," Stoker admitted. "Something about this doesn't sit right with me."

"You mean apart from the sick snowman thing?"

"I'm not so sure it was sick."

"Come again."

"I have a theory on why someone would bury a corpse inside a snowman."

"What is it, then?"

But Stoker shook his head. "I think first I should see the crime scene."

"Sure. I'll show you the way."

Stoker could sense Hart was losing hope with this, but he had not just been encouraging when he had told her she was handling the case well. She may have only ever dealt with the odd major crime, but Hart had been trained well and all her experience counted for something. She was a strong woman with a good heart and Stoker knew, given enough support, she could crack this case. Perhaps she even did not need him at all, other than for psychological reasons. She was better than she knew, and it was Stoker's job to make sure she realised this.

At the same time, he was also intrigued. This was an unusual case and the detective in Stoker wanted nothing more than to solve it. He thought back to Brenda then and knew she had been right. He could not afford to lose his head. He could not afford for the past to repeat itself.

There was a reason, after all, they had come to Barrowville. The past needed to be left firmly behind.

CHAPTER FOUR

John Stoker was a legend. Of course, Hart had never heard of him before he had come to live in Barrowville, but he represented everything she had ever loved above detectives. He could only have risen higher in her estimation were he to don a fedora and trench coat while narrating events, using flowery metaphors and words like 'dame'.

Hart did not know why she had always wanted to work for the police, but supposed it had something to do with her family. Her younger sister Gail had Down's syndrome, so took a lot of looking after. She had matured early in life and had come to realise the value of looking after people she loved. As she had grown into an adult, it had seemed natural to her that she should extend that philosophy to her working life and the police had been a natural career path.

But Barrowville was not somewhere she could work the type of cases she read about in the newspapers. The worst thing she had ever had to deal with was the occasional sexual assault, and they were harrowing enough. Actual murder was unthinkable in Barrowville; even angry neighbours stopped short of actually putting a hatchet in someone's head. When Stoker had first come to live in Barrowville, Hart had been more excited than she had ever been. She remembered finding reasons to see him, to talk to him about what he must have seen. But Stoker was reluctant to speak of much of it, and his wife never really liked the talk in her house, so Hart had generally gone away disappointed. But there was always a gleam to Stoker's eye when he spoke of the past and Hart would usually be able to get some form of story from him.

As far as work was concerned, she had never asked him for help. Sometimes she had gone to him for advice, especially on the worst crimes. He had always proven willing to help, and even seemed to enjoy sharing his experience with her. This was the first time she had ever asked him to come with her out into the field – literally in fact – and she was grateful he had not turned her down.

Now all she had to do was prove herself competent enough to at least help him solve the case. She could not stand it if he ever looked upon her with eyes filled with disappointment.

She had taken him to the remains of the snowman. A large portion of the field had been cordoned off. There were few officers in Barrowville, so there was only one constable standing guard. He looked freezing and she imagined his flask of tea had run dry long ago, but she had not thought to bring any more. The constable's name was Rob Manson and he did not need to see any identification from either of them to let them through. Snow had been falling steadily throughout the day; consequently the footprints left by the children who had found the body had been mostly filled in, while the snowman itself was all but merged into the landscape now. Like some fallen giant finally come to rest and slowly turning into a hill.

Stoker stood several metres from the snowman, his eyes searching the area as though he would be able to see something she had missed. It was precisely what Hart had brought him there for, yet there was a part of her which hoped he would not find anything. It would be a boost to her ego to think she had been thorough, yet would not help the investigation any.

"What did the children say?" Stoker asked at last.

"Not much. They were playing, they knocked over the snowman and found the body."

"What did they say about the ground?"

"The ground?"

"Was the snow disturbed at all? Were there footprints from the people who committed the murder?"

"Oh. Not that they mentioned. They said there was no evidence of anyone else in the area, so I would assume not."

"It's never a good idea to assume anything."

Hart felt a momentary twinge of resentment. "The coroner's still looking at the body, but it was out here for at least a few days, if that's what you're getting at. The snow would have filled in the footprints."

"I'm not trying to undermine you, Liz. I'm just trying to gather corroborating evidence. If there were footprints and the coroner is saying the body's been here for days, that would mean someone came back to the scene of the crime."

She had not thought of that and knew she should have.

"I'll talk with them again, but I did get the impression they thought no one was out this way. Truman has a reputation, you know. No sane kid would play in his field if they thought Old MacDonald was lurking in the area."

"That's a point."

Hart tried not to feel proud that she had thought of something Stoker had missed. This was not a competition but a murder investigation.

Stoker walked across to what remained of the snowman. He pulled the carrot out of the snow and held it up to her. "What's this?"

"A nose."

"Then why isn't it back at the station?"

Hart knew what he meant. The body and the stake had been removed, but she had not honestly thought the carrot would bear any significance to the case. "Because it's a carrot."

"And where did the carrot come from?"

"From a carrot patch," she said dryly.

From where he crouched, Stoker looked at her with a steady gaze. "If we can trace this carrot back to where it was bought, we may be able to put a face to the person who bought it. Maybe a bearded, young face."

"But it's a carrot. How are we supposed to track it?"

"Failing anything else, there could be fingerprints."

Hart did not like to say that there would be no fingerprints on the carrot. It was possible the cold had frozen some onto it, but she did not think the cold worked that way. The fact she did not know for certain, however, stilled her tongue. She knew she had made a mistake and felt like a rookie on her first walk of the beat. Thankfully, Stoker was not cruel enough to mention it.

Producing an evidence bag from her pocket, she took the carrot and dropped it inside. Stoker's attention had already moved on. She could see he was thinking and wondered what was going through his mind.

"I think it's time I saw the body," he said at last, rising and brushing the snow from his legs.

Hart did not like to say, but this was an odd order of conducting an investigation. They had already interrogated their first suspect and Stoker was only now looking at the scene of the crime and the body. She knew what he would reply should she bring it up with him, however. He would tell her this was her investigation and he was just lending a hand. While that was technically true, she had not knocked on his door because she had wanted someone to hold her hand through this, but to fill in all the blanks she would miss.

"I'll take you to the morgue," was all she said.

It was a long walk back to the station. Ordinarily they would have driven, but the roads were thick with snow and even if they could have got a vehicle through, they would have only ended up getting it stuck. Trudging through on foot may have been slow going but, with her wellington boots, Hart was more than willing to walk ten times the length of the village if necessary.

The station was small and had little in the form of staff. The coroner had been and gone, having left his notes behind. Hart had discussed the findings prior to going out to meet with Stoker, although there was nothing conclusive on offer yet. She led Stoker to the morgue out the back. Barrowville was odd in that its emergency services were all positioned next to one another. Years ago some eager architect had knocked out several walls in an attempt to join them all together. It had not worked out entirely as expected, but it did allow easy access from the police station to what passed for the Barrowville hospital. They had no surgery, of course, but they did have a doctor and some basic facilities. One of those facilities was a mortuary, which every settlement needed. This was the first time Hart had needed access to a corpse during an investigation and was glad she could pretty much just find her own way to it.

The body had been left out on a bed, a sheet covering it for decency. Hart was reluctant to remove the sheet. There was no decomposing stench to the air and she assumed the body had been tended to in whatever professional manner was normal. Hart did not hang around dead bodies and had no idea the processes in dealing with them.

"I guess you've seen corpses before," Hart said, if only to make conversation in the thick, cloying air.

"A few, yes."

"Do you get used to it?"

"You mean did I gain professional detachment?"

Hart nodded.

"Yes."

She noted he did not meet her eyes as he said the word. There was something more and she was debating whether to press.

Eventually she decided she probably needed to know, if she had any hope of solving this case. "You don't sound too sure," she said.

"There's only one time I got emotional when viewing a body, Liz. When I had to identify one."

"An informant?"

"My daughter, Sue."

Hart wished she could sometimes just keep her nose in her own business. "Jesus, I'm sorry, John."

"You shouldn't be. You didn't kill her. Now," he said, taking a deep breath, "show me what I need to see."

Hart removed the sheet so he could see the body, inner disgust at her thoughtlessness overriding any sense of nausea she might have felt in the presence of the corpse. The coroner's notes were sitting on a table, alongside the various items connected to the murder, such as the pole to which the man had been tied. She knew she probably should have them locked away in the police station, but she had commandeered this room as her base of operations while she considered the case and she needed to have everything at her fingertips for her to think properly.

Stoker examined the corpse with a calm detachment. He even touched the body, at which point Hart had to look away and pretend to be busy doing something else. Stoker took his time, being more thorough than Hart felt he needed to be; but he was the experienced officer in this kind of thing.

"Do we know who this chap is yet?" Stoker asked at last.

"No idea. He's not from Barrowville, that's for sure."

"Look at this. Here."

"Do I have to?"

He gazed at her with an expression halfway between bemusement and disappointment. "Only if you want to do your job, Liz."

Offering a sarcastic smile, Hart forced herself to look at the corpse. Stoker was of course pointing directly to the head wound. "What do you think caused this?"

"Luckily I have the coroner's report for that." She flicked through the notes, although she had already read them; it gave her the perfect opportunity to take her eyes from the body. "Blunt instrument. Likely a hammer."

"Does this look like a hammer wound to you?"

Reluctantly, Hart looked at the injury. It was a medium-sized hole formed of a semi-circle where something heavy and blunt had cracked through the skull at a downwards angle. "Yes," she said. "That looks just like a hammer blow to me."

"Good. Because that's what it is."

She narrowed her eyes at him. "If you agree with the report, why did you make me look at the body?"

"Because bad things happen in life, Liz, and people like us don't have the luxury of ignoring them. By the end of this investigation you may see far worse than this poor fellow and you need to be prepared for that."

"You think there will be more bodies turning up?"

"That depends why this one was killed."

Hart did not like the way Stoker was manipulating her, treating her like his assistant and playing with her fears and loathing. She had to remind herself that she had gone to him. "You mentioned you had a theory," she said. "Fancy sharing that yet?"

"First, the evidence. What's the stake?"

Hart had already examined the stake, but did not mind doing so again. "It's a fence pole. It could have come from anywhere. There are fences all around this place, what with all the fields. If the snow wasn't so bad we could work out precisely where it came from, but my guess is it will be from somewhere close to the field where the body was found."

"And the other evidence?"

"There is no other evidence."

"You're forgetting the carrot."

"You're seriously considering the carrot to be important?"

"Everything's considered important until it's been ruled out."

Trying not to sigh, Hart produced the carrot. It was still cold as she set it on the table, not removing it from its evidence bag. "So we have two things to examine now," she said.

"Hopefully one of them will provide some answers."

"John, your theory?"

"Yes, my theory. You're not going to like it."

"I don't doubt that."

"I think we were meant to find the body."

"What?"

"Just not yet."

"How do you mean?"

"If you'd killed someone and wanted to hide the corpse, you'd shove it in the river or bury it somewhere in the woods. Instead, these killers built a snowman around it. Snowmen thaw. If this was a normal winter, in a few days, a week at the most, the snow would have thawed enough for the body to start showing, at which point someone would have noticed."

"But the snowstorm's getting worse, John. That snowman could have conceivably stayed out there for weeks."

"But our killers wouldn't have known that. My theory is that they killed this man, stood him in a field and hid him in this unique fashion; then they fled Barrowville, knowing by the time their crime was discovered, they would be halfway across the country."

"So they're gone?"

"No."

"No? John, you're not talking sense."

"It's like you said," he replied seriously. "The storm's getting worse. I think our killers intended to flee, but found they couldn't. Vehicles aren't getting in or out of Barrowville. Unless they left on foot, they're stuck here. And how far's the next village?"

"Too far," Hart said, her heart sinking. "This guy's not from around here, so I'm guessing his killers aren't either. You're telling me there's a group of murderers hanging around someone's barn somewhere?"

"It's worse than that, Liz."

"Oh, do go on."

"They intended to be long gone by the time the body was discovered, but when they holed up they must have figured things the way you did: that the snowman could conceivably have stayed there for weeks."

"But it didn't. It was just by chance those kids found it."

"I reckon the killers would have been keeping an eye on the field. Maybe checking it once every day or something. I think it's a sure bet our murderers know we're onto them. Even though we have no idea who they are, they know we're looking for them now."

Hart's heart sank a little lower. Barrowville had never before had to deal with this kind of thing, but it looked as though the murder had only been the beginning. She realised with horror she was going to have to find these killers before the killers found her.

The entire village was relying on her to save them and she got squeamish just looking at a dead body. Stoker was right: before the investigation could be closed, she was destined to see far worse things indeed.

CHAPTER FIVE

Their first stop was to see Larry Millar. Millar ran the local greengrocery and if anyone knew where the carrot nose had come from, it should be him. It was a ridiculous thing to even consider, but Hart had to admit she did not have much in the way of leads. Even Stoker was giving the impression it would not amount to anything, but he insisted every small possibility had to be properly investigated. What he had said back in the mortuary still hung heavy on Hart's mind. As she walked through the village on her way to the grocery, she could not help but look at all the houses she had known her whole life, think about all the people who lived within those houses and wonder how many of them might not still be alive two days from then. Hart did not know every single person in Barrowville, but she was in a job where she knew more than most. Millar was in another such role, and between them she was hoping they might be able to work out whether any strangers had passed through recently. It was, perhaps, the only thing she expected to get from interviewing the man.

She entered the shop with a smile. Ordinarily, Millar's produce would be outside on show, but the snow was keeping him inside, along with most of his customers. She was glad to see him still open, however, but had not expected otherwise. Larry Millar was a cliché pillar of the community and would never let his neighbours down.

"Morning, Liz," Millar said when he saw her. He was aged in his fifties and had been running the greengrocery for more years than Hart could remember. He had a son and daughter who generally helped him, but they were nowhere in sight. A portly man with a friendly disposition, Millar's smile faltered somewhat when he saw her company. "Trouble?"

"Yes," Hart said, "unfortunately. John's helping me look into it."

"Not my Tony again?"

Hart smiled. His son had been pulled in a couple of times for antisocial behaviour. Nothing serious, just being drunk in the street and trying to start a fight. He was a good enough lad when he was working, but was one of those people who really should lay off the drink since he obviously couldn't handle it. "No, Larry," she said. "There's been some trouble in Truman's fields."

Millar grunted. "His dogs attack someone?"

"No, we don't think Truman's involved."

"If you can arrest someone for forgetting their pleases and thank yous, go right ahead."

"Truman comes here?" Stoker asked.

"Sure. Everyone comes here, even hermits. Old MacDonald has to eat, same as everyone else, and he can't grow all his own produce. He's self-serving that one; sells his wares without involving the rest of the village, but still comes here for his luxuries."

"And what does Truman consider luxuries?" Stoker asked.

"Whatever he can't grow. Toilet paper mainly. Buys the stuff in bulk so he doesn't have to come here too often."

"And groceries?"

"Of course groceries. Everyone comes here for their groceries."

"Have you had any strangers through recently?" Hart asked.

"Strangers? Now and then. Relatives of so-and-so, friends of such-and-such."

"We're after a group of men, possibly around three. One would have had a beard. They may have been fairly young."

Millar scratched his chin. "Well, I'm not saying they didn't come in, but I don't really remember anyone like that. When are we talking about?"

"Maybe about a week ago?"

"Before the snow?"

"No, this would have been around the same time as it started getting really bad."

Millar continued to think. "I don't know. My memory's not too good."

"Maybe Tony or Clarissa served them?"

"Clara's concentrating on her schooling lately so she hasn't been working in the shop. Tony might have, yes. Hold on. Tone! Police!"

Hart winced. "You're going to scare him."

"Sometimes that boy needs scaring. Tone! Police want to question you! There are two of them so it's serious!"

There were a few moments of silence and then they heard movement upstairs. Frantic movement at first, then begrudgingly a figure poked his head around the door. He was aged somewhere in his early twenties, thin and terrified.

"Lady wants to ask you a few questions," his father told him.

"Hi, Tony."

"Ma'am."

Hart smiled. "Sorry, it's nothing to worry about. We're investigating something and you might be able to help."

"I'm not in any trouble?" Tony flicked his eyes to his father.

Millar laughed soundly. "I don't get much fun in life, don't begrudge an old man."

"Mr Millar," Stoker said, addressing the younger. "We're looking for three men who might have come into this shop around a week ago. They may have bought groceries."

"Everyone buys groceries here, sir," he said.

Touché, thought Hart. She said, "They would have bought a carrot."

"*A* carrot?" cut in the elder Millar.

"Well, they might have bought more, we don't know that. But they certainly bought one."

"*If* they came in here, you mean?"

Beside her, Hart heard Stoker chuckle. He clearly knew what was coming and thought it just as ridiculous as she did. "Specifically," she said, producing a bag, "this carrot."

The two Millars looked at the bag, no doubt wondering what planet she was on.

"Uh," the elder said, "why?"

"It's evidence," Hart said. "This carrot was used for the nose of a snowman. We need to find out who put it there."

"Why?" the elder Millar asked. "Has the snowman made a complaint?"

Hart would have laughed – the entire situation was indeed ludicrous – but for the fact there was a body in the morgue and the potential for further corpses to begin piling up at any moment.

"Someone got this carrot from somewhere," she said, "and I need to know whether it was here. Have any strangers come in lately and bought some carrots?"

"Actually," the elder Millar said, rubbing his chin, "now that you mention it, there was someone wasn't there, Tony? You said someone came in and bought one carrot. We had a laugh about it."

Hart's hopes spiked. "Tell me."

"It wasn't a carrot," Tony said quickly. "I said shallot. Someone bought one shallot, not a carrot."

"Shallot?" his father asked. "No, I'm sure it was a carrot."

Tony shook his head, keeping his eyes down.

Hart exchanged a glance with Stoker. She could see he was thinking exactly as she did: that there was something screwy about Tony's testimony. "Tony, look at me," she said. When he just shrugged, she said again, more forcefully, "Tony?"

He looked up and she could see he was setting his jaw firm. It would have been obvious even to the corpse in the morgue that he was hiding something.

"I'm going to assume you don't know how serious this is," Hart continued slowly. "You're a good kid, Tony. I know you've made some mistakes in the past, but if you know anything about this carrot, you need to tell me right now."

"I don't know anything," he said, his voice small. "I don't even like carrots."

Hart wanted to keep the news of the body secret if she could. Truman wouldn't tell anyone, but of course the kids who had found the body would have already told everyone they knew. The thought of these killers finding out about the discovery was making Hart want to keep as firm a lid on the secret as she could, but she knew if she was going to make any impact at all upon Tony Millar, she was going to have to shove the truth in his face and see how he reacted.

"We have a body in the morgue," she said. "The person who bought that carrot is very likely the murderer. So if you know a name, Tony, you need to tell it me."

Larry Millar gasped and turned angry eyes upon his son. But it was Tony's reaction Hart had been watching for. The younger man's eyes widened, he stopped breathing for a single moment. His eyes darted to his father, to Stoker, to Hart, all around them again before settling on nowhere. He had not known about the body, Hart decided, which relieved her no end.

"Tone, what have you got yourself mixed up in now?"

"Nothing, dad. Honest."

His father clipped him around the ear. Hart had never seen him angry.

"You tell the detective who bought that carrot."

"I don't know."

"Then," Stoker said, "you admit it wasn't a shallot?"

"No, it was a carrot. But I didn't know him."

"So it was one man?"

"Yes. No. I ... I don't remember."

Hart's eyes narrowed as she digested all this. Tony was the worst liar she had ever met. "How old was he?" she asked.

"Twenty-five, maybe thirty."

"Height?"

"Average."

"Clothes?"

"Normal."

"Accent?"

"None."

Hart resisted the urge to throttle him. "What did he say when he was here?"

"Nothing."

"He must have said something if you're telling me he didn't have an accent."

"Just regular stuff. He bought his carrot and his dog food and asked me how much."

Hart tried not to smile. "He bought dog food?"

"Yeah. I guess he had a dog."

Hart was certain now the people Truman had encountered in the field were the murderers. They had been seen heading away from the scene of the crime and they had bought a single carrot which had to have been the one in Hart's hand. Now all she needed to do was properly identify them.

"Would you like to continue this down at the station?" Hart asked Tony.

"No." He looked horrified. "No, I ... I don't know anything else."

"We don't need to bring him in, I don't think," Stoker said. "Keep a tight leash on your boy, Mr Millar. We have other avenues to investigate but we'll be back soon."

Millar nodded, still not having taken it all in. "Will do, yes."

Hart frowned at her companion but Stoker was already motioning her towards the door. Not wanting to argue in front of the suspect, Hart stepped back onto the street. The two of them walked several metres before she decided she would have it out with him. Before she could say a word, however, Stoker had grabbed her by the arm and dragged her into the alley beside the shop. He did not stop walking until they had gone all the way around to the back and she angrily shook the arm away.

"What are we doing?" she whispered harshly.

"Waiting."

"That kid knows something."

"Yes, but he wasn't going to tell us."

"So we just give up? We could have broken him at the station."

"That would have taken time. I think we'd be better off letting him show us what he knows."

Hart had no idea what he was talking about. Then she saw a window open on the upper level of the shop and watched as Tony Millar emerged. He had a little trouble working his way down to the ground and almost skidded on ice once or twice, but finally he was on the ground and walking.

"I can see," Hart said slowly, "why I called you in on this one, John."

Stoker was not smiling. "Let's just see where he leads us. Thank me when we're both having tea and laughing about all this."

If there was anything to even think of laughing about, Hart wished someone would share the joke.

CHAPTER SIX

Things were bad, and Stoker was certain his partner did not realise just how bad they were. It was strange to think of Felicity Hart as his partner. Before his retirement, Stoker had usually worked alone and had always scoffed at the television versions of the police where lifelong partnerships were formed. However, that was precisely how he felt working alongside Hart. He had never seen himself as an old veteran offering sagely advice, but that was the role he had fallen into, and the one which Hart needed. He tried not to think of what might happen should he fail Hart as he had failed his own daughter so many years earlier.

But that was not the attitude he should have been entertaining while on the job. They were following Tony Millar and with any luck would be able to make their arrests and no one else would be hurt.

Tony led them on a direct path and clearly did not even consider that he might be followed. Initially Stoker and Hart had kept as far back as they could, well aware they were leaving visible tracks in the snow, but since Tony had not turned around even once, they had closed the gap and reduced their chances of losing him. Stoker was not certain of the youth's destination, although could see Hart had already reached a conclusion.

"He's going to church," she said. "It's the only thing out this way."

Stoker found he had to concur. After everything that had happened to him in the big city, Stoker found he had little time for God any more. He had been inside that church perhaps two or three times during his years in Barrowville and fought to recall the layout. As a detective he had been trained to remember even the smallest of details, but since he was retired he had allowed the habit to die.

"You'd best take the lead," he told Hart. "But we should do this as quietly as possible."

"Should I have brought some weapons?"

"Why? Do you have any?"

"Only a truncheon and some pepper spray, and I already have those. I meant, if these people have killed already, maybe I should have called for backup."

"I'm not sure you even have any backup to call."

"I meant out-of-town backup. You know, cops with guns."

Stoker grunted. "The last thing you need in a bad situation is to add guns to it, whoever you put behind the trigger. Besides, we don't have any indication these guys are armed with anything worse than a hammer. Right now, though, we're just observing. If we can see who Tony's headed to, we can at least get a look at our killers. Then we can take things from there."

"You really think the killers are hiding in the church?"

"Either that or Tony's gone to confess his sins to someone who cares."

It was mere minutes later that Hart's assessment of the situation proved correct, for Tony entered the church grounds and moved to the front door. His two pursuers rushed quickly to the door so they would not lose him. Hart moved to open it immediately, although Stoker silently cautioned her. Opening the church door might cause an echo to resound through the large hall and send Tony running. In a whisper, Stoker counted down from fifteen and then opened the door as slowly as he could. The sound it made was probably nowhere near as bad as he had expected, although to his worried mind it was very much like an earthquake.

They stepped gingerly into the church, the eerie silence oppressive upon them. The main hall was long and spacious, tall stained-glass windows allowing the light of God to fill the area. Rows of pews took up all the nearby space, while at the end of the central aisle stood an altar. It was close to this that they could see Tony standing, arguing in whispers with Barroville's priest, Father Bishop. Unlike Truman's nickname of Old MacDonald, Father Bishop was the priest's real name. Stoker had always found it somewhat amusing and sometimes wondered whether Father Bishop took the coincidence as divine intervention.

Keeping low, Stoker and Hart hurried down the rearmost pew until they reached one of the support pillars. From there they made their way quickly down the side of the pews until they finally came to rest behind a pillar much closer to their quarry. From this position, they could hear and see everything.

Bishop, a thin man in his sixties, seemed both worried and adamant about something, while Tony was irate and almost on the point of exploding. If he made a move to throttle the priest, Stoker fully intended to leap in and arrest him.

"We have to put a stop to this, Father," Tony was saying. "Things are going too far now."

"You're talking as though you have any control over the situation," Bishop hit back a little haughtily. "As though either of us does."

"Well we need control," Tony snapped. "Talk with her, Father."

"I have. You know I have."

"Then talk to her again."

"She's not going to listen to me. She only talks to me because I'm her priest; if she thought I had a hidden agenda she'd disappear entirely."

"Then take me to her."

Bishop laughed. "We do that and we lose her entirely. She doesn't want to talk to you, Tony."

"She told you that, did she?"

"You know she did."

Stoker and Hart exchanged glances. They were hoping Tony Millar would have led them to three men and these two were discussing a woman. Unless the dog was female, Stoker reasoned they may have been barking up the wrong tree. He opted to keep the pun to himself.

"Then don't tell her you're setting up a meeting," Tony all but pleaded. "Just arrange to meet her and I'll be there instead."

"If I did that, she would never trust me again."

"We don't have any choice now, Father."

"There is always a choice, my son."

"Damn it, Father, they found a body in the field."

Whatever Father Bishop had been intending to say died in his throat. From his position, Stoker could not see the man's eyes too well, but he could see his skin paling. "Dead? Who?"

"I don't know," Tony said, running agitated fingers through his hair. "Detective Hart didn't say. She's with that old guy, the one from the city."

"Stoker?"

"Yeah. They found a body inside a snowman or something."

"Could the death have been accidental?"

"Unless the guy died standing up, was snowed over and some helpful passer-by put a carrot on his face ... no."

"Dear Lord."

"Father, please help me."

"Of course, of course." Bishop looked as though he was about to collapse. His mind was no longer quite with them, and Stoker would have paid good money to know precisely what was going through his head. "But if this goes wrong, we've lost her, Tony. Forever."

"I know that," Tony said in a small voice. "But we have to try one last time. Before hers is the next body to turn up."

The two men did not speak much after this and Tony left soon after. Hart made to step out into view, although Stoker held her back. Even as Tony left the church, Bishop disappeared out the back, leaving the two detectives to exit via the door through which they had come in.

Once they were back outside, Hart asked, "What was all that about?"

"I don't know." Stoker knew precisely what they would have to do now, although he was loath to suggest it. His primary goal in all of this was to protect Hart and if she agreed with his suggestion he would be surrendering all chance of being able to do that. However, it was what the investigation required and he could not shirk his duty just because he was afraid for Hart's safety.

"John?"

"We need to split up," he said. "One of us needs to grill Tony about what just happened in there; the other needs to follow the priest and see who he's arranging to meet."

"Good idea. Any preference which you take?"

Stoker knew which would be the more dangerous. "I'll take the priest."

"Right. If you find anything, give me a call, yeah?"

It was almost a joke, but it was also serious. Phone reception in Barrowville was not the greatest: sometimes it took a miracle just to get the television to receive signals from the channels you wanted. A temperamental signal in this instance could well cost lives, but it was all they had to work with.

"Please be careful." It was silly, but all he could think of to say.

They were also the final words he had ever spoken to his daughter.

CHAPTER SEVEN

He had expected Father Bishop to have found a quiet room somewhere to make a phone call, but it seemed the priest did not have any greater ability to receive a signal in Barrowville than anyone else. Perhaps, Stoker reflected, miracles were saved only for those who truly needed them. Instead Bishop was leading him away from the church, once more through the snow, and Stoker had no idea where they were going. He tried to think what was out this way, but there were so many fields in Barrowville Stoker had long ago lost track. He marvelled at how Hart's initial thought might have actually been true: that these killers were hiding out in someone's barn. If that turned out to be the case, he would literally kick himself for not having simply made a systematic sweep of everyone's barns.

Then he realised precisely where Bishop was headed. Aside from fields, there was only one thing in this direction, and because of the snow it would be closed today. In fact, if it had been open, the children would never have found the body to begin with.

Bishop kept his head low as he entered the school, Stoker following. Bishop did not dally, which meant he knew precisely where he was headed. Stoker had never been to the school and did not know its layout, but he reasoned it would be no different to any other. The playground was a large affair, and there were two buildings, probably one for younger and one for older children. Barrowville was nowhere near large enough to incorporate two schools. The building they entered was the smaller one. The corridors were narrow and lined with terrible blotchy paintings which could only have been done by five-year-olds. Peering through the doorways they passed, Stoker could see tables upon which overturned chairs lay dormant. Upon the walls behind the teachers' desks hung blackboards, several of which were scrawled with work left undone. It had been a long time since Stoker had been to school and he did not miss it. But the one thing he had always liked about school was that it was ordered. Life required order and, when done right, schooling dictated that order.

He saw the priest duck into a classroom and approached slowly, hanging outside the door. Crouching low, he poked his head around the doorframe and could see a young woman sitting in the teacher's chair, swivelling gently and looking very much in control. Stoker had brief visions of this girl being some kind of crime boss, although shook such thoughts away. He had chided Hart for watching too much television and here he was entertaining even more ridiculous thoughts than she.

"Thanks for meeting me," Bishop said, his voice laden with relief and fear. Stoker reasoned that meant the girl did not squat in the school, but that this was just a meeting place for them. It seemed Bishop had managed to send a message to her after all to meet him. Whatever he wanted from her, he certainly had not wanted to say it over the phone.

"Something on your mind, Father?" the girl asked.

Stoker looked at her then, ingraining her image into his memory. There was something familiar about her and he wondered where he had seen her before. She was around nineteen, he would have guessed, with short dark hair and striking green eyes. About her neck there rested a pendent which cost far more than she could have earned at her age, while a silver bangle adorned her wrist. She was dressed in jeans and a jumper which would keep out the cold but not ruin her image by making her appear gaudy. She did not even seem to have brought a jacket. Stoker's initial impression of her was a young woman who cared more for her image than her safety. They were, in his experience, the most dangerous people in society: to themselves and to everyone who loved them.

"There's talk in the village," Bishop said. "Someone's dead."

"Dead?" the girl asked, glancing at the blackboard.

"I take it by your reaction you already knew that," Bishop said dryly. "Were you there?"

"No. I ... he fell."

"And you know that even though you weren't there?"

"He fell and Dom panicked. Said there was no point in phoning an ambulance because he was already dead."

"So what did he do with the body?"

"I don't know. Threw it in the river maybe."

"And you think Dominic is a respectable pillar of the community to be throwing the bodies of his friends in the river?"

"Leave Dom alone, Father. Is that why you wanted to meet? So you could remind me how much you don't like Dom?"

"I'm worried, child. I'm worried you're in over your head. Come talk with the people who love you. No pressure, I promise, but you need to get their opinions."

"I know their opinions, thanks." She had become defensive by this point. "That's what you wanted, wasn't it? You want me to confess my sins or something? I didn't have anything to do with what happened to Joe. He slipped on a ladder and hit his head on a rock. It was an accident, so before you start accusing Dom of murdering his own friends, I'll stop you right there, Father."

"Your brother is worried."

"My brother is always worried. But then he's never done anything in his life and he's never going to. That's why he drinks, Father, because we're stuck in Barrowville doing nothing of anything. Well, I'm not going to be here forever, Father. I have plans, I have dreams. And when Dominic takes me out of here I'm going to see the country, maybe even the world."

Suddenly Stoker realised why the girl was so familiar. He had indeed met her once or twice, but it was her father he knew better, and more recently her brother. This was Clarissa Millar, who was apparently concentrating on her schooling at the moment. That had likely been a euphemism by her father for 'she's run off with a murderer', unless her father really had believed her lies. That she was indeed presently in a school was somewhat ironic, but Stoker was not there to laugh at the little coincidences of life. All he knew was that this girl had named the victim and knew where the murderer could be found. This girl was the linchpin from which the entire investigation could be solved; and if played properly he might be able to wrap up this entire thing and not have to involve Hart save to hand her the killers bound in a pretty Christmas bow.

"I'm not getting into the rights and wrongs of young love," Bishop told her. "But if you took a step back you'd see you need to get away from this situation."

"Joe fell," she replied icily.

"I'm not saying he didn't. Maybe he did. But a man is dead and the police will have to investigate."

"They'll blame Dom. He's a stranger here, and the police always blame strangers."

"Is that what Dom told you?"

"You don't know him, Father. Now, was there something else you wanted or can I get back to him now?"

Bishop sighed. "I'm desperately trying not to preach at you, Clarissa. I was young once too, you know. I even remember some of it." He smiled, trying to look sympathetic but only coming across as desperate. "Just promise me you'll consider what I'm saying. The best thing you could do would be to convince Dominic to come in and explain how Joe fell."

Clarissa snorted.

Stoker decided he had heard enough.

"Stay right there," he said, stepping into view.

Clarissa started, almost falling from her chair as she got back to her feet. Her confusion quickly passed, transforming into hatred directed towards the priest. "You brought the cops?"

"No, I …"

"I followed him," Stoker said. "Miss Millar, I need to talk with you. I need you to take me to Dominic."

"You're not getting him," she said, breaking into a run. Stoker went to follow but remembered the only exit was through him; the windows would not open wide enough to let her out. It was a fire hazard, certainly, but it was also extremely helpful in this situation. Clarissa ran about the room for several moments, frantically searching for a way out, but he knew soon enough she would realise she was trapped. And then he would have to deal with a trapped animal in heat.

"Whoever killed Joe was sick," Stoker told her. "You need to tell me where your boyfriend is and you need to tell me right now."

Clarissa shrieked and snatched up a chair. Stoker winced as she hurled it at a window. The chair bounced off the glass, the entire pane rattling in its frame. Stoker had seen people try that trick before and it seldom worked.

"Calm down," Stoker told her.

She looked at him then. Her chest was heaving, her eyes terrified and wild, her stance suggesting she was fully prepared for a fight. Father Bishop was on his feet, holding up his arms and trying to placate her. Stoker watched as the girl lowered her shoulders and charged him. She struck the priest head-on, forcing him backwards to slam directly into Stoker. The three of them went down in a flailing mass of limbs. Stoker attempted to grab out at her ankle but Bishop's elbow went into his face, obscuring his vision. By the time he had scrambled back to his feet, the girl was gone.

"Well that worked," Bishop said, rising also. He still looked worried, but there was fury to his eyes as well by this point. "What were you thinking?"

"That I could solve a murder."

"That has to be the worst attempt at talking to a teenager I've ever seen. You do know what teenagers are, right?"

Stoker rubbed his cheek, where the priest's elbow had struck. "Who is this Dominic? Does he have a surname?"

"How should I know? I'm just her priest."

"A man is dead, Father."

"I know. So people keep telling me." He shook his head angrily and sat upon the edge of a desk. "I don't know much. I've been Clarissa's priest her whole life and she's always been a devout young girl. I had a rapport with her, a connection even her brother doesn't have. Of course, I think that's been destroyed now, don't you?"

"I'm sorry. I only want to end this before more people die."

Bishop's laugh was strangled. "Oddly enough, so do I. These people are a bad bunch and I was that girl's only lifeline. Now I have no idea what will happen."

"Tell me what you know."

Bishop looked him over with disdain, but clearly understood Stoker was his only way out of this now. "A group of them came to the village just before the snows got really bad. They drove in, apparently, and intended to be out rather quickly. The only names I know are Joseph and Dominic, and no I don't know any surnames. I doubt Clarissa knows them either."

"Where did they come from?"

"Somewhere larger than Barrowville, which isn't hard. I get the impression they only meant to stay the night, but this Dominic took a fancy to Clarissa and wanted her to run away with them. She said no, and he stayed an extra day to change her mind."

"Then the snows hit and they were unable to drive out," Stoker surmised.

"Which is where Joseph fits in. She only mentioned him once, said he was getting antsy about being here. She said Dominic got into an argument with him, that she was afraid it would come to blows."

Stoker considered this new information. "Why would Dominic be getting antsy? What were they doing here in the first place?"

"I don't know that either."

If they were just passing through, they would not have been bothered by staying longer. That meant the group had done something illegal prior to coming to Barrowville, or at least were on the run from something. "So Joseph blamed Dominic for staying too long," Stoker said, "tempers flared and Dominic smashes Joe's head in with a hammer."

"That fits in with what I know of Dominic, yes."

"Do you have any idea where he's hiding?"

"No. If I did, I'd tell her father."

"Larry Millar doesn't even seem to realise his daughter's off the rails."

"That doesn't surprise me. He's always seen her as an angel. He should try taking confession from her from time to time."

Stoker had never been a teenage girl but did not envy the priest his job. "What's your deal with the brother, then?"

"Tony? He loves his sister and doesn't want to see her ruin her life."

"He's been in trouble with the law."

"Nothing too bad. Barrowville is a very small community, Mr Stoker. Young people yearn for what they don't have, and television and magazines show them all the things they're missing in the larger world."

That made sense of the drinking comment he had overheard. He tried to think of a way to salvage this mess but there was nothing. He had messed up his end of things and Hart was going to have to pick up the pieces. "I don't suppose," he asked offhandedly, "Clarissa ever mentioned a dog?"

"Bruno?"

"That the dog's name?"

"Yes, she loves Bruno. She plays with him a lot, takes him for walks."

"Walks?"

"Well, it's a dog. Someone has to walk it."

"Anything else?"

"Not really."

"Which means there's something."

Bishop thought a moment. "Well, just a couple of comments really. She once said Bruno loves to chase the ducks. She also said with so many trees around it was difficult to get him to walk anywhere."

"So they're camped in the woods?" That was not something Stoker had considered.

"I've always thought so. But they cover such a vast area it would be impossible to search it all. Plus, the woods aren't exactly the easiest place to get around, what with all this snow."

That was true, but it was all useful information. "I have to get back to Liz."

"Then go. Just try to think next time before blundering into situations."

Stoker knew he deserved the comment, and as he departed the school he wished he could say he had not done more harm than good. He attempted to call Hart but could not get a signal so gave up. He could not imagine she would have gained any useful information from Tony Millar that he had not already gained from the priest, but at least Hart was out of harm's way. If he was doing only one thing right, it was that he was keeping Hart safe. A part of him even considered combing the woods without her, but this was her investigation and she would never forgive him if he took it away from her. At least she would be alive, though.

He slowed in his walk, not yet having reached a decision. Whatever else he thought about the case, he hated the choice he found himself forced to make.

CHAPTER EIGHT

He had proved very helpful and, after the smallest bit of prompting, Tony Millar had told Hart everything. At first Hart had a difficult time believing that Clarissa would have been stupid enough to have gone off with a group of strangers, but Tony had explained that Hart's perception of Clarissa had been coloured by their father's glowing praise of her. Hart had to admit she had seldom spoken to the girl and that Tony was right; she had never formed her own opinion of her. The more the situation flooded out of Tony's mouth, the more Hart realised he was only looking out for his sister.

"She listens to Father Bishop," Tony said. "He's the only one who can get through to her."

"Then let's hope my partner has more luck his end."

A dull beep sounded from Tony's pocket and he pulled out his phone. Hart never seemed to be able to get reception so if this was Clarissa calling him she would be the first down to the church to offer praise to the Almighty.

"Clara?" Tony said. He listened to whatever she had to say, then said, "No, I ... who? Stoker. Yeah, he came to see me as well. Him and Detective Hart." He glanced her way. "No, no, I didn't say anything. He followed you? Well that was silly."

Hart could not have known the full story but realised Stoker had made things worse. She quickly fought for a way to set things to rights before Tony finished the call. She needed to meet with Clarissa, but doubted the girl would agree to it, especially if she had noticed Stoker following her. Then an idea struck her and she struggled frantically for a piece of paper. The two of them were standing on the street, however, and she had not brought a notepad with her. Her eyes looked frantically about for some form of writing implement, but all they found was snow.

Snow!

Crouching, Hart ran her hand across the top of the snow to make it smoother, then began to scrawl a message. Tony watched her, and when she was done looked at her with raised eyebrows. Hart smiled encouragingly and Tony rolled his eyes.

"Uh, Clara?" he said. "Look, I'm not going to tell you what to do, but I've found out something I think you ought to know. It was something Detective Hart said, when she was asking me about you. She said ..." He paused, glancing over the message once again. "She said she had DNA evidence for whoever killed that guy. She said she was keeping it back at the police station and that it didn't matter where the gut ran ... I mean where the *guy* ran, with his DNA on record she could find him wherever he wert." He paused. "Wert? I think I mean went."

Hart thumped her forehead against a wall.

"Sure," Tony said. "No problem, Clara. You take care."

He hung up a little despondently and Hart asked, "Well?"

"That's the first time I've ever lied to my sister, Detective."

"If it saves her life she might thank you for it. Did she take the bait?"

"She seemed worried. When she tells her friends, I'm sure they'll come to you, yes. Although, you do realise it's an obvious trap, right?"

"That all depends whether she trusts you. She'll fight your corner and make these people believe her."

"Which makes me feel so much worse that I was lying to her."

"Hey," she said, placing a hand on his shoulder. "You're doing what's best by your sister, Tony."

"Sure," he said with downcast eyes. "So, what do you want me to do now?"

"Go home. Go home and stay there." Hart erased the message in the snow. "I need to contact John and get a trap set up at the station."

"Clara's not going to get hurt is she?"

"She'll be fine. Trust me. There's no party in any of this that has anything against your sister."

Tony did not look convinced, but there was nothing she could say which would have changed his mind. She knew if it was her sister in this situation, she would be thinking precisely as Tony was. She watched him slowly walk back home, with his head hung, and wished she could have allowed him to help further. But he had done his part and now she needed to do hers. But first she had to find Stoker and compare notes. There was a good chance he had been able to find out something useful from when he had cornered Clarissa.

Heading back to the station, Hart thought about how she would prepare for the arrival of Clarissa's boyfriend. Turning the station into a death-trap would have been a good idea, and she thought back to the old cartoons with Roadrunner or Tom and Jerry. Even if such would feasibly work, the preparations would have taken far too long, and she knew she was going to have to settle for something far less grand. While she walked, she considered the idea of setting up a wire fence and running a current through it, but doubted that would even be legal.

"Liz."

She had not noticed Stoker coming the other way, and she waited for him so the two of them could head back to the station together. He quickly informed her of everything that had happened with Father Bishop; then she told him everything she had herself done. Stoker did not seem particularly happy with the way she had handled things, which was somewhat crass considering he was the one helping her.

"Well, it's done now anyway," she said. "So we have to get back to the station and fortify it before we receive company."

"Liz, you've invited a gang of murderers to your doorstep."

"To familiar territory. What would you prefer, that the two of us head off into the woods and we have it out there?"

"We need reinforcements."

"This is Barrowville. We don't exactly have paratroopers on hand. Out here we work with what we have. I'll call Rob and get him away from the crime scene. I can't imagine what's left of that snowman's worth guarding any more anyway."

"I hardly think Constable Manson's going to tip the balance if it comes to a shoot-out."

"Then you haven't seen him shoot."

"He can use a gun?"

"Well, no. I was being metaphorical."

"Metaphorically, we're like a beetle under someone's foot, without anywhere to fly."

"No, that's a simile."

Stoker shook his head and Hart tried hard to think of when this had become a game of one-upmanship.

"I had to make a spur-of-the-moment decision," she said. "Anyway, at least I'm doing something. So come help me fortify the station or something."

Hart was still angry when they arrived, although she fully intended to put that anger to good use. The police station was not built to withstand a siege, but Hart knew how to improvise. The first thing she did was move the Christmas tree so it wouldn't get ruined; then she set about saving their lives. Together they moved any furniture they could find, positioning it so they could force the killers to come a specific way. Hart and Stoker were tucked away behind the main desk, where they had a full view of anyone as they entered. So long as the killers did not have any firearms, they would have no room to manoeuvre and Hart could tackle them one at a time. As formidable as this Dominic may have been in hitting someone in the face with a hammer, Hart had training in how to take down aggressors with her extendable truncheon. If it looked as though she was getting in trouble, she would drop to the floor and Stoker would blast the offender in the face with pepper spray.

It was a well-thought-out plan, and one which even had a fair chance of success.

Crouched behind the desk, they waited in silence for someone to show.

Twenty minutes later, Hart was beginning to feel her legs cramping.

"When I was six," she whispered, "I had a party. No one turned up. This kind of reminds me of that."

"I can't believe you weren't a popular kid, Liz."

"I looked after my sister a lot, I didn't get to socialise too much. And I guess I grew up quickly and saw my school-friends as ... well, a little childish."

"You were six. You're allowed to be childish."

"Technically I was five. It was on my sixth birthday they didn't come."

"If you kept correcting them over things, it's no wonder they didn't turn up."

Hart could hear the tension in his voice. Stoker was worried. He did not like this plan and he was afraid. She had never seen Stoker afraid before today, had never really thought he could have been. He always approached a situation with such calm detachment for which she had always striven. It was strange, finally being on the job with him, but she had the feeling he would not appreciate her gushing in his presence.

"Tell me about Sue," she said instead.

"Sue?"

"I get you want to protect me because of what happened to your daughter. I just ... I'm not her, John."

"No, you're not."

She did not know how far she should push him, but she was insanely curious. He had never once mentioned his daughter, not in all the time she had known him. It was as though he had tried to forget her, as though that was the only way he found he could cope with losing her. It was a terrible thought to have, but one she honestly felt was true. And if his dwelling on his daughter was going to affect his actions here, she felt she needed to know. That and she was nosy.

"Sue was the best thing that ever happened to me," Stoker said. "And then she died. There's not much more to say."

"I'm sorry. What happened?"

"There'd been a bank robbery. Nasty business, two people put in the hospital. I was investigating the case and knew it was going to end badly. Sue got a lead and she looked into it without waiting for backup. I guess she wanted to impress me, I don't know."

"You daughter was on the force?"

"Constable. A bobby on the beat. I told her she should progress through the ranks but she was happy where she was, dealing with the public: being the face of the law."

Hart knew the feeling. While it was true she was a detective, her most satisfying aspects of the job came through her interaction with the public. Wisely, she did not say as much. She had a feeling Stoker saw her enough as his daughter as it was.

"They caught her snooping," Stoker continued. "So they took her. Then they started making demands, as though they actually thought they were going to get anything. They threatened to shoot her if they didn't get what they wanted, stuck a gun to the side of her head and expected us to back down." His voice drifted off and Hart thought she might have lost him. He continued as though she was no longer even there. "They took me off the case, of course, and not just because I was related to her. I wasn't trained to deal with hostage situations, so I left it to the professionals."

"They couldn't get through to the bank robbers?" Hart guessed.

"I don't know what happened. I never did find out, but it doesn't matter. Shots were fired inside the building where they were holed up, so the armed police moved in. Officially, the shot that killed Sue came from one of the gunmen, but I had a friend in ballistics who told me otherwise."

"Good Lord," Hart said. "She was shot by a police officer?"

"That doesn't look good in the media. Bad enough a constable dies, but that she was killed by one of the people who went in to rescue her?"

"Was there an investigation?"

"Probably. Likely someone was reprimanded, maybe even sacked for it. I didn't want to know, because I didn't want to find out the name of the person who killed my daughter. I knew I wouldn't be able to trust myself if I ever found out." He inhaled deeply. "So I threw it all in and retired. Brenda and I came to live here, in Barrowville, where bad things don't happen to good cops."

She could feel his eyes on her and wished he would understand she wasn't his daughter. But the more she thought about that, the more she realised that was the role she had been unconsciously trying to fill. She had always wanted to impress Stoker and had taken this as her opportunity to do so. She felt a sudden shiver to think she might well end up dead, and knew Stoker would take it terribly.

Hart opened her mouth to speak, but her heart leapt as a shrill noise blasted through the room. Forcing down her panic, she reached for the phone sitting on her desk. "Detective Hart," she said.

"Hart?" It was Father Bishop.

"Father, what's wrong? You sound upset."

"Hart, I have Tony here with me. The silly fool warned his sister off."

"He did what?"

"Says he didn't want to betray her: he's a right mess now. Anyway, that's not the point."

Hart felt her entire body go numb at the very thought of what Bishop might say next. If Tony had warned his sister of the trap, it meant Dominic would know the police were onto him. And that meant he would be about to do something desperate.

"They're here," Bishop said. "They're here at the church. I don't know what they want, but I don't think they ..."

There was the sound of a scuffle and the line died. Hart did not bother to shout Bishop's name.

"That was bad," Stoker said, "wasn't it?"

"Dominic's at the church. He's taken Bishop and Tony hostage."

"As they can't get out of the village, it's a logical step."

"How can you be so calm?"

"Because when cops get emotional, they barge in and people die."

Hart reached a decision. "I'm going in alone. I'm not having you there with me, John, no arguments."

"Well I'm certainly not letting you walk in there alone, Liz."

"No arguments," she insisted. "You can wait outside, but I go in alone. This is still my investigation and thank you for your help but your part in this is over. Now it's time for me to go do my job."

"Hostage negotiation isn't the job of a detective."

"Out here it has to be. John, please don't fight me on this."

He clearly wanted to argue, but Stoker merely grunted. She had no idea whether that was acceptance of her decision, but she had made up her mind regardless. The situation had turned about as bad as it could go and now it was time for her to solve the problem entirely. Steeling her nerves, Hart prepared herself for having to talk to a gang of murderers and convince them to turn themselves in.

If this was what life in the big city was like, Hart at last decided she didn't want any part of it after all.

CHAPTER NINE

She knew the people of Barrowville, she knew the church and she knew the entire village was depending on her to protect them. Detective Felicity Hart kept repeating these things to herself as she approached the church but knew none of it would make any difference. She was still a small-time cop dealing with big-time criminals. But she would do her best and pray it was good enough. Inside the church, perhaps her prayers might even do her some good.

A crowd was forming outside the church by the time she got there. Apparently, the strangers had been seen entering the church and had kicked out anyone who was in there at the time, taking the priest hostage in the process. The news had shot through the village in minutes and the crowd was worried and afraid. It fell to Hart to calm them down, but all she could really tell them was that she was going to sort the problem and get their priest out of there. They also confirmed what Father Bishop had said over the phone: that they also had Tony with them. Some of the crowd thought Tony was working with the criminals, others did not seem too certain. Hart suspected assumptions were being made, but she would not vilify Tony Millar until she had more proof against him.

Before going inside the church, she asked about the strangers. There were three, aged somewhere in their thirties, and one of them had a beard. She was given such a variety of descriptions that she figured the best way to be certain of what these men looked like was to wait until she confronted them.

Wishing she had more time to think of a better plan, Hart walked to the church door and entered.

The first thing she noticed was the noise. Hart had spent a great many hours in this church and always had its silence been impressed upon her. Even when Bishop was speaking, there seemed to be a quiet ambiance which listened intently to every word he spoke. Now there was tension in the air, angry shouting and commotion. Hart absorbed the setting as much as she could, knowing at any moment things could turn nasty. Bishop and Tony were seated on the pew at the front of the church. They were not bound but sat in such a way which denoted they had been ordered not to move. Clarissa was standing nearby, leaning against the pulpit, her arms crossed. She looked nervous, but had an air that she was trying to seem as though she was still in control of herself. Hart surmised she was worried about her brother: perhaps a threat had been made against him. Also, this situation was far beyond anything Clarissa had ever imagined and she was probably having trouble being so far outside her comfort zone.

It was the other three men upon whom Hart focused the most.

She had never seen any of them before. They were dressed in jeans, which reminded Hart they had not expected to stay here through a snowstorm. Two of them looked just as nervous as Clarissa, although the third, the one with the beard, had manic eyes and was in Hart's opinion on the verge of snapping. Whoever these people were, wherever they had come from, they had a carefully laid plan which had been disrupted by the snow and their leader was at breaking point.

Hart could see no firearms, of which she was grateful, but all three men were armed with long knives and baseball bats. Hart had not been aware baseball bats were even available to buy in England.

"Hands where I can see them," the man with the beard said. Something told her this was Dominic.

"Detective Hart," she said, slowing her approach but not moving her hands at all. "You're under arrest. I'd advise you to come quietly."

"I said hands."

Hart ignored him and looked to the prisoners on the pew. "You two all right?"

They nodded slowly, uncertain what game she was playing.

Dominic laughed. "You're not what I expected, Hart. Clarissa said you'd be a pushover."

"Did she now?"

Beside the pulpit, Clarissa shifted uncomfortably.

"All right," Dominic said, "now you're here and can see we're serious, it's time to lay down our terms."

"There are no terms of surrender. You hand yourself in and it goes better for you."

"Terms of our walking out of here. Don't push it, Hart. I like your bravado, but I have a temper."

"And a hammer," Hart said. "Unless you were clever enough to toss it in the river."

He grunted. Hart was not all that certain what the sound in this instance even meant.

"You're not getting out of here," Hart told him. "And, before you explode at me, that's not me being difficult. The roads are still blocked, so unless you're prepared to walk a very long way, you're as stuck as you were before you murdered Joe."

Dominic stiffened and Hart realised she probably should not have mentioned Joe's name. If Dominic thought she had any way of identifying any of them, he might not be so amenable in this negotiation.

"I can get you a helicopter," she relented with a deep sigh.

"You can?"

"No, leave off." She looked at the three men and tried to put her training to use. During hostage situations it was always best to make the criminal think he was in control. However, in poker the winner was usually the one who held chip power and the air of authority. If she could project confidence, she would disarm her adversaries and their resolve would falter. In theory. Of course, having such an honest attitude to life, she had never been any good at poker.

"I wouldn't play games with us," Dominic said.

"No offence," Hart replied, "but what do you actually hope to gain here? I can't get you any form of transport to take you out of Barrowville. You're holed up in a church and the snowstorm's not showing any signs of letting up. About all you can do here is confess your sins and pray for forgiveness." Her eyes flitted to the other two men and noticed with rising hopes that they were already faltering. She imagined they were not happy about what Dominic had done to Joe and knew either of them could be next. They could also likely see the hopelessness of their situation, even though they still did not want to accept it. If she could point things out to them as clearly as possible, she might be able to get them to turn on their leader.

"I want a tractor," Dominic said. "One of the ones with big wheels. That'll get us out of here."

Whatever Hart had been expecting, that certainly had not been it. "A tractor?" she asked flatly. "Are you serious? You're going to escape the law on a tractor? Do you have any idea what the top speed for a tractor is?"

"I don't care. We'll get past all the snow and ditch the thing before the cops show."

"I am a cop."

"I mean the real cops."

Hart narrowed her eyes. "I can think of a few flaws in your plan there." She glanced again to his companions to make sure they were still wavering. She decided to hold up some fingers. "One: I'm not sure a tractor would get you through the snow; two: you're assuming the snow's confined to Barrowville like we're the village that time forgot or something; three: I'm not giving you a tractor."

Dominic held his knife before him. Hart could see his arm was far from steady and feared the situation had unnerved him. His eyes were wild, but his mind for the moment was still lucid. "You'll do what I tell you," he said.

"Why did Joe have to die?"

"What?"

The question had thrown him, so Hart pressed it. "Poor Joe, he didn't stand a chance, did he? Is that what happens when you get angry, Dominic?" She made a conscious decision to throw in his name: it might help convince the others to surrender if they thought she knew all about them. "Sorry, I forgot," Hart continued, "Rob fell, didn't he?"

Dominic glanced to Clarissa, who looked away.

Hart noticed Clarissa's pendent then, hanging about her neck. Stoker had mentioned it, along with the silver bracelet she wore, and something clicked in her mind. She had been wondering why these people had come to Barrowville, why they had felt the need to hide. They were clearly on the run from something, and if Dominic had some convenient jewellery to give to the girl he was courting, there was only one logical answer.

"You robbed a jewellery shop," Hart said before she could stop herself. Since she had said that much, she continued. "You robbed a jewellers and ran through Barrowville, intending to only stay the night. Now you're stuck and probably looking at a charge of murder."

"We didn't kill anyone," Dominic said.

"Except for Joe. Is that how you're going to split your profits, Dominic? A four-way split, until you decide to cave in the heads of your partners? Or maybe when you took a shine to Clarissa you figured one of the others had to go. Was it a random choice, Dominic? Could poor old Joe have been any of these others?"

"You think you're clever, don't you?" Dominic said. "You're trying to turn my boys against me, I can see that. Joe wanted out. He wanted to betray us, to give himself up. So yeah, I hit him. I didn't mean to kill him, just shut him up. Then, when he died, we figured we had to hide the body."

Clarissa gasped. Hart knew she had genuinely believed Dominic when he had told her Joe had fallen and died accidentally. Hart had been a teenage girl one time but was always too busy to be young and in love. She understood the principle, however. So long as the group hadn't actually done anything illegal since Joe's death, Clarissa would be in the clear.

"You're such a nice man," Hart said. "So, you want a tractor. Anything else? A bag of groceries from Clarissa's shop?"

"Don't make fun of me," Dominic warned, waving his knife, his baseball bat in his other hand, by his side. "Just get me that tractor."

"Sure, all right. First let the boy go."

"What?"

"You want the tractor, fine. But I need a show of faith. You have two hostages, you don't need them both. Let the boy go and you still have the priest. I get the boy, you get the tractor."

"No."

"No? What do you mean no? You intend on letting him go eventually. I mean, you're not going to hurt him anyway."

"Get me that tractor or I'll show you how much I can hurt him."

It had been the response Hart had wanted. If Clarissa had been in any doubt as to her new boyfriend's intentions, threatening to kill her brother should have expelled them. She did not risk a glance at Clarissa and was thankful the girl did not react in any way. It was possible Clarissa was so callous that she did not care what happened to her brother, but Hart had known her for a long time and could not believe that for a moment.

"All right, I'll go enquire," Hart said. "It might take a while to find one and get one here, though. I'm telling you, those things aren't designed to travel through snow. No sane farmer tends his fields when it's snowing."

"Stop giving me lip, woman, and get me that tractor."

She could see he was on the verge of snapping and decided she had pushed him far enough. She could probably get him a tractor fairly easily, but was loath to give it him. She would have to think of something along the way, but at least she had bought herself some time.

"Let him go," Clarissa said, and Hart froze, hoping the girl wouldn't be stupid enough to confront him now.

"What?" Dominic rounded on her. "You too?"

"He's my brother, Dom. Let him go with her."

"He's my hostage, of course I'm not going to let him go."

"You're not going to hurt him."

"Don't you tell me what to do. What is it with women telling me what to do?"

Suddenly Hart could see what Dominic's main problem was and felt perhaps it would have been better for Stoker to have come in her place after all.

Clarissa had started towards him, seemingly oblivious to the knife he was flashing around. There was confusion in her face, but there was also anger. Clarissa was a young woman and if there was one thing young women did not like it was men playing their heartstrings. Hart briefly wondered whether Clarissa had slept with him yet, whether that would make things worse. Then she realised things probably could not get much worse.

"Everything you've told me has been a lie," Clarissa said. "Everything."

"Most things," Dominic said snidely. "There's a difference. Now get back there and shut up."

Clarissa lunged for him before anyone could stop her and Dominic easily pushed her away. Hart watched his arm come around, saw the knife flash, and reacted. Throwing herself at him, Hart grabbed the wrist holding the knife, twisted it and forced the blade from his grip. Dominic screamed in pain even as, on reflex, he brought his left arm around. It all happened so quickly Hart did not even see the motion until she felt something hard slam into her side. She released him, falling back, Dominic's free fist smashing into her face and sending her sprawling.

An explosion of sounds erupted about her as Hart fought to crawl from her attacker. She could hear shouts of panic and fear and anger, could feel her head pounding with pain even as she tasted the blood of her split lip. Her brain was hazing as she watched the wraithlike figure of Dominic approach her, hefting his baseball bat, and she felt a bizarre relief that he had not thought to collect his knife.

Placing her feet beneath her, Hart charged for him, catching him about the waist and pushing the both of them backwards. But Dominic did not fall. Whether it was fury or the gym or drugs or desperation, Dominic's body held a strength Hart simply could not match and he shrugged off her grip, spinning with his bat and smashing it with all his might against the side of her head.

Hart fell, her mind reeling, her brain screaming at her to get up. She could see Dominic towering over her. He grunted, spat at her and brought his bat around over his head. She could see he really didn't like women telling him what to do.

Her mind worked on instinct as she drew her extendable metal baton and swung it at him. The weapon caught him on the shin and arrested his downward thrust. Hart forced herself to her feet, even though her brain was insisting the whole church was moving around her, and swung at him again with the weapon even as she attempted to draw her pepper spray from her pocket.

Dominic moved far more quickly than Hart believed possible and her hand was suddenly throbbing with pain, the spray clattering way. He swung the bat as though he was semi-professional and Hart knew he had good practice in using it on anyone who annoyed him. Concentrating on her baton, Hart kept an eye on the baseball bat, determining when her opening would come.

A hand closed upon her throat and she realised she had once more underestimated the man's speed. She could hear Clarissa sobbing, could hear the priest shouting, but it was all a jumbled mess. As Dominic held her in the air, she struggled to breathe and felt her throat collapse. Staring down into the manic eyes of a killer, Detective Hart knew she had at last faced a proper criminal.

As black spots sliced through her vision, she thought about Sue Stoker and of how against real criminals, the police did not always win.

She blacked out, oblivious to anything further the monster could do to her.

CHAPTER TEN

Detective Hart had been gone a long time and Stoker was beginning to worry. Thankfully there was no way he was going to just wait around for Hart to solve the problem alone and had stumbled across what he considered to be a secret weapon. Holding it firmly in both arms, Stoker approached the church and decided he would have to help Hart whether she wanted it or not. He paused only momentarily to leave something just outside the church door, hoping it would be enough to tip the balance in their favour.

Entering the church, Stoker quickly assessed the situation. Confusion hung heavy in the air, along with the unmistakable sharp tang of spilled blood. Panic rose in Stoker, although he fought it down. He could see three men arguing. All were armed with knives and baseball bats, and none of them seemed in a good mood for negotiation. Sitting on the front pew he could see Tony Millar consoling his weeping sister. To the side crouched Father Bishop, huddled over a bleeding form and attempting to stem the wounds with cloths and holy water.

Felicity Hart was barely conscious. Her clothes were torn, her chest stained with blood, and there was a nasty gash to the side of her head which was spilling blood everywhere. Stoker forced himself not to look at her too much because he knew he had to concentrate on Dominic and his criminal friends.

When they saw Stoker strolling towards them, they stopped arguing. The man with the beard stepped forward, a range of emotions to his eyes. Stoker instantly pegged him for their leader, which meant he had to be Dominic. Only the group's leader would have drawn Clarissa into their fold. Stoker tightened his grip on the secret weapon in his arms.

"Bruno," Dominic whispered.

"Nice dog," Stoker said. "I reasoned this was the only thing you cared about in your whole life, Dominic, so let's talk."

"Give him to me."

"Or not. Let the kids go."

"Give me my ..."

"No." Stoker did not shout, but his voice carried well in the high ceiling of the church hall. "The Millars," he said forcefully. "They walk free right now or I walk out myself and take Bruno here to the pound."

"I ..."

"No negotiation. Kids. Out."

Dominic's face twisted but Stoker knew he had him. "Out," Dominic said. When they did not move, he shouted the word and they scrambled to their feet.

As they passed Stoker, he gave Tony a nod. He could see confusion in Clarissa's eyes and was grateful the girl had come to her senses. He could not see either of them was injured, which was at least one good thing. He heard the door close behind him, which meant he was left with only Hart and the priest to set free.

"Now," Dominic said, "give me my dog."

"Not so fast," Stoker said.

"But you said ..."

"I didn't say anything. Father, how's Liz?"

"Not good," Bishop replied. "She's conscious, but that animal hit her pretty bad. We need to get her to a hospital."

"She goes," Stoker told Dominic.

"No. She stays."

"She goes or I don't make any deals."

"Looks to me," Dominic said, "you love her as much as I love Bruno. The priest can go if you like, but the cop stays."

It was not what Stoker wanted at all, but it saved one more hostage. "All right."

"No," Bishop said. "I'm not going anywhere."

Stoker looked at him.

"I'm serious," Bishop said. "I've known this girl since she was knee-high, I'm not leaving her here to bleed to death. Just pretend I'm not here," he said to Stoker. To Dominic he said, "That would be right about the same time you're pretending this isn't a house of God."

Stoker had not had any respect for religion since the death of his daughter, but felt a great deal of warmth in that moment for Father Bishop. He realised he still didn't even know the man's Christian name.

"Right," Stoker said. "So, now we have ourselves a situation, Dominic. I'm sure this wasn't precisely what you wanted when you came here. But then Barrowville's not exactly what anyone expects, is it? We city folk have a strange conception of small, rural communities. Everyone knows each other's names, each other's business, right? Strangers walk through the door and everyone stops and looks up?" He laughed. "Strange thing about Barrowville is some of that's actually true."

"I want a tractor."

"The other thing ... you want a what?"

On the floor, Hart wheezed a laugh, blood flecking her lips. "He wants to ride out on a tractor, taking his jewels with him."

"Ride out on a ... that's the most ludicrous thing I've ever heard." However, Hart had also mentioned jewels, and that was something Stoker should have realised sooner. Dominic and his friends had clearly robbed a jewellers before coming to Barrowville. It was good Hart had already figured that out, but right at that moment Stoker had other things on his mind: he could pat her on the back later.

"My dog," Dominic said again. Stoker could see he was becoming irate and decided it would be safer to let Bruno down.

Slowly, Stoker set him to the floor, but Bruno made no move to run to his master.

"Get over here," Dominic barked at the animal. Bruno seemed to prefer it with Stoker. It seemed Dominic loved Bruno more than Bruno loved Dominic, which backed up something Stoker had learned lately. There was more to taking care of a dog than buying it food and getting your new girlfriend to take it for walks. Dominic was a domineering man with intense anger issues and Hart was not the only one who had felt the brunt of his aggressions.

He was suddenly glad Hart had left him behind. He had taken the opportunity to accomplish so much.

"I don't think he likes you," Stoker said. "Sorry. Anyway, you want a tractor?"

"What have you done to him?" Dominic demanded.

"Done to him? Nothing. Bruno just has good taste. What do you beat him with, by the way? My expert says it's a stick."

"Bruno. Come here, boy."

Bruno backed away and Stoker knew this was the moment of truth. The dog was scared of its master and didn't want to be anywhere near him, but that had not been enough for Stoker. That was why Stoker had left some dog food in the church doorway. He needed Bruno to run in a specific direction. For the entire plan to hinge on the actions of a dog was not a sign of good planning, but it was all Stoker had.

"Bruno," Dominic said, still moving towards the dog. Bruno continued to retreat, then broke into a loping run and headed for the door. Stoker noticed Dominic's two accomplices were uncertain what to do. From looking at them, he got the impression they had held their doubts about Dominic for a while now. Killing Joe had not helped their indecision any, and Stoker's hope was that if he could take Dominic out of the picture, the other two might just surrender.

Bruno had decided to cower against one of the pews and while Stoker was silently urging the mutt on, he did not seem to want to go any farther. Dominic caught up with him and cuffed the animal with the back of his hand. Stoker judged the distance between Dominic and the door to be around ten metres. It was greater than he had wanted, but it would have to do.

"Now!" Stoker shouted.

The door exploded inwards and Dominic physically jumped. Surging into the church came two devils: angry, fierce beasts with fires burning behind their eyes. Dominic screamed and attempted to bring up his bat, but the dogs were too swift and were upon him. Stoker winced as he saw one lock its jaws about Dominic's wrist and did not look to see what the other was doing.

He turned to the other two men and said, "I'd give up right about now if I were you."

The two men looked at one another and dropped their weapons, placing their hands behind their heads.

Rushing to Hart's side, Stoker could see Bishop had done some good work with tending her injuries. He clearly had some experience in the field and for this was Stoker thankful. She managed a smile and winced as she tried to get to her feet.

"Easy," Stoker cautioned.

"She's not as bad as I made out," Bishop admitted. "Dominic was intent on beating her to death, so I convinced him she was near to it. Even Dominic could see it was a bad idea to kill a detective, so he backed off."

"Looks like you have things well in hand," Hart said. "Those Dobermanns are familiar."

Just then a cranky old hermit walked into the church and shouted for his dogs to come back to him. Stoker was pleased to see Bruno go with them. Dominic was left on the floor, shivering in shock of the sudden attack.

"That was a little unconventional," Hart said.

Stoker shrugged. "I've learned to work with what I have, Liz. I went back to speak with Truman about Bruno. Him being an expert on dogs, I thought he might be able to offer something. He was only too eager to come. Turns out the old grouch is an actual dog-lover, instead of just being someone who beats animals when they don't do what he tells them."

"Community spirit," Hart said, unsteady on her feet but determined not to be held up by the priest. "We all pull together when we need to. Should we be cuffing these guys?"

"They can run if they like, but the Dobermanns might rip out their throats."

"True enough." She paused and he could sense she wanted to say something but was not certain whether she should. He hoped she felt herself close enough to him to say anything she pleased. "You did well," she said at last. "Thanks for saving my life."

"Welcome."

"You're a good negotiator, John. I know you'll never get over what happened with your daughter, but if you weren't here, today, this would have ended very badly for me."

He knew what she was trying to say, but it was an awkward thing to voice. She was telling him he had allowed someone else to negotiate last time and Sue had died. This time he had done it himself and had saved a life, and in the process perhaps even saved something of himself. With Hart he did not have to hear all her words to understand her meaning. They understood one another perfectly.

By this point, Constable Manson had entered the church and was taking Dominic into custody. He motioned for the other two men to accompany him and with a wary look at the giant dogs they complied. Truman sniffed at them as they passed, and Stoker imagined that was a dog's equivalent of swearing or something.

"Thanks, Mr Truman," Stoker said. "We couldn't have done this without you."

Truman shrugged. "Not many people call me Truman, Stoker. Eee-aye-eee-aye-oh and all that. You all right, Miss Hart?" He spoke as though he did not care, but if that was the case he would not have asked at all.

"I'll live," she said.

"What are you up to tomorrow?" Stoker asked him. "My wife's cooking Christmas dinner a little early. You're welcome to come."

The old hermit looked offended. "I have a hermit's image to maintain, Stoker. I'm keeping the dog, by the way."

"Nothing to do with me," Stoker said, "but I couldn't think of a better home."

Whistling to his dogs, Truman departed the church. Stoker did not envy the man walking directly into the crowd, or the fact the media would be all over him as soon as they got wind of what had happened.

"What about you, Father?" Stoker asked. "Fancy a Christmas dinner?"

"Thank you, but no. I have too much to do here now. Just cleaning up all this blood will take forever."

"Sorry," Hart winced, holding her side. "My bad."

"That was heartless of me, Felicity; I'm sorry."

"Not half as sorry as Dominic will be when we bang him up. So, what about me, then?" she asked Stoker.

"You? How do you mean?"

"This Christmas dinner you're inviting everyone to. Where's my invitation?"

"I wasn't going to invite you."

"Oh."

"I figured you were already coming. I didn't think I had to invite family."

He saw the warm smile light up Hart's face and knew in that moment it had all been worth it. They had caught some jewel thieves, solved the murder of a snowman, helped a teenage girl through her bad-boy crush, rescued a dog in distress and made a hermit happy. But Stoker did not care about any of that. All he could see before him was a smiling young woman who could easily have been his own daughter had he been able to properly look after her.

"Come on," Stoker said, feeling happier than he had in years. "You can come help me untangle my plastic bells."

"Sure. Right after I see a doctor."

Stoker had almost forgotten her injuries had not all been faked. Helping her to the church door, they walked out into the street. Some semblance of the crowd was still milling around, but most had probably either followed the criminals to the police station or got cold and gone home for some tea. Stoker paused, gazing out at something happening across the street, where the snow was even now still falling.

"What is it?" Hart asked from where she was leaning against him.

"Nothing," Stoker said and resumed walking. "Just thinking about cycles, Liz. How everything always seems to come back around eventually."

He did not look back at the scene as he took Hart in the other direction. Oblivious to having been observed, three children were busy laughing, making a snowman; only this one was far more snow than man.

MURDER WHILE YOU WAIT

CHAPTER ONE

Technically, it wasn't murder. However, as Suzie Locke stared down at the body pumping blood into the carpet, she could see how other people might have seen it that way. It was odd how her senses had been suddenly sharpened as she stood there, unable to look away. She could smell the rich, almost sweet, aroma of blood and sweat; could taste on her tongue the bitterness of words left unspoken. She surprised herself by not being distraught, for being able to stand there and coldly assess the situation. She wondered whether she would ever be able to get the stains from the carpet.

What surprised her most was that she did not much care that Harry Slade was dead.

Moving away from the body, Suzie went to the bathroom to wash her hands. There was no blood upon them, for when she had smashed him over the back of the head with the table lamp he had fallen forward, away from her. But she washed them anyway, convincing herself she should scrub as hard as she could, as though she was some modern-day Lady Macbeth. The truth was her hands were clean, at least physically, and by the time she came to dry them she still wasn't even trembling.

Stepping back into the living room, she figured she would have to do something about the body. Then, and only then, would she think about what she would tell the police if they came knocking.

Fetching a few bin bags, Suzie began cutting them up while she thought about Laura. An hour ago she had not even known Laura existed, but somehow Harry had thought it was about time she found out. It turned out Harry Slade was more the man of mystery than Suzie had expected; and not in a good way. Harry Slade was married to Laura Slade and through his somewhat babbled explanation, Suzie had found out she was nothing more than his bit on the side. Bit of what? she had asked. Harry's face had fallen when she'd asked that. It seemed he genuinely expected her to be happy that he had decided to leave his wife for her.

It was after the resulting argument that Suzie had bashed him over the head. She wondered whether she would ever regret it, wondered whether it made her a bad person that she didn't think she would ever care. She also wondered why anyone ever thought of hiding a body in a bin bag.

Entirely surrendering that idea, her eyes found the settee in the centre of her living room. She had never liked that settee and, since she now didn't like Harry either, decided to let the two have one another. Fetching a knife from the kitchen drawer, she sliced open the material at the front of the settee, exposing the gaping hole beyond. For the first time since she had bought it, she was rather glad about the thing. No, she realised, she wasn't glad at all. She wanted to feel glad, but she still wasn't feeling anything.

Harry fit snugly into the settee, as though the thing had been designed with a mind to hiding dead bodies, and Suzie began the laborious task of sowing the material back together. She was good at sowing, but then she had always liked the domestic arts. Being a modern woman did not mean she had to hate sowing, cooking and cleaning. It was, she reflected, perhaps what Harry had found attractive about her. Maybe his wife refused to even load the dishwasher. While she worked, Suzie decided she should have clobbered him with the iron; it would not only have been ironic but would have been a good pun for the tabloids to use.

But the tabloids were not going to be using anything, because they were never going to find the body. Even while she was finishing her sowing, she was thinking ahead to what she would do next. She knew a good way of getting the stains out of the carpet – she had a foolproof method for almost every stain imaginable – but getting the plush coffin removed was going to be difficult. She reasoned she could just buy a new settee and have the old one taken away, but sooner or later someone would wonder what the smell was and cut it open. Same thing if she asked the council to take it away. She could take it to the dump, but that would only buy her a little extra time before someone found it; and somehow they would be able to trace it back to her.

As she made the final stitch, she realised she had reached the only decision she really could have. It was not exactly the ideal solution, but she had never before murdered anyone, so did not have any experience to fall back on. Next time she would get it perfect, assuming there was ever a need for her to kill anyone else. Besides, she had made the trip once before and had got away with it, even though there had been no body back then.

The first thing she did was fetch a clean pair of trousers. She had a feeling she was going to need them.

Getting the settee to her van was going to be a problem. That she had a van at all instead of a car was fortunate, but then it all came full circle so it wasn't that much of a coincidence. She needed the van for one of her jobs (she sold cleaning products); it was her job which gave her all the domestic knowledge (or her domestic knowledge which had made her go into the business); and her domestic knowledge which had attracted Harry to her in the first place. Looking at it that way, the poor guy had guaranteed she would have the perfect means to dispose of his body. She assumed, of course, he had never given a moment's thought to the possibility she might one day kill him.

Taking one end of the settee, she dragged it across to the living room door and down the hall. As she opened the front door, she planned her route to the van. She lived on a busy road but thankfully had managed to park outside her house, so there was not a great distance to drag the thing. It was a chill November afternoon and as she got halfway to her van she considered going back for her jacket. Leaving the settee in the middle of the pavement, however, did not seem the best of options, so she pressed on. It was as she opened the back of her van that she realised she would have a problem lifting the settee to get it into the vehicle.

"Suzie."

She had not noticed her next-door neighbour but he was approaching now with a beaming smile. There was a newspaper tucked under one arm and, since he was heading back to his house, she supposed he had just been to the newsagent. His name was Jack Eddings, but she always called him Oddings. Not to his face, obviously. He was always taking too much of an interest in her affairs, asking her how she was and what she was doing at the weekend. At first she had assumed he was trying to chat her up, but she had long ago reached the conclusion he was just making inane small talk. Suzie was not a fan of small talk, especially since most of it contained a hidden agenda.

"Afternoon, Jack," she said.

"Need a hand with that?"

Her automatic reaction was to say no, she had it fine thanks. But she did not have it fine and there was no way she was getting the settee into the van without help. Reluctantly, she nodded.

"Right-o," he said, taking one end and hoisting it to rest upon the floor of the van. "This weighs a ton, Suzie, and the weight's lopsided."

"It's not a very good settee," she said flatly. "That's why I'm getting rid of it."

Oddings didn't say anything and between the two of them they managed to shove the settee into the van. Suzie closed the doors, not even feeling relief they could lock without much effort.

"Thanks," she said mechanically and Oddings beamed before continuing onto his house. He truly was odd.

Climbing into the driver's seat, Suzie shoved her spare trousers on the passenger seat and took a moment to look in her mirror, but there was no sign that anyone had paid any attention to her shoving her furniture into the back of her van. It was the normal thing to do if she was looking to get rid of it, and everyone at some point got rid of their old furniture.

Suzie did not think of much as she drove. She knew where she was going because she had been there to dump furniture before. This time was no different, and she had not been caught the last time so doubted there were cameras in the area. It was possible the body would be found eventually, but by that point there should be nothing connecting her to the crime.

Crime.

She thought about that word then. Harry would have loved to hear her use that word. But then Harry had always been obsessed with crime and criminals. He liked to find out precisely how people did such terrible things to each other, and why. She thought he would have found it funny he was himself now a murder victim.

Murder.

Murder was pre-meditated. Harry had told her that. She had not pre-meditated his death, just clonked him over the head and that was that. It was barely even manslaughter, but that was only because Harry could only loosely be described as a man. Pest control; that was more like it. If a rat wandered into your home, you were within your rights to kill the thing. Harry Slade had been a rat and she was rid of him.

The road became a little bumpy, but she was expecting that. Travelling through the dirt tracks between fields was never pleasant, but she knew the end would be worth it. She could even see her destination approaching and found a good place to park. Stepping out the van, Suzie cast a quick glance about, but there was no one for miles. That was the good thing about fields in November: no one tended them.

Opening the back of the van, she struggled to get the settee out, but managed it even without Oddings. It fell into the mud with a sickly squelch and she got behind it and gave it a mighty heave. It took more effort than Suzie had ever expended upon Harry in life, but finally the settee hit the water and then it was somehow easier to push. Suzie felt water slosh over her shoes, but she needed to make sure it went deep enough into the river not to be discovered.

Once the water reached her waist, she could no longer see the settee and decided she had pushed it far enough. Dragging herself back out of the cold water, Suzie looked over her handiwork. There was no sign of the settee, or of Harry, and snow was predicted next week so with any luck the river might freeze over. That would stop anyone finding him soon; in the meantime, the fish might start eating him.

Returning to the van, Suzie stripped off her wet trousers and put on the clean ones. She struggled with the clasp and remembered she had not worn them for several months. Finally managing to fasten them, she felt something poke her in the leg from an inside pocket. She pulled out the offending item and discovered it was something Harry had lost a year ago. Something he had got in a lot of trouble for losing. Suzie did not know how it had managed to get into her trousers but reasoned she must have stolen it. Why she would have done that she had no idea, but the point was a tad moot now.

Tossing the thing into the river, Suzie got back into the van and started the engine. It may not have been a particularly good idea to leave identification with the corpse, but she had to be fair to Harry. After all, every detective should always carry his warrant card.

CHAPTER TWO

Detective Ruth Hayden put down the receiver and felt far more depressed than she had been ten minutes earlier. It was freezing in the office but heating seemed to be something her employers didn't care much about. Outside, the snow was thick upon the ground and still coming down in light sprinkles. She had no idea how she was going to be able to drive home through it all, but that was not something she would have to think about for a few hours yet. Christmas was also not something she would have to think about just yet, but it was December 18th so she knew she could not put it off too long. Rich wanted them both to spend Christmas with his parents but they had done that last year and she wasn't too eager to repeat it. She would not say the day had gone down as a complete disaster, not now they were all back on speaking terms, but it was a situation best avoided. He had asked her what she wanted to do this year, but Hayden had never much cared for Christmas anyway so was happy to ignore it. Either that, she had said, or go to Honolulu. This was the first time in years the both of them would have the entire day off; she had spent so many years treating it as just another day, that was just what it had become. They didn't even give each other presents any more, but that had been an entirely different disaster she really did not like to talk about.

She leaned back in her chair and closed her eyes. The phone call from Laura Slade had not done much to brighten her spirits.

A month ago, Laura's husband had disappeared without trace. Detective Harry Slade had been a popular character around the station, but Hayden had known the man had issues. In the police everyone had issues, it's what the job did to you, but Slade had seemed to have more than his fair share. He drank too much, gambled too much and from the way he leered over women he likely had a few girlfriends his wife didn't know about. But, aside from all that, he acted like a decent enough guy. He was good to his friends and was always reliable. That he had upped and left one day should therefore have been surprising, but Hayden only found herself disappointed. She didn't much like him and Harry Slade was certainly a snake, but he was a pleasant enough snake.

Something plopped onto her desk and she knew even without opening her eyes it was a strong coffee.

"You look like you need it," Tremens said as he perched himself on the edge of her desk with his own mug. "Need to share?"

Hayden tried not to sigh. She tried not to sigh because Tremens always told her she sighed enough to sail a steamer across the ocean. She never had the heart to tell him steamers didn't have sails. Hayden and Tremens were very similar. They were both in their late thirties, both physically fit and dressed smartly for work. Neither of them had much of a life, which was probably why they had drifted together. They had been lovers for over two years now but Hayden was not entirely certain either of them was actually in love. It was a terrible thing to say about her relationship, but at least it was consistent in how it reflected their lives.

"Laura again," she said, wrapping her hands about her steaming mug. It was strange how the warmth from a simple drink could infuse her entire body but still leave her soul feeling chilled. "Rich, what do you think happened to Harry?"

Tremens shrugged. He shrugged as much as Hayden sighed and she long suspected he did it just to annoy her now. It was his trademark way of saying he didn't know and didn't much care. Tremens and Slade had never been especially close, which was odd because Hayden had always believed lads stuck together and respected any of their male friends who could get away with the things Slade did.

"Maybe he's dead," Tremens said, sipping his coffee.

"Rich, that's horrible."

"True though."

When Slade had vanished a month earlier, there had been a lot of talk. Most of his co-workers thought he had just had enough of his wife and left her. That he had also left his job had not been all that surprising considering it wasn't that much to abandon. There had been an investigation but nothing conclusive had been discovered. His passport was missing, along with a bag and some of his clothes. A month later, no one had heard a word from him, so the rumour of his death was becoming more prevalent. Either that or he really just didn't want to be found. Hayden had assumed he had run because of gambling debts, but the investigation had not turned up anything of the sort. He gambled too much, true, but he didn't owe anyone any money.

"I reckon he just didn't like Laura," Tremens said.

"What's wrong with Laura?"

"Well, she's a little domineering."

"So it's her fault her husband ran away?"

"Unless he's dead, yes."

"Why do men always side with men?"

"Same reason women always side with women."

Hayden knew this was an argument she was not going to win. She remembered having talked with Laura during the investigation. The poor woman had been distraught and could not stop crying the entire time. That was not the reaction of someone who didn't care for her husband; and if she could react that way, she did not deserve such a louse for a husband to begin with. There had even been hushed talk that Laura might have killed him to stop him wasting all their money, and such talk had infuriated Hayden no end. She was not herself married, but could not believe that the job could so destroy a person's soul that they could not be happy for those who were.

"Maybe we should look into it more." Tremens said. "Someone somewhere must know where Harry is."

"I thought you thought he was dead?"

"Yeah, but that doesn't mean I can't hope he isn't. Where could we start looking? And, before you say it, I'm not talking to Laura. That woman does my head in."

Tremens had a lot of work on. Hayden knew precisely how much because her workload was just as full. To take on a missing person's case would be ridiculous, even if that missing person was a fellow detective. However, a month without any sign of the man was worrying and Hayden liked to think someone would do the same for her should she vanish.

"We can get the case notes," Hayden said, "but we're not assigned to the case. Whatever we do will have to be off the record, Rich."

"Sure. At least that way it means we won't have to fill in any reports about what we do."

He was hiding it well, but Tremens was worried. Hayden always knew when Tremens was worried because he began making jokes about paperwork.

They requested the case notes through an unofficial channel. With an officer missing, it presented an opportunity for everyone to forget about correct procedure and do everything possible to get said officer back. Hayden considered sifting through the notes at the station, but the atmosphere was so bleak and oppressive she knew the only conclusion she would reach would be that Slade was far better off wherever he was. She therefore suggested the two of them head down to the local café. Given the opportunity, Tremens would have lived in that café, so he offered no argument.

Grabbing her jacket, Hayden stepped outside into the blasting December cold. The snow had slowed to a mild flurry, but even that was mainly just what the wind was blowing around, while underfoot her shoes crunched through the soft layers, leaving an unsightly white rim which no doubt would be the devil to remove. Hayden had never much liked snow, even when it was in the soft, harmless stage. It was, so far as she could see, pointless. Snow did nothing for the environment, did nothing to help life along, and to her mind it was something to be fought. If she could slap an ASBO on snow she would gladly have done so, but she did not like to think about it too much. If she did, she would only return to the fact she hated the winter and everything it brought with it. She knew Tremens was more open to the winter months, which was one of the reasons she did not like to discuss Christmas with him. Tremens was a boy at heart, which always surprised her considering how soul-destroying their lives were.

They moved quickly to the café, neither of them wanting to spend any more time in the cold than necessary. Decorations clung gaudily to lampposts and railings: sickly displays of quasi-religious cheeriness. Some of the lights were on, others knew not to illuminate during the day, while some had died years ago but their corpses were dragged out each winter to make everyone feel better about themselves. As they entered the café, it was to discover a low undercurrent of Christmas music which was nowhere near as annoying as it could have been. The café itself was fairly small, with only a dozen or so tables, all bolted to the floor. It was cheap, served nothing that was any good for the human body, but above all it was warm. Hayden found a table beside one of the radiators and knew after a few minutes she might even stop shivering.

Tremens did not even glance at the menu. Hayden wished the owners would one day change the choice and give him the shock of his life.

"So," Hayden said as she set down the notes, "what makes us a better investigation team than the officers actually assigned to the case?"

"We don't miss what's obvious," Tremens said, giving his order to the waitress he had already called over. Hayden had learned he knew all the staff by name, which meant he used the café far too much to be healthy.

She realised then the waitress was waiting for her to order something, and she went with egg and chips even though now they were there she wasn't all that hungry.

"We should start," Tremens said, "by eliminating everything that's already been covered. They spoke with Slade's family, right?"

"Nothing from any of them," Hayden said, sifting through the paperwork.

"And his neighbours."

"Same. No one saw anything, heard anything, noticed anything."

"Talking to his co-workers would be next, but that's us and we sure don't know where he is."

"So then we come to his vices," Hayden said. "Gambling, womanising, drinking. Nothing conclusive from those, either."

"If it was gambling or drinking," Tremens said, "we'd be able to find a trail. There would be clues."

"So you're saying it has something to do with his womanising?"

"I'm saying it's easier to keep a woman secret than a gambling problem."

"And you know this from experience?"

Just then the waitress appeared and saved him from having to answer. She plopped two coffees on the table, her eyes lingering as though she wondered what they were working on, before she drifted back to her work.

"We have to break this down to the basics," Tremens said. "There are only two things that could have happened. He could have disappeared voluntarily or involuntarily. If the latter, he's probably dead. And yes, I think it has to do with a woman."

"Why?"

Tremens shifted uncomfortably and suddenly Hayden realised there was something he was not saying. Something he knew about

Slade he had never told her. Something perhaps more people at the station knew.

"Spill it," she said. "Slade told you something, didn't he?"

Tremens shrugged, and this time Hayden actually thought he likely hadn't realised he had even done it. "Harry *was* seeing someone else."

"You mean for definite?"

"He told me."

"Have you told the investigating officers?"

"Of course, what do you take me for? But I never knew her name, never knew anything about her actually. I just know he was seeing someone."

"Does Laura know?"

"I doubt it. Unless she found out and she was the one who killed him."

Their food arrived at that point. The waitress smiled, sliding their plates before them. Again she seemed to take her time leaving their table and Hayden was beginning to get annoyed with her.

"What?" Tremens asked.

"What, what?" Hayden asked. "What's that waitress keep hanging around us for?"

"She's our waitress; she's serving our food."

"And?"

"And? And what? You think I'm having an affair with the waitress now?"

"You tell me. You're in here a lot and you seem to be keeping other things from me."

Tremens ignored her and started on his meal. He was angry, which was a sure sign he wasn't hiding anything. Hayden turned to her own food and the two of them ate in silence for some minutes. She knew she was frustrated about the missing detective and that she should not be taking it out on Tremens. But it was eating at her that they did not know what had happened and that until they found out, it could perhaps have been any one of them who had vanished.

"We need to find out who Slade was having an affair with," Hayden said at last. It was not an apology, but since she was talking about the case again it was the best Tremens was going to get.

"No one's been able to figure that out," Tremens said, his tone suggesting he had not forgiven what she had said but had decided to forget it. "Maybe we need to talk to Laura after all."

"You mean tell her about the affair?"

"It's the only angle I can think of that hasn't been covered yet. Maybe it'll get us somewhere."

"It'll surely get Laura somewhere; just not anywhere pleasant."

Tremens stopped eating, which was never a good sign. "I feel terrible already, but it needs to be done." He pulled out his wallet and Hayden was glad she was sitting down because he hadn't finished his food and did not seem as though he intended to. He signalled the waitress and gave her the money. She smiled and thanked him, entirely ignoring Hayden.

Stepping back into the cold, Hayden tried not to glower.

"What?" Tremens said. "Not the waitress thing again."

"No, of course not," Hayden said more icily than the air. "Just be careful, Rich."

Tremens scowled. "Sure, whatever."

"Richard," a voice called and Hayden saw the waitress hurrying out of the café with something in her hand. Without her jacket she was likely freezing but Hayden didn't care, for at that moment all she wanted to do was shove the girl's face into the snow. "You forgot your change," the waitress said.

Tremens looked flustered as he explained she could keep it. The waitress veritably beamed and almost moved to hug or kiss him. She must have caught Hayden's glower because she restrained herself. "If I don't see you before Christmas, have a good one, Richard."

"You too," Tremens replied sheepishly.

Once the girl was gone, Hayden folded her arms and stared, saying nothing.

"She's a sweet kid," Tremens said. "And a lot of the guys from the station use this café. We all know the staff."

"All?"

"Well, obviously you don't. But you don't have anything to worry about, Ruth. There's nothing going on with me and Suzie."

Suzie. Hayden filed the name away. She had a feeling that come the future, Suzie was going to be causing them a great deal of problems indeed.

CHAPTER THREE

Laura Slade did not know anything. Hayden had met her a few times over the years but would not have called her a friend. Since her husband had disappeared, Laura had latched onto Hayden as her point of contact at the station. Perhaps it was because she was a woman, perhaps because Hayden did not judge Laura like other officers might have; whatever the reason, Hayden was the closest thing Laura had to a friend at her husband's work.

Hayden found herself in the kitchen, making tea. She did not ordinarily drink tea, but Laura was a traditional woman who loved nothing more than to share a pot of tea and a plate of biscuits with her guests. Hayden did not want to do anything to unnerve the woman further and if she could adhere to Laura's routines it might help her remember something. Tremens was in the living room making small talk with her, which was always laughable. Tremens was a good detective but he was not exactly what Hayden would have called a people person.

The water boiled and Hayden poured it into the teapot before carrying it into the living room. The Slades had a decent-sized house in a fairly nice neighbourhood, which was more than Hayden and Tremens had. There were no Slade children, so the arrangement of the house was entirely Laura and Harry. There was a DVD cabinet and a small CD rack which were probably Harry's, but aside from that Hayden could not see anything which presented the property as belonging to anything other than a single woman. The ornaments on the mantelpiece, the animal doorstops, the flowery design on the curtains; none of it seemed to say anything at all about Harry. She had thought she had known Harry fairly well, but it seemed she had no idea about his social life at all.

She realised she was standing in the doorway, her mind wandering, and moved in to set down the tea.

Tremens, she noted with a little glee, looked extremely uncomfortable.

"Laura was just running through what she told the other officers," Tremens said.

Hayden poured the tea. Whatever Laura had told the other officers would not interest the two of them. If there was anything to be found in her statement it would have already been picked up on. They had to go through the procedure, however, to make Mrs Slade more comfortable. If she was relaxed she might remember something or even say something she did not feel was important, but which could crack the case for them. Hayden decided she would have to say something to Laura: something that would make them bond. She had no idea what that might have been.

Then she realised something was missing from the house and decided that was perfect. "You haven't decorated," Hayden said as she reached for a biscuit. "Gaudy tack, isn't it?"

"When your husband's missing, presumed dead, you don't much feel like decorating."

Hayden's hand stopped with the biscuit halfway to her mouth.

"There's probably not a lot of room in there for the biscuit," Tremens said, "what with all the room being taken up by your foot."

"I'm sorry, Laura."

But Laura waved it off. "Harry's said much worse. It's the job, you know. It plays with your mind. All those hours you work without proper time to sleep in between. Do you know Harry well?"

"No," Hayden said. "Well, I thought I did, but I really don't know." She took a sip of tea to calm her nerves.

"So you weren't sleeping with him, then?"

Hayden spluttered, her tea going everywhere.

"Sorry," Laura said. "Bad moment to ask that. I just wondered whether it was you, that's all."

"You know your husband was having an affair?"

"I suspected. Well, yes I know. I just didn't want to admit it to myself, and I didn't want to ask him because I didn't want to hear the answer. If he said yes that would have destroyed me, if he said no it would have been worse because it would have meant he couldn't even be honest with me." She stared into her tea. "Honestly, do you think he's dead?"

"I've no idea," Hayden said truthfully. "And until we can figure out what happened to him, no one does. Uh, you want me to grab a cloth or something for the tea?"

"There's some cleaning stuff in the bathroom."

Hayden exited the living room as quickly as possible before she could say or do anything to make matters even worse. She hoped she would be able to find a cloth without too much rooting around: she didn't want to make it look as though she had been searching through the victim's bathroom for clues. As she opened the bathroom door, however, she stopped in shock. It was not a large room, but its two shelves were loaded so heavily with cleaning products she thought it might collapse at any moment. In the shower she could see at least half a dozen different shampoos and conditioners, while on the floor about the sink there were four different types of toilet cleaners. She reached tentatively for the room's only cupboard and cleaning products poured out onto her like someone was throwing them at her from the other side. There were hard soaps, liquid soaps, fruit-smelling soaps; toothpaste tubes, toothpaste pumps, dozens of spare toothbrushes; mint mouthwash, fruit mouthwash, plain mouthwash; handtowels, bath towels, flannels.

Shuddering, Hayden felt more than a little afraid she had stepped into the home of the most obsessively clean couple who ever lived.

Returning to the living room with a damp cloth, Hayden made a half-hearted attempt to sponge out the tea stains before Laura took over. She noticed Tremens was slowly working his way through all the biscuits and wondered whether that was the entire reason he had come.

"You certainly have a well-stocked bathroom," Hayden said, unable to stop herself from enquiring.

"That's Harry for you," Laura said as she finished with the cloth and put it to one side. "He gets it cheap somewhere. Wholesale or something. I don't really ask."

Hayden was under the impression there were a lot of things Laura Slade did not like to ask her husband about. "Anything else he gets wholesale?"

"What are you insinuating? Harry doesn't get things which fall off the backs of lorries."

"No?" Hayden asked. "Look, I'm not trying to accuse him of anything, but the more we know about his lifestyle the more avenues are open to us. Believe me, all we care about is finding your husband alive and well. The official investigation team has looked into his gambling and nothing came of it. That means it's something the team didn't know about. If he was getting things on the cheap, maybe the distributor found out he was a cop and got worried."

She could see some of Laura's instinctive aggression fading, the wall breaking down brick by brick. "I don't know the name of the company," she said. "Harry never brought home receipts or anything. He'd just stay out all night and then drive home with a car full of cleaning products."

"He's not a flowers guy, then?" Tremens asked.

Hayden really wished sometimes he would just shut up.

"You think they're from his fancy woman?" Laura asked, and from her tone it was clear the thought was not so alien to her.

"Well, it does seem a bit weird," Tremens said, "but he might use it as an excuse to see her. You don't have any idea who she might be?"

"No. And if you find her, I still don't want to know. I don't want to meet her, don't want to talk to her. She has nothing to do with my life, whoever she is."

They did not get much more from Laura Slade and by the time Hayden and Tremens left they were even more in the dark than when they had begun. Hayden drove them slowly home, giving them a chance to think, to sort through whatever they had learned.

"About all I can conclude," Tremens said, "is that Slade's life is a bit screwed-up."

"Which Slade?"

"Both of them, actually. All right, let's look at this logically. Harry's having an affair and in the morning brings back toilet cleaner. Sounds stupid, but it's still the most plausible thing we can surmise. Question is, who's the weirdest party in all of this? Harry, who expects it to work; Laura, on whom it does work; or this other woman, who thinks women love cleaning products."

"You start bringing me fresh towels," Hayden told him, "you can look for a nice couch to sleep on for the rest of your life."

"We find this woman," Tremens said, "we find Slade."

"So you don't think he's dead any more?"

"I think he's run away with his other woman. No offence to Laura, but she was asking for that."

Hayden glanced away from the road. "Excuse me?"

"Knowing Harry was having an affair and not even confronting him about it? Guy was obviously bored with his wife and she didn't care enough to ask him about it?"

"I think she was trying to save her marriage, Rich."

"You don't save a marriage by not talking to your partner."

"I can see why we're not married."

"Why do you pull apart everything I say?"

"Because everything you say is, on some level, offensive. Or stupid. Or both." Hayden did not mean to take anything out on Tremens, but the entire situation was ridiculous. None of it made any sense at all, yet that was all they had to work with. She could not shake the image that Harry Slade was out there somewhere, lying on a cruise ship with his mistress, sipping cocktails and laughing at everyone he had left behind in his old life. For one fleeting moment, she spitefully hoped Tremens was right and that Slade was dead. It was a horrible thought and made her a horrible person, but at that moment Hayden's seasonal goodwill was all but exhausted.

They drove the rest of the way home in silence.

CHAPTER FOUR

"One Happy Christmas breakfast," Suzie Locke said with a beaming smile.

The detective, Richard Tremens, looked down at the food she had dropped in front of him. It was morning and he was in for his usual full English. She had been afraid yesterday he wouldn't come back, that his partner would not have allowed him to. Suzie knew all too well how annoying co-workers could be, how they tended to think they had every right to run your life for you. Tremens was one of those men who had his own mind but had enough experience not to use it. Suzie had been wondering for several months now whether he was seeing anyone. He did not wear a wedding ring, but that did not necessarily mean he was single. She had never seen a wedding ring on Harry's finger either, but it seemed he had just been careful to remove it whenever he came to see her. It still irked her to think of how the man had treated her. She knew she would always have a clear memory of how he had announced he was willing to leave his wife for her; the wife he had until that moment never thought to mention.

She vowed she would not make the same mistake with Tremens. She would find out first whether he was attached to anyone. She would play this one carefully. For one thing, she had only recently had her new settee delivered and could not afford to lose it just yet.

"Thanks, Suzie," Tremens said, taking up his knife and fork. He seemed distant, as though he was distracted by his problems. It was probably that case he was working on with that icy woman he had come in with yesterday.

"Nothing a good breakfast can't solve," she said, sliding into the seat opposite him.

"Why's it a Happy Christmas breakfast anyway?" Tremens asked as he ate.

"I reckon this is the sort of thing Jesus ate at the Last Supper."

"Uh, the Last Supper was at Easter."

"You sure?"

"Yeah, it was just before they killed him."

"Oh. Wasn't that Christmas?"

"No, Christmas was when he was born." He paused, confused. "Are you playing with me, Suzie?"

"Sure," she said, beaming. She would look it up later to make sure, but she was certain she had it around the right way. "Still freezing outside, isn't it?"

"Yeah." He resumed eating.

"Still, not as cold as around that woman from yesterday."

"Ruth? Yeah, if she comes in again, could you tell her I only come in here occasionally?"

"Why?"

"She doesn't like me coming here so much. Thinks it's bad for my health."

"Sure, Richard. Anything for you." She offered him her most dazzling smile but he was busy dropping sugar into his coffee. She coughed to get his attention, but his concentration really was elsewhere. "Hard case you're working on?" she asked.

"Sorry, can't talk about it."

"Maybe I can help."

He went to refuse again, but reconsidered. "A lot of the guys from the station use this café, right?"

"Yep."

"What about a guy named Harry Slade?"

Suzie was glad she was sitting and somehow managed to keep a vague trace of a smile to her face. "Gary Slade?"

"Harry."

She put on her best pout as she shook her head. "Nope. Sorry, don't know him. If he comes by, maybe you could point him out to me."

"If he comes by I won't much care because it means we've found him."

"You and Ruth ... you're looking for Slade?"

"Yeah. He's disappeared. Just wondered whether he might have mentioned something while he was here."

"Oh." She thought hard. "I think he said something about heading north for a while. Maybe to see family?"

"Thought you said you didn't know him?"

She realised she was an idiot. "Oh. No, I don't. But I saw your paperwork yesterday. It said something about gambling debts. There's only one detective I know with gambling debts, only I never knew his name."

"So you do know Harry Slade?"

Suzie wished she had never begun to dig her own grave in the first place. "Well, a little. Never tipped, that one, so I didn't pay much attention to him. Tips keep a waitress happy, you know? Saves her having to supplement her income doing other things."

Tremens laughed. "How many jobs do you have exactly?"

Sensing a way to break away from talking about Slade, Suzie said, "Just the one more. I sell stuff. Have myself a market stall when I have the time to use it. I sell rather a lot of …"

"That's nice, but back to Slade?"

"Ah."

"You said he said he was heading north?"

"I'm not sure. Like I said, I didn't pay much attention to that one. Maybe he did, I don't really remember. He's disappeared, you say? Any leads?"

"Would I be sitting here asking you if I had any leads?"

"Well, there's no need to be rude about it."

"Sorry, Suzie. Just having a difficult time with this one, and it's not even my case."

"Then why are you on it at all?"

"Ruth. Detective Hayden insists."

"And you don't want to find Slade?"

"Don't get me wrong: when one of our own disappears, I'm more than willing to pull out all the stops. Whatever that means. It's just, I never liked him much to begin with. I reckon his arrogance has finally caught up with him."

"How do you mean?"

"Like I said, the man had problems. Problems of his own creation. I'm not saying anyone deserves to be killed, but he was a rough character. I was told this morning his description's been put out now. Hopefully someone somewhere will have seen him, dead or alive."

"But he wasn't killed. He just headed north."

"So you think you heard. But considering you didn't even know his name I'm not putting much faith in that theory. No, depending on who he annoyed, Harry Slade is likely holding up a bridge somewhere."

Suzie tried to think that through, but if it was a well-known metaphor it was something she had never heard before. "I'm sorry," she said at last. "Holding up a bridge?"

"Hmm?" Tremens gulped his tea. "You know, mob killing. It means his body's probably in the river."

Suzie felt the colour drain from her face. She thought about how much her new settee had set her back and how it was a waste of money if the police already knew what had happened to Slade.

"You all right?" Tremens asked.

"Sure. Richard, do you mind if I ask you something personal?"

"Shoot."

"If it turned out the woman you were seeing was married, what would be a normal response?"

"Normal?" He half-laughed. "I don't think I've ever given a normal response in my life, Suzie."

"Humour me."

Tremens thought a moment. "Normal response would probably be to shout at her and never see her again. Go out and get hammered or something."

"And your response?"

"Honestly? It would depend where we were at the time."

"Say ... say you were at your place."

"We in bed?"

"No, we're in a café."

"Cute. I meant in the theoretical scenario."

"Oh. Sure."

"Then I'd take all her clothes and throw her out the front door. She can scream and pound on my door all she wants, but it wouldn't be me suffering."

It was something Suzie had not thought about. Perhaps she should have done something similar to Slade. Perhaps killing the man had been a little over the top after all. At the time it had not felt satisfying, but she could imagine throwing him out naked into the snow might well have done. Richard Tremens could have had a good influence on her life had she fallen for him instead of Harry Slade.

"Why anyway?" Tremens asked.

"Oh, no reason. Just trying to sort through some personal issues." What she was hearing was terrible. At the time, she had thought what she was doing was perfectly normal and entirely acceptable. Harry Slade was a cheating rat and it was not illegal to kill a rat which entered your home. Now it seemed she might have overreacted, that perhaps bashing his head in could have even constituted murder. She wanted to ask Tremens but feared the answer. If it turned out to actually be murder, he would arrest her. She did not want to go to gaol, even though she was certain it would not come to that. But she needed to make sure, needed to be certain she was in fact in the right. And if she could not tell Tremens precisely what she had done, perhaps she could show him. After all, it was only a matter of time before someone found her settee. They would have a tough time connecting the body to her but the police were clever. They would make the connection eventually. She needed to know beforehand whether she had actually done something wrong.

"Rich," she said slowly, "could I ask you a favour?"

"Sure. What?"

"Would you take a ride with me?"

"Is that a euphemism?"

"In my van. There's something I want to show you. Something I think you need to see."

A strange look came over his face then. It seemed as though he was on the verge of making a crude joke, but he must have seen the seriousness to her face because he nodded instead. "All right. When?"

"Now, if you're free."

"Not really, but I'm intrigued. Will it take long?"

"Maybe half an hour, round trip."

"All right." He looked wary, but also incredibly curious. I'll just let Ruth know where I'm going."

"Couldn't you do that when you got back? I ... this is a little personal."

Tremens looked as though he was about to argue. Then he smiled reassuringly. "Only because I trust you."

Suzie returned his smile, but inside she was a bag of nerves being shaken like a carbonated drink. Once her lid came off, she had no idea what might happen. She hoped Tremens would laugh when she showed him Slade, but if it turned out she had actually done the wrong thing, she always kept a few tools in the van. Among them was a wrench. Richard Tremens was such a nice guy, but she had to protect herself.

With any luck, she was worrying over nothing; but she had a sneaking suspicion in the eyes of the law she had done something very, very wrong indeed.

CHAPTER FIVE

She had been neglecting her actual work and Hayden knew she would have to immerse herself in it the entire day if she had any hope of keeping her job. It was after midday now, which meant she had not seen Tremens for a couple of hours. The two of them had agreed they would just get on with their separate workloads today and try to figure out Slade's disappearance once they got home. Rather than allow him to do that, however, Hayden had followed him. He had gone precisely where she knew he would: to that café down the road. She knew it was irrational to think he was having an affair with the waitress, but Hayden had not been sleeping much lately and she always became paranoid when she had not slept enough. The fact that the waitress – Suzie – was younger and prettier than she did not help her state of mind any. But no; she knew Richard Tremens simply could not say no to a bacon and sausage butty. The only way Tremens would cheat on her would be to run away with a pig.

It was not a trust issue, therefore, which saw Hayden pop out to the café for a coffee. Since she had not been sleeping, she needed more coffee, which was a perfectly reasonable argument. Having found no trace of either Tremens or the waitress, Hayden returned to the station and tried not to think about either of them. It was then she realised she had forgotten to buy her coffee; which proved she had indeed been following him. Not that she would ever have admitted it.

"Excuse me, do you work here?"

She almost collided with a middle-aged man hanging around the doorway.

"No," Hayden said. "I just heard there was a fan club forming at the door so I thought I'd wait for an autograph."

The man did not seem to even understand her joke, which was fine because she wasn't sure she did either.

"Detective Hayden," she said. "Can I help with something?"

"Well, I'm not sure. I ... Well, it's silly. I just thought I might be able to provide some information and I didn't ... I'm probably just wasting your time."

That explained why he was hanging around the door. He did not want to be laughed at for wasting police time, or arrested or something. Why he had not just phoned in the information he was certain no one wanted was beyond Hayden. He was probably one of those goody-two-shoes characters who always wanted to phone Crimestoppers but never had anything worthwhile to say. That meant she did not want to talk to him, but could not very well turn him away.

"Tell me what case it involves and I'll get someone to talk to you," she said. It was always best to get someone else to sort out the things she did not want to know about.

"This missing detective."

Suddenly Hayden was interested. "Slade?"

"Yes. I knew him. Well, I say knew him and I really ..."

"Do you know where he is?"

"No."

Hayden's hopes fell. "Oh."

"But I saw him a lot. He's seeing my next-door neighbour. I haven't seen him around for a few days, though."

"Seeing ...? He's having an affair with your neighbour?" Hayden's heart leapt at the possibility she had finally caught a break.

"An affair? Oh, I didn't realise he was married."

"What's your name?"

"Jack. Jack Eddings."

"Mr Eddings, I want you to think very carefully. When was the last time you saw Harry Slade?"

"The twenty-first of November. They had an argument, you see. I heard shouting, but it didn't last. There was proper screaming, though. Something about a woman. I suppose it must have been Slade's wife."

"Supposition's a fine thing, but I need to know facts. What time did he leave?"

"I don't know. I didn't see him leave."

"When did his car pull out?"

"It vanished the next day. I remember thinking that odd, because her van left the day of the argument. I helped load it. I remember wondering why Slade's car was still there if the van was gone."

"Helped load it? With what?"

"A settee. She was throwing it out. It didn't look that old, although it had been sown up good and proper. I didn't like to say anything. The replacement didn't arrive for weeks, though, so I don't know what she did in the meantime for sitting down."

"Mr Eddings, your neighbour. She wouldn't happen to be a bit OCD in the cleaning department, would she?"

"OCD? No."

"Shame."

"But she does sell cleaning things. She has a market stall, you know. When she's not waitressing."

Hayden's heart sank. "Waitressing? Mr Eddings, what's the name of your neighbour?"

"Locke. Suzie Locke."

Suddenly Hayden decided she should have punched the woman in the face when she had wanted to yesterday.

"I'm terribly sorry to waste your time like this, detective."

"No," Hayden said quickly, her mind racing. "No, you might just have solved ... Richard!"

Eddings looked about him silently.

"She has Richard," Hayden said.

"Oh. Is that bad?"

Hayden's instant thought was to run back to the café, but they would be long gone. "Come with me," she said, grabbing Eddings by the arm and hurrying him back to the street. "Which one's your car?"

Eddings indicated and she pushed him inside, scrambling in beside him. "Where are we going?" he asked.

"Locke. Get me to her house. Quickly!"

Eddings asked no further questions and simply drove. A thousand scenarios shot through Hayden's head. There was no indication this Suzie Locke had killed Slade; perhaps their affair had ended and Slade had just chosen to disappear. What Eddings had said about the settee, however, had made her think a little too hard.

They shot through a red light and almost collided with a lorry coming the other way.

"Jesus! What are you doing?"

"Urgent police business," Eddings said. "Do you have a spare blues-and-twos for the roof?"

"Do I have a spare ...? Slow down."

Eddings looked at her, which was not a good idea considering the speed he was travelling. Finally he slowed.

"Better," Hayden said, buckling her seat-belt and deciding the man could run courses in safety awareness.

Soon enough they arrived at Eddings's home and Hayden looked over the house next door. She could see no sign of movement and there were no windows open, but she was hardly going to let that stop her.

"Are we going to break in?" Eddings asked. "I have a credit card handy."

"You watch a lot of cop shows, right?"

"Yes. You?"

"That'd be like getting home from school and watching Grange Hill."

"Are you going to kick the door in?"

Hayden decided sometimes she hated the public. "Do you know where Locke went to get rid of the settee?"

"No."

"Damn."

"But I know where she got rid of her last settee."

"You ... She makes a habit of this?"

"They were going to charge her for taking away her old one, so when she got a new one she dumped it." He leaned closer to whisper conspiratorially, "Illegally."

"She dumped it?"

"That was why I was surprised she was getting a new one already. Couldn't have had the old one more than a year."

She wished he would stop mentally wandering off places. "Where did she dump it?"

Eddings looked a little uncomfortable. "I wouldn't want to get her into any trouble."

"I think she killed Slade and right now she might be killing my partner."

"Are you sure? She seemed like such a nice girl."

Hayden bit back her reply and said instead, "Maybe I should check. Better safe than sorry."

"Quite, quite."

"Eddings, where did she dump the flaming body!"

Eddings physically jumped and Hayden could see some curtains twitching now; but she was seething and did not much care. There was still a chance she was completely wrong and had just defamed the woman's character to all her neighbours. If that was the case, she would sort it out later, but right at that moment all she cared about was finding Tremens.

"The river. There's a shallow part where it meets the fields."

"How do you know that was where she dumped it?"

"Because she told me afterwards. She was worried she'd done a really bad thing. She tends to do that, you know. Does things on the spur of the moment, then worries about them later. She's her own morality police, you know."

"Just tell me about this river."

"Well, you go to the Field and Fountain and there's a track behind it leading off through the fields. Just follow that and you're there."

"What's the Field and Fountain when it's at home?"

"A village pub."

"You seem to know a lot about what Locke does, Mr Eddings."

"I went with her, after she'd dumped the first settee. She'd convinced herself to go get it back, so I went with her. But when we got there it had sunk and we couldn't get it out."

"So you've driven there before?"

"Yes."

"Is the address of this pub in your sat nav?"

"Uh, yes."

She held out her hand. "Keys."

"Keys?"

"Car keys. If you're such a fan of TV cops, you'll know I'm commandeering your vehicle for police purposes."

"Oh, right. Certainly." He dug through his pockets and took far too long to come up with his keys. When he found them, Hayden snatched them from him and climbed back inside the car. Eddings was still talking, but she slammed the door on him and tore away from the kerb. She finally had a destination; now it was time to discover whether she was already too late.

CHAPTER SIX

Gazing out across the river, Tremens could not help wonder what he was doing there. When Suzie Locke had asked him to come with her in the van, he had not quite known what to expect. That she would take him through a field and to the edge of a river had not quite been on his list of best guesses, however. The river was shielded by a great number of weeping willows, the green sludgy water not enticing him to go for a swim. There was a winter chill to the air and in places he could see the water had begun to freeze.

What they could have been doing out there was beyond him.

"You said you wanted me to see something. Uh, is this it?"

"Sort of."

She looked more nervous than he had ever seen her, and he began to wonder just what the problem was. "Are you in trouble, Suzie? Is it something I can help with?"

"It's about Slade."

"Has he threatened you?"

"Threatened me?"

It had been a stab in the dark, but Tremens had felt it worthwhile asking, if only to gauge her reaction. If anything, she became even more nervous. "How well exactly do you know Slade?" he asked.

She looked down at her feet. "Well."

"Well? Well as in well, well?"

"Well as in ... well, sort of ... well enough."

"Well, well, well."

"Was that a joke?"

"Just a realisation. You were having an affair with him, weren't you?"

"It wasn't an affair," she snapped, then controlled herself. "Or, at least I didn't realise it was."

Tremens thought through that. "He hadn't told you about his wife, right?"

"No." A look of anger flitted across her face, followed by the strangely disturbing flash of a smile.

"So all those questions about what I would do if I discovered someone was cheating on me? It was all about Harry Slade?"

"You said you would have chucked him out into the cold."

Tremens snorted. "Too right I would have. But then with a snake like Slade I never would have invited him into the warm to begin with. Why are we at the river?"

"My life had fallen apart. I should have been angry, should have felt something. But I didn't. Not really. I told myself I was angry, but I wasn't."

"That's … nice."

"Is that a normal reaction, Richard?"

"To not feel anything?" He shrugged. "Probably. If you're not angry, you're numb. There's nothing wrong with that. So, where is he? You told him to take a hike and he went north?" Her story did not make any sense, but he still had no idea what she had brought him all this way to tell him. She had been having an affair with Slade, sure, but that didn't help find the guy.

"I've never been cheated on before, I didn't know how to react. I thought it was the way anyone would have reacted, thought it was normal. But if it was normal, you wouldn't be looking for him so hard, would you?"

Up until that moment, Tremens had thought of Suzie Locke as a nice young woman. He had known her for a while now and she would slip him an extra rasher of bacon when the boss wasn't looking. She was good-looking, sweet and sincere. It had been this façade that had prevented him from looking much further. Now he was beginning to think he perhaps should not have come all this way alone with her. She had yet to say anything truly incriminating, but he was getting a bad feeling all the same.

"Is Harry Slade dead?" Tremens asked.

Suzie looked away. It was probably the worst response she could have given him.

"Is he in this river?"

"It was a bad decision, wasn't it?" Suzie asked.

"Killing a guy? Yeah. You … you can't see that, can you?"

Suzie was trying not to cry, but it was difficult for her. Tremens almost reached out a consoling hand, before remembering what she was crying over.

"I'm an ordered person, Richard. I like things to be right. Clean. Septic. Everything has its place, you know? People are no different. Men belong with women and women belong with men."

"Well, that's a debate in political correctness if ever I heard one."

"You know what I mean," she snapped. "A man belongs with *one* woman, and a woman belongs with *one* man."

Tremens did see now, and it scared him. Pleasant little Suzie Locke was a nice girl, so long as the world worked the way she thought it should. But as soon as something happened she didn't agree with, or didn't understand, she would panic and lash out to correct that mistake. If she had genuinely not felt anything when she killed Slade, it only told Tremens she had some kind of problem. But sociopath or not, she had still killed a man, and for that there would be consequences.

"You need to come with me to the station," Tremens said, keeping his voice calm. So far, Suzie had not shown any violent tendencies, and he wanted to clear this up before that could change.

"Are you arresting me?"

"Not at this stage. But I do need to ask you some questions about what happened to Slade."

"Then ask."

"You might want a solicitor present."

A look of genuine sadness overcame her then; it was as though she had still been hoping he might agree with the decision she had made. "I thought you'd understand, Richard."

"What exactly made you think that? Because I eat the food you serve me?"

"I thought we had something between us. I guess I'm going to have to be grateful I brought you out here."

"Yeah, why did you bring me out here?"

"To clean up."

Before Tremens could say another word, there was something being sprayed in his face. He had not seen her produce the canister and cursed himself for a fool that he had not expected it. He had thought she might pull a knife or something, not spray him in the face with some form of chemical.

He fell to his hands and knees, his eyes stinging fiercely. He had no idea what he had been hit with, but while he was incapacitated Suzie could be doing any number of things. Tremens flailed with his arms, trying to keep her at bay, but since he was kneeling on the ground he doubted he presented much of a threat. He tried to listen to whatever Suzie was doing, but the burning in his eyes consumed his senses and he was no longer even certain he was facing the right direction.

"Sorry, Richard," she said, her voice flat. That was not a good sign. If she had delved into the same psychological temperament as when she had killed Slade, it meant she no longer believed she was doing anything wrong. Tremens knew nothing about psychological conditions, but Suzie Locke was nuts.

"We need to talk about this," he said, trying to stall her attack with whatever he could.

"We did talk. You told me I was in the wrong."

He could hear her moving, perhaps fetching a weapon. Desperately, he fought to think of what he had to hand, something he might use to defend himself. But he had brought nothing, not even his own car. Nor was there anything in the area he might use. There was a field and a river: there weren't even any people about should he shout for help.

His eyes itching like mad, he realised one of those could be useful after all.

Dropping his hands to the ground, he madly scrambled for whatever he could find. His fingers closed upon small stones and he tossed one to the left. Another he threw ahead of him, another to the right.

To the right, he heard a dull splosh.

Raising his left leg, he propelled himself to the right, charging until his foot struck the water. Leaping, he threw himself into the dirty river, ducking his head beneath the surface and rubbing furiously at his injured eyes. The water was near freezing and filled with scraggly weeds which clutched eagerly at his clothes like some faerie river monster, but Tremens knew the river was his only chance at survival. Blinking rapidly, continually rubbing water in his eyes, he was at last able to see again. His eyes still burned terribly, but as he crouched in the river he could make out colours and shapes once more.

And he could see Suzie Locke standing on the shore, holding a plunger.

He did not even want to think about how she intended to kill him with that.

"I must say, Richard, you're being very unreasonable."

"Congratulations, Suzie. You've just convinced me you're not all there."

"Look at it from my point of view," she said. "I'm losing one of my best customers."

"What a shame for you." Tremens took a few steps back. His foot caught in something which wasn't a plant. Feeling behind him with his hands, he discovered something large under the water. It felt like a settee, which meant Suzie was not the only person who had been dumping things in the river.

"I wish you could agree with me," Suzie said, "but it looks like you're all the same."

He had no idea whether she meant the police or men in general, but he watched her walk away and disappear from sight. He had no idea where she was going but doubted she was just leaving him. His eyes were beginning to feel a little better but if he was going to survive this he needed something to use as a weapon.

Remembering the settee, he reasoned that there would be wooden supports inside. If he could somehow cut through the material, he might be able to pull out the framework and fashion a makeshift club. Reaching beneath the water, not able to see much of what he was doing due to the murkiness of the river, Tremens was able to find a hole in the seam. Pushing in a finger numb with cold, he widened the hole and tore into the piece of furniture. His spirits lifting, he used both hands to reach inside, groping for the wooden supports. His hands found something else and his fingers squelched as they passed through something decidedly gooey.

That was when he heard the engine.

Turning away from the settee, he watched in mounting horror as the van reversed towards him at speed. Its back doors were open and he could see it was filled with all manner of cleaning equipment. The van did not stop at the water's edge but barrelled over, shooting straight towards him. Trapped in the water, there was nothing Tremens could have done to evade it.

CHAPTER SEVEN

It had not been the way she had wanted to do things, but Suzie knew the police would be all over her anyway. She had never thought they would have been able to connect her to Slade, but that had been her own fault, really. She had said too much to Tremens, foolishly believing he would understand what she had been forced to do. Tremens had wanted to arrest her, which meant it probably had been murder after all. Suzie was not a bad person, and if she had done something wrong she knew she needed to be punished. She still could not understand what it was precisely that she had done wrong, but Tremens was a detective and if he said it had been wrong then she believed him.

As she had stood at the edge of the river, plunger in hand (because killing someone with a wrench was definitely wrong), she had come to realise there was only one thing she could do. If killing Slade was so bad, assaulting Tremens was also bad. So she needed to remove Tremens, make sure he was in no condition to tell anyone what she had done. But that would not punish her: it would only exacerbate her crimes. She could not continue with her life, knowing she had committed such wrongs.

So she had returned to her van and reversed it towards the river. Making sure Tremens did not tell people what she had done was vital, but so was paying for her sins. She hardly felt the jolt as her rear wheels left the ground, but a few moments later the vehicle had stopped moving and she could feel it sinking. Water began to coat the floor and Suzie removed her hands from the wheel. She made sure her seat-belt was buckled and then closed her eyes. All she had ever really wanted out of life was a little happiness, but she had never been able to find it. Several times now she had thought she had, but something had always happened to destroy it for her. Now she did not much care. She had broken the law and she would pay, just like the law declared.

Glancing out the window, Suzie could see the river water frothing, strange coloured clouds working their way through the murky depths. She remembered her van had been filled with cleaning products and that they had all spilled out into the river, some of them splitting open. She smiled, but there was no mirth to the gesture. This was probably the first real clean the river had ever had.

"No!" someone cried. Suzie was pretty sure it wasn't her.

Looking out the forward window, she could see a car had pulled up. It was odd because it belonged to her neighbour, Oddings, but as the door opened a woman stepped out. She recognised her immediately as that annoying woman partnered with Tremens. That she was driving Oddings's car meant she had already worked out Suzie's part in all of this, which meant she could not afford to drown just yet. She could not die knowing someone could still expose her.

Besides which, she was getting the impression her van wasn't going to sink any further.

The detective had jumped into the river by this point and was tearing open the driver's door. "Where's Richard?"

"Having a bath," Suzie said.

The detective paused; then punched Suzie in the face and dragged her from the cabin. "Detective Hayden," the officer said. "I'm arresting you for murder. Now tell me where Richard is before I make that two."

"You can't have him back, Hayden," Suzie said flatly. "I didn't do any of this so you could have either of them back."

"So you admit you murdered Slade?"

"So I'm told."

There was more uncertainty, more nervousness, in Hayden than Suzie would have expected. The detective grabbed her by her collar and threw her into the water. "Just tell me where he is."

In that moment, Suzie understood that Tremens and Hayden meant something to one another. When Tremens had said they were partners, he had not been talking about work.

Another man had done it to her again.

"He's gone," Suzie told her, bitterness creeping into her voice, even though she always convinced herself she did not feel any emotion at this stage of things. "The river claimed him."

Hayden released her, her eyes tracking the surface of the river, but there was no movement at all. There were reeds, toilet cleaner, an old settee jutting out of the water, but nothing else. Suzie had not realised the settee had even been visible, but supposed she must have hit the thing when she had reversed her van into the river. She briefly thought of Slade, still trapped inside and dead. She almost wished she did feel something for him, but she did not. Nor, she was not surprised to discover, did she feel anything for having killed Tremens. About the only emotion she was feeling was anger towards Hayden and everything she represented as the other woman in her life.

Her attention focused on listening for sounds, Hayden did not stand a chance. Suzie launched herself at her, tackling the detective about the waist and sending them both sprawling into the river. Hayden thrashed, attempting to stay above the water, but Suzie had the advantage of position and grasped at the detective's neck with both hands. Hayden tried to punch her again, but lacked the best angle and the blow, had it landed, would have been weak.

Suzie knew she should have felt something, even if it was just remorse that she had continually done the wrong thing. She tried to work out why she did not feel anything, why she never felt anything. She did not like to consider it too deeply because she knew she would only come to the conclusion that she was a monster. It was not something she wanted to discover, not something she even really wanted to think about. Tremens had told her she was wrong, but Tremens was dead and if she was really as wrong as he had believed, she would not have got away with it twice.

Beneath her hands, she could feel Hayden struggling. She had not even realised she was holding the detective's head beneath the water but did not stop now. Just a few more moments and Hayden would have swallowed enough water to fill her lungs. A few moments after that, she would have been in long enough to kill her.

Then what? Suzie's intention had been to die in the river alongside her victims, but she wasn't so sure she wanted to do that any more. She was taking her inability to sink as a sign: a sign that she was not destined to die today. She would take the van and drive, get away from her life and start afresh somewhere else. It was what the sign was telling her, and she always listened to signs.

The settee shifted slightly and Suzie glanced over to it. It was probably settling in the mud, she reasoned. She had struck it when she had reversed her van, she supposed, which was why it was moving now. Then it moved again and she could see it was turning onto its side. As it did so, more of the settee was revealed. Suzie could now see the gaping hole in which she had stashed Slade's body. The material had been cut away, the hole revealed for all to see. She watched in awe as something emerged from the hole.

Suzie released her grip upon Hayden, the detective tearing her head through the surface and spluttering uncontrollably. But Suzie forgot all about her as her eyes focused upon the great form rising from the foetid water within the settee; a shambling cadaver returned to life to exact vengeance on her for her sins. Tremens had been right. What she had done truly was wrong and now she was paying for her crime.

The figure turned towards her, sludge dripping from its body, and Suzie felt her heart freeze. Slade had returned a monster, to show her she was nothing less.

Hayden's fist came out of nowhere and this time Suzie went down hard.

CHAPTER EIGHT

Hayden did not know why Tremens was even now being kind to Suzie Locke, but supposed some of the girl's sweet innocent charm was still playing around in his heart. Either that or he was at last paying her back for all the extra rashers of bacon she had slipped him.

It turned out when he had seen the van reversing towards him, Tremens had taken refuge in the only place available: the settee. Trapped in there with a decomposing body, Tremens had been covered with all the sludgy detritus which had collected over the last month or so. Even as she was herself exploding from the water and gasping for air, Hayden knew Tremens had been exploding from the settee doing the same. That Locke had seen something she wanted to see, rather than what was actually there, was not surprising. She had likely been doing that for a number of years now.

Taking Locke into custody, Hayden and Tremens had gone home. Neither had any intention of going to the hospital and had by far enough medical experience to treat one another. It turned out neither was injured very badly, not as badly as Locke's mind anyway. Slade, of course, was the real casualty in all of this; both Harry and Laura.

"At least we solved the case," Tremens said once they were both patched up. They had settled in front of the television, although the sound was down low since neither of them was watching it. White noise and familiarity were always good in times of stress. That they were huddled on a settee was doing nothing for her nerves.

"Now if only we can solve our own cases," Hayden said. "Why'd you do that for her anyway?"

"Do what for whom?"

"Rich, I'm not in the mood."

"Sorry." He sighed, which she found annoying considering that was always what she did to wind *him* up. "I guess I just wanted what was best for her."

"She murdered Slade."

"I know. But no one ever liked Slade and I'm not going to pretend I do now he's dead. We had a responsibility to find his murderer and we did that."

What he was saying was true, but Hayden did not say anything. Suzie Locke had justified everything she had done. She had honestly not been able to see anything wrong with what she was doing, but at least she had believed in her actions. Hayden and Tremens had taken it upon themselves to discover Slade's murderer out of a sense of duty, nothing more. They did not care about Slade, did not stop to think about the right and wrong of the situation. They did not care about what they had done, which was what made them so different from Locke.

Still, Tremens putting in a good word for her was not something he needed to do and it had surprised Hayden.

"So you're not going soft on her, then?" Hayden asked.

"On the crazy woman who tried to kill me? Please."

"Good. Wouldn't want to think you were weird or anything."

"Nothing weird about me. Here."

Hayden looked across to see Tremens was handing her something. It was a box. More specifically, it was a badly-wrapped box.

"Happy Christmas, Ruth," he said.

"Rich, you shouldn't have. I mean, you really shouldn't have." She did not know whether she was annoyed, although felt like she should have been. "We don't exchange gifts."

"Exchange gifts. That's such a septic term, Ruth."

"A septic term for a commercial time of year."

"Are you going to open it?"

She sighed, not even realising she was doing it any more. Wordlessly, she undid the wrapping. Removing the lid from the box, she found two slips of paper. Curious, she picked them out and examined them in shock.

"You best not be joking here," she said.

"You did say you didn't want to spend Christmas with my parents, right?"

"You got tickets for Honolulu? Can we even afford this?"

"After spending even a few minutes in a settee with a rotting dead guy, I'm not sure I much care."

Hayden laughed. It was a good, strange feeling. She had always felt she stayed with Tremens because they had become lumbered with each other, because their unsociable hours had forced them to find someone with equally unsociable hours; but then he would pull something like this and she would understand there were other reasons they were together.

"You now what?" she said as she got comfortable resting her head on his arm where she was sprawled. "You're a good man, Richard Tremens."

"Sure. Just remember; I need someone new to make my breakfast, and extra bacon never goes astray."

For his sake, Hayden could only hope he was joking.

ONE-WAY TICKET TO MURDER

The Detective

There were four witnesses; and one of them knew far more than they realised.

Outside, the steady sounds of bustling people provided an almost soothing backdrop to where we were. It was as though the rest of the world was continuing as normal, not even aware I had sectioned off one waiting room in order to conduct my investigation. The only window in the room was on the door, and anyone peering in would see little more than the 'out of order' sign I had managed to find in a pile on one of the platforms.

The four within the waiting room caught glimpses of spectral forms beyond that window, hurrying about their daily business. Such wraiths would make them understand that for the next hour or so they had become separated from the rest of humanity, that they'd been plucked from reality and would be returned only once this was settled.

Nearby, a horn blasted across the platform, followed by the frantic chug-chug of the train passing through. The train which could not have had any bearing on my investigation because it had thought twice about stopping there, at that station.

The train that interested me had already made that stop and among all the bodies disgorged there were only four I cared about.

Only these four had seen my prey.

"Do we not even get a coffee, Detective?"

I kept my expression neutral as I looked at the tall, thin man resplendent in his grey suit. With his black tie, shiny shoes and tidy briefcase there was nothing genuine about this man. He lived for his work, strove to succeed, and had few other concerns. Perhaps he was married, perhaps he had children. If so, his life with them was sterile, septic. He kissed his children goodbye each morning, picked up the sandwiches his wife had made him, worked until late evening and returned home (sometimes) in time to see his children before they went to bed. His life had drained him of purpose, but the money rolled in and he considered himself a success.

"No, Mr Holding," I said. "I think it best not to allow any of you to leave until we have the truth."

"This is a breach of my human rights," Holding declared huffily as he paced. His annoyance stemmed mainly from the break in his schedule. Every minute he lost was time not spent in the office. Money was everything to that man, and helping in a police investigation was not earning him money.

"Then why don't you begin?" I asked. "The sooner you each tell your story, the sooner I can let you all go."

"Story?" he asked, his mind still on how late he was going to arrive at the office. "We don't have a story, Detective. We were all on the train going to work, there's no story to that."

I cast my eyes about the group. Of the four of them, only two of them had been on their way to work. One was already at work, while the other likely did not even have a destination. It did not matter what they had been doing on that train, however, only how much attention they had been paying while they were there.

"If you have no story," I said amicably, "then this won't take you long, Mr Holding."

I knew an interrogation's greatest ally was always patience. The truth would come eventually, and I could have sat there waiting for it for far more hours than Holding was willing to spend.

"All right, all right," Holding said, sitting and trying to think of the quickest way to get his case across. "I got on the train on my way to work. Then you pulled me in here."

Under less serious circumstances I may have smiled at the man's inability to even recognise there were other people in the room. "Mr Holding," I said, "might I remind you why I've gathered you here? A criminal boarded that train and the four of you spoke with him. I need to know everything you remember. What did he look like, how was he acting, what did you speak about? Everything, Mr Holding. And then you can go."

For a moment it looked as though Holding was going to find fault even with that, but even he could see my words made sense. "All right," he said. "I'll go first."

"If you would."

The Businessman's Story

I was late for work. People complain about the trains all the time, but to be honest during rush hour they're so close together I always end up getting one on time, just not the one I was going for. Today though, the trains were really screwed-up. They hadn't told me what it was, of course. It's funny how they never tell you at the time. Leaves on the line, the wrong type of snow, cow on the track. Those are the things you find out later, but on the day all you hear is a garbled message. Unless of course it's signal failure or delays caused by earlier delays. For some reason you can always hear them when they're admitting to failure of their trains, but never when they're acts of God.

So I was running late, but had managed to get onto a train at last. It was packed, but since I got on at the first stop from the depot I managed to get a seat. I checked the time and drummed my fingers on the briefcase on my lap. Eventually the train pulled out, but I could see I was going to miss my connection. It meant I was going to be at least twenty minutes late into the office, and that's twenty minutes of sales I was going to lose. I sat there knowing there was nothing I could do about it, but it still grated on my nerves that I wouldn't even be able to claim some money back from my ticket because the train hadn't been late enough. It annoyed me to have wished the train was just a few minutes later than it had been.

"Morning."

I looked up at the man seated opposite me. He was frightfully cheery and at first I just ignored him. I was angry and had no desire to start an argument on a train, especially when I was going to be on that train for another half an hour.

"Good morning," he persisted.

Perhaps it was that extra word that made me answer him. "What's good about it?"

"Oh, lots of things." He was probably still in his twenties, wearing unsightly stubble and dressed in a T-shirt and raggedy jeans.

I'd seen his type before and knew he wasn't on his way to work. In his lap there was a bag of some sort, a rucksack I think. Maybe the queue for the job centre was so long nowadays that he felt the need to pack a picnic.

"Pardon me," I said, "but my day's bad enough already without someone talking to me on a train."

The fellow laughed, as though he thought I was joking. "My day's going great."

"Bully for you." I was in too much of a mood to read the paper I always pick up, but I opened it just to indicate that I was done talking.

Again, he did not seem to care. "You see," he said, "I was all nervous this morning, thought it was all going to go wrong. But it went right, yeah? Righter than I could have dreamed."

"Better."

"What is?"

I gave up any pretence of reading the paper and folded it. As I stared at him I felt as though I should have been charging him for tuition. "*Better* than you could have dreamed."

"That's what I said."

"No, you said ... What do I care what you said?"

He sniffed, his good mood momentarily broken. "You sound just like that teacher." Then he brightened again. "Only I'm not giving you anything pretty, no offence."

"You're still in school?"

"No. Don't need to be in school to have yourself a teacher."

I did not understand, but nor did I want to. "Was there something you wanted?" I asked tiredly.

"Got everything I wanted right here," he said, jostling the rucksack he was clutching in his lap. "Now I just got to decide where I'm going."

"You mean you haven't bought a ticket?" I asked, incredulous. There's nothing worse than a job-seeking scrounger who travels without a ticket; and sits in a seat no less.

"No, I meant where I'm going in life," he said. "Going to London. Once I'm there, who knows?"

"Well, what are you going to London for?"

"Same as everyone goes to London. To make my fortune."

I started to tell him I for one wasn't going to London to make my fortune, but I supposed that was precisely what I was doing.

"If you could go anywhere," he asked, "do anything, what would you do?"

"I'd get to work on time."

"I didn't mean work. I meant … if you didn't have to work."

"You mean if I signed on to benefits?"

"No, not benefits." His face was still illuminated by a euphoric sheen. If I wasn't so annoyed about the train delay I might even have been happy for him myself. "Say you won the lottery," he continued. "Say you didn't have to work no more."

"Any more."

He grinned. "What would you do?"

It was around this point I realised he wasn't going to shut up the entire journey, so I figured I might as well answer the fool. The old 'what would you do if you won the lottery' question was about as old as 'who'd win in a fight?' and was equally as pointless. "I'd invest it," I said. "I'd buy some shares, some stocks, and put the rest in a fixed-term bond."

"What if you'd already won more money than you knew what to do with?"

"Then by the end of the two-year term I'd have a lot more money than I'd know what to do with."

"There's no amount you'd be happy to reach?"

"There's never a point you should be happy to reach." I honestly could not understand what he was talking about.

"But there's only so many houses you can buy, so many cars. What would you do with the rest?"

"Stick it in a savings account."

"Have it sit in the bank doing nothing?" He frowned. "Doesn't that just give the money to the bank?"

"Well, yes. But it's also my money."

"Not if you don't spend it. If you leave it in the bank untouched it's the bank's money. And they're laughing at you for it."

I went to tell him he was being a fool, but what he was saying actually made a certain kind of sense. "What would you spend it on?" I asked.

He laughed. "I haven't decided yet."

"Well at least I had an answer."

"Well, I just didn't like to get my hopes up beforehand."

I gathered from the way he was speaking he was either a dreamer or he had received a sudden windfall. Whichever the case, it was not getting me to work any quicker. "What are your interests?" I asked.

"I like a good gamble."

"Then buy a racehorse. Invest in something like that and you might lose all your money, but you might make a fortune."

"I don't know ..."

"Thought you said you liked a good gamble?"

His face broke into another annoying grin. "So I did. I like you, sir. You have a mind for this sort of thing. A racehorse, yeah. That'd be a good thing to start with."

"Tickets, please."

Grumbling, I found out my train pass. Why ticket inspectors have to come around during the rush hour I'll never know. I showed the fellow my pass even as I watched the lad opposite me fumbling in his pockets for a ticket I knew he didn't have. The inspector waited patiently, holding on in the gentle sway of the train.

"This service is appalling," I told the inspector while he waited. "I'm late for work now."

"It'd be ironic," the inspector said, "if *I* was late for work because of the trains."

The youth had found his ticket by that point, and it seemed he had bought one after all. He dropped it as he went to hand it over, but I caught it. Taking a quick glance to make sure it was in date, I saw he had indeed bought a single to London. So he had been telling the truth about not knowing where he was going afterwards. Still wasn't going to a job though.

As the inspector vanished, I said to the youth, "You should think more about where you are, instead of where you'd like to be."

"Probably. Say, you've been real helpful to me, Mr. A true gentleman."

I pretended to read the paper again.

The train pulled into Lewisham soon after. I was continuing to Waterloo East, but thankfully the youth had decided to get off already. I remember thinking that was weird, since he'd bought a ticket for London and we hadn't got that far yet. He said something about it being a pleasure meeting me; then he excused his way to the door and got off the train.

I didn't give the young fool another thought.

The Detective

"So he went to buy a racehorse?" I asked.

His story finished, Holding had gone back to being evasive. Telling the story had helped him blow off some steam, but once he was done he had fallen back into being angry that I was keeping him from getting to work.

"I don't know where he went," Holding said. "All I know is he got off at Lewisham. See? I told you I didn't know anything useful."

"Everything is useful, Mr Holding."

"Fine. Can I go to work now?"

"Not yet. I think it's best we listen to all the other stories first."

A cloud passed across his face, but there must have been some ingrained respect for the law in the man because he did not put up any further fight. Indeed, he simply slumped into his chair in the waiting room and, for want of a better word, sulked.

"Did he tell you his name?" I asked.

"I didn't ask."

"Tell me something about his rucksack."

"What about it?"

"What do you think it contained?"

"How should I know?"

"Well, how was he holding it?"

"How was he holding it?"

"You said you had your briefcase on your lap, and he had his rucksack on his. How were you holding your briefcase?"

He paused. "Well, I wasn't, as such. I just sort of sat it there."

"You didn't put it on the floor?"

"Floors are dirty. Besides, I like to keep it handy in case I need to open it. For my paper or if I want to go over any work."

"So your briefcase was sitting there, fairly loose."

"I guess."

"And the rucksack? Was he holding it loosely? Did you get the impression he didn't put it on the floor because the floor was dirty?"

Holding grumped. "His bag was dirtier." He paused. "He always kept at least one hand on it. Come to think of it, he usually had them both on it. He had one of the straps wrapped around his wrist, actually."

"So if someone made a grab for it, they wouldn't get away with it so easily."

"I suppose."

"Do you value your work, Mr Holding?"

He seemed incredulous that I might suggest otherwise. "What kind of a question is that?"

"A simple one. You said you sometimes catch up on work, so you must have some work papers in your briefcase. So, do you value your work?"

"Yes."

"And if your briefcase was stolen?"

"I'd lose the work inside, yes."

"So, if the youth was holding onto his bag more tightly than you were your briefcase, that would indicate he valued the contents of his rucksack more than you valued the contents of your briefcase?"

Holding hesitated.

"It's a fair assessment," I said, informing him it had not really been a question. "And what did the young man value?"

Holding snorted. "Money."

"So, what do you suppose was in his rucksack that he valued so highly?"

Holding's eyes widened. "He went on about winning the lottery. You think he had money in the bag?"

"He also told you he was a gambler. Large lottery wins don't pay out enough in cash to fill a rucksack, but perhaps gambling does."

"That would have to have been a big win."

"Which indicates it was an illegal game, if so much money was handed him in cash."

"Is that why you're after him?" Holding asked. "Because he's an illegal gambler?"

"No. Because he's a murderer."

Silence fell upon the waiting room, which was precisely as I had intended. Suddenly this all became more serious to them, and even Holding stopped grumbling so much about being kept from his work.

"Perhaps we should continue," I suggested. "You mentioned a teacher?"

"Yes, he said something weird about a teacher. His correction officer?"

I assumed he meant probation officer, although why he thought a probation officer would insist on correcting the young man's grammar was not relevant to my investigation. "I think perhaps it was not *his* teacher," I said, "just a teacher he happened to meet not long before he got on that train." I turned to another of the four I had pulled off the train. "Perhaps you could enlighten us as to the next part of the mystery, Miss Robinson?"

Holding looked to the woman sitting next to him. She was short, pretty, aged somewhere in her thirties, and dressed smartly enough, but was not suited for the office as was Holding. She also looked uncomfortable, for which, after hearing Mr Holding's testimony, I could hardly have blamed her.

"All right," she said, "but I don't think I know even as much as Mr Holding here."

I forced a smile in order to reassure her. "Just tell us what you know, Miss Robinson, and let me be the judge of that."

The Teacher's Story

The train was late, but that was all right because I was running late as well so I'd already missed the one I was going for. I was standing down near the ticket office, waiting for the display screen to cycle back to the first page so I could see when the next train was going to come in. Why they have to show you all those other screens is beyond me. It was while I was standing there that someone walked into me. I stumbled, but caught myself.

"Sorry," the man said. He was a few years younger than me, dressed in jeans and a T-shirt. He looked a little frazzled, but I couldn't picture why. It was as though he was moving away from something rather than towards anything. He was also in a hurry, but he took the time to apologise, which was kind of him. Most people running for a train just barrel through and swear abuse at you for having been in their way. Come to think of it, he didn't even look up to the screen to see when the next train was.

"It's all right," I said. "I'm used to people not looking where they're going."

"I said I was sorry. Are you sure you're all right?"

The question threw me, and any anger I might have still had for him dissipated. "Yeah, I'm fine. But I meant at school I get people haring down corridors all the time."

He looked me up and down strangely. "School? But you must be early twenties."

I laughed. Thirty-three was more like it, but I wasn't going to tell him that. Extending my hand, I said, "Sue."

Something in his eyes told me he didn't quite want to accept the hand, but I could see he wanted nothing more than to do so. After a moment he surrendered and shook. "Gary."

I remembered some baby name polls someone had released recently. "Not a common name any more."

"Well I wasn't born yesterday."

It was a good answer, and as I glanced back to the screen it was to see all the trains were now marked as 'delayed'. "You want to grab a coffee, Gary?"

"I probably shouldn't."

"Married?"

"Who?"

"Uh, you?"

He pulled a face, as though it was something he had never even considered. "All right. Coffee. But I'm buying."

I wasn't going to argue with that. Thankfully most of the crowd waiting for the trains were still heading up to the platform, so we were able to find a seat in the coffee shop by the ticket office. Gary bought me a coffee and one of those weird caramel biscuits they sell. We didn't talk about anything really, just stuff. I told him I was a teacher, he told me he was a student. I asked him what he was studying, but he was very vague.

"So, what do you teach?" he asked.

"English."

"I know English."

"Surprising what you can still learn. You headed to university?"

"Hmm?"

"The train."

"Oh, the train. No. I have … I'm not sure where I'm going actually."

I noticed the rucksack he'd placed against his chair leg. "Not running away I take it?"

"Sort of," he said, sipping his coffee. "Just needed to put some distance between me and my uncle."

"Family problems?"

"Not now." He laughed. I smiled along with him, but I didn't know why.

"You don't give much away, do you, Gary?"

"Nope. Me and my uncle, we're close, you know? Dad doesn't like him, but that's only because he's been inside."

"Ah. But now you're running away from your uncle?"

"Yep. He had a good idea, but then he always has good ideas. It's just I've never listened to them before."

"You need any help with anything? I mean, you want me to call the police or something?"

He looked at me strangely.

"Because your uncle's after you?" I said.

"Oh, that. Nah, he wouldn't hurt me. We're family." He did not sound at all convinced.

"Well, just so long as you're all right then."

"I'm good."

"Good." I tried to work out what he was talking about, but he still didn't seem to want to reveal much. Which was strange, because I could see in his eyes the burning desire to tell someone a secret. I could certainly have been a good sounding-board for him. "Tell you what," I said, "I'm on my way to work right now, but what are you up to later?"

"Depends where I'm going."

"Friday."

"Friday what?"

"I'm free."

He still didn't seem to understand what I was saying, but then he suddenly got it. "Oh, Friday. Yeah, I might be free Friday."

"Depends where you're going," I guessed.

"Sure. But I could come back."

"Back from running away?"

He looked confused, which only made him more endearing.

"Look," I said, taking up a free newspaper and a pen. "Here's my number. Give me a call or don't. Just make up your mind first whether you're running or hiding or whatever."

"I ..." He looked down at the newspaper and I could see something weird in his eyes. Then he tore off the section with my number and shoved it into his jeans. "Sure I'll call, Sue. Can't run forever, can I?"

"Depends if you're actually running in the first place. You sure you don't want me to call the police?"

"Nah. Here." He leaned down, unzipped his backpack and ...

Anyway, by this time we'd finished our coffees and the trains were starting to run again, so we headed up to the platform together. At the ticket barrier someone shoved in front of me, and this guy didn't even have the decency to apologise. To make matters worse he was wearing a uniform and I'm pretty sure he actually worked for the train company. Then my ticket didn't go through the machine for some reason and I had to show it to the attendant. By the time I was through the barrier, Gary had disappeared in the crowd. I got to the platform and couldn't see him anywhere, but a train was just pulling in so I jumped on board.

He was a good-looking guy, but as I looked for and entirely failed to find a seat, I thought about how he had pretty much turned me down. And I couldn't help but feel what a jerk he was.

The Detective

"So you met a murderer and ten minutes later gave him your phone number?"

"Well at the time I didn't know he was a murderer."

I could not make any comment as to how good a teacher Susan Robinson was, but as a woman she certainly had a long way to go. I'm sure if I had made any such comment to Miss Robinson she would have given me a retort about it being a modern world where women were free to do as they pleased. Looking into her eyes, I could even see the words forming.

"You were lucky," I told her.

"Who did he kill?"

"It's probably best if I don't prejudice you with information you don't know. He didn't give you his phone number then?"

"No," Robinson said. "Oh God, that's a point. He has my phone number."

"Has he tried to contact you?"

"No. I'm going to have to get a new number aren't I?"

"That depends on how many random strangers you intend giving your new number to."

She did not look at all pleased by my comment, but that was good since it had been designed to rattle her.

"It's interesting he mentioned his uncle," I said, pressing on before she could say anything. "I wouldn't have thought that was information he would be throwing around."

"Is that the person he killed?"

"No. No, his uncle is very much alive."

"But if you know who his uncle is, surely you must know who Gary is."

"Yes. I know who Gary is."

"But I thought …?"

"That I didn't know anything before stepping into this waiting room? Believe me, I know more about this man than the four of you combined. But there was a part of your story you glossed over."

"Was there?"

"He reached into his backpack and ...? What?"

"Oh." Robinson shrugged. "Nothing. I just meant he picked it up because we were leaving."

"So if I was to ask you to turn out your pockets I wouldn't find any jewellery?"

"None that I hadn't brought out with me, no."

"Only Mr Holding's testimony indicated Gary had met a teacher on the platform and had given her something. Something pretty, was it not, Mr Holding?"

Mr Holding nodded, saying nothing.

"Miss Robinson?" I asked.

"All right," she said. "So he gave me a trinket. It was a bit strange. He just unzipped his bag, reached in and brought out a brooch. Made me wonder what else he had in that bag of his."

"May I see the brooch?"

She produced the piece of jewellery without comment and handed it over. I made a point of examining it very slowly, although I already knew precisely from where it had come.

"Gary's uncle," I said, "reported several items missing, along with a substantial amount of cash. This brooch is one of those items. But, then, I suspect you already know that, Miss Robinson. Otherwise you wouldn't have been trying to hide it from me."

"I just wanted to keep it," she grumbled. "It's a nice piece, and it looks expensive."

"Oh, it is."

"So Gary robbed his uncle and ran away?" she asked.

I smiled as I slipped the brooch into my shirt pocket. The expression told her I had no intention of answering any of her questions. "Did Gary give you any indication of which stop he was getting off at?"

"No. But he got off at Lewisham."

"So Mr Holding says, yes."

Holding stiffened at this. "He did get off at Lewisham."

"I didn't mean to call your word into question," I told him. "No, I'm just trying to piece together his movements. We know that once he left Miss Robinson he boarded the train. And, since you both got on at the same stop, we also know he went straight from Miss Robinson to Mr Holding. It's what happened to him after he left Mr Holding that interests me now. Because I don't believe he got off at Lewisham." I held up a hand to forestall any further argument from Holding. "Again, I insist I am not questioning your word. But we must remember that here we are dealing with a diabolically clever young man. He's already committed robbery and murder and now he's talking to people as he makes his getaway. That's a ridiculous thing to do, would you not say?" There were nods all around. "So, as a gambler, I suggest he began employing some gambler's strategies."

"Like what?" Robinson asked.

"Making sure the other players thought one thing, when in fact quite the opposite was true."

After a moment's pause, Robinson said, "I don't follow."

"Then we come to our third witness," I said, casting my eyes upon the girl who had until that moment been sitting very quietly indeed. She was only fifteen years old, but carried her own rucksack which I knew was not filled with school books. She had already told me her name was Karen Ashcroft, and I had been eager to hear her side of things ever since I had gathered everyone together. "Miss Ashcroft?" I asked.

With a sigh, she looked me in the eyes and spoke.

The Runaway's Story

I was wedged into a corner, standing close enough to a window that I could see the world going by. I wasn't doing much of anything, just thinking over what I was doing, where I was going. The whole journey I'd kept to myself, as people do on the train, wishing I'd brought a book or something, but I don't think I would have been able to concentrate anyway.

We got to Lewisham and a lot of people got off, finally giving me some room. Then a lot of people got on and I was back to being cramped. Just as the doors were closing this guy jumped on, looking relieved he'd made it. He was in his twenties, I guess, and had that rugged, unshaven look that can't be carried off well by a lot of folks. As the train began moving again he shucked off his backpack and held it before him as he found a pole to hold onto. This brought him close to me and we found ourselves facing one another. He smiled, and I could tell he was having a good day.

"Nearly there," he said.

"Nearly where?"

"Waterloo East. That's where the new life begins."

I suppressed a little shudder, fearing he'd somehow reached into my mind and plucked out my darkest secrets. "Maybe I'm just on my way to school," I told him. "Just because I'm fifteen and on the train with a rucksack, it doesn't mean I'm running away."

"You're running away?" He laughed. "Running from or running to?"

"Beg pardon?"

"*I'm* running away," he said. "Running away from someone who wants to break my legs and shove me into a skip. You have anyone back home who wants to break your legs?"

"Uh, no."

"So you're probably running *to* something."

"I'm running away from home."

"Teenage girls who are serious about running away from home take their music with them."

"I *am* serious," I said angrily. "I'm running away from home."

"Sorry. Didn't mean to offend. But you don't run away from home. Home will always be there for you if you want to go back. If you change your mind you can go back to the way things have always been. Me? If I go back ..."

"You'll have your legs broken. You said." He was a curious man, and I found myself intrigued. Most adults would have told me I was being a stupid spoiled girl, would have told me to go straight home and would have either phoned the police or my parents. This guy, whoever he was, seemed to understand me. Which I found interesting, especially since he seemed to be in something of a similar position to me.

"Why are you running then?" he asked.

"Long story, wouldn't want to bore you with it."

"Short version?"

"You don't want to guess? You don't want to assume I have a bad stepfather or that my parents don't understand me?"

"Sounds like you've had too many people say those things already. If I said them as well, would it make a difference?"

"No."

"Then I won't say them then. Honestly, why are you running?"

I sighed. Opening up to a complete stranger was an odd thing, but it felt freer than anything I've ever done. Talking to friends, teachers, parents, counsellors; none of it was quite the same. Those were almost scripted, as though there were things I knew I would never dare mention. But with a stranger, someone I knew I would never see again five minutes from then ... I guess I just thought why not?

So I told him everything that was going on in my head, in my heart, in my soul. I told him all of that in about thirty seconds, but obviously I'm not going to go through it all with you because that'd defeat the object of having told one person I knew I'd never see again.

It all boiled down to one thing, though.

"You want to see the world," he said. "I can understand that."

"Life's too constricting," I said.

"I know what you mean."

I could even see that he did. Having talked at length about me, I felt fired up, eager to get on with life, adrenalin pumping through my veins. But I also knew next to nothing about him. All he had told me by that point was the vague nonsense about someone wanting to break his legs. "If you're running from something," I said, "where are you heading?"

He glanced out the window, for we had just pulled into London Bridge, which meant there was only one more stop, two maximum, before we had to leave. "I don't know, but I might buy a racehorse." He thought about that and laughed. "Nah, I'm not buying a racehorse."

"Why would you want to buy ...?" I shook my head. "Who wants to break your legs anyway?"

"A convicted criminal."

"You keep nice company."

"Well, he *is* my uncle."

"Why does your uncle want to break your legs?"

"Because of the contents of this bag."

I looked down at where his rucksack was held protectively between his feet, one hand never leaving the strap. "What's in there?"

Before he could answer, if he even was going to answer, a ticket inspector came around. As I handed across my one-way ticket, the unshaven guy said, "You already saw mine."

"I don't think so. Ticket, please."

"In the last carriage? I was sitting opposite the guy with the briefcase?"

"Lots of people with briefcases on this train, sir. Ticket, please."

A few people were staring by this point so he got out his ticket and showed it to the inspector.

"Thank you," the inspector said and continued on his way. "Tickets, please!"

"Job's worth," my new friend grumbled as he put away his ticket. I could sense his mood had soured, but we were only a couple of minutes away from Waterloo East so I wouldn't see him for much longer anyway.

"I don't suppose," I said, "you could recommend a good place to run away to?"

"That's the thing, you see. Our cases are different. All I care about is getting away; I'm not too bothered about where I end up. Where you, all you want to do is see the world; you're not bothered about what you're leaving behind."

It was a harsh way of saying it, but it was also pretty much true. I hadn't given a great deal of thought to how my family would feel about my running away. I guess I'd tried not to give it any thought at all.

"You're saying I should go back," I asked, "aren't you?"

"I wouldn't dream of ever thinking I could give out good advice. And anyone who listened to any advice I gave should have their head examined."

"You should have more faith in yourself."

"This from the runaway?"

An announcement came over the train to inform us we were arriving at Waterloo East and the next stop would be Charing Cross. It was annoying, because I really could have done with another five minutes.

"I'm not a bad person," I said.

"I never said you were." He paused. "Did you say you were?"

"No."

"Then you don't think you are?"

"No."

He smiled. "Good. Go out and see the world. Enjoy yourself. Don't look back."

The doors opened and people began to step off. Taking up his rucksack, the guy joined the crowd, and I stayed in the corner, thinking about what he had said. He hadn't said anything against my running away, but that almost made it worse. If he had been like everyone else, if he had told me to go home and stop being so selfish, I could have dismissed him. But what he had said touched me, made me realise maybe there was time to see the world later, that maybe I should go back home and sort out all my problems first.

I stepped off the train, determined to buy another one-way ticket. This one was going to take me home.

The Detective

"Interesting," I said. The girl was back to looking at her shoes when she finished telling her story, and I could hardly blame her. It takes a lot for a fifteen year old runaway to be honest with the law and I was grateful for what she had given me. I wasn't going to tell her that, however. I also wasn't going to mention that it took about ten minutes to get from Lewisham to London Bridge, so whatever she confessed to her new friend had certainly taken longer than the thirty seconds she had told me. "So he told you outright that his uncle would break his legs if he caught up with him?"

"Yes."

"You didn't just tag that bit on when you heard everyone else tell their bit?"

"No. Why would I do that?"

"Because he's a fellow runaway and you want to help him escape? Telling us his uncle is a bad man is a good way of getting sympathy."

"What would be the point in that?" she asked. "They've all gone before me."

"We still have one more to hear from."

"Oh. I assumed he was just hanging around because he brought us here."

I looked over to the final man. "He is. He's also a witness. But I'll get to him in a moment."

Ashcroft shrugged in that nonchalant way only teenagers can. "Can't see what else I can tell you."

"I must say, you're not showing the right attitude here, Miss Ashcroft. Don't forget, this man I'm chasing is a murderer."

"So you said. Who did he kill?"

"Can't you guess? But we're getting ahead of ourselves here. Which way did he go when he left the train?"

"I don't know, I wasn't stalking him. He went along with the crowd, but I didn't see where he went."

"I find it difficult to believe you weren't watching."

"I had other things on my mind."

"Ah, yes, his little talk. Did he convince you?"

"To not run away?" She gave another of those shrugs. "Yes."

I carefully considered my next question. "Did he mention what was in the bag?"

"I thought you already said, it was money."

"But did he tell you that?"

"No. He didn't say what was in there, just that his uncle wanted to break his legs for it."

"And he didn't give you anything from the bag?"

"No."

"So he could have been lying."

"Lying? He never said there was any money in the bag. You did."

"There was the brooch," Miss Robinson put in.

I could feel the brooch burning a hole in my pocket, directly into my heart. "Yes, the brooch."

"Are we almost done?" Holding asked crossly. "I think I might have mentioned this once or twice already, but I'm rather late for work."

"I shan't keep you too much longer," I promised. "We just have one final person to hear from."

We all looked to the last, silent person in the room. There was one man on the train who had not been a passenger, a man whom I had approached just as the train pulled in. A man who, I hoped, was going to make my investigation worthwhile. Otherwise, it would have been a terrible shame indeed to have gathered all those people there for no reason.

The Ticket Inspector's Story

"Tickets, please!"

I always liked to practise that in the mirror, and as I straightened my uniform and made sure my card reader was straight, I thought about all the fun I was going to have that morning. The trains were up the spout and everyone would be in foul moods as they forced themselves onto already packed carriages. The perfect time for a ticket inspector to work his way through the train, trying to catch the fare dodgers. It not only means there's nowhere for the little scroats to run, but it also annoys the hell out of everyone.

Having spent so long before the mirror, as I stepped out onto the concourse I realised there was a train on its way in. I had felt certain there wouldn't have been any trains for at least the next ten minutes, and I was determined to get on the one approaching. It would be the first in, so would be by far the most crowded. They're always the best to force my way through, because no one argues with a ticket inspector. Well, that's far from true, but since I'm allowed to call the police for even verbal abuse I don't have any grounds for not being as obnoxious about things as I can.

A crowd was already moving through the barrier by the time I reached it. There was a scruffy man ahead of me, with a prim and proper woman who was desperately trying to keep up with him; and I use the word desperate on purpose. I figured the meanest thing I could do would to separate them, make my best effort to force her to miss the train he got on, so I pushed in front of her and made sure I got through the barrier before her. She swore at me, loudly, and I could not hide my grin when I heard her swear at the barrier for rejecting her ticket. That would have slowed her even more, and I was satisfied she had lost her friend, even if they did manage to somehow get on the same train.

Moving up to the platform, I could see it was crowded indeed, but I managed to get on, at the expense of an elderly woman who might have made it if I wasn't more sprightly. As the doors closed, I lowered my voice and said in a flat tone which I knew would annoy everybody, "Tickets, please."

Then I bathed in the collective groan I could feel washing upon my jagged rocks of a heart.

It took me a while to work my way through the carriages, but all the looks, all the grumbles, all the veiled yearning for my death made it all worthwhile. It was not long before we reached Lewisham that I came across a man sitting with a briefcase on his lap. Opposite him was the same scruffy individual I'd separated earlier from his girlfriend. I felt glad he hadn't got off the train yet, because it meant I could annoy him all over again.

"Tickets, please."

The man with the briefcase was not happy, but he was not my target. The scruffy man seemed to have some trouble finding his pass, and while I waited I felt immense elation at the very thought he might be a fare dodger. He certainly looked the part.

"This service is appalling. I'm late for work now."

It took me a moment to realise the briefcase man had spoken to me. Ordinarily I would have absorbed his anger with glee, but at that moment he was not my target.

"It'd be ironic," I said, "if *I* was late for work because of the trains."

Just then the scruffy man found his ticket and I checked it thoroughly. I did not show him my annoyance that the thing was in date and moved off to check other people's. It was a shame I couldn't make the man's life miserable, but I felt I would have to settle for just having separated him from that woman earlier.

We reached Lewisham and, as usual, a lot of people escaped while a great deal of fresh meat was introduced into my slaughterhouse. Continuing my rounds, I eventually made it to the next carriage, where I was somewhat surprised to find a familiarly scruffy man, talking to a sad excuse for a teenager who was clearly running away from home.

I approached with a gleam to my eye, deciding fate had been kind to me and I was going to get a second chance at making his life hell.

"Tickets, please."

The scruffy man looked very annoyed with me that I had interrupted his conversation. The girl showed me her ticket, but I only gave it a cursory glance before asking the scruffy man for his.

"You already saw mine."

"I don't think so. Ticket, please."

"In the last carriage? I was sitting opposite the guy with the briefcase?"

"Lots of people with briefcases on this train, sir. Ticket, please."

People were staring by this point, which is always an added bonus. I had no idea why he had moved onto this carriage from the last, but I hoped somewhere along the way he had ditched his ticket. With pure venom to his eyes, he shoved it in my face.

"Thank you," I said, knowing I would sleep soundly that night. Moving along the carriage, I once more called out, "Tickets, please!"

It was not long after this that we arrived at Waterloo East and as I got off I saw you hurrying towards me, flashing your badge.

"Have you been through the carriages?" you asked.

"Wouldn't be much of a ticket inspector if I didn't walk through …"

"I'm after a man. I had a tip-off that he'd be on this train. Twenty-six, unshaven, wearing a T-shirt and jeans, carrying a backpack."

"The scruffy gentleman." I beamed. "I found him rather memorable."

"Where is he?" You looked about us at the crowds pushing past, as though you were going to be able to spot him.

"Gone."

"Damn. Did you talk with him?"

"Me and several others, yes."

"Others?" Your eyes took on a suspicious look. "What others?"

"Three that I know of, detective."

"Which three? Tell me."

You grabbed hold of my arm, and I said, "Steady, detective. I can find them for you. That man who just passed us. The one with the briefcase? He was one of them."

"You! Stop!"

As you ran to accost the man, I glanced into the carriage to see the teenage runaway was only now stepping off the train, deep in thought about alcohol abuse or Take That, or whatever teenage girls think about. She didn't seem to be in any hurry to move, so I scanned the oncoming crowd for the scruffy man's girlfriend. As a ticket inspector I've always been good at picking people out of a crowd, but in all honesty I didn't expect to find her. Statistically speaking, she was likely staying on until Charing Cross. I whooped with joy when she almost bumped into me.

"Sorry, miss," I said. "Detective wants a word."

By that point you had come back to me with the briefcase man and I was able to point out the others to you. I had a happy feeling I was going to make the scruffy man's day a whole lot worse. I had no idea why I had decided to pick on him, but I was mighty glad I had. Now, I knew, the real fun was going to begin.

The Detective

I looked at the ticket inspector in something approaching horror. "You really are an odd man."

He beamed. "Thank you."

"So that's it," Miss Robinson said. "You've heard all our testimonies and you're still no closer to finding Gary. I take it we can all go now and you'll contact us again if you need us."

"No," I said. "The problem is, Gary Kensing spoke to all of you, but he didn't actually tell any of you anything. None of you knows anything at all about him, other than what I've just told you."

"Well, no," Holding said.

"And by bringing you all together I've just given you more information on him than any of you even wanted to know. You would have gone on with your lives, not even giving the man a second thought. You certainly wouldn't have known were Gary to simply disappear."

"Well, no," Holding repeated. "Considering none of us even knew him."

I sighed. "Then I should apologise. I thought you were all witnesses, that you had vital information which could have led me to him; or information which could have led the police to me. But you weren't witnesses. You were just casual train acquaintances. By bringing you together I have, ironically, made you all witnesses."

"Uh," Ashcroft asked, "what do you mean led the police to you? You *are* the police."

"If I was the police," I said tiredly, "I wouldn't legally have been allowed to interview you without your parent or guardian present."

I pulled the gun before any of them could react. My choice of room was good, since with the only window blocked no one outside could have seen the movement. My four captives gasped like something out of a comedy film. They were all so obsessed with their own lives they had not even imagined the move could come.

"You're Gary's uncle," Robinson said.

"That's right," I told her. "As Gary mentioned, I've been inside for a stretch. Jewellery heist, you see. When I got out I wanted Gary to help his uncle on his next job. The lad didn't want to come with me, and I couldn't persuade him." I could feel my anger burning. "Then, after I'd done the job alone, he stole all the money and jewels from me. He wouldn't help me, but he'd certainly steal from me."

I realised I could not allow my anger to cloud my judgement, lest one of them attempt a break for the door.

"You can't just shoot us all," Holding said, distraught. "I have to get to work."

"And I have to get back to my parents," Ashcroft said.

"And I have people's lives to ruin," the ticket inspector said.

I waited for the final whinging voice and when it did not come trained my gun upon Miss Robinson. "Nothing you want to get back to?" I asked airily.

"Paperwork," she said. "Shedloads of it. It comes with arrests."

"Arrests?"

"Brian Kensing, I'm arresting you for armed robbery, kidnapping and attempted murder."

I blinked. "You're not an undercover cop, don't be ridiculous."

It was just as I spoke those words that the door burst in and an army of screaming, shouting police officers startled me into hesitating too long. They had my gun in moments, and before I even realised what was going on I was in handcuffs.

"What, no," I said, my brain still refusing to believe any of it. "No."

Robinson smiled as she approached. "Gary came to us to say you were going to commit armed robbery. Unfortunately, you were quicker than we anticipated and since we didn't know which jewellers you were going to hit we didn't manage to protect them in time. But Gary asked to help and the next thing we knew he'd shown up at the station with a bag of loot. At first, I have to admit, we panicked. Then I saw an opportunity. So we packed him off on a train, letting you know which train he was getting." She fished the brooch from my pocket, the one I had taken off her following her interview. "So I brought a bugging device for the armed police to listen in on while we awaited your confession."

"So your story was made up?" I asked, as though that was the worst thing that had just happened.

"Of course it was made up. But if it makes you feel any better, Gary played along as well, which is why he was able to tell people about the teacher he'd met. Mr Holding, we'd like to talk with you a moment but then you can go back to work. Mr ... ticket inspector? I'm sorry, I don't know your name."

"I have no name."

"Ooo ... Kay. Uh, same with you anyway. Miss Ashcroft? It's good to see Gary did more good here than just catch a bad guy."

Ashcroft looked a little shaken. "I think catching a jewel thief is more important than bringing home a stray."

"In my job, miss, I find them both rewarding."

It was around this point my brain allowed itself to catch up and I finally realised I was heading back to prison. The others were filing out the room, and as the armed police dragged me back onto the platform it was to the sound of a train's horn blaring as it sped through the station. The one thing which annoyed me most about all of it was that even after interrogating my four suspects I was still no closer to tracking down the whereabouts of my nephew.

The trains, of course, only seemed to laugh.

THE MURDER OF LOYALTY

CHAPTER ONE

"Come on, love, what does a score get me?"

Jennifer Appleton had been having a good day. Her sister had phoned to tell her she was getting married, her work had accepted her Christmas holiday request and when she had gone to book the flight she discovered the price had dropped two hundred pounds since yesterday. Plus, it was Friday, so Jennifer Appleton had no complaints at all. When John had called her to ask whether she wanted to go out for a drink or two, she had even begun to think now might be a good time for her to drop some not-so-subtle hints herself about when precisely the two of them should be getting married. After all, her sister was younger than her and, if John didn't want to make her feel old and left out, he would have to pop the question soon.

The pub they had chosen was large, spacious and part of a chain. And, typically with such pubs on a Friday night, it was crammed with people who had spilled out from their offices surrounding the river. Jennifer knew John preferred such environments, although she could not imagine why. She would have gone for a quieter, more personal place, but so long as she could get her hints dropped, she wasn't all that bothered where they were.

Things were all going well – they had even found a table – when a drunken lout had leered over her, asking her what a score could get him.

"Excuse me?" she asked, not being able to think of anything else to say.

"Girls like you are only with guys like him because he's paying you." The man was clearly drunk, she could tell as much from his eyes and the way he wavered. He produced his wallet and began counting out notes there and then. "I got ... twenty. That get me a really good time?"

John was halfway to his feet, murder in his eyes, but Jennifer's hand snapped out and caught him at the wrist. She looked at him pleadingly, but it did nothing to calm him.

Thankfully at that point two other men appeared, one either side of the drunk, and took him by the arms.

"Sorry," one of them said sheepishly. "Too much to drink, Harry. Come on, man."

Harry tried to shake away his friends' hands, although they were less drunk and far more insistent. Together, they managed to steer him away.

"Sorry," one of the men said over his shoulder as the three disappeared into the crowd.

John seemed to want to go after him, but Jennifer did not let go. She knew his temper was matched only by his protectiveness of her, and that should the two ever combine, it could only end in something ugly. John followed the trio with his eyes, but Jennifer could not imagine he could even see them any more.

"Just ignore him," she said. The good mood had vanished from their table and she knew it would certainly not be a good idea to begin dropping hints as to their impending engagement. It annoyed her no end, but at least the incident hadn't collapsed into a fistfight.

The two of them spent the next half hour talking of nothing. John still hadn't calmed down and Jennifer was beginning to wish they had chosen a different pub after all. Short of suggesting they leave, however, there was nothing she could think of to do about it. John was not a man who liked to admit defeat in anything, and leaving just because of that drunken lout would have irked him for days, weeks even. Jennifer had seen him in such moods before; they were, in fact, the reason her sister had never been keen on the man. He was violent and he was unpredictable, her sister had said. The truth was John may have had a temper, but he had never been violent towards Jennifer; and being unpredictable was not exactly a bad character trait in a future fiancé.

"What say we go get something to eat?" she said at last. She had been trying to think of a way to get them out of the pub, and food was always a good magnet for John. If they ordered from his favourite Chinese, it might even make him forget about the drunk.

"Sure," John said. "I could do without the chance of running into that guy again anyway."

That had been the other thing Jennifer had been afraid of. John was a large man and spent a fair amount of time in the gym. She was always afraid that if he got into a fight he would kill someone.

They finished their drinks and headed outside. It was still early evening and there were crowds of people awash upon the street. Jennifer could sense John was still in a bad mood and it annoyed her slightly. After all, she had been the one the guy had been leering over, and she would have happily forgotten about the whole thing by now. It wasn't that John especially bore grudges, but it certainly did take him a while to forget things.

John stopped walking so suddenly that Jennifer thought he must have collided with an invisible wall. Her heart was racing with the uncertainty of what he was playing at, and as she looked about she took in everything around her. To the left were two other pubs, each with their own crowd of patrons outside. The rest of the area to the left was taken up by walls forming the backs of whatever buildings lined the river. To the right, Jennifer could see the river flowing gently, a metal rail barrier preventing anyone from falling in. There was a single boat moored on their side of the river, but there was no one on it and she could not imagine John would have much cared for it.

Then she saw what had made him stop and her heart almost stopped with him.

Leaning against the railing, swaying gently and slurring lewd comments at any woman who passed him by, was the drunken lout Harry. His two friends were with him, all of them drinking and laughing. Neither of Harry's friends appeared especially apologetic for his behaviour this time.

"Don't go over," Jennifer all but pleaded.

"It'll only take a moment."

"John, please."

He shook off her arm and slowly walked to the river. Harry continued to harass anyone who came near, and Jennifer could see one poor girl stumble over her own feet as she attempted to get away quickly. Harry laughed and one of his friends high-fived him. Jennifer immediately understood that the entire incident in the pub had been a sham, that Harry had perhaps even been dared to say something stupid to her. When they had taken him away, his friends had not been sorry at all, which meant they had all been laughing afterwards.

Before any words had been spoken, she knew this was going to end in bloodshed.

One of Harry's friends noticed John approaching and said something to his companions. They were all grinning like fools, which Jennifer knew was only making the situation worse.

"Evening, lads," John said flatly. "Having a good night?"

"So-so," Harry replied. "I spent that score, though." He made a show of rooting through his pockets and came out with some loose change. "I got ... sixty-seven pence. What can I get for sixty-seven pence?"

John stared at him in stony silence. Jennifer stood several metres behind him, holding her breath and knowing this was about to turn sour. Harry was laughing, his two friends were laughing, and none of them understood just how badly things were about to go. She wished she could warn them, wished she could get them to run away and not look back, but she was frozen. She had seen this happen before; only once, but it had been enough for her to fear it ever happening again.

"Sixty-seven pence," John replied slowly.

"Or," Harry said, looking either side at his friends, "we could have a whip-round. I think we should be able to ..."

John slapped the money out of his hand so quickly and violently that Harry didn't even see the move coming. But John did not follow through on his attack; he just stood there watching them, waiting for them to make the next move.

One of Harry's friends lost his smile, but Harry and the other man seemed to think it was the funniest thing they had ever seen.

"Don't have no money at all now," Harry said, then lowered his voice to a conspiratorial whisper. "Any chance of a freebie?"

John launched himself at Harry and Jennifer shrieked. About her, people stopped to stare, but no one made any move to contact the police. John had grabbed Harry about the throat and his two friends were struggling to get him off. The four of them swayed this way and that as though they were one body, emitting shouts of rage from John and a strangled gurgle from Harry. Jennifer watched in horror at the scene but could not even find her voice to scream at them to stop.

She watched as John was pushed backwards as finally Harry's friends managed to tear his hands away. Harry was choking, but as he crouched on the floor Jennifer could see he was sobering. His two friends threw punches at John, but John was too big a man and too experienced in fighting for them to even connect. Throwing himself forward, John slammed his fists into the two men. It was not an attack designed to especially hurt either of them, but to get them out of his way. One of them men fell, the other stayed on his feet and took another swing; and John belted him across the face, sending the man sprawling in an arc of blood.

Murmurs shot through the gathering crowd and Jennifer stood with frozen eyes, wishing someone would do something, wishing someone would at least phone the police. But in these situations no one ever did anything. They just stood there and watched, like spectators at a cockfight who hadn't put down any money.

Harry was shouting by this point, angry at what John had done to him. One of his friends was still on the floor and didn't look as though he was going to be getting up any time soon; his other friend looked terrified. John lunged for him and the man turned and ran, leaving Harry and John alone.

This was precisely what Jennifer had been afraid of. In a one-on-one fight, John was going to kill him.

John lunged forward, grabbing Harry by the collar, but Harry was too pent up with fury to allow him to retain his hold. He slammed his head forwards, his forehead cracking against John's nose with such force they both staggered at the impact. John's face boiled with a crimson fury, lava bubbling behind his eyes, his entire body trembling in rage. It was what Jennifer always referred to as his volcano look, and she knew precisely what was about to happen.

Harry squealed as John lunged for him, his fist slamming into the man's face. Jennifer heard something crack and knew it was John's knuckles: the best way to break your fingers was to punch someone in the jaw. Harry fell, his cheek torn open by one of John's rings, but John did not stop there. He swung his left fist at Harry, knocking him with such force that he slammed into the railing bordering the river. John grabbed him with both hands, twisting him about and hurtling him to the floor.

Breathing heavily, his rage still burning, John placed his back to the railing and stared down at the now sober Harry.

"John!" Jennifer shouted, her body struggling to run over to him but her mind refusing to allow her any movement at all. She could hear the tears to her own voice and hated the fact she could be so afraid of the man she loved. "John, please."

Harry spat blood, his face filled with panic. He knew there was little chance of him walking away from this with his legs intact and the realisation spread a change across his face. His panic darkened, became anger, and as Jennifer watched she could see at last she was watching two furious combatants who had no intention of relinquishing any ground at all.

Launching himself from his position on the ground, Harry slammed into John, his arms encircling his midsection. John thumped down with his fists upon Harry's back, but Harry seemed to have become insensate to pain and continued pushing. John's back struck the railing and he gasped at the unexpected impact. Jennifer could see the shock in his eyes and knew it was going to give him at least a second's worth of hesitation.

A second was all Harry needed. His left fist cracked against John's chin, his right came around a moment later to strike his face. Jennifer could see John's shock deepening as he entirely failed to counter any of the attacks being made against him. Harry had him pinned to the railing and was hammering blow after blow upon him. Blood spattered the ground as John fell, his hand tightly grasping a rail as he attempted to drag himself back to his feet. Harry was screaming, probably unaware even of what he was saying as he unleashed all his aggressions upon his attacker.

Then John shoved forward; a final, feeble attempt to place some distance between them. Harry took only a momentary step backwards before dropping into a crouch and throwing himself again into his foe. His shoulder struck John's belly and his arms once more encircled his midsection. An instant before they struck the rails, Harry straightened his back and with an almost superhuman effort used the railing to lever John into the air. John's eyes widened as he realised his predicament, but Harry was still screaming at him. Jennifer felt her heart collapse as she saw John's arms flail uselessly, his anger gone, his eyes now filled with terror.

Harry pushed and John disappeared over the railing. Slowly stepping backwards, Harry laughed sickeningly, his legs promising to stumble beneath him.

Jennifer was only half aware of the commotion around her, of the crowd's varied reaction. Some had decided the show was over and had turned to go home, others had rushed to the railing to peer down; for the most part they stood there staring. Jennifer felt her legs buckle and suddenly she was on the ground, her tears flowing, her world collapsing. She could feel her brain swimming and dark spots appeared at the edges of her consciousness.

The voices around her blurred, and then they were gone as Jennifer quickly slipped into merciful unconsciousness.

CHAPTER TWO

She did not have a great deal to do at the scene, but then Constable Caroline Lees did not get too involved with the actual detective work. That was, understandably, for the detectives. It was a career path in which she was certainly interested, but sitting her exams had proved the most difficult thing she had ever attempted. She had already failed them once, but was determined not to mess them up a second time. There were only so many years she was willing to spend in a uniform and, if she was going to work the long hours and receive all the abuse that went with being a police officer, she may as well be doing something she actually enjoyed.

Standing at midnight in the rain, holding an umbrella over a crime scene and the detective working it, was not her idea of doing something she enjoyed.

There were several uniformed constables on the scene and most of them were loitering about the police line stretched around the area. Lees had never much seen the point of the long slice of material upon which 'police line, do not cross' was emblazoned, since all it did was encourage people to want to cross it. She supposed television had a lot to do with that. She had seen so many programmes where someone would approach the line, be told not to cross, only to flash a badge and, not looking at the constable, stride boldly through; usually taking along any civilian they wished just so long as they did so with the phrase 'it's all right, (s)he's with me'.

In the opinion of Caroline Lees, television had a lot to answer for.

"This one's not going to take a whole lot of brainpower to figure out," Detective Barden said from where he crouched, examining the blood spatter. Lees could not understand what staring at the pattern would achieve, but then perhaps that was why she had failed her detective's exam. In his late thirties, Barden was about ten years older than Lees. He was a decent guy and had helped her through some of her preparation; he had not even offered platitudes when she had failed, since he knew her well enough to realise it would annoy her. The only person who got away with being nice about it was her boyfriend, and even that was a stretch for her to accept. Barden was good at reading people, which was his greatest strength, and it was a skill Lees had always envied.

He was the one man at the station over whom she didn't mind holding an umbrella, even though it meant she was herself getting soaked.

From what Lees understood of the situation, there had been a fight between a group of people coming out of a pub a few hours earlier. Being Friday night, that was hardly a surprise. One man had ended up in the river, while everyone else had run away. The man in the water had disappeared and there were officers dredging the river even now. Lees had suspected that anyone falling into a river would just come back up again; she could not believe the currents of any subsidiary of the Thames to be that strong. Since the man had vanished, it showed she knew next to nothing about rivers. Perhaps, she reflected, there were a lot of things she needed to learn if she wanted to pass that detective's exam any time soon.

"When can we get out of the rain?" she asked.

"If you don't like standing out in the rain, Carrie, you're not going to make a good detective."

"Holding an umbrella over you isn't exactly what I call good detective work, Ray."

"You're not holding it over me; you're holding it over the crime scene."

"Makes me feel so much more useful."

"And you're holding it over the crime scene because?"

Lees was cold and wet and more than a little hungry. She had no time to even consider stupid questions like that. "To prevent contamination."

"Nope. Try again."

She frowned. "Why else would I be standing here in the rain, holding an umbrella?"

"That was what I just asked you."

She thought about an alternative answer, but nothing sprang to mind. Logically, the only reason to hold such a thing was to keep the rain off someone or something. There was no other purpose for umbrellas. "I give up," she said. "There's nothing else an umbrella does."

"Well, originally they were used to keep the sun off, not the rain. Chinese invention, umbrellas. Useful for so many things. Even for keeping your friends close."

"So you've got me standing here holding this thing because you want me close to you?" Now she was really confused.

"No, because you need me close to you." He looked at her some more, waiting for her to catch on. Then, with an exaggerated sigh, said, "Because the more time you spend with me at the crime scenes, the more tips you can pick up; and the more tips you pick up, the better you'll do next time your exam comes around."

"Oh."

"You need to think more optimistically, Carrie. The whole world is *not* out to get you."

It was something she had already known she had to work on. Lees would not have said she mistrusted people, it was just that she didn't especially like many of them. Interacting with the public, therefore, was always a chore for her, but it did mean that catching villains proved an especial pleasure for her. Knowing each arrest could effectively ruin someone's life was the greatest feeling she had ever known.

She had, she hoped, not mentioned any of these feelings during her detective's exam.

"So," she said, "what can I learn on this one?"

"That there's blood on the floor," Barden said. "Which confirms there was a fight."

"What, the crowd of witnesses wasn't enough for you?"

"Not always. People see what they want to see, Carrie. Sometimes people choose not to see what's obvious. Mainly because they don't want to get involved, but sometimes they make that decision for other reasons."

"You're talking about Appleton, aren't you?"

Jennifer Appleton was the girlfriend of the man who had fallen in the river. Barden had spoken with her and had sketched out a very vague outline of what she had told him. It had not been much, but then perhaps the young woman was still in shock.

"You think she's involved?" Lees asked.

"In arranging for her own boyfriend to take a dive? Not likely."

"Then what do you mean?"

"What do I mean? Nothing. I'm just saying people do things for lots of reasons. We can't afford to assume anything here."

Lees did not like it when Barden spoke so cryptically, but she had the impression he didn't actually know anything. "Right," she said. "Well, have fun with it."

"I've requested you help me on this."

"Me?"

"You need the experience. It's been okayed, by the way, so don't think you have to clear it with your duty sergeant."

"Then I'm officially helping you with this investigation?"

"You are."

"So why am I still holding the umbrella?"

Barden smiled. "You know, we'll make a detective out of you yet."

Lees was not all that certain whether he was being facetious.

"So, fill me in, then," she said. "What do we know about the fight?"

"Only that there were three of them and one of him. John Tanner was thirty-three, in excellent shape and the size of a bear. Someone insulted his girlfriend – according to the girlfriend – and the argument spread outside, where Tanner was thrown into the river. We don't have any names for the three attackers except the one who threw him in. Name of Harry."

"Hold on, I thought three of them threw him in."

"By that point one had run off, and the other was in a daze."

"So this Harry was a human tank?"

"No, just lucky, by all accounts."

There were several accounts, Lees knew, and if they all pretty much matched, it had to have added up to the truth.

A constable called over to them and they moved to the river. One of the police divers had surfaced and was shaking his head.

Barden's grip tightened on the railing. "I don't think he's down there. They would have found him by now."

"So what's the next step?"

"Without a body, it's still not murder. I'm assuming Tanner managed to swim to a ladder or something and hauled himself out. If we contact the girlfriend later today, I wouldn't be surprised to discover he's turned up."

"Or maybe he never went missing at all and she was covering because she knew he'd be in trouble."

"Maybe. Actually, yeah. That's happened to me before and it's always annoying."

"So this isn't necessarily even a murder investigation?"

"Don't sound too disappointed."

"Sorry. Just need something like this. Makes me look good if I've helped solve a murder."

"It probably wouldn't even be classed as murder anyway, but that's the vagueness of the law for you."

"Maybe he's down there, caught in reeds, and they can't find him because it's dark."

Barden looked at her strangely and she grinned.

"I think we should call it a day," he said. "We have everything we need from the crime scene and I have a lot of paperwork to get moving in on before we pick up again tomorrow. You want to help me with that?"

"With the paperwork? No thanks, I get enough of my own without doing yours as well."

"Ours. This is our investigation, remember. Everything I find out, I pass on to you."

"And, if by some miraculous intervention I find something out, I'll pass that onto you. But I'm still not doing your paperwork."

Barden grunted, but he said, "Fair enough. Get yourself home. We'll start again in the morning."

The crime scene would stay there without her, and it felt strange for Lees to be heading out before everything was entirely settled. She had done more than her fair share of standing in the rain doing little of anything, telling people to move along. She even used that phrase quite a lot purely because it was what people expected. 'Move along, nothing to see'.

She decided she was herself going to have to stop watching quite so much television if she was the one coming out with such rubbish.

Barden drove her back to the station, where she had her own car parked. As she drove home, protected from the dark and the rain, she wondered what could have happened to the body of John Tanner. That he was still alive was not something she was even going to entertain, and as she sat at a red light, her wipers slicing through the rain pelting her window, she thought about how this was going to be her chance. Her big chance to prove herself. This was going to make a name for her, and for her to do that, she needed for John Tanner to turn up dead somewhere.

She jumped as someone beeped her from behind, and realised the light had turned to green. Continuing her journey, she shook such destructive thoughts from her mind. She should not have been wishing people dead, it was not exactly the image the police wanted to project. But it certainly would have been a help.

Arriving home, she was pleased to find a parking spot outside her house. Grabbing her bag, she hurried inside and out of the rain, closing the door on the terrible night. Walking to the living room, she dropped her bag and collapsed into a comfortable chair, closing her eyes and knowing she probably should go straight to bed. She had a big day tomorrow and she would need all the rest she could get.

"Carrie?"

She opened her eyes, surprised her boyfriend was still up. She saw him then, sitting on the floor in the corner, his back to the wall, his legs tucked up to his chin. He was wet and trembling. His clothes were torn and his face was a mass of dried blood. He looked at her with wild, almost vacant eyes.

"Harry?" she asked. "What happened?"

Then she remembered the only named assailant of John Tanner. The man who had fought him and thrown him in the river had been called Harry.

Constable Caroline Lees had a sudden desire to see Tanner turn up alive after all.

CHAPTER THREE

He had worked on some difficult cases in the past, but Detective Ray Barden always seemed to end up with the ones without evidence. Occasionally it vanished (which was always worrying), but sometimes it simply wasn't there at all. This was the first case he had ever worked on, though, where he was investigating a death and did not even have a body. Perhaps what he had said last night to Lees was right, he thought; maybe Tanner had simply scampered out of the river and gone into hiding. He knew Lees had a somewhat twisted sense of morality in hoping the guy was dead, but Barden was beginning to agree with her. Drunken fights caused him so many headaches that he almost would have preferred for them sometimes to end so badly.

Almost. That was the difference between himself and Lees.

Barden had not slept much and had decided to get an early start. He knew even if he stayed at home he would only have been worrying through the case, so he had gone back to the station to review the evidence. Officers had taken over thirty witness statements, and they all said basically the same thing. He was sitting at his desk, slowly going over them while he tried to discern some discrepancy. Someone somewhere knew something, and he firmly believed that should he stare hard enough at the reports, he would be able to find it.

Across the floor, he could see Lees approach. She moved slowly, as though there was something on her mind. She was also still wearing her uniform, and he supposed he had not told her not to bother while she was working the investigation with him. That she was approaching him at all meant he had spent far more hours staring at the witness statements than he had thought, so he pushed them aside and leaned back in his chair as she arrived.

"Sorry I'm late," she said distractedly. "Had some things to do."

If she was apologising for being late, Barden didn't even want to know what the time was.

"There's nothing in the statements," he told her. "Divers still haven't turned up a body."

"So he's likely still alive. We should leave it until he turns up. Might be nothing."

Barden could feel himself frowning. Yesterday, Lees had been eager for it to be a murder investigation, but she seemed to have grown a moral backbone overnight. Still, they could not simply leave the investigation on the off-chance nothing became of it.

He shoved the papers across the desk to her, noting she was still standing rather straight. "Fresh pair of eyes," he said.

Lees glanced down at the paperwork but did not seem inclined to handle it, as though putting her fingerprints on the statements would somehow implicate her.

"What's the matter?" Barden asked. "Too much starch in your washing powder? Sit down and take a look."

Lees obeyed and as she leafed through the paperwork, Barden noticed a speck of blood on her sleeve. It had likely come from the crime scene the night before; the rain was so hard it had flung some of the victim's blood onto her whenever she had crouched. It meant she hadn't changed her uniform since the previous night, which showed Barden just how rattled she was.

He softened in his approach with her then. This was clearly affecting her a lot more than she had shown last night. It seemed sleeping on the matter had only brought her nightmares. If she was going to become a detective, that was something she needed to beat out of herself, but it was not Barden's duty to do so. There were some things Lees had to solve for herself.

Still, he resolved to be a little nicer to her because of it.

"They're all the same," Lees said at last. "They all say the same thing."

"Which likely means they're all true. Trouble is, we only have the one name to go on. Harry." He noticed she winced slightly at this, and reminded himself he was treading softly with her. "Don't let that bother you," he said. "Most investigations, I don't even have that much by this point. We also have the descriptions: one scraggly and lanky, with untidy hair, one more muscular with gelled hair, and Harry." He paused again before describing him. "Who's described as average everything, so not likely to be caught easily. The photofit guys are mocking up portraits for our three suspects, but I've never much trusted to those things. No one ever turns out to look like their photofit, or at least no one from any of my cases."

"Are we sure the name's right?" Lees asked. "Harry. Could it have been Barry?"

"Could have been Carrie for all I know. That was a joke," he added when she straightened. "God, you're tense this morning."

"Am I?"

"Yeah, what happened in the night? Your cat die?"

"No, I ..." She composed herself. "Sorry, just not used to all this. I'm good though, you can rely on me."

"Good. Because I'll need you if we're going to find this killer."

"Potential killer. We don't have a body."

"Nice to see you're back to thinking straight. Question: the witness statements aren't telling us anything, so what do we do?"

"Give up?"

"Aside from give up."

"Get more statements?"

"No. I think we have more than enough to annoy us."

"I don't know, then."

Barden could see she really didn't. "We go talk to the one person who might be able to offer some insight into this."

Lees shook her head. "And that would be?"

"Carrie, are you being particularly stupid today?" He knew he had intended to be pleasant to her, but enough was enough.

"The girlfriend," Lees said. "We go visit the girlfriend."

"That's right. Honestly, Carrie, whatever's eating you, you need to push it aside and get on with your job."

"You're absolutely right, Ray. I need to focus or we're going to make mistakes here. After all, we wouldn't want to arrest the wrong man."

"That's right." He did not understand why she brightened so much in suggesting they would do such a thing, but so long as it got her moving, he was more than willing to accept the change in her. "I'll drive. I'm not sure I trust you behind the wheel at the moment."

Lees offered no argument and the two of them headed out. They did not talk much during the journey but, from what conversation they did have, Lees did seem to be back to her old self. Barden had too much to worry about as it was, without having to deal with the strange mind of Caroline Lees. Still, they were friends and he was concerned for her. He would talk with her about it after, he promised. Once they had put this assignment behind them he would take her down the pub and get a few beers inside her. She always opened up after a few beers and generally felt better for it afterwards.

They pulled up at a house and Barden evaluated it in seconds. It was small and terraced, with a compact front garden consisting of a scattering of plants in pots and a broken statue of a gnome. As Barden pressed the doorbell, he thought about how they were going to approach the interview. He had intended to let Lees lead, but she had seemed such a mess when she walked in to work that morning, he was not certain he entirely trusted her to do it right. Besides, if his superiors discovered he had allowed her to be the one leading the investigation, it would be his body they would be dredging the river for.

He refrained from saying such aloud to Lees. He did not feel in her current mood she would have taken it as a joke.

The woman who opened the door was sleight of build and had a lost, gaunt look to her eyes. Barden had seen that look in many different faces. Grief was one of the unifying forces which swept across all classes and cultures. As a police officer, he had tried long and hard to become immune to seeing it etched upon people's faces, but he felt the instant he stopped caring was the instant he ceased being human.

"Detective Barden," he said, showing her his identification. "Constable Lees. Miss Appleton, may we come in?"

She did not answer in words, but moved away from the door and did not close it, so Barden took that as an affirmative. The two officers entered slowly, cautiously, for the house held the scent of grief: the empty, lonely air of longing and wishful thinking. Barden had long believed being an undertaker would have been a cheerier job than dealing with grieving or frightened relatives.

They moved into the living room, where the distraught young woman had made some attempt to keep house. Going through the daily motions was a good way of taking a person's mind off tragedy, apparently. Barden did not believe it for a moment, yet it was one of those things people always said to him.

"Can I get you some tea?" Appleton asked. She looked spaced, distant, and Barden wondered how much she'd had to eat and drink since her boyfriend's disappearance.

"Thanks, no," Barden said, although he did take the seat she offered. Lees remained standing and folded her arms. She looked agitated and he wished she would just calm down a bit. "There's no news about John," Barden said to start things off. "You haven't had any contact with him?"

"Is that how the investigation's going?" Appleton asked. "You wait for his body to turn itself in?"

"In my experience, Miss Appleton, this sort of incident usually has a happy ending." He had never before dealt with someone falling in the river, but she did not need to know that. The truth was, most drunken brawls ended up with blood and bruises, maybe a broken bone or two, but seldom a fatality. It was this statistic he was determined to hold onto as long as he could. It was his lifeline of hope, and something with which Jennifer Appleton could no doubt sympathise.

"It was supposed to be a happy evening," Appleton said distantly. "My sister's getting married, you see? I was going to drop some hints, get the ball rolling." She slowly shook her head. "Not so happy after all, was it?"

"Tell us again what happened," Lees said. It was something Barden would have avoided if he could, but Lees had not heard it directly from Appleton and perhaps if she did she would see something he had missed.

"Really?" Appleton asked.

"I haven't heard it yet from the horse's mouth."

Barden sensed something odd in the way she said that. It was almost as though Lees was intentionally insulting the other woman. He wondered what had got into her and hoped she knew what she was doing.

"We were sitting there minding our own business," she said, "when …"

"Sitting there in the pub?"

"Uh, yes. This guy came over. Drunk. He said something to me, something about money."

"You don't remember what he said?"

"Not exactly, no. He was asking me how much it would cost to hire me, told John he was only with me because he was paying me."

"But you don't recall the exact words?"

"What? No. Does it matter?"

Lees paused. "Then what happened?"

"His two friends pulled him away. One of them apologised."

"Then you eventually left the pub. And?"

Appleton was fighting to keep up with the interrogation. Barden desperately wanted to jump in, to tell Lees this was not the way they should be speaking with the victim's girlfriend, and again he just hoped she knew where she was going with this.

"And," Appleton said, "we saw them. John went over."

"To start a fight?"

"I don't know."

"Come on, guy insults his girlfriend, of course John wanted to start a fight."

"Maybe, I don't know. But he didn't start the fight. He just talked."

"Who threw the first punch?"

"I ... don't remember. It's all blurry."

"So it could have been John?"

"I ..."

"It could have been?"

"It could, I don't ..."

"And did you hear anything these three men said to John or what John said to them?"

"Not all of it, some of it."

"How much had you had to drink?"

"How much? What does that have to ...?"

"How much had you had to drink?"

"I ... a couple."

"So John's been drinking, has been insulted in the pub, and when he leaves he sees three men and goes over to pick a fight with them."

"It wasn't like that."

"No? This drunk man: were his two friends still dragging him away?"

"No, they were laughing with him."

"So they were all drinking and all laughing?"

"Yeah. Said something about loose change or ..."

"So the three men were acting completely differently outside the pub from when they were inside?"

"No. I ... well, two of them."

Barden decided he had been silent long enough. "Constable, is there something you're getting at?"

"Just wondering one thing, sir," Lees said. "Something no one's taken into consideration. These three men inside the pub and the three outside; who's to say they were the same three men?"

"They were," Appleton all but wailed. "I saw them."

"But you're not even sure what the drunk man said to you in the pub, so maybe you're not sure what he looked like, either. Maybe you'd had one or two more drinks than you thought you did, steady your nerves after being insulted, so that when you went back outside you latched onto the first trio of men you happened to see. After half an hour, what are the chances of bumping into the same people in so big a crowd?"

"That's enough," Barden snapped, then realised he would have to gain control of the situation while at the same time reassure Appleton that they were still doing everything they could to find her missing boyfriend. "Theorising is good, Constable, but right now all we're interested in are the facts."

"Of course," Lees said. "Sorry."

She did not sound very sorry.

Barden continued the questioning, although he kept it far lighter. In truth he did not expect to be able to discover anything new, but sometimes memory resurrected something forgotten. Jennifer Appleton was in such a state, however, that Barden doubted he would have been able to get anything useful out of her even if he felt she might have known something.

He cut off the visit as soon as he could, noting they were leaving the poor woman in a worse state than when they had arrived. He did not say anything to Lees until they got back to the car, and even then he drove away from the house before confronting her about what she had done. Five minutes from earshot of Jennifer Appleton, Barden stopped the car and turned to Lees with a glower.

"What was all that about?" he barked.

"She's hiding something."

"She's not hiding anything."

"No? They were a lot more drunk than she's making out. Those three men Tanner attacked were innocent bystanders. So Tanner ends up in the river? If a giant man like that attacked me, I'd shove him in the river and run away."

"That's not what the other witnesses say."

"The only witness we have who was there for the very beginning is Appleton, and she admits she didn't hear everything that was said. They were afraid for their lives, Ray. That's why they fought back."

"Or they could have been the same three."

"Could have been, yes. But we know from all the witnesses that Tanner threw the first punch. At least admit I could be right. Maybe he was drunk and attacked three strangers."

Barden did not like to admit any such thing, but what she was saying was true. Tanner and Appleton had been the only two to have seen the three men in the pub, and since Tanner was missing, they only had the word of a distraught girlfriend to go on. Perhaps Tanner had indeed picked a fight with the wrong crowd. And yes, if a giant of a man was starting a fight on a group of drunk lads, they could indeed have thrown him in the river and then legged it.

Still, it was not the way investigations were handled.

"A bit of warning next time," he said and restarted the engine.

"Which means," Lees pressed, "this name might be wrong as well. Did any of the witnesses hear the name Harry being spoken? In Appleton's original statement, she said she heard the name spoken in the pub. Maybe she just thought she heard it repeated outside."

That was also something to look into, Barden knew. He had studied those statements over and over and had never seen the name Harry appear in any of them.

"So," Lees continued, "Harry could be innocent. Innocent of everything, that is, except for approaching a woman whilst drunk and making lewd comments at her. His friends led him away and probably took him straight home."

"Which means we don't even have a name to go on." Barden did not like what he was hearing, but it did make sense. "We're farther back than ever now."

"At least we don't have to waste time chasing down bad leads."

"Still, I want to find this Harry anyway. Maybe he wasn't the same guy, maybe he was. But I want to find him and talk to him. If nothing else, he can give us information on Tanner and Appleton. If his friends were more sober than him, they could tell us how many empties were stacked in front of Tanner. If we can prove Tanner was extremely drunk, at least that's a step forward." He did not like to approach the investigation by suspecting the victim, but as a detective he had to cover all angles.

There was something else he should be admitting to as well.

"You're not a half bad detective, Carrie," he said. "If nothing else, you've made me see this case in a different light."

"It all helps to get me that promotion, Ray."

The promotion had been what had driven her to help him before, but this time Barden could sense there was something else. It was as though Lees had a personal stake in this, as though she had something against Appleton, or maybe even Tanner.

But that was not something he had to worry about now. First he would solve the case; then he would deal with the mystery that was Constable Caroline Lees.

CHAPTER FOUR

She did not have long, but Lees needed to check on Harry. Making an excuse to Barden which sounded feeble even to her own ears, she headed back home with all haste. The night before had been hectic and filled with panic. She had torn Harry's clothes from him and shoved them into the washing machine. She would likely have to burn them as well, but if they were washed before they were burned, there would be virtually no chance of anyone getting DNA evidence from them. She had told Harry in no uncertain terms not to leave the house until she got back. He had likely spent the past few hours going out of his mind, but she did not care. The more she investigated the case, the worse it was looking for him. As far as Barden was concerned, she knew she had put him off Harry's scent for a while, but he would be back on it soon enough; and then he would realise the trio in the pub really were the trio John Tanner attacked.

She and Harry had spoken so very little the night before, but that was one thing he had confirmed when she had insisted he tell her the entire chain of events which had led to his coming home in such a state.

Harry all but pounced on her as she walked through the door. She could see a hunger in his eyes unlike any she had ever known before. He was so eager for news, she could imagine he had been pacing ever since she had left him. In the time they had been apart, he did not appear to have even had a proper wash. His face was still bleeding, although some of the cuts had dried, most noticeably where Tanner's ring had cut him. One cheek was a welt of bruising and she could imagine it was extremely painful for him.

She raised a finger and poked him in the cheek.

"Ow!"

"Serves you right," Lees said. "You're a mess, Harry. Haven't you even cleaned yourself up yet?"

"I'm trying, but it won't stop bleeding."

She could see he was shaking, and the last thing they needed was for him to go into shock. But he could not go to a hospital, which meant he had to take care of the injuries himself. Or, more likely, she would have to once she came home from work. If he could just stop bleeding over the house, she would have been a bit happier.

She noticed something else which annoyed her.

"Shoes," she said. "You're wearing the trainers from last night."

"So?"

"Burn them. Hold on, you haven't been walking around the house in them, have you?"

"So what?"

"God, you idiot. I'll have to deep clean all the carpets now. You'll have stepped in Tanner's blood, you fool."

"There's no blood on my shoes, Carrie. Tell me what happened."

"There are always traces. You want to put your faith in my forensics guys not being able to do their jobs properly?"

"I am *not* burning these trainers. Do you know how much they cost me?"

"They'll cost you twenty years if you don't burn them."

Harry backed down. The threat seemed to have mollified him somewhat, but she had not been saying such things to make him angry. This was far more serious than he seemed to be taking it and it was good to see he understood the importance of what she was trying to do for him. She was trying so hard to become a detective and instead was harbouring the primary suspect in a potential murder investigation.

"I'll burn the shoes," he said meekly.

"You do that. Later. Tanner's body hasn't turned up yet. We're still hoping it won't. Maybe it's washed out to sea, maybe he's still alive, I don't know."

"He has to be still alive. Falling in the river doesn't kill you."

"No, because no one in the history of the human race has ever drowned, have they?" She knew she was becoming facetious, but his idiocy was driving her insane. "We have to calm ourselves, stay in control. It's the only way we're going to see this through. Calm and controlled. We have to think through every step logically, stay one step ahead of the investigation."

"Yeah, we have to fool the cops."

"I am the cops, you idiot."

In all the confusion it seemed Harry had forgotten that. It was something Lees found she had to continually repeat to herself in order for it to stay firmly in her mind.

"All right," Harry said. "Logically, then. There's no body. Logically, they can't charge me with anything even if they did manage to catch me. Do they know what I look like?"

"There were enough witnesses for Ray to come up with a good idea, yes."

"Who's Ray?"

"The detective who's going to put you away if we make even one bad move. It's Appleton we have to worry about. I think I've convinced Ray that she doesn't know what she's talking about, but that won't last forever."

"Who's Appleton?"

Lees's mind was working so frantically she had forgotten Harry was not present with her all through the morning. His name had come up so often it was as though he had been watching over her. "The girl you leered over. Why were you leering over girls in bars anyway?"

"How should I know? I was plastered."

"She says it was about money."

"I thought we weren't taking her word for anything because she's confused?"

"Don't toss my words back at me, Harry. Is this how you spend Friday nights with the boys? Picking fights with people bigger than you and making crass comments to women?"

"I wasn't picking a fight with anybody. Can we just get back to saving my neck?"

"If it was worth saving, maybe I would. I went to see Appleton this morning. You know what struck me about her? The one thing I noticed?"

"Shock me."

"She's a pretty thing. Of all the girls in the pub for you to leer over, it has to be a pretty one."

"So I'm cheating on you now? Is that it?"

Lees did not know what she was accusing him of exactly, but shouting at each other was a good way of venting steam. As soon as she realised that this was all she was doing, she realised also it was a waste of time. She had come home briefly for a reason, and it wasn't so they could get into an argument. And she would have to get back to Barden very soon, else he was going to wonder what had happened to her. The last thing she needed was Barden suspecting her of something.

"Here's what we're going to do," she said. "I'm going back to meet with Ray. With any luck, he won't have any leads and nothing's ever going to come of this. Some cases are just never solved, Harry, and this could become one of them. That means you can never meet Ray Barden, I can never talk to him about you, all right?"

"Fine with me."

"What I want you to do is stay here. Don't go outside for any reason. Get rid of those shoes, but don't burn them outside because that's something the neighbours will see and remember." She thought quickly. "The bath. Burn them in the bath, along with your clothes. Are they out the wash yet?"

"I don't know."

"Don't tell me you've left them in the machine."

"I don't even know how to work the thing."

Lees shook her head in resignation that she would have to do everything herself. "Get your clothes out of the machine, put them over the radiator until they're dry, then burn them in the bath as well."

"I can't take them straight out and burn them while they're wet?"

"I'm going to pretend you didn't just say that."

Knowing Harry would somehow mess it up, she went to the washing machine and pulled out the clothes herself. The wash cycle had finished hours earlier and she was annoyed as she dumped the wet, heavy garments into a basket. They should have dried by now, should have already been on their way to clothing heaven, but Harry did not seem to know how to look after himself. She began to wonder how he had ever managed before she had met him.

"Your two friends," she said as she shoved the basket into his hands, impacting into his stomach with an 'oomph!'. "What are their names?"

"What? Why?"

"Because I need to know in case Ray finds either of them. Come on, what are their names?"

"You're not going to turn them in then?"

"How could I turn them in without turning you in as well?"

"They wouldn't give me up if they were arrested."

Lees stared at him with a look that was half sympathetic, half despairing. "Yes. They would. Stop being so weird and just tell me their names."

Reluctantly, Harry gave her what she wanted. Sean Mullin and David Straw. She would have loved to talk to them both herself, make sure they understood the seriousness of the situation, but if she was going to get back to Barden this side of Christmas, she didn't have the time. That meant, unfortunately, she was going to have to trust Harry to do it for her.

"Have you called them today?" she asked.

"No. You told me to stay here and not do anything."

"Call them once I'm gone. Tell them nothing, but just warn them the police might be looking for them. Hang about, one of them had run off before you threw Tanner in the river, right?"

"I didn't throw him in the river."

"Don't be pedantic. Whoever ran off didn't see a thing. All he could do would be to confirm you were at the scene, which is enough to put you in the frame but not enough to damn you. Which one ran away?"

"Sean."

"And the other was on the floor in a daze, so he didn't likely see anything either." Her mind was working quickly. On one hand things suddenly did not look quite so bad, yet on the other she knew either man could still condemn him. Just positively placing him at the river would be enough to corroborate what all the other witnesses had seen.

"Talk to them," she said, "but just tell them to shut up. They can't mention last night to anyone, and I mean anyone. If they've already told people, we could be in trouble."

"Why? Even if they've told someone they had a narrow escape, no one's going to even know the guy fell in the river. It's not like it's going to make the papers or anything."

"That all depends how he's found."

Harry said nothing and Lees could see he was again thinking. It was good to see him thinking for a change, and perhaps if they could make it out of this mess together he might emerge a better person.

"Anyway," she said, "I have to go. Ray's going to be wondering where I've got to, and I can hardly tell him I came home to see you."

Harry nodded and thankfully remained silent. Lees was beginning to feel they might make it out of this yet.

Her mobile sounded in her pocket and she answered it quickly.

"Just on my way back, Ray," she said. "Sorry about that, I got caught up in ... Oh."

She listened to what Barden had to say, made appropriate noises of her own, then hung up. She could see Harry was eager for news, that he even had the intelligence to understand it was something bad. She thought about breaking it to him slowly, but the idiot did not deserve her being so kind to him.

"That was Ray," she said. "They've found a body."

CHAPTER FIVE

Detective Barden had seen a lot of corpses in his time and that of John Tanner was no different. That it was Tanner was not in doubt, for while he was waiting for Lees to return he had brought in Appleton to positively identify the body. Appleton had come and gone, and Barden was somewhat glad Lees had not been there for it. She had not, after all, been especially pleasant to the woman, and Appleton had been upset enough as it was. Where Lees had got to, Barden could not say, but if this was how she treated her job, he could see why she had failed that detective's exam.

The coroner had left him alone with the body, allowing him time to think through the situation. Barden did not know much about dead bodies, so most of what the coroner had told him had gone over his head. However, he understood what he needed to, and it gave him more than enough to be thinking about.

The door to the mortuary opened and as Lees walked in he could see she was haggard, distressed. Barden did not even feel the case had been an especially harrowing one, but perhaps it had just become commonplace to him. He could not remember ever being quite as Lees was now, but he supposed there had one time been someone in his place looking at him in much the way he was now looking at Lees. Since he had turned out all right, he decided to do what his own mentor had done and not mention it.

"Sorry," Lees said. "Had something that couldn't wait."

"It happens. Anyway, here's John Tanner. Shame, but he's not turned up alive."

Lees stared at the body as though electricity might shoot through her eyes and awaken the monster. "We sure he's dead?"

"Are you feeling all right?"

"I meant are we sure it's Tanner?"

"Appleton identified him. And yes, I'm sure he's dead."

She did not take her eyes from the corpse. At first he thought she was staring in horror, her mind aghast at what was lying before her;

but then he realised she was examining the injuries. She was already moving ahead to the actual cause of death, which meant she had put her insecurities aside and was getting on with putting a villain behind bars.

"The injuries are consistent with a fight," Barden said. He did not mention he had obtained all his information from the coroner; if she had been here on time, Lees would have found it all out herself. "Nothing professional, just a brawl. Bruising and cuts to the face, mainly. A broken nose consistent with the head-butt Harry supposedly gave him. And cracked knuckles from where he's obviously punched someone in the face."

"Backs up what we know, then," Lees said.

"Yes."

"And also what I suggested."

"That Tanner was the antagonist?"

"The knuckles show he hit someone, hard. Are there any signs that he was punched anywhere near as hard as the one he gave?"

"No. The worst injury, as I said, is the broken nose, but that would have been the head-butt. Harry's fists don't seem to have left quite as much damage as Tanner's would have. It would be interesting to see the other guy. Harry's probably a mess, you know."

"Then we need to find him before he can get himself cleaned up. We should check the hospitals. It might take time, but it's our best place to look."

"Already put in the calls. There were a couple of possibilities, so I sent uniform to have a look. Neither was our man."

"How do you know? We should go ourselves."

"One was too old, one wasn't white, and all the witnesses said Harry was white."

"Still, we should be sure."

"I trust uniform," Barden said, "and considering you *are* uniform, you should trust them too."

"Right. Sorry. Just eager to get a result, I guess."

"Admirable. You want to ask me the cause of death?"

"I assumed it was drowning."

"No. He was still alive when he hit the water, but he didn't drown."

"How did he die, then?"

"This is what killed him." Barden indicated Tanner's side and saw Lees's eyes widen. There was a narrow slit in the skin which had bled out into the water. It was, to someone of Barden's experience, unmistakable.

"That's a knife wound," Lees said.

"Our man Harry carries a knife."

"No."

"How's that?"

"Well, none of the witnesses said anything about a knife."

Barden eyed her curiously. She had been acting very strangely since all this had begun, and there was no way he believed she had reacted like that because she was thinking about the witness statements.

"Do you have any familiarity with this case, Carrie?" he asked.

"What? No, of course not."

"So you're not working on it with me?"

"No, I'm working on it with you. I thought you ... I thought you meant do I know any of the people involved."

"Good, because that's exactly what I meant. Have you ever met Appleton? You seemed to hate her."

"I don't hate her."

"Tanner, then? Or the suspects?"

"No, of course I don't know anyone. I just ..." Her voice drifted off.

"Just what?"

"Something similar happened to me when I was a teenager. I was just a witness, but my friend's boyfriend was set upon. This is just bringing a lot of that back to me."

It was a plausible enough answer, but she had never mentioned the incident before. Still, Barden did not like to call her a liar and decided he would trust her. "What was the result?" Barden asked. "Anyone die?"

"No. Just a fight. I guess that's what guys do best, yeah?"

"Not all guys get into drunken brawls, Carrie."

"I didn't mean to suggest they did. What else can the body tell us?"

Barden knew a deflection when he heard one, but at least she was talking about the case now. "Not much. I'm assuming Harry was clever enough to toss the knife away. I'm hoping we might find it in the river, but it doesn't look too good for that."

"Where did the body surface?"

"About a mile away from where he fell in. I'm getting some people working on identifying the type of knife used, so until then we have to try harder to find the killer. I have a lead."

"You do?"

"And a possible name. One of the witnesses worked with someone who seems to have recognised the description we put out. I got a call about half an hour ago giving me a name. I was about to go pay him a visit, if you're ready."

"Sure," she said a little stiffly. "What's the name?"

"Sean Mullin."

"If he ran away, we won't even be able to charge him as an accessory."

"How do you know he's the one who ran away?"

"I don't. That's why I said *if*."

"Oh. Well, actually he is the one that ran away. But, even though he wasn't there for the end, we can still bring him in. That's how police work goes, remember? We question people and they lead us to other people, and sooner or later we get to a suspect and we arrest him. You know, standard police procedure."

"Please don't patronise me just because I'm having a bad day."

It may have been a bit of a low blow, but Barden did not feel bad for having struck it.

Barden had already found out Mullin's address so they headed over there immediately. It was still only half a day since the fight, so there was every chance Mullin did not even know there had been a body thrown in the river. Mullin had fled the scene before the fight got really bad, so he had probably just gone to bed and woke up with a hangover. He may not even have given a single thought to the fight as yet, which meant Barden could leap on him and get whatever he wanted.

From what Barden had learned, Mullin lived with his parents in a quiet neighbourhood. He always felt bad about arresting people in front of their parents, but when he was investigating a murder it was not something to which he gave much thought. Pulling up outside, they strode to the house and Barden knocked on the door. He could see there was a bell, but everyone expected the police to knock on the door so that was what he did.

After a few moments, a woman answered. She was aged somewhere in her fifties and was clearly Sean Mullin's mother.

Barden flashed her his identification and said, "Detective Barden, ma'am. I'd like a word with your son, if I may."

"Sean?" She looked confused. "He's not in. He went out this morning. Is he in any trouble?"

"Hopefully not, ma'am. Did he say where he was going?"

"Oh, no. What's he done now?"

"Witnessed a fight, ma'am. I really do need to speak with him."

"You might try his friends."

"Could you tell me their names?"

"Oh, I don't know their names."

"Could you tell me what they look like?"

"I've never met them. But if you find them, they might know where he is."

Barden had a strong dislike of people who stood at the door and gave him no information whatsoever. "Do you mind if we came inside?"

"I suppose not. You want to check he's not in his room, I assume?"

It was precisely what Barden wanted to do, and he was surprised she was canny enough to have realised. "If I may. I hate not believing a lady, but it's my job to check."

Mrs Mullin was fine with them searching through her son's things, although they did not spend long there and found nothing at all of interest. CDs, magazines, computer games: Sean's room was just the same as anyone else aged in his early twenties. Nor were there any discarded clothes from the fight last night. Barden got the impression coming to Mullin's house had been a waste of time after all.

"Thank you for your time, ma'am," he said as he and Lees left. "When your son comes back, could you get him to give me a call at the station?"

"Certainly, Detective."

Barden also hated people who were too polite when he was trying to arrest their children.

"Dead end," Lees said as they approached their car.

"Maybe, maybe not. Mullin will now know we're onto him and that may spook him, make him make a mistake." He frowned, for he could see Lees was looking over his shoulder at something. Turning, he saw a young man walking towards them or, more specifically, towards the house. He was tall and scraggly, with a mop of untidy hair and trousers just a little too long. He did not match Mullin's description, but he certainly matched someone else's.

"David Straw?" Barden asked casually.

The man blanched, turned with a stumble and ran. Barden smiled. This was more like it.

"Caroline, go!"

Barden ran, knowing every second he wasted was allowing Straw a greater chance of escape. Straw was younger and had fear on his side, but Barden seldom lost a chase and wasn't ready to now. He did not stop to see whether Lees was following, but hared down the street after the only lead the investigation had thus far turned up. After only twenty steps or so, Straw stumbled and Barden closed the gap, grabbing the younger man at the shoulder and twisting so he lost his balance. Straw fell clumsily and Barden placed a knee on him while he got the youth's hands behind his back. As he dragged Straw back to his feet, he was barely even breathing hard.

It was only then he noticed Lees was still a few paces behind him, but it did not matter. They had a body at last.

"David Straw," Barden said. "I think we'd like to talk to you down at the station."

"I didn't do anything."

"Never said you did. You OK?" he asked Lees.

"Fine. Just not as fit as you." She bent over, holding her hands to her knees. They had only run for about ten seconds, if that, and she was already worn out.

"You need to get yourself to the gym," he said, shoving Straw ahead of him. But none of it mattered. They had someone in custody at last; now the real work could begin.

CHAPTER SIX

Lees had never felt as sick in her life as when she sat in the interrogation room. Beside her, Detective Barden was psyching himself up for the interview, while across the table sat the scruffy, nauseated form of David Straw. She did not know whether he had a hangover or whether his fear had made him turn pale, but she could tell this was his first time in a police station. She and Barden had checked his record and had found it clean, which was another indication that he had never been inside a police station; but Lees was trying to use her instincts a little more. Lees was glad of Straw's fear, for the more he sweated, the less Barden would likely notice her own discomfiture.

There was a duty solicitor present, but she seemed content to let the officers ask their questions, which was always a bad sign. Lees realised then she did not even know the solicitor's name, which was also a bad sign because it meant she had been told but had forgotten. It was something she would not admit to Barden.

"Where were you last night?" Barden asked. Lees knew he began with the question because it was standard and something everyone expected the police to ask. Perhaps Straw had even already fabricated an alibi, or perhaps he would tell the truth. Either way, the answer would be interesting.

"I don't remember."

All right, Lees reconsidered, the answer hadn't told them much of anything.

"Let's try to narrow it down, then," Barden said diplomatically. "Were you at home, or were you out?"

"I was in the pub, yes, but I don't remember much of it."

"Which pub?"

"The one you're talking about."

"I haven't mentioned any pub."

"Detective Barden," the solicitor said with the voice of an oily snake, "let's not bait and trap here. Mr Straw is willing to cooperate, but he's very nervous. He knows full well why he's here and what happened at the river, but he's still confused. So let's not treat him as a suspect, but a witness."

He was technically both, Lees knew, although she did not say as much. She also knew Barden did not like to be told what to do or how to think by solicitors, but he was clever enough not to let his emotions show.

"Certainly," he said. "Mr Straw, we can agree then that you were in the ..." He checked his notes before naming the pub and the street. Since it was a chain pub there was no reason for him to have forgotten the name: not that Lees believed for a moment that Barden would ever forget anything. It was a tactic, one of many Barden implemented. As nervous as she was, Lees realised she was indeed learning a lot from this experience.

Straw nodded that he was indeed there.

"Tell me what happened," Barden said. "And, if you're intending to be very cooperative, please don't leave anything out."

"Harry went over to them, and ..."

"To whom?"

"The big guy and the girl."

"Do you know their names?"

"No."

"Did you know who they were?"

"No."

"Did Harry?"

"I don't know."

Barden paused. Lees wanted to say something, but she was too afraid to.

"Go on," Barden said at last.

"Harry was drunk and he said something to her. Something about offering her money."

"Why did he do that?"

"Because he was drunk."

"No other reason? You see, it's been suggested there might have been a bet involved."

"A bet?" Straw frowned in genuine thought. "I don't remember a bet, I don't make bets. We might have dared him or something, I don't know."

Lees sensed he was being honest and a glance to Barden confirmed he did too.

"So, Harry approached the girl," Barden said, "and made some crass comments. Then what?"

"We pulled him away. I said sorry to the girl and we took Harry outside."

"Then what happened?"

"He sobered up a bit. The air got to him, I reckon and we had a bit of a laugh over how close we'd come to the big guy tearing into us."

"Sounds hilarious."

"Everything's funny when you've just escaped death."

It was a little extreme, but a fair enough comment for a young and confused man to make.

"How long were you outside?" Barden asked.

"I don't know. Might have been twenty minutes? Forty? I lose track of time when I'm drinking."

That much, Lees reflected, was also true.

"But eventually," Barden said, "the two came out. The big man and his girlfriend."

Straw looked down at the table. "Yeah. I didn't see them at first, not until the guy started talking to us. He wasn't being aggressive, but I could see he was angry. But Harry ... Harry didn't seem to care."

"He wasn't too drunk to notice?"

"Not by that point. We'd gone back to drinking again, but only just. We were all a little plastered, don't get me wrong, but I could feel something inside me ticking away, like I knew we were on a timer or something."

"Who started the fight?" Barden asked.

"Harry, I guess. The other guy threw the first punch."

"Tanner, you mean?"

"That his name?"

"Tell me about the first punch."

"Harry offered him money and Tanner knocked it out of his hand. Then Harry lunged for him."

"So Harry attacked first?"

Straw seemed confused, and even Lees was trying to figure out whether slapping money from someone's hands constituted assault. She knew she was trying to defend Harry, but things were looking grim.

"Sean laughed," Straw said. "I couldn't believe he was doing that, it was just winding the guy up. I don't remember much after that. There was a fight, I didn't do much but tried to help where I could. Then the big man – Tanner – went for me and I fell."

It was how they had been told already, but Lees had not been dreading anything up to this point. It was where the questions would go from there that had her concerned, because now Barden would ask about Harry, about what his surname was and where he lived.

"Let's talk about Harry," Barden said.

"Harry," Straw repeated. "I don't know much about him but I'll tell you what I can. Lucy says ... says Tanner died?"

Lucy Fisher! That was the solicitor's name. Lees noticed they were all staring at her then and she wiped the huge smile from her face.

"Tanner died," Barden confirmed. "He was stabbed."

"Stabbed?" Straw asked, aghast.

Lucy Fisher shifted her weight where she was sitting. Lees understood the woman's frustration: she had already told her client all of this but in his confused state, Straw was taking in only a portion of the information presented him.

"Does Harry carry a knife?" Barden asked.

"Harry carry?" Straw asked without even meaning to, his brain still trying to catch up to the situation.

Lees felt the blood drain from her face. She had been trying so desperately hard not to have her name linked with Harry's, and suddenly wished she insisted everyone call her Caroline.

"Someone stabbed Tanner," Barden said, "and I need to know who it was."

"I ... I didn't see a knife."

Lees opened her mouth, not even knowing what she was going to say even as the words came out. "None of the witnesses mentioned a knife," she said, "so it's not likely he did, but we have to cover all aspects." She realised she was once again defending Harry too readily, so for Barden's benefit added, "Or maybe things moved so quickly you didn't see the knife."

"I don't know."

Barden seemed curious as to his partner's angle of questioning, but did not berate her. "Does he generally?" he asked.

"I don't know him."

That answer surprised Lees and even offered her a little hope.

"What?" Barden asked. "What do you mean you don't know him?"

"I only met him last night."

"You what?"

"Sean, I know Sean. Sort of. Haven't seen him for about a year, but I bumped into him last night at the pub. He was with his mate, Harry."

"Why go to Mullin's house if you haven't seen him in a year?"

"Because of what happened yesterday. I don't have Sean's number, but I remembered roughly where he lived. Found his number in the phone book and decided to go see if he was all right, ask him if he knew anything more than I did about last night."

Barden did not look pleased, while Lees was trying to hide her relief.

"So," Lees said, "until we jumped you, you didn't even know Tanner had ended up in the river?"

"No."

"So why'd you run?" Barden asked.

"Because you looked like cops and when you said my name I just panicked."

Barden held the bridge of his nose with thumb and forefinger. "I don't suppose," he said tiredly, "there's much point in asking whether you know Harry's surname?"

Lees felt her heart stop ...

"Sorry."

... and continue.

Barden did not have many further questions and they wrapped up the interview quickly. Lees was under the distinct impression he wanted to get rid of Straw so they could concentrate on something productive.

"What a waste of time," he said when they were alone once more. Straw had been taken back to a cell while Barden and Lees had retired to the staff canteen to bury their sorrows in badly made coffee.

"What are we going to do with him?" Lees asked.

"Straw? Nothing. He didn't do anything. Dragged his drunk friend away from a fight when they were inside the pub; got knocked down in a fight outside. He may have thrown a punch or two but, like he said, he was just trying to help his friends. That he was there when Tanner went over the rails means we could look at charging him as an accessory to something, but if he was barely conscious at the time I don't see the point. Well, to be fair, we could try, but we couldn't make it stick."

"So we let him go?"

"Eventually. He can stay in the cell for a while. No, it's these others we want. I get the feeling, though, that when we pull in Sean Mullin, we're going to be faced with the same problem. Guy ran away before Tanner was thrown in the river, so his lawyer's going to argue he can't be an accessory either. That'll be an even worse fight for us, since Straw was at least there when it happened."

"So," Lees summarised, "what we really need is Harry."

"Right. No Harry, no case. I'm beginning to wonder whether even Mullin knows who this Harry character is."

Lees did not know any of Harry's friends, but she had certainly never heard him mention anyone named Sean. It was a possibility. Up until recently she wouldn't have believed it to be an especially good one, but then again she had thought it was all over when they were interrogating Straw.

"Back to searching for Harry, then," Barden said. "You have any connections you could try?"

Lees sensed this was the perfect opportunity to get away. She needed to ask Harry about Sean, whether he knew his surname, where he might have gone running off to. "Sure," she said. "Even uniform have their informants."

"Go check with them. We'll meet back here in a couple of hours. Keep your phone on, in case speak no evil or hear no evil grow a conscience and hand themselves into the front desk."

Lees had no idea why Straw was designated see no evil, since he could well have been any of them, but Barden was tired and likely didn't know what he was saying.

They parted company a few minutes later and Lees got in her car and headed straight home. As she neared the house, she had visions of Harry out in the front garden, burning the carpet, but thankfully there was no activity at all that she could see. Turning her key in the lock, she could hear voices, which meant the idiot had invited someone around. Storming through to the living room, she found Harry sitting there with a can of beer in his hands, his trainers still on his feet, a companion sitting opposite him. It was then she noticed they were also watching the football and she almost screamed.

"What are you doing?" she demanded fiercely. "I've been spending all morning saving your neck and you're sitting here drinking."

"Carrie," he said, "I think you need to talk to this guy."

She rounded on him, becoming more aware with each passing moment that she now had two targets upon whom to vent her aggression. The man was clearly vain: physically fit, with gelled hair. "And who the hell are you?" she asked.

"I think you've been looking for me," the man said, raising his beer in a toast. "My name's Sean. Sean Mullin."

CHAPTER SEVEN

Sean Mullin was in her house. Sean Mullin and Harry Gorman were the primary – the only – suspects in a murder, and they were both sitting in her front room, drinking beer and talking football.

"I don't know why I bother trying to save you," she said, rounding upon Harry.

"Sean came round when I phoned him," Harry said. "After you'd gone, I remembered I don't actually have Dave's number, so I couldn't call him."

"We have him at the station," Lees said.

"We?" Sean Mullin asked, some of his smug demeanour dwindling.

"Oh, good," Lees said snidely, "Harry's forgotten to tell you who's investigating the murder. Murder? That word sinking in yet?"

"Murder?" Harry asked. "It was an accident."

"You threw him in the river."

"Yeah, but only accidentally."

"He was also stabbed."

It was Harry's turn to lose some of his surety. "Stabbed."

"Yes, stabbed. Someone jabbed a knife in him and it killed him. So, which of you was it?"

"I didn't stab him," Harry said.

"Hold on," Mullin said seriously, "you're a cop? Harry, you never said your girlfriend was a cop."

"What does it matter?" Harry asked. "Neither of us stabbed the guy, Carrie. Maybe he caught himself on something under the water."

"I think Ray might have thought of that."

"Who's Ray?" Mullin asked.

"Detective Ray Barden," she replied. "He's the one in charge of finding the two of you."

"And you say you have Dave?" Harry asked.

"He was useless. Doesn't know anything, so we'll let him go. But we went to your house," she told Mullin, "so don't go back there."

"Oh perfect," Mullin said. "I can't just hide low. Eventually I'll go home, and when I do the police will nab me. You have to do something, girl. You've got to get me off this."

"For one thing, don't call me girl. And what do you expect me to do? Frame someone else?"

"That's one option."

Lees was shocked to silence. She had been spending so much time trying to divert the investigation, she had never considered pushing it forward and making sure someone else got sent down for it. Ethically, it was far from sound, but Lees had never much cared for ethics.

"Appleton," Lees said without meaning to.

"Appleton?" Harry asked.

"The girlfriend. I keep telling Ray she knows more than she's saying. I could blame her, but I don't know whether I could frame her. What I need is the knife."

"Can't you just use any knife?"

"No, it has to be the one with the blood on, you idiot."

She could see Harry was tiring of her calling him an idiot, but she wouldn't have to if he stopped acting like one.

"I'm supposed to be out looking for the two of you right now," she said. "Since I can't find either of you, I'm going to need to take something back to Ray."

"How about we kill Sean," Harry said, "and you can tell him Sean and Tanner killed each other."

"Actually," Lees said, "that's not a bad idea."

Mullin raised his beer can in a threatening manner.

"I didn't mean kill you," Lees snapped. "Tanner was clearly murdered. I reckon he clambered out of the water and got into another fight. It's obvious he was murdered. So what if it wasn't murder? What if it was self-defence?"

"I'm not following," Harry said.

"We stab one of you and tell Ray that Tanner came after you with a knife. You managed to wrest it off him and stuck him with it."

"That's still implicating one of us in the death," Harry said.

"But self-defence isn't murder. I think we have to accept here that we're not walking away from this totally untouched."

"So which of us are you offering up?" Mullin asked. "I'm assuming that would be me."

"You're the logical choice," Lees told him, "since Ray already knows where you live. If you don't mention Harry, they'll never catch him."

"Charming," Mullin said. "So I go to prison and you two breathe a sigh of relief?"

"It could be worse," Lees said. "Harry can say he saw you stab Tanner. I have access to Tanner's body and it won't be too difficult to coat a knife with the man's blood. It won't stand up to scrutiny of course, but remember who I am. I can rush things through, maybe even have the knife conveniently disappear once we've all verified the blood was Tanner's and that it was found in your house. Your choice, Mullin, is going down for murder or chance getting let off entirely with a plea of self-defence." She paused for effect. "No, really, it's your choice. You have to choose."

"I don't have to listen to this," Mullin said, tossing his beer can at Harry. Lees winced as she saw dregs splash across the carpet, but because of the possible bloodstains she had already decided to deep clean it anyway. "Typical pigs, setting me up for something."

"You've had trouble with the law before?"

"Like you haven't looked me up already."

It was something Lees probably should have done, but her mind had been on other things. Besides, looking someone up on the police database likely left a trace, and if Barden checked her progress he would wonder why she was looking up Sean Mullin to begin with. The last thing she wanted to do was give Barden precisely what he wanted.

"Or," Lees said as he moved for the door, "I could arrest you here and now."

"Then Harry would be in for it as well."

"Then how about I cuff you and leave you here while the two of us head down to the station and blame everything on you?"

"You wouldn't."

"I would. We're back to my finding a conveniently blood-stained knife, by the way. Uniform would be along in about an hour to arrest you, so with any luck," she said, glancing at the television, "you might get to see the football result as your final act as a free man."

She could see the anger boiling within Mullin. He was not a physically strong individual and Lees knew enough self-defence to be able to take him down. Plus there was Harry, who would not side with Mullin if he knew what was good for him. Lees had no doubt at all that if this turned into a fight, it would be Mullin who came off the worst for it.

"Have it your way, then," Mullin said and headed once more for the door.

"Hold on, where are you going?"

"To the station, like you just told me to."

"Then I'm coming with you."

Lees hastened into the hall, where Mullin was already disappearing out the door. It did not take a genius to tell he was up to something and she did not believe for one moment he was handing himself in. It took her a few moments to realise he was parked outside; he had the car door open before she had even properly assessed how much of a scene she was willing to make in front of all her neighbours.

"You're doing a runner, aren't you?" she asked.

"No. I'm doing what you told me. God, you people are never satisfied, are you?"

"The police?"

"Women. It's like we have to bleed gold before you're happy with us."

He slammed the door and drove off. Lees considered following him, but her priority was that Harry seemed to have wandered out the door after her. Scooting him back inside, she closed the door and said, "Your friend has anger issues."

"Well, he's not exactly my friend."

"He's what?"

"I only met him last night. He was a friend of Dave's."

"Hold on, he was what?"

"Yeah. I'm lucky I had his number so I could call him about last night. I got it from Dave when I dragged him out of there. Figured it was a good idea to be able to stay in contact in case there was any comeback. Come to think of it, I could have got Dave's as well while I was …"

"No, go back. You don't know Sean Mullin?"

"Well, not before last night, no." He paused. "You're looking a little pale, Carrie."

"David Straw said … he said he didn't know you, that you were a friend of Sean's."

"Really?" He frowned. "I wonder why he said that."

"How long have you known David?"

"Since last night."

Now Lees really was confused. "Harry, you need to start making sense. Did you know either Sean or David before last night?"

"No. I met them in the pub. I was out with the lads and I sort of ended up by myself. And I was a little drunk. Then I met Sean and Dave and we had a few laughs. They dared me to go over and make trouble with some hot girl and I was in such a mess I figured what the hell?"

"So they were together when you met them?"

"I'm not sure actually. It's all pretty much a blur."

Lees did not understand what was going on, but she had a feeling there was more happening than she realised. Straw hadn't looked up Mullin's name in the phone book, and he hadn't run from Barden just because he'd panicked. One thing of which she was certain, however, was that they needed to speak with David Straw again before he was released.

"Stand there and be silent," she said as she punched a number into her phone. Barden answered it on the second ring. "Ray? Don't let Straw go. I have some questions for him."

"Ah," Barden said. "Might be a problem there. His solicitor insisted we either charge him or let him go, and we didn't have anything to charge him with."

"Damn."

"What do you have?"

"Not a lot, other than that Straw lied to us. I have a few more leads to check, so I'll talk to you later."

As she hung up, Harry looked annoyed. "Dave was protecting me by not saying anything, you know."

"Possibly, but I don't think so. There's something going on here, Harry, and I mean to get to the bottom of it."

"That's the policewoman talking."

"I am a policewoman, you dolt."

"Well maybe you're more a policewoman than my woman."

"I'm not your woman, and if you weren't my man you'd be in a prison cell by now. Do you understand that?"

Harry backed down and nodded meekly.

"I'm going out," Lees said angrily. She had nowhere she really needed to be, but away from Harry Gorman would have been a good start. "I'll say this again: do not leave the house until I get back. Do you think you can do as you're told, or do you fancy organising another party?"

"I'll stay."

"And burn those damn shoes."

She stormed out, angrier at herself than she was at Harry. She was trying to make something of herself, trying to establish a proper career in the force, and Harry was all set to screw that up for her. He wasn't worth it, he really wasn't worth it, but it was too late to do anything about it now. As soon as Harry was arrested, her chance of promotion was over. She had to save the man, but that did not mean she had to like it.

For the want of somewhere to go, Lees drove back to the station. Maybe there was a chance Mullin had handed himself in after all.

CHAPTER EIGHT

"Harry Gorman," Barden beamed, slapping a written statement onto the desk. Lees's eyes widened, her lips parted as she grabbed the paperwork and devoured it eagerly. Proud of himself, Barden leaned back in his chair and even thought about putting his feet up on his desk. "Now that," he said, "is having good contacts."

"I ..." Lees was staring at the papers, but Barden could see she was not reading them. Her hands were shaking and she was hardly able to take in the concept, let alone the words. "Who's the girl who made this statement?"

"Arlene Jeffers," Barden said, watching his partner carefully. "It took a bit of effort to track her down, but I knew there was something more to all of this. I spoke to witnesses, informants, I even went to see my priest and got a few confessions off my chest. Short story is I eventually turned up a name. Arlene Jeffers. It seems Jeffers was at the pub that night as well, but she wasn't there alone. Harry Gorman had gone there with her; she was his date."

"Harry was on a date?"

"Well, whatever you'd call it. It's been a while since I was down with the kids, but that's what we used to call them. He took the girl to the pub at any rate."

"He didn't just meet her there?"

"Nope. Gorman and Jeffers went to the pub together, had an argument and Jeffers stormed off, left him to it. Only she stayed in the pub, so she saw him approach Appleton as well."

"What was the argument about?"

"Is that relevant?"

"It might be."

Again, he could see she was nervous and he made himself as comfortable as possible. "Gorman's girlfriend," he said. "Turns out he already had one and let something slip while he was there. The argument, come to think of it, was probably the reason for his getting stinking drunk and then aggressive with the first pretty lady he saw. That and being urged on by his two friends of course."

"Harry was ... The cheating ..."

Barden raised an eyebrow. "Of course, we still don't know where Harry Gorman is. If we knew that, we could move in and arrest him."

"I can't believe he's ..."

"So if we knew someone who knew where he was? Even anonymously would be fine."

"All this time I've been ... and he's been ..."

"Like, for instance, if we knew who was hiding him. Quite innocently, of course. After all, you can't be arrested for hiding someone, so long as you give them up when the situation turns to murder."

"That rat-faced ... Say what?"

Lees was looking at him now, her face etched with the expression of a cat which has just wandered into the wrong exercise area in Battersea Dogs' Home.

Up until that moment, Barden was not certain whether he was having a good time, but murder was a serious business and he could no longer afford to let Lees play this however she saw fit. "You didn't read the whole report," he said, tapping a particular section of Jeffers's statement. "Harry's other girlfriend is called Caroline." He leaned back. "Not that I didn't already know, of course."

"There are plenty of Carolines in ... Already know?"

"Come on, you've had guilt plastered across your face ever since this thing began. I knew you were involved somehow; I was just praying you didn't have anything do to with Tanner actually going over the rails. A while back I figured you knew Harry, that you were hiding him. Then I remembered you mentioning one time the name of your boyfriend and I didn't need much more."

"You ... If you knew, why didn't you say anything?"

"I was kind of hoping you'd come to me on your own." He was angry, but there was no sense in showing it. He had himself done some pretty stupid things in his time, but hiding suspected murderers was not something he had ever even considered. "We're on the same side, Carrie. And, unless you didn't realise, cops don't have a particularly good name any more. The fewer criminals we hide, the better it is for our image."

"I'm sorry."

To be fair to her, she did look sorry. She also looked a little lighter and he could see just how badly the thing had been holding her down. With any luck, now it was all in the open, she might actually show him what a good police officer she could be.

"Remember, Carrie, we're a team. I share with you, you share with me, and hopefully along the way we avoid any more murders."

"Harry didn't kill anyone."

"Right. So, we're getting back to work at last. You said you suspected Straw of something else?"

"Straw and Mullin know each other. Harry only met them last night."

"Straw said the same thing."

"I know. But I believe Harry."

"Why? He's been lying about everything else."

"Because Harry's never been able to lie when I ask him a straight question."

It was not a good enough reason, but if Lees believed it, it was something Barden knew he was going to have to accept. After all, he had been the one who wanted them to work as a team; and disregarding her intuitions and decisions was not a good basis for that relationship.

"I think I should talk with Harry," Barden said. "But I'm giving you the opportunity to bring him in yourself."

"Arrest Harry?"

"Or have him come in of his own accord. In case you really can't see how serious this is, your boyfriend tossed someone in the river. All right, you say he didn't stab anyone, but we know for a fact he threw Tanner in the river. And for that, yes, I have to talk to him. So either bring him here or I'm going to go get him."

It was something, he could see, that Lees had already herself considered many times. When she spoke, it was with a resigned voice. She knew this was over. "You're right. Of course you're right, Ray. I'll drive home and fetch him."

Barden's desk phone rang and he picked up the receiver, noticing that Lees had stopped to see what it was. "Barden," he said.

"Detective? Detective, please, he's here."

The woman's voice was terrified and familiar. "Miss Appleton? Who's there? Someone's in your house?"

He heard a crash, a scream and the line went dead.

"Miss Appleton?" Barden called, but there was no answer.

"What's happened?" Lees asked.

Barden was already on his feet and grabbing his coat. "Someone's attacking her. We have three suspects so it could be any of them."

"How could they even know her name, though?" Lees asked.

"You tell me. You happen to tell any of our suspects the name of the victims?"

Lees blanched.

"Great," Barden said. "We're taking my car."

While Barden drove, Lees put in a call to uniform to get some bodies their way, but Barden knew he and Lees would arrive on the scene first. They did not speak during the journey, for there was nothing to say. Lees had screwed things up and did not need the lecture that went with it. What this would mean for her future, Barden could not say, but right at that moment he was more concerned with the woman being attacked in her own home.

"What are you doing?" he asked when he saw her produce her mobile.

"Calling Harry."

"Leave off." He grabbed her phone and tossed it on the back seat, never once taking his eyes off the road down which he screamed. "One in three chance he's the one attacking her and you want to phone him?"

"Harry's not a murderer," Lees said defiantly.

"Tell that to the guy he tossed in the river."

No further words were spoken and Lees made no attempt to retrieve her phone. They pulled up outside the house of Jennifer Appleton for the second time that day. The front door was open and there was already a small crowd outside; the ghouls who always gather but never find courage enough to venture inside to see whether they can actually help. Barden and Lees charged in, heedless of any danger, and found the house silent.

Stopping in the hall, Barden listened hard, but whatever travesty had occurred, it was all over. His eyes trailed through the hall, taking in the tidiness of the shoes lined up like dutiful children, the pictures hanging from the wall without a single degree's tilt. There were several photographs sitting atop a small cupboard, depicting Jennifer Appleton with a woman of marginally lesser years. That, Barden knew, was Jennifer's sister. They were so happy in the picture that he prayed they would be able to have many more such photos taken.

His heart was racing as he prayed for a kidnapping but, as he took a few more steps, he detected the sharp, coppery scent of blood in the air.

They found Jennifer Appleton in the bathroom. There was blood pooled upon the floor, dirty red stains streaking across the tiles where she had flailed with useless arms, her bleeding fingers finding no purchase that might help her. The porcelain sink was slick with goo, blood slowly draining down the plughole. Appleton's body lay in a crumpled pile on the ground. Her clothes were saturated with blood, her hair was matted and untidy. Her eyes stared out sightlessly, vital fluids pumping out the side of her head where someone had cracked it against the sink as though it was an egg.

"Ambulance," Barden told Lees, knowing it was already too late. "Lees, ambulance!"

Lees tore her eyes from the body and called in the request on her radio. She stepped out the bathroom to do so and Barden knew what she was feeling. This was her fault. Not totally, of course, but it was enough her fault for it to make a difference. Someone had killed Jennifer Appleton and Lees could have prevented it, or at the very least not told the murderer the name of the woman to go after next.

He walked from the bathroom and found Lees in the kitchen, head over the sink in case she needed to throw up. Barden perched himself against the counter beside her. "Rough day."

"This wasn't Harry," Lees wheezed.

Barden had at last had enough. "Carrie, I don't much care who it was. We have three suspects and I'm pulling them all in. We leave here and go straight to your place. I want three men in three cells by the end of the day and I don't want any more bodies turning up. And you, you little idiot, are going to pull yourself together. Do you understand that? You're not going to be any use to me if you keep on like this."

"You're still using me on the investigation?"

"I don't have much choice. You know at least one of the suspects and you're familiar with the case. My options are to carry on as we are or arrest you for stupidity and go on alone."

"I won't let you down."

"This is beyond letting me down, Carrie. Let me get this straight; what you've done is hamper a criminal investigation and the result is lying on the bathroom floor. This isn't a second chance for you, this isn't a way to make amends. This is damage limitation. You told a suspect the name of the next person he should kill, and he went and killed her. Right now you're a resource and that's all. Now go wait in the car; and if you even think of calling Harry Gorman I'm going to personally see you're sent down for murder."

Lees was wise enough not to reply and Barden did not feel at all bad when she ran from the house, her head bowed. This was hard for her, but he did not care. A woman had died and there was no coming back from that. The investigation had become a whole lot messier and Detective Barden knew from this moment on the only person he could rely on was himself. Constable Lees was finished, and if he protected her now it would be no different to how she had protected Harry Gorman.

Yet Barden still had no idea whether he was quite ready to abandon her entirely.

CHAPTER NINE

Her hand hurt from where she had punched the steering wheel. It had not made her feel any better, but it gave her something else to concentrate on. Lees had never ruined anything in her life as badly as she had Barden's investigation. Only a few hours earlier this had been a simple brawl. A man had fallen in the river and Harry needed to stay out of trouble for a while. Then a body had turned up, stabbed, and now another. If she had known this would happen, she never would have covered for Harry to begin with.

Especially if she had known from the outset he was cheating on her.

The car door opened. Barden dropped into the driver's seat and buckled on his belt. The paramedics had arrived and pronounced Jennifer Appleton dead, which meant forensics could now get on with examining the crime scene and seeing what DNA evidence they could pull.

Without a word, Barden drove and did not stop until he had reached Lees's house. "Get him out here," was all he said.

"You're not coming in?"

"He sees me coming towards the front door, he'll do a runner out the back. Get him out here and don't tip him off."

Lees made no remark about not trusting her. She was lucky she was still in the same car with Barden and knew from now on she would have to do precisely what he told her to, as soon as he told her. She left the car and walked to the front door, trying to remain as casual as she ordinarily would have done. She missed the lock with her key several times before cursing herself for her nervousness. When she finally managed to open the door, she found Harry standing there looking anxious.

"Come with me," she said, trying not to allow her voice to crack.

"You said not to leave the house."

"And have you?"

"Have I? Of course I haven't. Carrie, what's wrong?"

"Just come with me. Things have got worse."

"Worse? Worse how?"

"Just come with me, Harry. Now."

He opened his mouth to argue further, but there was nothing to say. She stepped back out the door and he followed, looking around sheepishly, as though dark clouds were preparing to strike him with lightning. Lees kept in front and purposefully did not look him in the eyes. She walked slowly towards the waiting car and Harry had no idea he was walking into a trap. She watched as the car door opened and Barden casually emerged.

It was only when Barden grabbed his arm and twisted it that Harry gave a shout and realised he had been set up.

"We meet at last, Harry Gorman," Barden said, cuffing him before shoving him towards his car. "Now get in."

"Carrie?"

"Don't you Carrie me, you two-timing louse. And get in the car before I start interrogating you here on the street."

She could see the fear in Harry's eyes and knew it had all been true. Everything Arlene Jeffers had said in her witness statement: it was all true.

"Carrie," he said, "let me explain."

"I don't want to hear it."

Barden grunted. "And I could certainly do without hearing it." He shoved Harry again and got him inside. "Now sit down and shut up."

Lees climbed into the back seat with Harry and obeyed, even though she wasn't sure which of them he was speaking to. She knew her house was going to be searched soon for a bloody murder weapon, but first they would interrogate Harry, or at least Barden would. Inviting her to the interview would have been a serious error on Barden's part, and Detective Barden did not make errors. She was surprised, therefore, when she realised they were heading in the wrong direction.

"We're not going to the station," Barden told her before she could ask. "We take Gorman to the station, that's it for you. Before I kill your career, Lees, I want to make sure I have the right man. That might well be Gorman, but it could easily be one of the others. If it's Gorman, you're both going down; if it's not, I don't know what I'll do yet."

Lees could not believe what he was doing, but then she had never been able to predict what Barden was going to do. "If anyone finds out about this …"

"I know. And I shouldn't put my own job on the line for you, but that's precisely what I'm doing. So have the decency to shut up a while."

Being a constable, Lees knew the area well and after a short while reasoned she knew where Barden was headed. Harry did not seem to have worked things out yet, which was good, although when he caught the first glimpse of the river, Harry's eyes widened in panic.

"Don't cause a fuss," Lees told him. "Detectives aren't going to stab you and throw you in the river, Harry." She paused in thought. "Constables, though, are a different matter."

It was not the same area of the river where Tanner had fallen in and Lees doubted it was the same area from which he had been recovered. But the river was long and vast, and there was so much filth at its bottom there might well have been any number of bodies down there that no one yet knew of.

Barden parked and told them both to get out. Lees dragged Harry out and looked around. They had come to an industrial area devoid of traffic and pedestrians. There were large, bleak buildings surrounding them whose broken windows and unkempt appearance indicated the only people inside would have been squatters. The river itself was wide at this location, tumbling along beneath them. Striding across the concrete and weeds, Barden reached the old railing which prevented people from falling in. There had been so few people passing through this way in the last few years that even from Lees's distance she could see it was rusted through.

"Nice view," Barden said while he gripped the railing and slowly twisted it. "Tell me where to find Straw and Mullin."

He was to the point, which Lees had always admired about him. Harry, his hands still bound behind him, did not seem to know what to say, what to do. Lees stepped away from him, almost hoping he would try to make a run for it. She would have been gladder than ever to see Barden chase him down.

"I don't know where they are," Harry said imploringly. "I told Carrie, I really don't know them."

"Did you stab John Tanner?"

"What? No."

"Did you ever meet Tanner or Appleton before last night?"

"No. Look, I told Carrie all this, if she just ..."

"I prefer to form my own opinions," Barden said, and Lees could see he had unscrewed one of the rusted metal rails. He was holding it in both hands and there was enough menace to his eyes that Lees honestly had no idea what he was about to do. "Did you," Barden continued slowly, his eyes boring into Harry's, "murder Jennifer Appleton?"

"Appleton? No, I ... She's dead?"

"Did you kill her?"

"No."

Barden brought the metal pole up so quickly Harry stepped back, stumbled and fell on his backside. "Someone tried to make an omelette out of Appleton's brains," Barden said. "Was that you?"

"No, I ..." Harry was desperately trying to scramble backwards, but with his hands cuffed behind him he could hardly even move. Lees took another step backwards, afraid herself and only glad she was not the object of the detective's fury.

"One of you killed her," Barden said. "If it wasn't you, it was either Straw or Mullin. Give them to me and I'll work out who to throw away for a double life sentence."

"I can't give you them. Wait, I ... I have Sean's number."

Lees suddenly remembered that was true, and if she had been thinking clearly she would have already mentioned it. She opened her mouth to confirm, but closed it when she realised she would only be implicating herself further. So far, Barden did not know that Lees had ever met Mullin. If she could continue to hide that from him, he could not hold her entirely responsible for everything that had happened.

"Call him," Barden said dryly. "Arrange to meet him. Tell him the cops are asking you about Appleton and that you think Straw's gone off the deep end." He paused. "Bit of gallows humour for you."

"I can't call him."

"Why? Because your hands are tied?"

"I can't squeal on him to the cops."

"Oh for the love of ..." Barden lunged for Harry, who revealed he certainly was able to squeal, but Barden didn't touch him and came away with the man's phone, which he tossed across to Lees. "You call him."

"Me?" Lees asked, which was a stupid question. "Mullin's going to know it's a set-up. He knows I'm police, Ray, and he doesn't trust me."

"How does he know you're police?"

Saying any more would have condemned her, so Lees quickly said, "Harry told him, I think. Quiet now, I'm making the call."

The phone rang several times before it was answered. On the other end, Lees could hear a dull rumbling which sounded familiar, but was not loud enough to disrupt the call. "Harry?" Mullin asked, sounding very suspicious before Lees had even said a word.

"Close," Lees said. "Harry's at the station, there was nothing I could do to stop them picking him up."

"So they've taken you off the case?" Mullin laughed. "Bet you loved that."

"You listen to me, you stuck-up, cop-hating jerk. Not too long ago, my life was fine. Now Harry's up on a murder charge and I think we both know he didn't do it."

"So who did? The Easter Bunny?"

"Straw. Barden had him but he let him go. You heard from him lately?"

"Dave? No. He's probably out there losing another fight as we speak."

"He killed Jennifer Appleton."

"He what?"

"The girlfriend of the guy Harry threw in the river? She's dead, beaten to death in her home. Well, Barden has Harry so he's trying his damnedest to make the charge stick on him. But you and I know better, don't we? We know it was Straw, so if I can find Straw I'm going to be a happier bunny than anything hopping around at Easter."

There was a pause on the other end. "How do you figure it was Dave? Could well just as easily have been me."

"Could have been, but I spoke with Straw, sat in on the interview. There was something about him I didn't like. Something creepy, something sinister. He might lose a fight with a six-and-a-half-foot strongman, but he's not the type to shy away from beating in the head of a defenceless woman."

"Well, he always was weird. What do you want me to do about it exactly?"

"Ideally, hand yourself in, but I doubt you're going to do that."

Mullin laughed. "I told you when I left your house I was on my way to the station. Just didn't say what type of station."

"Hold on a ... Are you leaving the country?"

"Station, not airport. I'm on a train right now, heading up the country. There's no way you have any idea where I'm going."

"So, if you're gone, help me find Straw. If he's taking out all the witnesses, it won't be long before he comes after you."

"You really do live in a dreamland, don't you? Look, all right, I'll give you something. Not because I like talking to pigs, but because I feel a little bad about what we did to Harry. Didn't think I would, but the guy invited me round and gave me a beer so I guess I owe him something."

"What are you giving me?"

"It wasn't a coincidence. None of it. Someone wants something out of this, Constable. Someone stands to gain."

"Would that someone be you?"

"No, but I gained as well. Not much, but some. A hundred quid doesn't seem worth it now."

Lees glanced to Barden, who could only hear half the conversation and was eagerly waiting for more. "Wait a minute," Lees said. "You're saying you were paid to kill Tanner?"

"No." Mullin laughed again. "We were paid to cause a nuisance. Ruin the mood, pick a fight and throw him in the river."

She stared hard at Harry. "And was Harry being paid as well?"

"Nah, he was our scapegoat. Me and Dave were being paid a hundred each to toss the guy in, but we didn't want to be arrested for it. So we convinced Harry it would be a good laugh. He gets the blame, we get the money. Easy."

"So what went wrong?"

"Guy turns up dead. Someone knifed him, I've no idea who. Maybe Dave, maybe Harry, certainly not me."

"If it wasn't you, come sort it out. You can't run forever."

"Sure I can. Listen, I'm going now. Probably going to toss my phone, so don't bother calling again. Just bear in mind the fact someone stood to gain far more than me."

"Why are you telling me even this much?"

"Because I figure I got stiffed. A hundred isn't worth the upheaval. So I'd like to see other people get a bit of upheaval, too."

He hung up and Lees wished she knew what he was talking about. She glanced to Barden but glowered at Harry. "You take any money for throwing Tanner into the river?"

"Money?"

"Harry and Dave were being paid. You were their patsy. How's it feel to be used, Harry? How's it feel to be lied to and abused?"

"This is about that girl, isn't it? Look, I wasn't cheating on you, Carrie. I saw her once, that was all."

"So you only cheated on me once and that makes it all right?"

"I didn't cheat." He seemed genuinely angry. "We didn't even do anything. I only met her a couple of days ago. So I took a girl to the pub on a Friday night: we honestly didn't do anything."

Lees opened her mouth to lay into him again but Barden said, "Hold on. Gorman, you met this girl two days ago?"

"Yeah, so?"

"And she suggested the venue?"

"Yeah."

"Where you had an argument with her?"

"I told you that already."

"Over what?"

"What?"

"What was the argument about?"

"I don't know. Nothing."

Lees snorted. "Clearly wasn't nothing."

"It wasn't about anything," Harry said. "She just got angry and started shouting. So I told her where to get off. She told me I drank too much, which was rich considering she'd insisted we do quite a few shots that night."

"So," Barden continued, "she got you drunk, then left you?"

Again Lees opened her mouth to say something, but Barden held up a finger.

Harry shrugged. "So?"

"And you just happened to fall into the company of Mullin and Straw," Barden said, a small smile appearing on his face. "Caroline, I think we have a suspect."

"We do?"

"This girl. She brought Gorman to the pub, where her hired goons were waiting. She made Gorman drunk and annoyed, and the two men took it from there."

"So this girl's behind it all?" Lees asked, uncertain. "So, who is she?"

They both looked to Harry.

"I don't know," he said. "She said her name was Jezzie. Short for Jezebel."

"Not made up at all then," Barden said. "Would you recognise her if we showed you pictures?"

Lees grunted and mumbled, "Depends if you have pictures of women's chests."

"Yeah, I'd recognise her," Harry said, a little annoyed at Lees's constant attacks on him. "I can tell you now what she looked like. Short, braided blonde hair, dimples, freckles around the cheeks."

"That on the level?" Barden asked.

Lees could sense the sudden change in him and it took her a few moments to understand just what it was. "You know this woman, don't you?" she asked.

"I should do. Only spoke to her today. And, idiot that I am, saw her after that and didn't put the pieces together. You," he told Harry as he turned him around, removed the handcuffs and gave him a rough shove with his foot, "disappear."

"You're letting me go?"

"I take you in and Carrie goes down with you. Right now I'm not convinced you're the murderer we're after, so you get to walk. Don't go far, don't leave the city and don't talk to anyone about anything. Go back home and sit in front of the TV: seems to be all you're good for."

Harry tried to say something to Lees, but she held up a hand. "One word and I throw you in the river myself."

Silently, Harry turned and meekly trotted away. Lees watched him go, but was far more interested in whatever Barden had figured out.

"Who is this woman?" she asked now they were alone.

"I don't know how it all fits in, Carrie, but Jezebel told me her name was Arlene Jeffers. And since photos never lie, I can tell you her real name is Jodie. And her sister was named Jennifer Appleton."

CHAPTER TEN

Unsurprisingly, Jodie Appleton was not at home. Instead they found a lavish apartment owned by a man named Morgan Flax. Barden had never known why such palaces were called apartments, considering they were so much larger than Barden's entire house; he doubted he would have himself been able to afford to run even the porch. Barden did not have any feelings at all towards people with money. It was not his business whether they had earned it or inherited it; if Barden tormented himself with coveting everything other people had, he would never be able to sleep at night.

"This is quite serious, yes," Barden said. He had of course not told Flax anything about the case, but had phrased things in such a way that made Flax think it was in everyone's best interests for his fiancée to contact the police immediately. It was something Barden was good at, which he should have been, considering how much practice he had had over the years. Lees did not say much during the interview, for which Barden was thankful. She had been forced to take in a lot over the past few hours and in truth he felt she was holding up pretty well. It did, of course, not excuse anything she had done, but if she could help him catch David Straw and Sean Mullin, he was even still considering covering for her. That Mullin had vanished up north was a possibility, but Barden intended to keep his options well and truly open.

"Is she in danger?" Flax asked. He was a fairly average-looking man and seemed a decent sort. Barden could not believe he knew anything of what his fiancée was really like.

"Difficult to say," Barden replied. "I noticed there wasn't a car parked outside."

"I don't drive. Nor does Jodie. Is that a problem?"

Barden had been hoping the lack of car might indicate Jodie was driving around somewhere. If they could get her registration number, he could have people look out for her; but if she didn't drive, he could not even do that little. Ignoring Flax, he said, "Tell me, do you know a man named John Tanner?"

"John?" Anger took hold of Flax's face then. "Great, what's John done now?"

"You know him, I take it?"

"He goes out with Jodie's sister. I've never met him, but I know Jodie hates him."

"Why does she hate him?"

"Because he's a violent, drunk sponge."

"And how do you feel about him?"

"I don't. But he upsets Jodie just by being with her sister, so I don't like him too much myself. What's he done?"

"Died."

Flax stared in shock.

The Appleton murder was not Barden's case so he had not got too involved, despite it being linked to his own. He knew the officers dealing with her death would have notified the family, which could well have been why Jodie was not at home; but surely she would have at least left a message for her fiancé.

He decided he would hold back on telling him Jennifer Appleton was dead as well. There was nothing to gain through total disclosure.

"We're looking for a man named David Straw," Barden said instead. "Do you know the name?"

Flax shook his head, thinking.

"How about Sean Mullin?"

"No. Sorry." He paused. "But I caught Jodie talking to a guy the other day. I made a joke of it, like I was jealous, but she got defensive so I had to tell her I was only kidding. Anyone could see I was kidding, but she was wound up tight about it."

"What did he look like?"

"Uh, tall, skinny. Could have done with a haircut about six years ago."

That, Barden decided, was David Straw. "What were they talking about?"

"I don't know. She got rid of him when they saw me. Was he the one who killed John?"

"We don't know, but we'd certainly like to ask him."

Flax looked from Barden to Lees and back again. "Wait a ... You think Jodie had something to do with this, don't you? You think Jodie and this guy killed him?"

"I never said he was murdered."

"So you've just come around to let her know the sad news? I don't think so."

"Why's that, Mr Flax?"

"Because you wouldn't have told me he was dead in such a deadpan tone."

"Oh, it would surprise you how deadpan I can be, Mr Flax."

"When did you last see Jodie?" Lees asked, the first thing she had said since talking to Flax. Barden had been wondering when she would pluck up enough courage to say something.

"This morning."

"And where is she now?"

"I don't know. She was supposed to be here, but she's not."

Barden toyed with the idea of telling him Jodie was behind it all, just to see what reaction he would get. Instead he asked, "Could she be at work?"

"That's where she's come from, yeah. But she should have finished a couple of hours ago."

Barden had a horrible feeling Mullin may have been on that train after all, and that he had not been alone. But it always paid to check these things. "Give us the address of where she works. And if she comes home, let me know immediately."

Flax gave them the address and Barden gave him his number before he and Lees departed. He had believed Flax, but that only meant his fiancée was more manipulative than any of them suspected.

When they arrived at Jodie's workplace, they received the answer Barden had pretty much expected.

"Jodie?" the woman at the office reception said when Barden flashed his identification. "She left ages ago."

"Did she seem tense or anything?"

"No more than usual. She's getting married; that's enough to stress anyone. Mind you, all that shouting's not good for her, either."

"Shouting?"

"With her fiancé. You know, I've never actually met him, but he's nothing like she described."

Barden desperately tried not to let his excitement show. "And they argue a lot?"

"I wouldn't know. First time I saw him was today. But they were outside screaming about something. I think he dropped by to offer her a lift and she didn't like it. Still went with him, though."

"Mr Flax drove by to pick her up?"

"That's right."

Mr Flax, who could not drive.

"Describe him to me."

The receptionist shook her head like a disregarding gossip. "Too thin for one thing, and what's with that mop of hair? If I was marrying him, he'd be shearing that off before the big day, let me tell you."

"Thank you for your time," Barden said. "Constable, back to the car please."

They did not speak until they were driving once more. Barden had not known how useful speaking to the receptionist would have been, but some of his theories were turning on their heads even as he thought them.

"You don't seem too unhappy by what we didn't find out," Lees said. "Jodie and Straw seem to have had an argument about something, but it didn't stop her going off with him though."

"You're letting your anger cloud your judgement here, Carrie."

"What are you, a Zen master?"

"Straw didn't just drop by to cause her grief. Jodie Appleton's been kidnapped."

Lees was shocked enough to confirm Barden's suspicions that she had not worked that out for herself. "Then I reckon she's going to be the next one to turn up dead."

"Maybe, maybe not. Straw's many things, but he's not stupid."

"What are you getting at?"

"Let's assume for a moment it was Straw who killed Tanner. Somewhere along the way he stabbed the guy, but no one saw him do it. That tells us he's sneaky, that he didn't want to be caught."

"I think that goes for most killers."

"Then he attacks Jennifer Appleton. Again, no witnesses. If he was going to target Jodie, why wait outside her work, then have a blazing row for everyone to see?"

"You're saying he didn't come here to kill her?"

"I think he came to talk. If she did indeed hire him to kill Tanner, perhaps he wasn't happy he was being stiffed on the pay. Mullin said he was paid pittance, and maybe Straw just wasn't the type of guy to take that lying down."

"So we're believing Mullin's word on this?"

"Until I have a signed confession I'm not believing anything, but I'm not about to throw out any intelligence, either. Villains panic, Carrie. It's one of the things every detective learns very quickly. And when they panic, they turn on each other. Mullin's out of it now, so that leaves only Straw and Jodie. I can imagine wherever they are right now, they're having a whopper of an argument."

"So we should just follow the sounds of shouting?"

"There's not much we can do to find her unless Straw makes a mistake. Sooner or later he will, so it all depends whether any more bodies have turned up by that point."

A sound filled the car and for a single moment Barden was going to tell Lees not to even answer it if it was Harry. Then he realised it was his own phone so pulled over as he dug it out of his pocket.

"Detective Barden," he said.

"Detective, this is Morgan Flax."

"What can I do for you, Mr Flax?" Barden tried not to sound tired, but he had not given Flax his phone number so the guy could call him every two minutes with questions about the investigation.

"I'm still in two minds about doing this, but … but you said Jodie might be in danger so I figured I'd trust you."

"Has she contacted you?"

"No. But I'm still in my apartment and I'm looking out the window. She's downstairs, getting out of someone's car. He looks like a scarecrow or something, and I don't like the way he's holding her wrist."

"Because they seem close or because it looks like he's kidnapped her?"

"Yes."

"Well which, man?"

"Detective, what's going on?"

"I'll explain when I get there. Don't do anything stupid and don't tell them you've contacted me. Just let them in, keep them talking and wait."

"Detective, I …"

"Listen. This is our prime suspect in the death of John Tanner. So, in answer to your earlier question, yes: I think your fiancée is very much in danger. Now, do what I told you and we'll be there to sort this mess out."

He hung up and pulled back onto the road. He knew Lees would probably have preferred that he answered the phone while driving, but he wasn't about to kill someone while on his way to save someone else. He was waiting so long for the comment to come that he glanced her way.

"No argument from me," she said.

Which meant he had been entirely right. If only he could read everyone so easily. If that was the case, he would have had this entire mess solved long ago.

CHAPTER ELEVEN

Becoming a detective meant a lot to Caroline Lees. It had been her goal for some years now and she had worked with it constantly in the back of her mind. When she had failed her detective's exam, she had taken some consolation in the fact it wasn't the end of the world. She could one day try again, and in the meantime she had a reasonably good life. Harry had been supportive, in his own way, and Lees had come to the conclusion life could have been worse.

Now she had all but thrown her career on the scrapheap because she had stuck by her man; only to find out he had hardly been worth the effort. She had lost Harry and she had probably lost her job; and all because she could not see what was staring her right in the face.

Lees had reached a decision: she would have made a poor detective.

As they raced back to Flax's apartment, all Lees was trying to concentrate on was the chance of doing the right thing before the end. She could not redeem herself, not enough to save any of her life anyway, but if she could put away a murderer she could at least finish on a high.

What she would do with her life afterwards was something she could think about later. If she was lucky – miracle-lucky – Barden might even support her somehow. Buy her a loaf of bread when she was starving, or something.

"The focus here is on saving lives," Barden told her.

"What? I didn't say anything."

"No, but you were thinking it. I can see it written all over your face."

"The man who has to pull over to make a phone call is watching my face while he's driving?"

"Carrie, I'm worried about you. I'm worried you're going to do something stupid."

"You mean leap in front of a bullet to prove my dedication to the job?"

"Something like that, yes."

"There's no heroine in me, Ray. And I'll take a hair follicle test to prove it."

They arrived at the apartment, but Barden was not foolish enough to pull up where Straw could see him. Lees had called for backup, but there was no sign of it so they decided to go alone. They had no idea how Straw was armed, but thus far there had been no indication of firearms. Certainly the man who murdered Tanner had a knife, and at that moment Lees would have placed good money on that someone being David Straw.

Barden raced ahead of her with far more stamina than Lees had ever possessed and it annoyed her somewhat that he was ten years her elder yet far fitter. He was not even breathing hard when they reached the door to Flax's home, while Lees was certain Straw would have been able to hear her own pounding heart as though it was her fist hammering on the door.

"You really do need to cut down on the pies, Carrie," Barden told her.

"A joke about my weight," she wheezed. "My bad day is complete."

They stopped at the door and listened, but could hear very little. Certainly there were voices coming from within, but there did not seem to be an argument, so they could not hear specific words. For all Lees knew, Straw, Flax and Jodie were all in this together and they were sitting inside having a nice cup of tea.

If they could have been certain the first strike would break down the door, they would have just kicked the thing and stormed in. However, bashing away at the door and not getting anywhere would have been the worst thing they could have done, so instead Barden did what Lees expected him to. He knocked on the door.

The voices within stopped, but only for a moment. They returned, frantic now, and Lees tensed as she heard someone approach the door. As it opened, Barden did not seem to be tensing himself to attack, so Lees tried to relax a little herself. It did not open far and the harrowed face of Morgan Flax appeared in the crack.

"Is Victoria in?" Barden asked loudly.

Flax now looked confused as well as terrified. "Vic ... Who?"

"Sorry," Barden said. "This is twenty-seven, I wanted thirty-seven. My mistake." Then he produced a credit card and held it up to the lock. As Flax closed the door, the latch caught on the card, preventing it from locking. Lees could not believe Barden had used a credit card like that. For one thing, it was one of those weird things which turned up on television, but mainly she couldn't believe it because she reckoned it would probably scratch his card. She certainly wouldn't be ruining her own property in the line of duty. If the police wanted her to use her credit card as a tool, they should be issuing their own cards for that; and while they were doing it they could offer good interest rates.

Barden waited for the voices to return to normal, for Flax to convince Straw that the man at the door had gone to the wrong flat. It was something Lees had not thought of trying.

Slowly, Barden pushed the door. No commotion sounded from within and when Barden got the door open by several inches, Lees was able to peer through. Several metres away, she could see three figures. One was Morgan Flax, sitting on a chair and looking scared and frustrated that he wasn't being believed. A woman Lees assumed to be Jodie Appleton was standing beside him, her hands by her sides, her fists trembling. She was angry, but far less fearful than Lees would have expected from the victim of a kidnap. The third man was David Straw: she would have recognised that scarecrow mess anywhere. He was also on his feet, waving his arms around theatrically, but did not appear armed.

Lees produced her police baton and flicked it so the metal length extended. Nodding to Barden, she prepared herself to run. Holding up fingers, Barden counted silently down from three, then threw open the door.

Lees shot into the room, shouting for Straw to get on the floor. It was designed to startle him, to make him hesitate and not place the hostages in danger. Lees was upon him before the man could even blink, her baton slamming into the back of his legs and forcing him to the floor. Grabbing his arms, she thrust them behind his back and shoved him forward so his face struck the settee and stayed there.

"Nicely done," Barden commented. "Mr Flax, Miss Appleton, are you hurt?"

"No," Flax said. "Who is he? Who is this man?" He was asking both Barden and his fiancée, knowing they both had the answer and wanting the answers to match.

Barden ignored him. "Your arrest I think, Constable."

Lees pulled Straw back to his feet. "David Straw, I'm arresting you for murder. You do not have to …"

"Murder?" Flax exploded. "So he did kill John?"

"Nasty business," Barden said. "Perhaps you'd like to stay here and leave us to it."

Lees tried not to smile. She knew what was coming and could see Barden was perhaps even enjoying it. Their case would only close with a confession and prosecution, but at least now they had some bodies to throw into a cell.

"Your arrest, Detective," she said.

"Jodie Appleton," Barden said, "I'm arresting you for murder. You do not have to …"

"What?" Flax said, making Lees wonder whether he intended to let anyone finish a sentence. "Murder? John? This is about John?"

"I didn't kill anyone," Jodie said fearfully. "I didn't do anything."

"Back at the station," Barden said, "would be preferable."

"I didn't tell them to kill anyone," Jodie said anyway. "Just throw him in the river. He was no good for Jenny, everyone could see that. I wanted him to get into a fight, to show her how violent he could be. I wanted him thrown in the river; I never told them to stab him."

Lees could see Barden was not happy with all of this coming out in the flat, but she had long ago learned that the truth came out whenever it wanted to. And it was better hearing it in the flat than never.

"So," Lees said, "why did you stab him, Straw?"

"I didn't. It was Sean. Sean stabbed him because Tanner scared him and made him run away. He didn't like being made a fool of, so he went back to the river and found Tanner climbing out."

So it was Mullin, Lees thought with a shudder. Which meant it was all her fault after all. She had Mullin in her house and she had let the man go. Then Mullin had gone on to kill Jennifer Appleton. If she had arrested Mullin when she had him in her house, Jennifer Appleton would still be alive.

"We're still arresting you both for murder," Barden said. "I'm not saying I don't believe you, but I don't believe you. Anyway, we can sort it all out with proper legal representation so everyone can be happy when the two of you are sent down for life."

They took them both in. Thankfully their backup had arrived by the time they returned to the street, so they didn't have to take the prisoners in Barden's car. They left Morgan Flax where he was; they had more than enough to deal with, without extra bodies complicating matters. While they were waiting for legal representation to arrive for the two prisoners, there was more than enough time for Barden and Lees to grab a coffee in the staff canteen. It could hardly have been called a canteen, Lees thought, but then what she was drinking could hardly have been called coffee, so it suited.

Across from her, Barden sipped his slowly, although his attention was on her.

"I know," she said before he could placate her with pleasantries. "I know it's all my fault. I had the opportunity to stop Mullin and I let him go. So Jennifer Appleton's death is on my conscience."

"You had Mullin?" he asked while he drank his coffee.

Lees realised she had not told him Mullin was at her house, but there was no point in hiding it now. "I was the one who told him Appleton's name, but you already know that. I was physically with him and could have arrested him, but I didn't."

"Glad to see you admit it at last."

"You already knew?"

"There's not much I don't already know. Carrie, you can't let it get to you. You can't think about what might have been. You screwed up and because of that a woman's dead. But you can't change it. So accept it, deal with it and move on."

She would have appreciated it if he had not been quite so blunt about it, but perhaps that was what she needed. Perhaps it was the only way to get her to put it behind her. "Have you ever messed up that badly, Ray? Has anyone ever died because you made a mistake?"

Barden seemed to straighten. It was only slight, but it was enough for her to notice. "Carrie, there are things about being a detective no exam can teach you. Sometimes making mistakes can make you a better soldier. That's what we are, in the end. Our job may be to investigate and make arrests, but essentially our role is to keep people safe. Sometimes people are killed through friendly fire. Should it happen? No. But every time it does, it makes us better soldiers because we're not going to make the same mistake again. Don't forget it, Caroline, but learn from it. The law is there for a reason. It doesn't matter whether we agree with it, it's there and we have to abide by it."

"Are you telling me to bring Harry in?"

"Mullin's gone and Straw never met you. He doesn't even know where you live. I don't see Harry could do that much good even if we did involve him. We nail a confession from Straw, we don't need Mullin or Harry. Which means the decision's taken away from me. It's down to you how you go on from this. If you want to come clean, I'll support you. Don't know whether I'll be able to do much to help, but I'll certainly not let you fight this alone."

"Thanks, Ray. You're much better for me than Harry ever was."

He offered a wry smile. "I'm starting to think that's not too hard."

In spite of everything, Lees felt herself relaxing. Ray Barden was a good man. Whatever happened, whatever she chose to do, she would not drag him down with her. Barden had a promising career; one which she would not allow him to sacrifice for anything.

"We should get on with this," Lees said. "Put the whole thing to bed."

"You still up for sitting in on the interview with me?"

"Should I? If it gets out that I know Harry, prosecution will have the case thrown out."

"I think we passed that point a long time ago. And I'd prefer you with me. There are a lot of sharks out here, Carrie, and I'd prefer to have a friendly dolphin by my side."

Lees looked at him strangely, trying desperately to work out what he was talking about. "That's the worst analogy I've ever heard."

"Yeah, it *was* pretty bad."

"I mean, you could have made some mention of your name being Ray, like a stingray, or something."

"I said I agreed with you, Carrie."

"Or you could have ..."

"Carrie."

She smiled. "You are so easy to wind up, Detective Barden."

Grumbling, he got to his feet. "Let's just go end this."

CHAPTER TWELVE

"I told you already, it was Sean."

David Straw was becoming irate, but Barden was still pressing the issue. Lees had watched the detective fight with Straw in the interview room, content herself to sit back and let him get on with it. Straw's solicitor, Lucy Fisher, was back and this time Lees even remembered her name. Fisher was not as cocky as last time, mainly because her client did not seem to have properly discussed what was going to be said during the interview. But Straw was sticking to his claim that it was Sean Mullin who had stabbed Tanner, which was convenient considering it wasn't Sean they had sitting across the table from them.

"I mean," Straw continued, "I told you that back at the flat."

"Jodie's flat," Barden said.

"Yeah, obviously."

"And what's your relationship with Jodie Appleton exactly?"

"She hired me. I told you that already."

"She hired you to throw John Tanner into the river."

"Yeah."

"But not to kill him? That was all off your own back?"

"No, that was Sean."

"Who killed Tanner because he made Sean look silly when he ran away?"

"Yeah."

"While you didn't feel silly at all being dragged away by Harry Gorman after Tanner had knocked you to the ground."

Straw paused, and Lees could see he had not expected the question.

Barden moved on. "Were you sleeping with Jodie?"

"What? No."

"Are you friends?"

"No. I never met her before."

"So a stranger comes out of the blue and offers you a hundred pounds to toss someone in the river?"

"No. She was a friend of Sean's."

This, Lees decided, was buck-passing at its finest.

Barden had agreed to allow Lees to ask whatever questions she felt appropriate and she decided they needed a more aggressive approach. Barden, of course, knew far more about this job than Lees ever would, but she had a feeling Straw would give them nothing otherwise. "Why'd you kill Jennifer Appleton?" she asked.

"I didn't. That must have been Sean as well."

"But you knew she was dead?"

"Jodie told me."

"I get the impression Jodie doesn't know."

"Oh, she knows all right."

Lees tried not to frown. Straw was suggesting Jodie Appleton had orchestrated the murder of her own sister, which made no sense considering this had all begun because Jodie had been trying to protect her sister from John Tanner. Only a truly warped mind would believe the best way to protect someone was to kill them.

"Let's start this again," Lees said. "Jodie doesn't like Tanner and wants him thrown in the river. You do that for her, then Sean kills him. You're saying Jodie wanted Tanner dead?"

"Well, it doesn't hurt her, does it?"

"So why didn't she pay you to kill him?"

"Because," Barden replied for him, "he doesn't want to admit he was paid to kill someone, even if it was Sean who did the deed."

"That makes sense," Lees said. "But everyone's blaming each other, so who are we supposed to believe?"

"What we need to do," Barden said, "is find out where Jennifer Appleton fits into all of this. We're concentrating too much on Tanner, but there's another victim here, remember?"

"Sure," Lees said. "Jodie did all this to protect her sister, so Jodie couldn't have been the one to have done it. That leaves the two guys she hired."

"And Harry," Barden said, "but he seems to have disappeared. And he was just a fall guy so it would have to have been one of the two Jodie hired."

"Right," Lees said. "One of them is a real sicko. Maybe he didn't like the fact her boyfriend knocked him down."

"Or made him look like a coward," Barden put in.

"But to go after the girlfriend? That's a bit low."

"Then we're talking about the lowest of the low, Constable."

"The lowest of the low who'd accept a hundred quid to toss someone in the river."

"Or to kill someone."

"You think they were paid to kill Tanner, then?"

"No," Barden said, "but when Sean stabbed Tanner, I think Straw realised they were both going down for murder. After all, they'd both accepted the same money."

Lees looked to Straw. "That's you, by the way. Feel free to jump in at any time."

Straw had adopted a nervous expression. Lees could see they had rattled him, which was a good start.

"Is that why you went to Jennifer?" Barden asked, leaning forward. "Did you panic when you heard Tanner had turned up dead? You asked Sean what happened and he told you he'd done it?"

"Sean *did* do it."

"And you realised the blood money would send you away. So you went to see Jennifer. Why though?"

"Because," Lees answered for him, "he knew Jennifer recognised him. You turned up at Jodie's work today, Straw. That makes other people see you, and it's not a clever thing to do, is it? Any other times you were with Jodie and someone just happened to see you? Did Jennifer ever just happen to see you? Not enough for her to remember you at the pub, but enough for her to remember you once her boyfriend turned up dead. You knew we'd bring Jennifer in and show her mugshots. You knew sooner or later she'd remember the scraggly guy with the unruly mop of hair from the river and connect him with a similar-looking guy she saw one time talking to her sister."

"I didn't kill Jennifer," Straw protested. "I didn't go over there to shut her up. I didn't do anything."

"You didn't mean to," Lees corrected. "You went to threaten her, no?"

"No."

"Silly me," Lees said. "Threatening her wouldn't have done anything except give her another good look at you. No, you went to blackmail her."

"No, I ..."

"Well, not blackmail, exactly," Lees interrupted. "You went to tell her everything. You went to tell her Jodie was behind it all, that it was her own sister that hired you and Sean. You wanted to make Jennifer understand if she put you away, you'd take her sister down with you." Even as she spoke the words, she understood it was a parallel with her own situation. She had protected Harry and now if Harry was caught they would both go down.

"I didn't kill her."

"You didn't take a weapon," Lees said. "So I accept you didn't *mean* to kill her. What happened? She screamed at you, got loud enough to make you nervous? And then you hit her?"

"By the way," Barden said, "we're getting DNA evidence together from the crime scene, so you might want to admit to at least being there."

Straw looked from one officer to the other. His solicitor said something to him about calming down, but Lees could see he was already surrendering.

"She slipped," he said. "I didn't hit her. She slipped."

"She slipped," Lees said, "with enough force to smash her brains out on the bathroom sink?"

Straw said nothing, but he did not need to.

"I think we have enough," Barden said. Lees was feeling elated they had a confession, but there was something off in Barden's voice. "Straw, give us Mullin or you're going down for both murders."

The solicitor made some remark about the legality of that statement, but Straw cut her off. "He's hiding out near the railway."

"Near the railway?" Lees asked. "You mean he didn't get on a train and go anywhere?"

"No. I can take you to him."

"Just give us the location and we'll find our own way, thanks."

Straw gave them detailed directions. He did so in a downtrodden fashion, but far from reluctantly. For the first time since the investigation had begun, Lees was beginning to feel they were at last getting somewhere.

They rounded off the interview shortly after and Straw was returned to his cell. They had a confession to the murder of Jennifer Appleton and a possible location for Sean Mullin. As they walked back to Barden's car, Lees felt in higher spirits than ever before. Barden, she noted, looked almost defeated.

"Why aren't you happy?" she asked. "We're well on our way to ending this. And ... Hold on, this means I'm off the hook. When I left Mullin, he didn't go off and kill Jennifer Appleton. My letting him go didn't do anything at all." She felt herself grinning like a fool. "I didn't have anything to do with Jennifer's death. I don't have to feel responsible."

"No," Barden said as he opened his car door. She did not believe she had ever heard him so defeated. "But I had David Straw in custody and I let him go. Then he went off and killed Jennifer Appleton, as you put it. You're not responsible for her death, Carrie. I am."

Suddenly, Lees did not feel so good about things after all.

"Just get in the car," he told her. "We'll go arrest Mullin, get a confession out of either him or Straw for the murder of Tanner; then I'm going to bed."

Lees said nothing and dutifully obeyed. It did not seem fair to tell her partner she was still relieved. If nothing else, this case had taught her the first person she should look out for in life was herself.

CHAPTER THIRTEEN

He had expected Mullin to be hiding out under a dank bridge or something, yet as Barden drove to the location Straw had given them, he could see the man sitting outside a pub, drinking a pint of beer. The name of the pub, *The Railway Arms*, was displayed on a sign directly over his head. Barden supposed this was a little joke between Mullin and Straw, but he did not find it especially funny. As Barden and Lees got out the car, they saw a train shoot past the pub on nearby rails above, for the pub was situated beside a small tunnel. He could imagine Mullin considered himself ingenious for having fooled the police.

With great prejudice, Barden intended to ruin his day.

Striding quickly towards him, Barden watched the man's face. He was so certain of himself, so confident that he had escaped the law, that he was not even paying any attention to anything around him. The instant he saw Barden his expression changed dramatically, for while he had never met the man before he could see Barden was the law. Noticing Lees striding along beside him confirmed his worst suspicions and Mullin was on his feet, stumbling over his chair and knocking the table over in the process.

Barden began to run, but Mullin was already moving, throwing his half-empty pint and entirely missing either of his targets. Barden did not believe he had ever seen someone flee in such a panicked fashion, but if Mullin was anything it was fast. As he and Lees gave chase, it became immediately obvious Mullin was going to get away unless they could do something drastic.

"I'll get back to the car," Lees said, "and try to cut him off."

"Wait," Barden said, seeing that Mullin was scrambling up a steep incline of dirt which led to the tracks above. "I think the idiot's slowing himself down for us. Find another way up and meet me on the tracks."

Without waiting for an answer, Barden launched himself onto the incline and scrambled up after him. Mullin's determination to escape lent him speed, but so too did Barden's determination to catch his prey. Several times he felt he could reach out and grab hold of Mullin's foot, but each time his prey eluded him. As Mullin reached the top and disappeared from sight, Barden knew he had to get over the rise in the next few moments or lose him for good.

He felt his foot slip and cursed, knowing his panic may well have cost him everything, and as he finally made it to the top he paused to take in the scene. Train tracks continued left and right, while on the opposite side there was a low wall, strewn with graffiti. Mullin could certainly have escaped over the wall, but it would have taken him a few moments to work his way over, and Barden had not been delayed enough for that. Looking both ways, he could see no sign of Mullin, but nor could he have escaped back down the incline.

Then Barden saw something else. To the left there was an area where the track split, ending after several metres in a buffer. Sitting against this was a cart or carriage of some kind which reminded Barden of a skip which had sat outside his house one time for months. It was filled with stones and grit and had enough weeds growing through it to suggest it had been there a long time.

It was the only place which offered any kind of cover for someone who wanted to hide.

"Mullin," Barden called as he started over the tracks. "Come on out, there's nowhere else you can go."

A head poked out from the side of the cart. "It was David," Mullin called. "David Straw's the one you want."

"For which murder?"

"Both of them."

"That's what he says, too."

Mullin paused. "Then why do you want me?"

"To testify that it was all Straw. You're a witness, Sean. The best witness we have."

"I'm not putting Dave away."

"It's either him or you, Sean. Your choice."

There were a few moments of silence, presumably while Mullin considered his situation. Then he said, "What evidence do you have it was Dave?"

"DNA," Barden shouted back, wondering why he was raising his voice. "We have enough to put him at Appleton's without a doubt, and without a knife we can't prove who stabbed Tanner; but if I can nail him for one I'll get him on the other through circumstance."

Another pause. "Are you tricking me?"

"No."

"But you would say that."

"Yes."

"So you are tricking me?"

Barden had dealt with frightened criminals before and always enjoyed it. "Whatever I say, you're not going to believe it. So how about you just come down to the station and find out? There's nothing much else you can do anyway. We know who you are, so unless you're going to flee to Spain or something, you might as well take the chance I'm telling the truth."

Again Mullin considered it, but didn't seem to believe him. Barden had never really expected him to.

"You can't come near me," Mullin said.

"Why? What exactly are you going to do?"

A rock hurtled over the top of the cart and landed on the track about ten metres from where Barden was standing.

"That's it?" Barden asked. "You're going to throw rocks at me until I leave?"

"I have plenty of rocks."

"And I have plenty of backup I can call in. If I tell them you're armed they might even come with guns." Another rock landed on the tracks and Barden did not even watch it roll away. "I'm sure they have better aim, too."

"Fine, I give up."

"Then come out."

"I can't. I've trapped my leg."

"You haven't trapped your leg. Now get out here."

"It's stuck."

Barden was not an idiot, but he also knew if Mullin wanted to keep to his story there was not much he could do. Lees was driving around somewhere, probably still trying to figure out precisely where they were, not having expected Mullin to just hide behind a rusty old cart. Calling in for backup was ludicrous and he would be laughed at for a very long time, even if there were officers spare. It all therefore came down to how much he wanted Mullin in a cell, which was very much so.

Grumbling, he started forward, keeping an eye on the side of the cart so he would be able to see if Mullin made any sudden moves. He could see the man's legs through the wheels and could not see either of them was stuck, but at least he now knew where he was standing. Crouching, in order to keep his eyes on Mullin's position, Barden reached the cart and began to move around it.

Then he heard a grinding sound and realised he had made a terrible mistake.

Leaping backwards, Barden saw the mound of rock and grit shift as though there was a gigantic demon mole within. Mullin had, unseen, pulled out the peg holding the cart's door in place and the entire content was coming his way. Barden cried aloud as black dust obscured his vision and pain shot through him as he felt the weight of the upturned quarry sliding over his legs like a pebbly beach coming in at high tide instead of the water.

As the dust settled, Barden was beset with a wracking cough, and he could see that while he had escaped the worst of the stones, his legs were pinned.

"Now who's trapped?" Mullin laughed as he came to join him.

"You're under arrest for whatever I can get you for," Barden wheezed, a second round of hacking catching in his lungs.

Mullin held out his wrists. "Fair cop, you got me." Then he laughed once more, although Barden could not see what was especially funny about it. He kicked at the spilled gravel and Barden raised an arm to shield his face. Mullin looked angry, although Barden could not see what he had to be angry about. He wasn't the one lying on the floor, having dirt kicked in his face.

"That's assault," Barden told him.

"You want to see assault?" Mullin drew a knife and Barden smiled. The sight must have disconcerted Mullin because his glee faded somewhat.

"That the same knife you stabbed Tanner with?" Barden asked. "Why bother asking? You're an idiot: of course it's the same knife."

Mullin stared at the blade and straightened his back somewhat. "I cleaned it, obviously."

"That counts as a confession. It also counts as idiotic, but that's a given."

"You really are looking for trouble, Detective."

Barden knew it was a gamble to make the man even angrier than he was, but he was buying time and so far it was working. "Here," he said, "have a rock." And he tossed one at Mullin with such force and accuracy that it struck him on the forehead and knocked him flat.

Scrabbling with his fingers, Barden tore at the detritus pinning his legs, knowing he only had a few seconds before Mullin recovered. He had not even freed one leg before Mullin was upon him, fists flying. Thankfully he seemed to have dropped his knife and in his rage had not thought to pick it back up before attacking. His fist found Barden's jaw, but the detective managed to catch the other and twisted so Mullin would lose his balance. Mullin fell on him but did not stop his attack, pounding Barden's face in a furious attempt to get him to let go.

"This was all going fine," Mullin was saying, "until David went and killed Jodie's sister. What was he thinking?"

Too busy in saving his face, Barden did not reply. If this was a confession, it could have come a little less painfully. However, he could see now where Mullin's aggression was coming from. It was never good when you couldn't rely on your colleagues.

Mullin flew backwards with a pained grunt and Barden lowered his arms. Lees was standing over him, holding onto some form of metal pole she had found by the side of the cart. Twisting the pole, she slammed it into the gravel about Barden's feet and loosened it enough for him to free himself.

On the floor, Mullin was moaning, blood pouring down the side of his face. Barden knew his lawyer would have a good time with the injury, but he did not mind the pain in his own face when he smiled at the thought of Mullin going to prison.

"Sorry I'm late; I couldn't find a way up," Lees said.

"Did you hear him confess to killing Tanner?"

"Sure."

Barden hesitated. "Did you?"

"It's handy if I did, so yeah."

Barden moved across to Mullin and cuffed him before he could regain his senses. "Care to tell us anything you can later deny?" he asked.

"Like what?" Mullin said, some of his anger dissipating now he knew he was caught. "You're police, you've probably figured it all out already."

"You mean about Jodie hiring you to antagonise Tanner?" Barden asked.

"Exactly."

"I get most of it," Barden said, "but there's still something that's annoying me. Straw killed Appleton because he lost his rag when he was blackmailing her; but why kill Tanner? Why follow him downriver just to stab him?"

Mullin looked confused. "Tanner knew about Harry."

Barden could feel Lees tense. "What about Harry?" he asked.

"He found out Jodie and Harry were together. That's why Harry set it all up. If Tanner told Flax his fiancée was already having an affair, he'd dump her."

"And?"

"You seen Flax? The guy's minted. Jodie's after his money. When she has it, she's going to disappear with Harry. That's why Harry knifed him."

"Hold on," Barden said, "you're saying *Harry* killed Tanner?"

"Of course he did. Why would I kill him? I'm not a psycho. I just kept the knife because I liked it. Like I said on the phone, Harry's the one who stood to gain from all of this." He glanced to Lees. "No one ever told me Harry's bit on the side was a cop, though."

Lees frowned. "What was all that other stuff you said on the phone, then?" she asked. "About Harry being your scapegoat, that you wanted him to take the blame?"

"I figured Harry was there with you."

"He was. So?"

"Guy had already knifed someone who could have grassed on him; you really think I'm stupid enough to put myself in the firing line?"

Barden turned him and gave him a shove before Lees could break down in front of him. He looked aside to see how she was holding up. "Sorry," he said. "I'm going to have to send uniform to pick up Harry."

"No," Lees said. "No you're not."

Barden sensed they were going to have a problem here. He could not imagine Lees was still sticking up for Harry Gorman, even if the murder accusation was not true. "Carrie, I …"

"You don't have to send uniform," she said flatly, "because I already called them while I was driving around looking for you. And, yes, I did it while I was driving. Shoot me."

"Carrie, I … I'm sorry it went down like this."

"I'm not." She shrugged. "Harry's a louse. It's just taken me a long time to realise that. He's manipulated me since the beginning. That story he told us about his girlfriend plying him with drink and then getting into an argument? Probably true, in case we dug deep enough to find witnesses to it. Which is also why he gave us an accurate description of Jodie Appleton: so the more we investigated, the less we'd suspect him. I reckon he might only have ever been with me at all because he knew I'd cover for him. What better way to foil the law than to have a cop in your pocket?" She was still angry, but was tempering it with logic. "It was probably a back door as well, in case we caught Jodie and she told us all about him. It was a way for us to think she was just lying."

Barden felt more relieved than he had since the entire mess began. "You know," he said, "detaching yourself from your emotions is a good start for every detective."

Lees held up a hand. "Save it, Ray. I did the right thing, I don't have to like it. Now I have to face up to hiding Harry all this time. Do you think they'll dismiss me?"

"I don't know. That's not up to me. But, when I'm asked, I'll tell internal affairs the truth. I'll say you committed yourself admirably to a difficult situation and that when the time came for total honesty and detachment, you did what needed to be done."

"They're not going to care, are they?"

"Probably not. But it's worth trying. We have to stick together, Carrie. I just want you to know I trust you. I trust you to have my back."

She seemed to smile at this, although he was not certain. "At least I have something left."

"And you know what? If you somehow get through this, I reckon you're going to make a fine detective."

They walked back to the car in silence. It only emphasised the fact neither of them expected there was even a chance Lees would ever be in a position to fail her detective's exam a second time.

THE WOMAN WHO CRIED DIAMONDS

CHAPTER ONE

"So, tell me about your day."

Ralph Watts looked over at me with an expression that could have soured holy water. Watts was the owner of the Teardrop, a diamond so oddly shaped it could have been called nothing else. He was in his late fifties, stocky, with a red face which was down to equal parts alcohol and stress. He was flustering badly by this point but I did not regret my comment. Call me cruel, but I've never passed up the chance to see someone almost explode with indignation.

"Mr Blake," he said from where he was sitting on a crate. "I'll have you know I don't appreciate such glibness after everything that's happened."

I glanced around. There were many ways to define 'after everything that's happened' and none of them were good. Even the promise that we were all going to die of asphyxiation was not helping me sort out the entire mess the investigation was becoming. One of them was guilty, I knew it. Proving it, however, had become something of a challenge.

But that was just my detective's mind thinking through the situation thoroughly and being somewhat optimistic. When we had walked into this room, Ralph Watts had no idea what was going to happen, of course, which only made the torment I was putting him and the others through far sweeter.

"Tell me about the Teardrop," I said, sitting comfortably on a storage box. "After all, there's nothing much else we can do."

My words did not placate him, but nor were they meant to. I knew all about the Teardrop, obviously. But talking would take our minds off our impending deaths so it was hardly a bad idea.

"The Teardrop is the ultimate in diamonds," Watts said. "It's 117 carats, with a finish as smooth as an angel's backside and the shine to match. Women would kill for that diamond, would do anything for it."

"That's a mightily low opinion of women you have there."

He did not look especially happy about my comment, but I've never much liked it when people gushed all over me about their weird loves. "The Teardrop," he continued slowly, with narrowed eyes, "is the most valuable artefact in this museum. Whoever stole it walked away with a fortune."

"To be fair," I reminded him, "whoever stole it is likely going to die."

"Conceded. But it's of little consolation."

"Hey," someone called, not kindly. "Why are you two still going on about that stupid diamond?"

I eyed the newcomer dispassionately. She had certainly seen better days. "Because, Miss Tarin, I am a detective and I'm going to find out who stole it." I paused. "If it's the last thing I do."

"You did not just say that."

I grinned, looked to where the inside of the door to the museum's vault prevented any of us from making a run for it. We all knew full well the vault was airtight, that we would all be long dead before the morning staff arrived to open the door. We also – all six of us – knew the thief of the Teardrop diamond was locked in the vault along with five innocent people. It may have been a contender for the greatest botched jewellery theft ever; but if I was going to die, I was certainly going to solve one final mystery before the end.

"If you'll get comfortable," I said, enjoying myself far too much to be healthy, "I'll begin."

CHAPTER TWO

It all began on poker night. Sally J always put on a great spread, but then Sally J's a real woman and knows how to look after her interests. She's also the best poker player I've ever known and most nights walks away with the contents of the pot. The rare times she loses, I reckon she does it just to make sure we all come back for a rematch. Sometimes she even sits out the game, because for Sally J it's all about getting people into her house and around her table. Sure, it's illegal since she takes a cut and doesn't have a gambling licence, but Sally J doesn't overcharge for the use of her house and I've always kept my ear to the ground for signs that anyone in the law even knows about her. There are no drugs on her premises, no alcohol is consumed during the game; no one's even allowed to smoke. It's a good, clean game where the winner walks away with a small fortune, minus the cut the house takes. And Sally J herself was always wonderful company. I could never quite place her age but there were a thousand quirky little things which made me suspect she was a lot older than the fifty-five I would have put her at.

I took what I liked to think of as a casual glance at the two cards sitting on the table before me, bending them so I could see them before letting them drop once more. There was nothing casual about it, however, since it was the half-dozenth time I'd taken a peek at them. It wasn't a good hand, but a pair of queens certainly wasn't a bad one. Nothing showing on the table was helping me, though, so I was all ready to fold just as soon as someone grew confident enough to bet anything. There was nothing special about the table – it was the same round table a million other poker players might use. The lights were always dimmed to create an atmosphere, but Sally J always liked to liven things up with candles or lava lamps or something. One time, at Christmas, she had on one of those annoying pictures with the flashing lights. Presently, she had a new lamp covered by a weird shade which gave off a rainbow effect. It wasn't putting me off my game as such, but I'm sure Sally J just does these things to annoy the players.

The man opposite me tossed in some chips and I folded, thankful to be out of the hand. Sally J was playing that night, but had not been doing so well herself. There were three other players – two of them folk I'd seen before, with one new face. That was the thing about games at Sally J's: she always made sure of the credentials of the players she invited, but the rest of us didn't necessarily know them. They weren't strangers as such, because Sally J would have been an idiot to have allowed strangers into the game, but if I'd never seen them before I had no idea what their technique was going to be like.

The newcomer was the one who had raised the bet and raked in a small pot. His name was Ralph Watts, which was all I knew about him. That and the fact he was in his fifties and looked like he could have taken better care of himself. He was flustered while he was playing, as though he didn't expect to be winning as much as he was, and I put this down as a great asset for him since it meant no one would be able to tell whether he truly was holding a bad hand. I couldn't shake the feeling I'd seen him somewhere before.

"I'd say beginner's luck," I ventured, "but I can tell you've played before, Watts."

Watts gave nothing away as the next cards were dealt. It was Sally J's turn to deal, and she did so silently, keeping a careful eye upon every player. She was good at that – it was one of the things which separated the bad players from the good – but I could not help feel she was watching less for the game and more for the potential fireworks. After all, Sally J knew Watts from somewhere and perhaps he had deeper issues than we wanted revealed when our money was on the table.

"I've been around," Watts said.

"You played a lot of poker dives?"

"A few." He glanced at his cards. There was the slightest frown to his brow which told me if he had indeed played a lot of live poker he had certainly lost a lot of money. I've never played any other venues myself. Sally J's a friend and since I like poker I play at her place. That's more than enough for me. The only other time I've played poker is with some colleagues at work, but that went down badly. I'd never recommend playing any sort of game with people you have to spend any appreciable time with.

I looked at my own hand but it wasn't anything to get excited about so I folded outright. It afforded me the opportunity to lean back and think some more about Watts. All I could think of was that he might have been someone from Arlene's side of the family; but since I had split from Arlene nearly five years earlier I'd pretty much forgotten the names of her family members, let alone their faces. Arlene and I had been one of those stupid cases of marrying when we weren't in love. We were both in our late twenties when Arlene got pregnant, so I was young and stupid enough to figure it the honourable thing to ask her to marry me. After Gemma was born, we both realised having children is the most stressful thing anyone can do. Sleepless nights did nothing to ease our agitation and soon enough we were shouting at one another. The separation was soon to follow and Arlene took Gemma and that was that. My temperamental work hours and the fact I'm a man didn't help me any and I was just lucky Arlene and I didn't hate each other, so I could still see Gemma.

There was only one person in Arlene's family I ever cared about and that, of course, was Gemma. I'm not sure I ever counted myself as a part of Arlene's family, even when we were married.

"Maybe," Sally J said while she raised the pot, "you recognise Watts from a line-up?"

"I never said I recognised him from anywhere."

"It's written all over your face, dearie."

Watts threw in some chips to meet Sally J's bet. "You're a cop then?" he asked me, trying not to sound nervous.

"An off-duty detective."

"Never much liked cops."

"Thanks."

"No offence."

"That has to be my favourite phrase."

Sally J tossed in her hand, which was odd considering I'm sure no one had raised the bet after her. "I'm curious now," she said while the cards were gathered for the next deal. "You ever been arrested, Ralph?"

It took me a moment to remember Ralph was Watts's first name.

"No," he said in a tone which indicated a yes.

"What for?" Sally J asked.

"Can we just deal some cards?"

We played in relative silence for the next few hands and knocked out the two players I haven't bothered to name. They both went home to explain to their wives why they had just lost a lot of money, but I didn't think much of them after they left the table. If they were stupid enough to gamble what they couldn't afford to lose, they deserved to go home broke. I wasn't a family man, and so long as I had enough money to look after Gemma there was nothing in the world I wanted. Gemma, rent, food – in that order. Every other penny I had could be gambled away and I wouldn't have cared for anything.

This attitude always gave me an edge when I played poker. The pay of a detective wasn't great, but it was enough to be able to lose a game every couple of weeks.

It was my deal and I tried to concentrate more on the game. After all, with only three of us left, there was a greater chance of me walking away with all the money. I was already resolved to Sally J winning the game, but after a swift chip-count I determined I was probably a little way ahead of her. Watts was still winning, but I knew either of us could break him down so long as we showed a little patience. Also, since he had discovered I was a detective, he had become a little anxious.

I dealt myself pocket kings; entirely randomly, I assure you. Before any of the community cards are exposed, two kings is the second best hand you can be dealt, so I was rather happy when Sally J made an initial bet. I was even happier when Watts called it, so I raised it and was called by both players. Sally J still seemed to be focusing on Watts, but I knew better than to think for one moment her mind was off the game. Watts himself wouldn't look at me, which was a sure sign he was some kind of criminal. But, like I said, I was off-duty and all I cared about in that moment was winning some money off him.

"Tell Matthew about the Teardrop," Sally J said in a quiet, flat tone which made me think she may have been talking to herself.

"He doesn't want to hear about the Teardrop," Watts said.

I overturned the first three community cards. Two, six and king, all unsuited. Things were definitely looking up for me; at that moment I had an unbeatable hand. Sally J checked and so did Watts, so I placed a bet. Sally J folded and Watts called.

"I sure would like to hear about the Teardrop," I said, not having any idea what it could have been. "What is that? A nightclub, a rocket ship?" I decided to throw Watts off his game as much as possible. "Kind of sounds like a new type of drug hitting the street." I turned over the fourth community card. It was another six, which was annoying. There were also now two hearts on the table, and since I wasn't myself holding a heart that could only work in Watts's favour. I needed to take him out before the final community card was laid.

"It's a diamond," Watts said absently. "Check."

I looked at the two hearts on the table. "Diamond? Where?"

"The Teardrop, not the cards."

"Right." I made a bet: a big one. "I'm assuming it's shaped like a teardrop," I ventured.

"Yes, and it's worth a lot of money. Raise."

I had not expected that and looked at the rather large stash of chips he had suddenly pushed into the centre of the table. For someone who had not made any bets on the hand up until this point, Watts was making an unusual move. I could only guess he was holding two hearts and was hoping for a flush. The only alternative was that he was holding two sixes and had just hit a four of a kind, which would have destroyed me. Or perhaps he was just a bad player and was holding a six, which meant he had struck three of a kind on the sixes, not taking into consideration I might have done the same with the kings.

Ralph Watts was either the greatest player I had ever faced, or the lousiest. If he had been playing as much live poker as he and Sally J had suggested, I was inclined to go more with the former.

But, like I said before, I can afford to lose a little money here and there. Usually it was to Sally J, but a loss is a loss. "All-in," I said, shoving everything forward.

Watts did not hesitate and called me. If he lost, he would still have a few chips remaining, but not enough to come back into the game as a major player. Not with an opponent like Sally J. His speed of accepting the all-in bet, however, gave me cause to think he would not have to worry about anything Sally J had to throw at him.

Hesitantly, I turned over the final community card. It was thankfully not a heart; nor was it anything which could have helped either of us. I was not about to feel any relief, however, until Watts showed me he was not holding anything that could beat me. That he was holding a pair of sixes was statistically not likely, but there had to be a reason for him to have gone all-in.

Looking annoyed with himself, Watts laid down his cards. I could see the redness in his face deepening, his sweat exploding from his pores. The tension and anxiety were over for him and there was no longer anything to hold back. I saw his cards then: two hearts. So he had been going for a flush after all. He had called my all-in knowing he at the time was holding the weaker hand. I had already made my three of a kind, while he was still waiting on a card.

It was things like that which separate the good players from the bad, which make poker a game of skill more than luck. Playing the odds is all well and good, but the fact was Watts did not have the winning hand and knew it. A bad player would have gone all-in on that; only a terrible player would have called someone else's all-in.

I realised in that moment what a truly awful poker player Ralph Watts was.

Showing my own hand, I gathered in my winnings. I now had immense chip power, while Watts was left with hardly anything. I've heard said that statistically you should only play one of every six hands, for poker is all about waiting for the good cards to be dealt you. Watts no longer had enough chips to wait those six hands, which meant he would be forced into playing half-decent cards, such as king-seven suited. I had no doubt at all within fifteen minutes Watts would be out of the game.

Sally J was a different matter entirely. By that point I had so many more chips than she it was laughable, but I never for one moment grew complacent about her. I had seen Sally J come back from being down to just enough chips to cover the ante.

For Watts, however, the game was over. He was a man a mile beneath the surface of the ocean holding his breath and frantically clawing in a dark direction he just hoped was upwards, knowing it wouldn't make a difference anyway since his lungs were about to burst.

I almost felt sorry for him.

Then I remembered the Teardrop.

"Cheer up, Watts," I said. "You still have that diamond. How much precisely is it worth?"

"More money than I'll ever see," he said despondently. Sally J had taken up the cards and was dealing slowly.

"Why do you even have a diamond?" I asked. "Are you a collector?"

"I was, one time. The Teardrop was my crowning glory. I hired it out to a local museum on a three-year contract."

"Is that how you make a living then?" I asked, glancing at my cards. "Buying expensive baubles and hiring them out to museums?"

"I used to, yes."

"Used to?"

He made a show of studying his cards. There was a possibility he truly was trying to figure out whether to play this hand, but the man was already broken.

"Used to?" I pushed. "You don't any more?"

"I've had some financial worries lately, Detective Matthew."

"Detective Blake actually." There was no need for me to say that, of course, but I figured I knew what the man meant. He had a gambling addiction, probably debts to go with it, and he didn't want to talk about it. I'd just taken the man's money, so I could respect his wish for silence. I tried to think of a tactful way to tell him not to play poker any more, especially since he wasn't any good at it, but didn't fancy being punched in the face.

"Two pair," Sally J said. I had not even noticed, but I'd absently been calling her bets. I glanced back at my cards to see I only had a pair with an ace kicker. I resolved to pay more attention to the game else Sally J was going to quietly take all my money from me while I was distracted.

"There's an interesting story behind the Teardrop," Sally J said in a relaxed tone. "It's why I fell in love with it."

"Do tell," I said. "Sally J seldom showed her emotions about the poker table and it was always a wonderful moment when she allowed people to gain an insight into her mind.

"There was once a princess of a faraway land," Sally J began. "She was young, beautiful and very much in love. She was also naïve and stupid, but that's beside the point. She fell for a knight of her father's court, the champion of the realm. Everyone believed the king would welcome the match, for the king saw this knight as his brother. But the king was a jealous soul who would not see his daughter wed to any man. So he sent the knight on a quest to win the hand of his daughter. He was to catch a rainbow and bring it back to court.

"Naturally, the king expected him to fail. But the knight set off determinedly towards the birthplace of rainbows and waited for the right weather conditions for one to form. There are a great many tales of the perils he had to face, of the monsters he had to slay, but suffice it to say once a rainbow appeared he fought his way through everything and with one mighty swing of his sword sent such a fear through the rainbow that it leaped into his outstretched sack. The knight brought the sack back to court and as he opened the drawstrings the entire palace was filled with such wondrous light that no mortal eyes had ever beheld.

"The king had no choice but to accept the knight for his son and preparations were made for the wedding. On the eve before the marriage, however, the king paid a visit to the knight and asked to see his rainbow once more. As the knight opened the sack, the light exploded outwards and, closing his eyes to the blinding display, the king slipped a knife through the back of the knight, killing him instantly.

"The princess burst into the room to find her beloved lying dead upon the floor and the king vanished. The rainbow, cowering in the corner, saw the princess's grief and was moved. In terror of the king's vengeance and in sympathy for the girl's sorrow, the rainbow entered her body and there it remained until she died many years later. Afterward, any time that the princess cried, her tears would be tiny prisms of diamond, shot through with magnificent colour by the frightened rainbow inside her."

It was a strange story and I was sure I could see some glaring holes in it. But we were in Sally J's house and it would have been rude to point them out.

"Lovely," I said. "If only Jack had found her up his beanstalk instead of the goose that laid the golden eggs. Would have given both stories a happier ending." Or was it Aesop? I wasn't sure, but we weren't there to discuss fairy tales.

Watts dealt the next hand and, after Sally J and I both checked, decided to go all-in. I was holding queen-jack suited so opted to call him. Sally J folded, so Watts and I both got to turn over our cards. He was holding ten-eight suited and everything went downhill for him from there. He did not even last five of the fifteen minutes I'd predicted for him.

"I should call it a night," he said, looking nowhere near as annoyed as I had thought he would. It only reaffirmed just how used to losing the man was. "Thanks for the game, Sally."

No one called her Sally. I don't know why, but no one even shortened her name to Sal. She was always Sally J. Whether J was her middle initial or the start of her surname, I had no idea. But that was what people called her.

Watts gathered his coat and left the room. I had never felt so sad watching a fellow player depart.

"He going to be all right?" I asked.

"He's had worse losses, Matthew."

"Sure, but that man really shouldn't be playing poker."

"No."

"How do you know him?"

A small smile creased her lips. "You know the rules, Matthew. I don't tell other players' secrets. Just as I wouldn't tell him about your secrets."

"That's fine. I don't have any secrets. Unless you wanted to get into my bad marriage, but I'm sure he wouldn't be interested."

"There's always Shenna."

I huffed. I've known Sally J for years and I'm always surprised by the amount of information she's managed to wheedle out of me without my knowledge. But then, she wouldn't be the perfect poker player if she wasn't able to do that.

The two of us continued playing, neither of us mentioning Ralph Watts or the Teardrop again. Over the following hour I watched my chips slowly walk across to her side of the table, to the point that we became pretty much even. Sally J dealt me two kings so I decided to risk everything and went all-in straight away. She called, and it turned out I had three more chips than she did. It was a make or break for either of us, but I could not help feel she was going to turn over two aces.

Sally J revealed her hand: ace-king, suited. I was winning, sure, but she had one of my kings and that ace was unsettling me, as were the two spades staring up at me. I was winning, but Sally J had far too many outs for me to be comfortable.

She somehow managed to avoid hitting anything on the community cards and her game went the same way as Watts.

"Almost," she said, leaning back as I packed away the chips for her.

"Who needs to eat anyway?"

"I'm not so sure my priorities are the same as yours, Matthew."

God, she knew that too?

She smiled again. There was something behind her eyes which I didn't like. She wasn't laughing at me as such, but Sally J always knew far more about people than they knew about themselves.

I left for home and found it had started to rain. Pulling my coat more tightly about my neck, I headed for the train station. It was not a long journey back home but the train was filled with all the drunks one usually finds on any public transport after eleven. I managed to block them out and was surprised to find I was thinking a lot about Watts. I had met men like him before, knew his type well in fact. I still couldn't figure out where I thought I'd seen him before, but by that point had decided I was just seeing him as a stereotype. So many people were torn apart by addiction, and gambling was always one of those no one seemed to be sympathetic to. I felt guilty having taken the man's money, even though next game it would likely go over to Sally J. Everything, eventually, always goes to Sally J.

When I got home, I went to bed. It had not been a good day.

Work the next day was a pain, but I had already planned my workload for the day so I wouldn't have to think too much about anything. I sat at my desk, going through the paperwork I was going to have to somehow reach the end of. I sat there for the first two hours in silence; it was only when a mug of coffee plopped on my desk that I acknowledged there were other people even alive in the office.

"Long night?" Holbrook asked.

"Yes."

"Lose again?"

"I don't always lose."

"No. But you don't always win either."

I looked up into the playful eyes of my fellow detective, Jane Holbrook. As usual, her round face was alive with passion. I would never have said Holbrook was especially pretty, but there's more to beauty than looks. I remember coming onto her one time I was very drunk, but thankfully she didn't even mention it to me afterwards. We had both turned thirty, neither with any prospects, so I knew I didn't have to feel bad about whatever terrible lines I had spun. I wasn't sure whether my guilt made me a decent human being, or just someone who knew he was a creep.

"Thanks for the coffee," I said, taking a sip. "Any chance of some digestives?"

"Well, if you buy some let me know."

"You sound annoyingly happy today, Jane."

"I have an interesting case, that's all."

"I'm not sure when I last found this job interesting, Jane."

"Not every day you get to investigate a jewel heist, though."

"A jewel heist? Which jewellers was knocked over?"

"Not a jewellers, Matt. This was a museum. When the curator was doing his rounds, he found this really expensive diamond had just vanished. No witnesses, no evidence, nothing. It's like a ghost whipped it away."

I could hardly believe what I was hearing but there was no need to ask the obvious. "This diamond," I said regardless. "It wouldn't have a fancy name would it?"

"Sure it did. It's called the Teardrop."

I sighed in dejection. Of course it was.

CHAPTER THREE

It wasn't my case, but I asked Detective Holbrook whether she wanted any help and she had never turned down an offer for help. I asked whether she had a list of suspects, and it turned out she hadn't been exaggerating when she had said the diamond had vanished. Our first stop should have been with the owner of the diamond, but I wanted to arm myself before talking to Ralph Watts. As such, I suggested to Holbrook we speak with the closest thing we had to a witness, and that was the security guard who had discovered the jewel had disappeared. From the notes Holbrook had passed to me, it seemed the cameras in that area of the museum had been knocked out, but we only had the guard's word that the diamond had done a disappearing act. I was not sure whether I actually suspected the guard of being a part of the theft, especially since it was too obvious, but it would still benefit the case to talk with him.

We arrived at the museum and were told he would be fetched for us, which was fine since it gave us the opportunity to examine the crime scene. The area had of course been cordoned off with a police line, with constables on guard and no access to the public. It was strange looking at the splash of colour against the otherwise stark whiteness of walls interspersed with garish paintings. It was almost as though the crime scene was a display; I could imagine there had been more than one attempt by visitors to photograph the area.

Passing beyond the police line always gave me a little thrill, I don't know why. Perhaps it was because I was doing something only a handful of people were allowed to do, that I could then turn and look at all the gawkers and know I had got one over them. That day, however, I was not paying much attention to what was behind me, but rather the somewhat foolproof measure of protecting the diamond. The plinth upon which the diamond had rested was about chest-height, allowing onlookers to lean in for a really close look. It seemed to be formed of wood, with an expensive-looking cloth draped over the top in a tidy fashion. There was even a dip in the centre to show where the diamond had been resting. The glass casing which had surrounded the jewel was rectangular and thick, with no markings to indicate anyone had cut through it. I could see no wires, but assumed there would have been some form of alarm hooked up to the thing.

It was only at this point I began to wonder how large the diamond was. I had never seen a diamond but had been labouring under the impression this one was the size of a football. But a diamond the size of an earring was of incredible value, so the importance of a much larger jewel was only then beginning to sink in. But my fantasies were running away with me, so I resolved to ask someone the size of the thing just so I could sleep at night.

One thing I was slowly coming to realise, however; at some point in his life, Watts must have been a very well-off man. It truly was saddening to think how far he had fallen because of his gambling problem.

"I take it we've dusted for fingerprints?" I asked Holbrook and saw by her expression how successful that had been.

"Nothing," she said. "They're pulling fibres from the cloth in case the thief touched it when they took the diamond, but I don't hold out much hope on that."

I stared at the glass casing. "How did they even get in?"

"I have no idea. It would take a master jewel thief to remove a diamond without touching the case."

For a moment, I thought Holbrook meant something by that comment, but I could see she was lost in thought as she examined the crime scene. So long as we weren't both thinking the same thing, she could make all the comments she wanted.

"Detective Holbrook?" a voice asked. There was an elderly gentleman being allowed through the police cordon. It would have been better were the constables not doing that sort of thing, but the damage was already done. The man was tall, with short white hair and a slow, slightly stooped walk. He wore a dark blue uniform which was pristine and well cared for. I would have placed the man somewhere at the tail-end of his seventies, but that was likely just me being mean.

"Bob Harkett?" I asked, extending my hand. "Detective Matthew Blake."

Holbrook shook his hand with a smile. "You were the one who found the Teardrop missing?" she asked due to politeness since we would not have called for him otherwise.

"Yes, miss. The strangest thing, it was. I almost didn't notice." He spoke slowly; perhaps because of his age, perhaps because he was wary while talking to the police.

"Almost didn't notice it missing?" I asked. "That's not something to admit to."

"I'm generally looking for intruders, sir. A missing painting's obvious, but I couldn't imagine someone taking a diamond without breaking the glass. Still can't."

Just because I agreed with him, it did not mean I valued his opinion. "Talk us through what happened," I said.

"Nothing really happened," he said. "I was passing through this room on my rounds. I saw the case was empty and raised the alarm."

"How do you do your rounds?"

"I walk through the museum."

"On a set pattern?"

"Usually."

"And how many times do you pass through each room?"

"Three."

"So, since you almost didn't notice it was missing, the diamond could have been stolen long before you realised it was missing? You could have walked through this room once or twice before realising?"

Harkett's initial response was to deny this, although he stopped to think. "Possibly, but I can't see I would have missed it completely."

"Do you check every exhibit?"

"No. But I do a proper job."

He sounded angry as he said this, although I hadn't been especially suggesting otherwise.

"How long have you been working here, Bob?" Holbrook asked.

"Forty-five years next month."

It was not an answer I had expected. It meant Harkett had been working at the museum longer than I had been alive. I could see why he would get touchy at someone insinuating he might have been remiss in his work. After so long, the job had likely enveloped his life. I could not imagine myself staying in the police quite so long, nor would I have wanted to.

However, there was something bitter in the way he had given his answer: something I could not quite understand. It was not that he despised those forty-five years, but something else.

"What can you tell us about the Teardrop?" I asked.

"I don't know anything about diamonds, sir."

"How big was it?"

"Oh, about the size of a golf ball."

Suddenly my football idea sank quicker than the Titanic.

"Did you ever notice anyone hanging around it?" I asked.

"Everyone hangs around the exhibits, sir. It's what people do in a museum."

I admit it was a stupid question.

"There's always Benny Shoreham," he said offhandedly.

"Benny Shoreham?"

"He started working here two weeks ago. Young kid. Doesn't fit in, though. Street punk, know what I mean?"

"Believe me, I know what street punks are. You say he hangs around this area?"

"Fascinated by the diamond. I've tried to talk to him a few times, but he doesn't have time for an old fellow like me." He paused. "Do you think he might have had something to do with stealing it?"

I could sense Harkett was annoyed at the possibility. To have someone working on the inside, right under his nose, was not something the old man had considered until that moment. It was helpful information and I filed it away as possibly useful.

"Do you know the owner of the diamond?" I asked.

"No, sir. Why would I know the owner?"

"I'm just trying to build a picture here, Mr Harkett. You say you've been working here for forty-five years. You must be coming up to retirement soon."

His eyes flinched and I was glad I had played a hunch and asked because I could see I had hit on something. "There's nothing wrong with me, sir," he said.

"I never said there was. Me? I'm looking forward to retirement. Chance to put my feet up and lie in the sun for a while."

"I don't need to retire, sir."

"I get the feeling there are people who disagree?"

"They say I'm too old to do the job, but I'm not. No one knows this place like I do. No one knows all the places a thief can get in or where he could hide."

It was a story I had heard before and it was always a shame when it happened. But the old man had admitted he had almost missed the theft and I was still not convinced he hadn't walked straight past an empty cabinet twice already. His position raised an interesting theory, however, for suddenly Bob Harkett had himself a motive.

I caught Holbrook watching me. By the mild frown she wore I understood she did not share my idea.

"How many thieves have you caught over the years?" I asked. "Must be a fair few, I'd wager."

"Not as many as you'd think, sir. It's not a glamorous job, but it's a good one. Steady, predictable, controlled."

I was fleshing out my opinion of Bob Harkett. He had spent so long in this role that it had indeed taken over his whole life, but it was more than that. He was one of those people that needed to lead an ordered life, who didn't like surprises. I could imagine he might get annoyed if something ever happened which went against his perfectly ordered system. A thief would not necessarily fall into that category, since it was his job to prevent thievery, but the sheer chaos thrown up by a thief should certainly bring out some reaction in the man. That he did not seem all that bothered suggested, to my mind, the possibility that the theft had not been outside of what he had expected.

We had few further questions for Harkett and then allowed him to get back to his rounds. Holbrook and I remained at the crime scene. We spoke quietly, even though we were only in earshot of the constables, and then only if we called over to them. I could see a cloud forming over Holbrook's face and knew what was coming before either of us even spoke a word.

"He wasn't involved, Matt," she said.

"How do you know that? Guy gives nearly half a century to a job and out of the blue it tells him he's no longer required? Maybe he helped the thief to show them why they need him as a guard."

"He shows them his ineptitude, you mean. Losing the diamond under his care isn't a good way of convincing his employers to keep him on."

"Then maybe he's just hidden it somewhere. Maybe he intends to whip it out and play the hero. It'd make all the papers; they'd have to keep him on then."

Holbrook sighed. "Matthew, you always see the worst in people."

"I see the truth in people. Everyone's at least a little bad, Jane."

"So what's a little bad about you?"

"What's not?"

Her entire body sagged. "You really do have a low opinion of everyone, don't you?"

"Everyone lets you down in the end, Jane."

"Even yourself?"

"Especially yourself."

A commotion sounded from the edge of the cordon then and we both looked over to see one of the constables struggling to prevent someone from passing through. The newcomer was in his fifties and, if possible, looked even redder than when last I'd seen him. It was only then I realised the problems Ralph Watts might cause me. After all, I could hardly hide my association with him, and I didn't want to be connected in any way with the crime since it would compromise the investigation. Also, our poker games were not entirely legal.

But I had made my bed, as it were, and couldn't now complain about who I'd invited to lie with me.

We walked over to meet him, since we didn't want him beyond the police line. The constable was visibly relieved to see us approach, but while Watts ceased trying to get through he did frown.

"Blake?"

Holbrook looked at me curiously. "You know each other?"

"We met last night," Watts said. "Blake, where's my diamond?"

"No idea," I admitted. "But that's why we're here."

"Bit of a coincidence," Watts said. "My diamond goes missing just hours after you take all my money. Now it turns out you're the one I have to trust to bring it back."

"Actually, it's not my case," I said. "I'm just helping out."

"Oh, that makes it so much more legit."

I could see his point. "Watts," I said, "I didn't steal your diamond. What would I want with a diamond?"

"Money, obviously."

"Money again," Holbrook said. "Mr Watts, what do you mean when you say Detective Blake took your money?"

"Poker," Watts said.

"Ah."

Taking money from someone at poker is not, of course, illegal, but the fact Sally J takes a cut while acting as the house certainly is. Even if I claimed ignorance and said I assumed she ran everything by the taxman, it would not have looked good for me. I very much doubted Watts knew about Sally J taking a cut, however, so I did not feel all that threatened by him.

"We'll find your diamond," I told him. "We've only just got started and already have a few leads."

"Which are?"

"Not something we can discuss with you at this stage."

"Pardon me," Holbrook said sweetly, "but I don't think proper introductions have been made."

"Ralph Watts," I told her. "He owns the Teardrop and loans it to the museum. What's your insurance like for something like this anyway?"

Watts was taken aback. "I hope you're not suggesting I had anything to do with this."

"Why is everyone so touchy today? No, I was just asking about insurance."

"Not a lot," Watts said, looking annoyed with himself. "I couldn't afford to properly insure it, but there hasn't been a successful theft from this museum in fifteen years so I figured I'd be safe with paying the lowest amount of cover."

I did not even have to check that to know it was true, although of course I would. Watts had likely lost so much money to his addiction that he was having to cut corners wherever he could. I knew what I would find when I checked his records: he would have begun with the best cover and slowly would have whittled it down to the bare minimal required.

"We'll be in touch once we know anything," Holbrook said. "Do you have a contact number?"

"Of course I have a contact number." He patted down his pockets and found a business card. He held it out to Holbrook, but I took it instead. I was curious why Watts would have business cards. It was old and dog-eared and was clearly a throwback to a time when he had been a success. Everything on the card confirmed what Watts had told me the previous night: that he had at one time been in the business of buying and selling expensive jewels.

"Mr Watts," I said, "do you have any enemies?"

"Enemies? What kind of question is that?"

"I just find it odd the diamond was stolen now, when your cover on it's so low. And why nothing else in the museum was taken. It's as though someone's targeting you."

I could tell from his face this was something he had not considered. "Why would someone target me?" he asked.

"That's why I asked about enemies. Maybe you owe money to someone?"

"I owe money to a lot of people, but none of them would break into a museum to steal my diamond. They'd take it through the courts and seize it legally."

That made sense, but it all depended on who he owed money to. The banks, obviously, would not send in their clerks, but if Watts had been borrowing from underworld figures they might not have been the type of people who favoured treading the legal path. It was something else to look into.

"Just find my diamond, Blake," Watts said. "Do your job and find my diamond."

He walked off in a huff, which was fine since I had no further questions for him anyway.

"Maybe it's not a good idea for you to help me on this after all," Holbrook said. "If you're connected to Watts, it's …"

"I'm not connected to Watts. Besides, when we find his diamond for him he's going to be the happiest man alive. I suggest we split up. You talk to this Benny Shoreham while I look more into Watts."

"Watts?"

"I'm interested in these people he owes money to. There might be something there we can use."

"If I'm talking to a suspect I need someone there with me."

The law was a frustrating thing sometimes. The word of an officer was not considered truthful unless there was a witness. Ludicrous as it was, Holbrook was right.

"Then just find him and bring him in," I said. "If we talk with him down at the station we might get him to crack."

"We don't have anything to arrest him on."

"Then don't arrest him. He's young and stupid. Make him think he's just helping us with our enquiries. He'll probably see it as a big adventure, until we pounce on him."

Holbrook did not agree with my methods, but I could see she was not going to argue. I had to remind myself this was her case and I was just helping, but it had become personal to me. Unless I could find the Teardrop, Watts would blow a fuse and this could all explode in my face. Holbrook was right when she said I should have taken a step back from the investigation, but the truth was I never should have involved myself in the first place. If internal affairs looked into any complaint Watts raised, they would discover I had volunteered my services only after I had learned the nature of the case. They would suspect me of all sorts of things and, even though I was innocent, all manner of nastiness could come out of it. I'd seen internal affairs tear someone apart before. He had been innocent too, but even after they had cleared him his career was in tatters. No one, not even his peers, ever trusted him again and eventually he transferred. I looked into him six months later and found he had resigned after being hospitalised for stress-related issues.

I was not going to become that person.

Leaving Holbrook to find Benny Shoreham, I headed back to the office. I had some research to be getting on with; research which, if done properly, could well save my entire career.

CHAPTER FOUR

It did not take much effort to pull up information on Watts. It turned out he was known to the police, which was interesting. He had an ex-wife named Elizabeth Payne and, while the details in the police report were sketchy, it seemed he had laid into her a couple of times when he was drunk. Perhaps Watts had more addictions than just gambling: perhaps he just wasn't a nice person. Either way, I sat at my desk wondering whether it might be an idea to talk to this woman. The arrest had been less than two years earlier and it seemed the charges had been dropped. Why the ex would have dropped charges was anyone's guess, but since it had only happened recently I figured she might still be able to give me an insight into the man. Finding a reason to talk with her was the problem, since Watts was the victim and not officially a suspect.

It was something I would have to put off for a while. We still had Benny Shoreham to interview, and then there was old Bob Harkett who might have nabbed the diamond in revenge for being forced into retirement. As much as I was interested in the man, Ralph Watts was going to have to wait.

With regards to his debts, I had less luck. I called around all the favours I could and threw his name out to all the usual moneylenders. No one had heard of him, which meant he had likely borrowed money from less than reputable sources. I knew I could talk to my informants and get them to ask around, try to figure out an answer for me, but I doubted they would have much luck. The only way I was going to get an actual name would be through Watts. If things got really bad and the investigation was going nowhere, that was when I was going to have to confront the man and get him to tell me. If he wanted his diamond back, he was going to have to cooperate fully.

It only occurred to me then I could have just asked him back at the museum and he may well have told me. Holbrook was right; I search so much for the worst in people, I invariably find it.

Gathering up some paperwork, I headed out to find Holbrook. I had a message that she had returned with Shoreham and was waiting for me. I went to the custody desk and saw a young man sitting nervously in one of the nearby chairs. He was about eighteen, nineteen, with the tall wiriness left over from his teenage years. He was dressed in the same uniform as Harkett, but I didn't need that to know this was Benny Shoreham.

"You set?" Holbrook asked, coming up behind me without me noticing. Shoreham looked up at that point and saw me. He did not look happy to be there and I could all but smell his guilt.

"Sure," I said and the three of us walked into an interview room.

I've always liked interview rooms. Their stark walls and lack of windows suck dry any ounce of personality or knowledge of the passage of time. They're like the casinos in Las Vegas, purposefully designed to make you sit at the blackjack table for a few hands, not realising four hours have passed by.

Shoreham sat opposite us without a solicitor – he was not under arrest, so didn't need one. That was not to say he could not have had one had he asked, but it wasn't a point I intended to raise with him.

"You want something to drink?" I asked, offering him a cordial smile.

"I'm good."

"I'm not sure anyone's good," I replied as I sat. "I was just a little while ago telling my colleague there's a little bad in all of us."

"And," Holbrook said, not happy with my manner, "a little good."

I shrugged but gave no verbal response.

"Benny," she said, "this is Detective Blake."

"Charmed," I said.

"You mind if we ask you a few questions about the diamond?" Holbrook asked.

"That's why I'm here."

"How long have you worked at the museum, Benny?"

"Not long. About two weeks."

"Do you like it?"

He shrugged. I leaned back and allowed Holbrook to lead the interrogation. I knew I tended to come across in a heavy-handed manner, but Holbrook was always my good cop.

"What's your job at the museum?" she asked.

"I clean."

"Clean what?"

"The floors."

"You don't have anything to do with the upkeep of the exhibits?"

He seemed to realise why she was asking for a distinction. "No. I don't restore or clean anything. Just throw soapy water over the floor and mop it around a bit."

I grunted. It was such a technical science. I could see why he hadn't set his sights higher when he left school. Holbrook glowered at me. We'd had this conversation before. She's of the opinion that so long as someone's hard-working, it doesn't matter what job they have. I'm more of a guy who measures success in a man's achievements. I've put away dozens of kids just like Benny Shoreham and in a heartbeat I'd put him away as well.

"When did you last see the diamond?" Holbrook asked.

"The day it vanished. Maybe four, five hours before."

"So you *have* seen it then?"

"Sure I've seen it."

"Do you pay much attention to the exhibits?"

He shifted uncomfortably. "Some of them."

"Can you tell me about any of the paintings hanging on the walls in the same room the diamond was kept?"

"No. Why would I look at paintings?" He seemed confused, but I could see in his eyes he knew he was being accused.

"What interested you about the diamond then?" Holbrook asked.

"You kidding me? That thing was massive. The way they had it in that case, it caught the light and shone like a little star. It made me think of those films, you know, where the jewel thief drops in on a wire and the entire room is filled with lines of light."

"You know a lot about being a jewel thief?" I asked, deciding that was a bad cop sort of question.

"No," he said too quickly. "Just what I see in the films."

"So," I continued, "you used to stand before the diamond, fantasising about the best way to steal it?"

"That's not what I said."

"Sure was."

"Well it's not what I meant, then."

I sat back again, folded my arms and let Holbrook take over.

"What made you take a job in the museum?" she asked.

"It came up. I figured I'd give it a few months while I found something better."

"Does it pay well?"

"No."

"Do you enjoy it?"

Shoreham looked at her as though she was an idiot. "Of course I don't enjoy it."

"Well," Holbrook said, showing him a smile, "now we've finished the nasty business of accusing you, we should move onto accusing other people. Have you seen anyone hanging around the diamond?"

"No."

"What do you think about Harkett?"

"Old Harkett? Nothing. Why? You think he stole it?" Shoreham laughed. "He'd take a bullet for that place. He wouldn't steal a pencil, let alone a diamond."

"Anyone else you could put in the frame?"

I knew precisely what Holbrook was doing because I'd used the same tactic myself on numerous occasions. She was allowing Shoreham the opportunity to drop someone else in it. If he seized that opportunity, it likely meant he was guilty.

Unfortunately, Shoreham was either innocent or too stupid to pick up on the hint.

"No," he said. "I have no idea who stole it."

"Then there's not much more we need you for, Benny," Holbrook said. "Thanks for coming. If we need anything else, we'll let you know."

"There was one thing," he said quickly. I found it strange he should look so anxious now that we had told him we were done with him. Nor could I believe he had just thought of something, which meant whatever he was about to say was pre-planned. He had been waiting for us to get it out of him, but now the interview was over he was all but blurting out his information.

"Go on," Holbrook said.

"There was a woman who came three days in a row to see the Teardrop."

"There must have been a lot of people through that museum. What made her stand out specifically?"

"You really want a guy to answer that?"

I grunted again. What he was saying actually sounded plausible, but it did not mean I liked it any better.

"What did she look like?" Holbrook asked.

"She was in her thirties, I'd say. Short, with curly red hair. I spoke to her on the third day, asked her what she liked about the diamond."

"What did she say?"

"No idea. I wasn't listening to her."

I grunted yet again but this time Holbrook agreed with me.

"I got her name, though," Shoreham persisted. "She said her name was Shenna."

I did not mean to react, but there was nothing which could have stopped me. I bolted upright, my arms uncrossed, and I stared wordlessly across the table at Shoreham. He visibly recoiled at my reaction and I could see genuine fear to his eyes. But he said nothing more and there was nothing I myself had to say to him on the matter.

"I see," Holbrook said as though the name had not affected her at all. "Did you get a surname?"

"No."

"I don't suppose you got her number?"

This time I snorted. "Leave off, did he." Shoving my seat back, I rose and left the interview room. I did not share parting words with Shoreham: there was little point in antagonising the situation. Nothing was being recorded, so I wouldn't have anything to explain to my superiors afterwards. I just needed to get away from Benny Shoreham, Jane Holbrook and anyone else.

Leaving the station, I walked to the railing overlooking the parking area. My mind was a haze, with too many conflicting emotions charging through me. Shoreham was lying, I knew he was lying. There was no way Shenna could be involved in this, no way she would have come back into my life in this way. It had been so long since I had seen her, so long since I had admitted to myself I even wanted to see her again.

But Shoreham's mention of her made me understand that I did want to, and I felt a thrill run through me that Shenna could have been somehow involved. She was the perfect suspect, of course she was, and even seeing her again in this capacity would have been better than nothing. Better, perhaps. Shenna Tarin in her prime was truly a marvel to behold.

"You all right?"

I did not turn at Holbrook's voice. "You get rid of Shoreham?"

"He's gone, yes." She spoke calmly and I knew she understood entirely what I was thinking. "There's more than one Shenna in the world, by the way."

"It's not the most common of names."

"Nor is it unique."

"It's her. Shoreham's talking about her, all right."

"He could be lying."

"He could be telling the truth."

She positioned herself against the railing beside me, leaning into it and gazing out into nothingness just as I was doing. "If it is Shenna, why would she tell Shoreham her name the day before she stole the thing?"

That was true. I clearly wasn't thinking straight if I hadn't even seen that much.

"Still," I said, "he didn't pick the name out of nowhere."

"Maybe he knows something about you. Maybe he's playing you."

I looked upon her with a frown and could see her worry.

"Matthew, I'm scared for you. If someone's been digging around your past ... well, people don't do that without reason. I don't know whether Shoreham's involved, whether he's just picked up something someone wanted him to pick up, or whether Shenna really is behind all of this. But whatever the truth, I think you're in trouble here."

"I'm always in trouble, Jane. Don't worry about me so much."

"If I didn't worry about you, who else would? You never take care of yourself."

"Never learned how to."

"Stop joking with me."

That tone of Holbrook's voice was something I never argued with. It was the reason I always thought it was a shame she had never tried motherhood.

"Shenna Tarin means more to you than all these half-rumours," she said.

"Meant."

"Means."

I ignored her.

"There's only one way we can be sure whether she's involved," Holbrook continued.

"And what's that?"

"Ask her."

I laughed, then realised she was being serious.

"I can't talk to Shenna," I said as though it was the most obvious thing in the world.

"Why not?"

"You know why not. If people started connecting us, I'd be in trouble."

"That was a long time ago, Matthew."

I did not reply to that. My relationship with Shenna Tarin was something I looked back on fondly, but it was also firmly in the past. Dredging up history was never a good idea, but I had no doubt she had been the Shenna Shoreham had mentioned; and that meant I needed to get to her before anyone else did.

"I'll talk with her," I said, reaching my decision.

"First you have to find her."

"That won't be a problem, Jane. I know precisely where she lives."

Holbrook looked at me quizzically. "You never let go, did you?"

That was a question I decided to ignore. At least until it was asked across the desk in an interview room.

CHAPTER FIVE

Walking back into Shenna's life after so long was weird for both of us. I didn't call ahead, didn't make any contact at all before knocking on her door. Shenna Tarin lived in a nice house with a spacious front garden and a lot of privacy. It was not the abode of a millionaire, but certainly Shenna must have been doing all right with herself. What type of work she had been doing since we parted company, I had no idea. I knew where she lived, but that was more so I could avoid her, not because I was stalking her. As I knocked on her door, I almost hoped she wasn't in; but when the door opened and I saw her for the first time in five years, I no longer cared about the missing diamond. Shenna Tarin was even more beautiful than I remembered. Short of stature, with a hardy, muscular frame without sacrificing any of her femininity, Shenna Tarin remained a goddess. Her large brown eyes were liquid pools of chocolate, her curly red locks framing her cherubic, rounded face in such a way it was though an angel was leaping through a hoop of fire. She was dressed in jogging bottoms and a blouse, which was Shenna all over. Her pert nose wrinkled slightly as she recognised me, although her eyes flared with a passion she could not hide.

"Matthew Blake," she said dryly. "It's been a while."

"Five years too long, Shen."

"Am I under arrest?"

"Uh, no."

"So this isn't business. You mean the great Detective Blake has condescended to pay me a personal visit?"

I looked away, embarrassed. "Actually, I ..."

She released an exaggerated sigh. "Should have known. Come on in, then."

She walked away from the door, leaving it open. I felt ashamed for having gone to her with accusations. We did not exactly part on bad terms, but at the time I didn't get the impression she wanted me to pop by for a chat any time soon. As the weeks turned to months and the months to years, I lost myself in my work and promised myself I would look in on Shenna soon. As with most good intentions, soon never came.

Stepping through the doorway, I closed it behind me and wiped my feet on her welcome mat. Her hallway was small, decorated with a single picture of a lion and furnished with a rack upon which shoes and an umbrella rested. I removed my shoes and added them to the rack. Just because I hadn't spoken to Shenna in five years, it didn't mean I didn't respect her.

I followed her to the living room, which was far homelier than I would have expected. There was a large settee and a couple of matching comfortable chairs. The carpet was thick, while what appeared to be a real fireplace sat dormant in the hearth. There were a few cabinets and chests, with an antique tea set on a table beside a chair. There was clutter, but in Shenna's natural way it was still tidy. Glancing about the walls, I found several original paintings, while the mantelpiece was filled with brass antiques.

"The paintings aren't stolen," she said as she sank into one of the comfortable chairs. "If that's what you're thinking."

I had actually been looking for evidence she had got on with her life, but there were no pictures of men. I wasn't sure how I felt about that but forced myself not to think too much about it at all.

"Nice house," I said. "Cosy."

"I know. You didn't come here to tell me I had a nice house."

"No. We had a guy down at the station. He …"

"I'm good, thanks. How are you?"

I bit my lower lip, wishing I wasn't feeling quite so shaky. "Sorry, Shen. I'm glad you're good. I'm … well, same old."

"How's Gemma?"

"You remember Gemma?"

"Cutest baby I ever saw."

"Still cute, but not a baby any more. Coming up to six now."

"Wow, time flies. What have you been up to the last five years?"

"Nothing much," I said. "Work. You?"

"Oh, broke into a few bank vaults, replaced the Mona Lisa with a forgery no one's discovered yet. That sort of thing. Can I get you some tea? I have digestives."

"You remember I like digestives?"

"I remember a lot of things, Matthew."

I looked around the room again. "Seriously, what have you been up to? You're doing well for yourself."

"Matt, sit down: you're making me feel like you're interrogating me."

"Sorry." I sat dutifully.

"Better," she said, pouring from the antique teapot into two china cups. I should have known better than to assume the set was for show. Shenna liked the best things in life, but nothing with her was ever just for show. If she collected stamps, I could imagine she would lick the back of the old ones she didn't like any more and send out postcards.

"Thanks," I said, taking the cup and saucer.

"I deal in antiques," she replied at last. "Buy and sell, that's me."

"If anyone would know what to look out for, it'd be you."

"When I got out, I reckoned it was time to put my skills to good use."

"You ever deal with jewellery?"

"All the time."

"Ever hear of the Teardrop?"

"Strange-shaped diamond kept in a local museum," she said, sipping her tea while keeping a cautious eye upon me. "Why?"

"Someone stole it."

"And that someone has to be me?" she asked calmly. "Or have you come to ask for my help in finding it?"

"I came because we pulled in a suspect and he mentioned you."

"Oh?"

"You ever hear of Benny Shoreham?"

"Should you be telling me that name?"

"No."

She laughed. It was a sweet sound. "Same old Matthew Blake."

"So you've never met Shoreham?"

"Nope. What did he say about me?"

"Have you ever been to see the diamond?"

"I've been to the museum, yes. And I saw the diamond. I stood there a long while trying to work out how I'd steal it."

"Shen?"

"No, I didn't steal it. I just find it fun to think of how I'd steal something sometimes. That's one pretty diamond; of course I'm going to work out how to steal it."

"And how would you have stolen it?"

She eyed me with curiosity and more than a little anger. "First tell me what he said about me."

I couldn't see that being unfair. "He said you were there, staring at the diamond. He said you came three days in a row and eventually he talked to you and you told him your name."

"That'd be stupid if I went on to steal it."

"That's what Holbrook said."

"Jane's still around? How is she?"

"She's fine."

"Good. Well, I wasn't at the museum three days in a row. I went there once, yes, but I didn't go back and I certainly didn't go around telling strangers my name." She paused, assessing me once more. "You ever move on, Matthew?"

"I never move anywhere. Why would Shoreham say he spoke with you?"

"No idea, never met him. You see much of Arlene?"

"Only when I pick up Gemma."

"She still a bitter cow?"

I sighed. Shenna and Arlene had never got along, understandably, but I didn't regret anything that happened.

"She was never good enough for you, Matthew. That's why you came to me. We had some fun, then you turned me in anyway and went back to work. Things like that could make a girl twisted, Matthew." She smiled. "But it sorted out my life for me, so I'm not going to complain."

"Arresting you was the hardest thing I ever did, Shen."

"And you were right to do it."

Arlene and I had always had our problems, but when I was investigating a string of jewellery heists, I met Shenna Tarin. I met her several times in fact, and knew she was the one committing the thefts. She toyed with me, always stayed one step ahead of me, and flirted all the way. I got as close to her as I could and for some reason she let me. That we became lovers was one of the factors which destroyed my marriage, and nailing Shenna for the thefts was a nightmare for me. She was the cleverest opponent I'd ever faced, but I managed to outfox her. As I took her in, I remember her laughter being warm and sincere. Aside from at the court case, it was the last time I ever saw her.

But it seemed since coming out of prison she'd turned her life around. That was good – amazing in fact. Shenna Tarin had at last turned her skills and knowledge of antiques to a legal advantage.

"So," I said, "how would you have done it?"

"Like I said; that depends why you're asking me."

"Because you've become a part of my investigation and I'm trying to figure out why." Shenna Tarin was the most dangerous human being I had ever encountered and it was never wise to tug a lion's mane. I didn't like to threaten her, but my work took precedence over my feelings. If it didn't, we might have still been together.

"The floor," she said.

"Come again?"

"The diamond was protected by a laser security system, but I'd have come in through the floor. That plinth it was on? Hollow wood. Cut a hole in the floor and you can squeeze through the plinth, unscrew the base the diamond's sitting on and the Teardrop would fall into my lap. Screw the base back on and no one would ever know the diamond was taken that way. Until they moved the plinth and found the hole in the floor, of course." She sipped her tea once more. "Have you checked yet for holes in the floor?"

Once again I was amazed at her genius. "I'm betting when we do, we'll find a great big hole."

"And an angry Ralph Watts."

That shocked me as well. "You know Watts owns the diamond?"

"Sure. I was the one who suggested he buy it."

"You what?"

"Honestly, Matthew, your research techniques are really letting you down today. What do I do for a living?"

"You buy and sell antiques."

"And what did I do when you met me? Apart from cat burgling on the side, I mean."

"You were an independent jewellery assessor," I said, trying to remember all the details. "You'd hire yourself out to wealthy people and help them value jewels they intended to buy, identifying faults and giving your professional opinion."

"I did a few jobs for Watts. He had a good knowledge of the jewellery industry, but everyone can do with a second opinion."

I did not like what I was hearing. Before coming to her, I had hoped Shenna would not have had any idea what I was talking about.

But not only did she admit to going to the museum to stake-out the Teardrop, she also revealed she knew Watts and helped him buy the thing? It was too much of a coincidence for me to like.

"Are you going to arrest me?" she asked, finishing her tea.

"I don't have any evidence for that."

"You have circumstantial evidence. You have a witness to place me at the scene of the crime and my confession to that. And I also know the victim and am very familiar with the best way to have stolen the jewel."

"But you didn't steal it."

"No. I didn't." I could sense the first trace of anger from her then and warned myself once more about making her angry. I knew I had to get her on my side. Shenna Tarin did not do anything by halves: she had been the worst enemy I'd ever had, and the greatest lover.

"Will you help me?" I asked.

"Help you?"

"You're the best in the field and someone's trying to muscle in on that."

"Don't try to engage my reputational pride, Matthew. I'll do it for you, not for me."

"So you'll help?"

"Of course I'll help. All you needed to do was ask."

I suddenly felt ten years younger, but Shenna had always had that effect on me. She was such a bundle of energy and joy I began to wonder how I had ever managed without her.

"So," she said, shifting in the chair which was suddenly too comfortable for one who had just discovered she was going to be returning to the high life of adventure, "where do you want me?"

She could not have more reminded me of her old ways if she had tried. The thing I missed most about my time with Shenna, I realised in that instant, was her happy flirtatiousness. Nothing bothered her, which was probably why she had always been one to take so many risks. And the greater the risk, the deeper the thrill. I don't know whether I was ever actually in love with Shenna, or just the thought of what she represented, but I could easily have not much cared about love if it meant keeping her in my life.

"I'm going to talk to Watts's ex-wife," I said.

"Ex? That would have been Elizabeth, right?"

"Do you remember her maiden name as well?"

"Not sure I ever knew it."

"What can you tell me about her?"

"Nothing much. She was a little younger than Watts, if I remember rightly. I always figured she married him for his money. If they divorced, could it be because he started running out?"

"Possibly. He also beat her up."

"Nasty fellow. What do you mean by possibly?"

"Watts is slowly gambling his wealth away. That diamond was pretty much all he had left to his name."

"And it would be tied to the museum by his contract with them." She nodded. "It's not like he could just sell it to raise some cash. His car, his home, his dignity ... all of that could be sold, but the diamond is a museum piece. Yes, it's his and technically he could pull it out and sell it, but he has a contract with the museum for it to be on display for another X number of years. If he broke that contract, he'd have to pay them a huge sum of money. Plus his credibility would be shot." She thought about it a moment. "I can see why you suspect him. And why you suspect his ex. She could have taken the term money-grabbing to a whole new level."

"I can't take you with me to see her."

"Of course you can't. But while you're talking with her, I can be talking to my own contacts."

"What contacts?"

"In the business. I buy and sell antiques, remember? Someone somewhere along the line might well try to sell me the Teardrop. And, if they don't, I may be able to find out who took it. No one takes a diamond just because they think it's pretty. You can't wear stolen jewels to a ball, after all."

"I hadn't thought of that."

"So you really did come to me just because my name was mentioned by Shoreham?" She sounded disappointed, and I knew it was not an act. "In this instance, Matthew, I'm the greatest resource you have. Use me."

I rose reluctantly. But if I stayed there I would never get any work done. "Don't tempt me, Shen. Thanks for the tea."

"Sure, Matthew. I guess I'm going to have to get some digestives in for next time."

I left without managing to convince myself I had gone to see Shenna about anything to do with the investigation.

CHAPTER SIX

I picked up Holbrook and together we paid Elizabeth Payne a visit. Along the way, I explained about my meeting with Shenna. Holbrook remained unusually quiet and I knew she was judging me. But then Holbrook was always judging me about something. If I asked her, she would say she just wanted me to be happy, and for the sake of our long friendship I chose to believe her. Personally, I just think Holbrook likes controlling people's lives, which isn't necessarily a bad thing in our line of work.

"You should stay in touch with her," Holbrook said once I'd told her everything. "After this is over, I mean."

"Even if she turns out to be the thief?"

"Is there anyone you don't suspect?"

"Maybe myself. But then you never know whether your doctor's well-versed in hypnotism."

"Do you suspect me?"

"No." I paused. "But it's always the ones you least suspect."

"I give up."

I don't know why I talk that way, especially to Holbrook. I don't like letting people get close to me, I know that much. That might have something to do with Arlene, Shenna or something else I've entirely forgotten. It might just be because I'm a grumpy old man without even being old. Whatever the case, I don't like talking about my feelings so I'm probably never going to know why I don't want people close to me. Or maybe that even answers the question.

To be honest, I'm not sure I even care that much.

As we drove through Payne's neighbourhood I noted how wealthy it was. Being divorced from Blake had certainly paid off, unless Payne had her own line of work. It was possible she knew as much about the jewellery business as her ex-husband, but I had no idea. It was probably, I reflected, something I should have asked Shenna about.

We pulled into a driveway formed of a million pebbles. There was no gate to protect her front garden, but said garden was not as large as those of some of her neighbours. The house itself was a mansion compared to anything I was ever going to afford, but again it was not as large as some of those around her. I was of course searching for a motive, and if Elizabeth Payne was a woman who liked to keep up with the Joneses, there was every chance she could have arranged for her ex-husband's diamond to be stolen. The trick Holbrook and I would therefore have to pull off would be to determine whether Payne was still bitter enough about her divorce to think Watts still owed her something.

"You want to do the talking?" Holbrook asked as we exited the vehicle.

"Depends whether the woman's a viper. Sometimes bad cop goes well with vipers."

"I can do bad cop."

"Well I can't do good cop, so we're not switching roles."

By this point we had reached the front door, framed by large stone sculptures of some kind of animal. As I rang the bell I realised I had half expected to find one of those big, elaborate knockers, but it seemed Miss Payne retained at least some of the throwbacks to bring her down to the level of us mortals. It was amazing how much I had judged her before even speaking a single word to her – before even seeing her, in fact.

The door opened and I don't know why, but I had been expecting a butler as well. The woman who stood before us was in her early-to-mid forties, with less-than-striking features but what I can only call a royal carriage. That's not to say she had horses pulling her forward, but that she carried herself in a royal way. Then I noticed the stone animal carvings outside her door were of horses and the image just wouldn't fade.

The woman was wearing jeans and I could not quite imagine this was Payne.

"Yes?" she asked with a frown.

I flashed my identification. "Detective Blake, Detective Holbrook. We're looking for a Miss Elizabeth Payne."

She held out her hand and I briefly wondered whether she was asking me to shake it. Then I saw her palm was facing upwards so I placed my identification into it. She took a step back, one hand still upon the half-open door, and read my card carefully. When she handed it back, she looked only marginally less confused. "How can I help, Detective?"

"May we come in?"

She considered a moment, then opened the door fully. "Yes, of course."

Holbrook and I walked in to an expensive abode and I unconsciously wiped my feet. It was the second such house I had been to that day and if I was going to continue the trend I would develop an inferiority complex by the time I got home. We were not offered tea and biscuits, which was a little disappointing, but I did take a seat unasked, so I like to think I got one over my host. The room, I could see, was spacious and devoid of character. Unlike Shenna's home, which was cosy and cluttered, Payne seemed to be someone who favoured a minimalist approach. There were one or two expensive paintings or sculptures about the room, but I got the impression she had spent all her money on these items and could not afford much in the way of personal luxury. The art would be to impress the neighbours when they came to visit, but pleasing them had restricted Payne in her own life.

I knew all of this could well have been totally untrue, but as first impressions went, it was certainly a clear one.

"Would you be Miss Payne?" Holbrook asked.

"I would. Please, sit."

Holbrook did so, Payne sliding into her own chair as though she had never bent her spine in her life. She looked upon me with the eyes of a tigress whose home had just been invaded by a particularly slouchy tiger. It was a good enough impression to have made on her and one I had spent long years trying to perfect.

"Do you know why we're here?" I asked.

"Why would I know why you were here?"

"Quite. When was the last time you spoke with your husband, Miss Payne?"

"Ex-husband."

"Quite."

She glared at me. I resolved to drop that word into conversation more often.

"I haven't seen or spoken with Ralph for a long time, Detective. What's he want with me? Is he suing me for something?"

"Does he do that often?"

"He's never sent the police around to me at all, actually."

"We're not here at the behest of Ralph Watts," Holbrook said. "That's not how the police do things. You have a nice home, Miss Payne."

"Is that a crime?"

I noticed she was unusually touchy and could see Holbrook had noted it also. That meant I wasn't just seeing the worst in people. Payne felt guilty of something, that much was definite.

"Do you know what the Teardrop is?" I asked.

"No. What?"

"Really?" I raised an eyebrow. Shenna had told me she had helped Watts purchase the Teardrop, and that would have been back when Watts and Payne had been together. "Your husband's had that diamond for years, Miss Payne."

"Ex-husband," she reminded me sourly. "And yes, I remember the Teardrop. It's a common word, Detective. If you want me to equate the word to a diamond you could just ask."

It was a fair enough point but I did not believe her for a moment. "What did you think of it?" I asked.

"The diamond? Nothing. It's a diamond."

"Are you in the jewellery business, Miss Payne?"

"The jewellery business? No."

"And what work do you do?"

"I'm a solicitor."

It explained the big house.

"Do you live alone?"

"No. I live with my fiancé. Roger Anderson. You want for me to call him so you can interrogate him as well?"

"And what would Mr Anderson do for a living?"

"He's a judge."

"Ah."

"So between us we know all the ins and outs of proper legal proceedings." She settled a little more comfortably at last; there was even a small smile to her face. "So, Detective, what can I do for you today?"

Holbrook took up the questioning. She was always better at spelling things out for people, since I had a tendency to delve into sarcasm.

"The Teardrop's been stolen," Holbrook said. "We're looking into who might have had a motive to take it."

"Anyone who wanted money, I'd wager. I appreciate you coming over to tell me, but I have no financial ties to the diamond any more. It was bought during my marriage, it's true, but Ralph was allowed to keep the Teardrop when we divorced. I'm sorry if you've had a wasted trip."

She was clever, this one. She had threatened us with her legal knowledge and then offered us a dignified exit. Dignity has never been something I've much bothered with, and I was glad when Holbrook said, "Be that as it may, we're actually here in the search for suspects."

Payne put on a thinking face, then made a theatrical display of realising what we were talking about. "Surely you don't mean you think *I* stole the jewel?" It wasn't a guilty display, just an insulting one. In the sarcasm department this woman could well have given me a run for my money.

"I suspect everyone," I told her. "Don't take it personally. I even suspect Watts, if it makes you feel any better."

She looked confused: the first genuine emotion I'd seen on her face. "You think Ralph stole his own diamond?"

"Heck, I'd suspect his cat if he had one. Does Watts have a cat?"

From that moment on, Payne decided to ignore me and spoke directly to Holbrook. "Tell me when the diamond was stolen and I'll see what alibi I can provide."

I laughed, just to annoy her. "If you've stolen it, you wouldn't have done it yourself."

"No," she replied tartly. "I would have hired someone like Shenna Tarin to steal it for me."

I shut up. From her wicked eyes I could see she knew all about my relationship with Shenna. Why she had not said anything about it years ago, I couldn't say. Possibly because I hadn't been accusing her of anything at the time. It was just one more threat to me, but this one was something which could potentially quail me.

"That name's already cropped up once," Holbrook said. I wondered what she thought she was playing at. "We've spoken to her, but she's not one of our main suspects."

"Whereas I am?"

"Not at all, ma'am. No, our main suspects work at the museum. It looks like a clear-cut inside job. We're just here to cover all angles."

"An inside job?" Payne asked. "Then you have someone in custody?"

"We haven't made an arrest, but we have people helping us with our enquiries. Between the three of us, one of those is very promising. Oddly enough, the one who mentioned Tarin to us, actually."

"Your prime suspect," Payne said slowly. "Does he have a name?"

Holbrook smiled. "One as well-versed in legal procedures as yourself should know we're not at liberty to divulge such information, ma'am. But I can tell you it's pretty much an open and shut case."

"I see." Payne paused. "The more I think about it, the more I think you might be right about Ralph, though. What if he engineered the theft himself? The man has addictions, don't you know?"

"Gambling addictions," Holbrook confirmed. "We know."

"They must have bled him dry around about now."

"I couldn't comment, ma'am. Does he have any other problems?"

"Aside from being a violent drunk?"

"I noticed that when we were looking him up. He was violent to you during your marriage, correct?"

"Ralph's always been a violent man, yes."

"I'm curious. Why did you drop charges against him?"

"Because I wanted to be rid of him. I know how long it takes for something to come to court and how long it gets dragged out afterwards. I wanted him gone from my life and pressing charges just wasn't worth it."

"It must have annoyed you to let him off though."

Payne shrugged. "He's lost more than I have."

"And with the Teardrop now gone, he's lost everything."

"I'm cut up inside."

Holbrook smiled slightly. "Well, from one woman to another, it's good to see you've become so successful since then."

"Believe me, getting rid of Ralph Watts was the best thing I ever did in my life." She glanced at me for the first time since deciding she hated me. "Men like Ralph Watts are better off out of everyone's lives."

I had no idea why she thought I was anything like Watts, but I've always made it a point not to be offended by anything suspects have to throw at me. And the more she spoke, the more of a suspect she was becoming. That, and she was annoying me.

"Oh, I agree," Holbrook said. "Still, we'll look into the Tarin angle, since you've mentioned her. I take it you haven't seen her since you split with Watts?"

"No."

"Good. I think that's everything. Blake, is there anything you want to add?"

I could tell by the way she spoke she wanted me to say no, so I fought very hard against my natural impulse. "No," I said through gritted teeth.

"Then thank you for your time, Miss Payne."

I did not speak until we were back on the road. Even then, I waited until Holbrook offered an explanation because I knew I would just explode at her otherwise.

"While you were with Shenna Tarin," she said, "I did some research into Benny Shoreham."

It was hardly what I had been expecting her to say, but I said, "Go on."

"His family's interesting. He was raised by his mother, Julia Shoreham."

"Fascinating."

"But his father was the one I paid more attention to. His father's a judge."

I was glad I had two hands on the wheel, since the investigation could have ended with the both of us wrapped about a tree. "Anderson?" I asked, eyes wide.

"Mmm. Elizabeth Payne is engaged to Benny Shoreham's father. Benny Shoreham just happens to have started work at the museum not long before the diamond is stolen."

"It's still a coincidence. It could also be Anderson wanting the diamond. We have nothing to connect Payne to the theft."

"Sure we do."

I waited for more and when it did not come asked, "What?"

"Shenna Tarin."

"Shenna?"

"Both Shoreham and Payne mentioned Tarin. That's weird, since Shoreham's only met her the once, according to him, and Payne hasn't seen her in years."

I kept my eyes on the road, trying to work out the mess. "That still doesn't give us much."

"It gives us a connection. And I don't know about you, but it makes me believe Shoreham and Payne were in this together."

"But Shoreham wouldn't have had the necessary knowledge to have stolen that diamond."

"No. Maybe the opportunity, but not the skills."

"So you're suggesting Shenna's involved as well?" I asked darkly.

"I'm not suggesting anything. Not at this stage. It would be nice to get everyone in the same room and hammer out some truths, but that's not going to happen."

That was, unfortunately, the way of most investigations. Even discounting Payne, Shoreham and Shenna, there were still Watts and Bob Harkett in the picture. I wasn't certain I trusted anyone's word, and even if I did they had all revealed motives.

"What if they're all involved?" I asked slowly, still trying to work out in my own mind what I was talking about.

"All of them?"

"It could explain why we're being given the run-around."

Holbrook pondered that possibility. "Talk to Tarin. See what she turns up."

"You don't want to come along?"

"You don't want some time alone with her?"

"I had that. Now we need to do this properly. If you're right and there's even a chance Payne and Shoreham have roped Shenna into this, I need to do everything by the book."

"I never said I thought Shenna was involved. No more than I suspect anyone else, anyway."

"No, but she could be. I may have been sweet on Shenna, but she's still a suspect."

"Sweet on her? Is that Blake-speak for being in love?"

I did not reply to that. If I was or ever had been in love with Shenna, that was none of Holbrook's business. Nor was it anything that should have impacted on the investigation. Besides which, Payne's mention of Shenna had triggered a defence-mechanism inside me. If she knew all about my former relationship with Shenna, I could be facing some serious problems.

"She's looking forward to seeing you anyway," I said.

Holbrook made that annoying half-laugh sound she always did when she couldn't believe the stupidity of something I'd just said but had every intention of going along with it. "Sure," she said. "What say we interrogate her next then? I get to be bad cop for a change."

Again, I did not reply. I'd been a bad cop for Shenna too often. The thought of putting her away a second time was not something I even wanted to contemplate.

CHAPTER SEVEN

Shenna smiled as she saw me but spread her arms and hugged Holbrook. "You're looking well," she said as she broke away. "No, you're looking really good."

"Thanks," Holbrook said. "Not so bad yourself."

We had arranged to meet in a café and arrived to find Shenna already there. The café was small, family run and far too expensive for me to usually think about using. I know I've never much cared for money, but I certainly didn't go out of my way to spend it frivolously. Shenna was just finishing a coffee she was drinking out of a china cup which likely would have cost me more than a day's work to replace, but as the waiter came over she ordered us all hot chocolates and encouraged us to try the home-made chocolate sponge.

Shenna and Holbrook then engaged in one of those inane and weird girlie chats I've never understood. It was odd, since the two women had never exactly been friends. When last they had met, we were chasing Shenna for a series of cat burglaries and were both incredibly proud when we caught her. But Shenna was never someone who bore a grudge and I could see she really did look back on our strange relationship with a deep fondness.

"Thanks for keeping Matthew afloat," Shenna said as our hot chocolates came. I had never had a hot chocolate in my life and knew I wasn't going to like it. As I took my first tentative sip all my inhibitions were confirmed. Why anyone would even think of drinking something like hot chocolate astounds me.

"It's been a chore," Holbrook said, and I picked up on their train of conversation with a little indignation.

"Hey," I said, "why do I need to be kept afloat? I'm fine."

"Sure," Shenna said with a wink. "Thanks to Jane here."

"No, thanks to me."

"No thanks to you, no."

Since it was an argument I knew I was not going to win, I decided to focus on my somewhat disgusting drink.

"You're an odd woman, you know that?" Shenna said.

"Odd?" Holbrook asked. "In what way?"

"Matthew here likes you, maybe even trusts you. And Matthew doesn't trust anyone."

I might have upped and left them to it, save for the fact I was still waiting for my chocolate sponge.

"Pleasant as all this Blake-bashing is," I said, "we did come here on business."

"Sure," Shenna said. "You talked to Miss Payne then?"

"You told her that?" Holbrook asked me.

I was reasonably sure I had. I was absolutely sure I didn't care. "She's a suspicious character, that one," I said. "Have you ever worked for her?"

"Nope. Well, technically when I worked for Watts. But no, not since the divorce."

"What about Roger Anderson?"

"Anderson? Hell, no."

I exchanged a look with Holbrook. "You know Anderson?" I asked.

"I should. He was the judge who sent me down."

I wasn't sure whether to laugh or cry. "Let me get this straight. You worked for Watts, who was married to Payne. Holbrook and I arrested you for jewel theft and Anderson sent you to prison. Now, years later, Payne and Shoreham might have dreamed up a scheme to steal Watts's diamond, name-drop you enough for us to suspect you, and it turns out Payne is engaged to the judge who sent you away?"

"She is?"

"Yes," I said dryly. "She is. All we need is for Harkett to be somehow tied into this little net and my head's going to explode."

"Bob Harkett?" Shenna asked. "Ooh, cake."

The sponge was placed before me and I instantly forgot about the conversation. Chocolate in a drink might be revolting, but in a sponge it's close to bliss. I shoved my spoon into the soft brown moistness and shoved a large portion into my mouth. As it began to melt, I smiled with a true pleasure I had not felt in a long while.

Then I remembered what Shenna had just said and the mood soured.

"Harkett?" I asked. "Why do you know that name?"

"You asked me to look into who might have stolen the Teardrop, right?"

"Right."

"No one's trying to sell it. That made me start to think that whoever stole it could be lying low with it for a while. You know, sell it on a few years from now, when all the heat's died down. I've seen that strategy before, although it lessens the risk so I never used it myself."

Shenna was never prone to rambling, so I could only surmise she was doing so to annoy me. "Go on," I said, having lost all interest in my chocolate sponge.

"A name did come up, though," she said. "Harkett. I assumed it was a pseudonym?"

"Probably not," I said. "Go on."

"Well, someone called Harkett has been trying to sell the Teardrop. Sort of."

"What do you mean sort of? He either has or hasn't."

"Well, he didn't have it at the time."

"At what time?"

"About six months ago."

"So six months ago someone called Harkett tried to sell the Teardrop?"

"He asked around for a buyer, then disappeared. No one wanted to touch it, obviously. It was clearly stolen, since it was in a museum. He even called it the Teardrop, so anyone he spoke to knew it was dodgy. No one's heard anything from this Harkett since then, though, so I guess he just gave up." She ate a spoonful of sponge. "Why? Who's Harkett?"

I thought about not telling her, but she was in deep enough with us as it was. "A curator being forcibly retired."

"Oh. I guess he found out six months ago and got annoyed."

"Annoyed enough to think about stealing the Teardrop," I said. "Or annoyed enough to actually do it."

"Maybe he changed his mind about selling it," Holbrook said. "Maybe he stole it after all but decided to keep it, or toss it in the river or something. If they took his job, it would be a matter of honour with him. Or maybe our initial hunch about him was right and he intends to whip it out and play the hero."

"I'm not sure I care any more," I said, pushing away my sponge and sinking my head into my arms on the table.

"So," Shenna said lightly, "anyone accuse me yet?"

"You expect someone to?"

"Hell, I expect everyone to. Ex-con and known jewel thief? If I thought it would do any good, I'd accuse myself."

I have always wondered just how much of Shenna's glibness was a cover for something, but since I've never been able to figure out what she might be covering it's not something I've ever had an answer to. Certainly she has never been lacking in regards to self-esteem, nor in skill or personality. But then again, I'm rather biased in matters pertaining to Shenna Tarin.

"The investigation continues," Shenna said. "But the question is, am I in or out?"

"To be fair," Holbrook said, "you never should have been in to begin with."

"But since you are," I said, "you may as well stick around with us."

Shenna smiled. "Much fun."

I cleared my throat. "I need to ask you something, Shen."

"Shoot."

I glanced to Holbrook, who took up the hint. "I'll go wait in the car. Thanks for the cake, Shenna."

We were alone a few moments thereafter but Shenna did not seem eager to have a private talk with me. I did not know whether that was an indication of her guilt or whether I should have felt ashamed for even contemplating that. She played her spoon about her hot chocolate, which I noted she had drunk a lot more of than I had.

"I need to ask you something," I said.

"You said that. You're either going to ask me something very insulting or you're going to warn me of the dangers of working this with you. I'm not sure which I'd find more offensive."

"I'd never warn you against any danger, Shen."

"So we're back to you not trusting me."

"Don't take it personally. I didn't trust you even when we were sleeping together."

"Is that all we were doing, Matthew?" She looked up at me. "Is that all we were to each other?"

"I thought that was all it was for you."

She shook her head very slowly, her eyes searching for something which she couldn't find. "You don't much understand women, do you?"

"I'm a man. If we understood women, the world would be a scary place."

"Don't joke with me, Matt. Not over this."

I wanted to glance away, but I respected her too much. "I don't know what we had, Shen. I don't fall for people I'm chasing to arrest. When we ... found each other, I figured it was just a heat of the moment response. I never thought much of it at the time. There was a jewel thief, a police investigation, media attention, a beautiful cat burglar. It was like some weird pulp novel come to life. And at the end of it all, the detective made his arrest and the beautiful burglar went to prison with a smile and a compliment for the amazing abilities of her pursuer.

"It was only afterwards, when you were gone, that the reality hit home. The buzz of the affair was over and I was back to my mundane job, sitting behind my desk and filling in paperwork. It was only then that I even considered you meant more to me than ... well, more than just the short time we had together."

Shenna did not reply for several moments. I could see she was seriously thinking about what I had said. It was strange to see Shenna serious about anything and it disturbed me. I did not know what I wanted from this encounter, did not even know why I was doing my version of pouring out my heart. But if there was one person I would admit my feelings to, it would certainly have to be Shenna.

"So," I said, "did you ever think about me? Afterwards, I mean."

"Would it make any difference whether I said yes or no?"

I paused. "Yes. It would."

Again she merely stared. Then she said, "What did you want to talk to me about? I think you were going to say something insulting?"

It was a brushoff if ever I'd heard one, and I had to respect her wishes. Sure, I'd opened up my chest and let her peer inside, but it did not necessarily mean she had to reciprocate.

"Payne," I said. "Payne and Shoreham both mentioned your name."

"Which they got from back when I worked for Watts, yes?"

"I need to make sure of something before we go any further."

"Before *we* go any further? Or before the investigation goes any further? I don't mind being a part of both, Matt – I've been there before. I just want you to be honest with me."

"I need to know the truth."

"You want me to promise you I haven't gone back to my former ways? You can't take my word that I'm honest now and you want to extract some sort of blood-binding promise from me?" She paused. "Feel free to deny any of that."

I gritted my teeth. "I know it's not a nice question."

Her laugh was strangled. "Not nice? Matthew, finding a dead fox in your back garden is not nice; having your roof leak during a storm is not nice; running out of digestives at the least opportune moment is not nice. Having the man you love accuse you of being a crook is downright rude," she shouted. Quickly, she collected herself, although I could see she was still seething. "I meant loved, of course. Past tense."

That she admitted to loving me at all broke my heart. It was the one thing I had never been able to admit to myself about her. And there could be no lasting relationship formed without trust. Since I didn't trust anyone, least of all myself, it seemed I was destined never to love again.

"I should go," I said, rising.

"Yes. You should."

"Shen, I ..."

"Now."

Bowing my head, I left her at the table, only afterwards thinking that I should have offered to pay the bill. I found Holbrook waiting in the car. She smiled as I approached, although that expression quickly died when she saw the thundercloud above my head.

"Sorry," she said. "I was hoping it would have gone better."

I turned the key in the ignition and ignored her entirely.

We drove without purpose, although I suppose I was headed back for the station. I no longer had any idea what I was going to do with the investigation, or with Shenna, but it was the first time in my entire career that I found I really didn't care. Whatever happened, it would end badly.

"You know something?" Holbrook said. I could tell by her tone she wasn't about to placate me with pleasantries, which was good considering the mood I was in. I hoped she had sense enough to talk about the case, since that was all I should have been concentrating on anyway. "I've been thinking about what we said in this car when we left Payne's."

I tried to think back, but there was an awful lot said back then. "What?" I asked.

"About getting everyone together? About sorting out this mess by shoving everyone in the same room and bashing some heads together?"

"I'm not sure we phrased it quite like that, but yes; it would certainly help matters some. I feel like just throwing the book at everyone and letting good old Judge Anderson arrange the nooses."

"Then let's do it."

"Let's do what?"

Holbrook smiled. "Let's get this investigation sorted in the weirdest style none of our suspects could ever anticipate."

That was the point at which I came to realise Jane Holbrook was sometimes possessed of a very vicious streak indeed. In the frame of mind I was in, I would have agreed to using cattle prods and a very deep pit, so whatever Holbrook had in mind I was already all for it.

CHAPTER EIGHT

I'd put in a few calls and knew the plan was going to take precision timing. Holbrook had decided to allow me to play the frontman, which was generous of her since technically it wasn't even my case. She was around, somewhere, likely getting into position, and as I arrived at the museum it was with a stomach churning in anxiety over everything that could go wrong. It was a good idea – I wouldn't have agreed to it if it hadn't have been – but it was also incredibly barmy.

I met Elizabeth Payne at the door. She did not look happy to have been dragged all the way to the museum, but when I called her I was betting on her being too deeply involved in this mess to easily back out. She gave me a greeting which was about as abrupt as I had expected, but the thought of tidying up this entire investigation in just one day kept me relatively happy.

"You said this was urgent," she said sniffily.

"I also said I couldn't explain everything right away."

She was nervous, but that did not make her guilty. I had a vague idea of what was going on with the woman, just as I had a vague idea of what all our suspects were involved in. Proving it all was why Holbrook and I wanted everyone in one place.

We entered the building together and I took Payne downstairs, which surprised her.

"We're not going to where the diamond was displayed?" she asked.

"I don't recall. Which floor was it displayed on again?"

She raised her chin and said nothing. It had not been my intention to make her reveal she knew more about the diamond's former location than she let on, but it was not a crime to have visited a museum once or twice.

Waiting for us on the stairs was Shenna Tarin. Her face fell when she saw Payne, and Payne drew herself up straighter.

"I didn't realise this was going to be one of those types of dates," Shenna said sourly.

"Detective Blake, what is *she* doing here?"

"Who's she?" Shenna shot back. "The cat burglar's mother?"

"I need her," I said once but looked at each of them in turn. My meaning was clear: I needed them both.

"Well," Payne said, "Just so long as you admit she's the likeliest one to have stolen the Teardrop."

"Just because I know how," Shenna said, folding her arms, "doesn't mean I did."

"Are we talking about diamonds or men?"

Shenna started then, probably would have struck Payne if I hadn't been suddenly standing between them. It was me Shenna had the affair with, not Watts, but I was getting the impression Payne may have thought there was something between the two of them. "We're not here to bash each other," I told Shenna. "Just trust me on this." I once more looked to them both in turn. "We do this properly and by the end of the night I'll have made an arrest. Are you both all right with that?"

Shenna seethed, but nodded.

"It's always good," Payne said, "to put criminals where they belong."

"Good," I said. "Now, come with me."

We continued down the stairs and came to a door marked 'staff only'. Here we met Benny Shoreham, standing there with his mop and bucket and trying not to look terrified.

"Hey, Benny," I said. "You set?"

"What's this respectable young man doing here?" Payne asked defensively.

"Benny's a cleaner here," I said. "He's been very helpful with our enquiries. Haven't you, Benny?"

"Yes, sir."

"That's a good lad. Shenna, I'm not sure whether you and Benny have met. It's been a long day and everyone's been a bit vague on whether they know each other."

"We met at the diamond, apparently," Shenna said, extending her hand to the young man. "Charmed, Mr Shoreham. And my apologies for having forgotten you."

He nervously took the hand and limply shook it. "Yes, ma'am."

I must admit to taking great delight in the next part. "Miss Payne, Mr Shoreham." I watched them shake hands as well, saw also the warning glower from Payne as she greeted her own future stepson.

"Now we're all acquainted," I said, clapping my hands, "what say we go through that door?"

"Where does it lead?" Payne asked.

"Down."

It was dark beyond the door, but I had brought a torch so it did not matter how deep we progressed. There was a lot of storage area down in the basement, with most of the artefacts boxed up or covered with protective sheets. I led my retinue through all of this, for I had a destination in mind and none of the exhibits meant anything to me. After a few minutes, we arrived at a large metal wall upon which was embedded a great wheel. Before the wheel, sitting on a packaging crate, was a red-faced middle-aged gambling addict.

"Blake?" he asked, his face falling when he saw my company. If possible, it flared even redder. "What are these people doing here?"

"Right," I said, relishing the introductions I would once again have to make. "Watts; Benny, Miss Payne, Shenna. Benny, Shenna, Miss Payne; Watts. Now we all know one another."

"Of course I know him," Payne said tartly. "This creature is my ex-husband."

"Well, you didn't recognise your fiancé's son, so I didn't want to presume."

"This is an outrage," Watts stormed as he got to his feet. "These must be all the prime suspects in the theft of my diamond. Why have you brought them all down here? Why have you asked me to meet you down here? What's *she* even doing anywhere near jewels?"

"You talking about me?" Shenna asked defensively.

"No, dear," Payne said, "I think he means me."

"Good to see we're all making friends," I said. "Now, hopefully we won't have to wait much longer for … Ah, Mr Harkett."

"Sir?" Bob Harkett said, appearing behind us then with a torch of his own. "I was instructed by my manager to come down here to the vault."

"That would be because I asked him to ask you," I said. "Come in, come in. Harkett; Miss Payne, Benny Shoreham, Shenna Tarin and Ralph Watts. Everyone; Bob Harkett. Now, how about that door?"

"The vault door, sir?"

"Yes, Mr Harkett. The vault door."

"I regret I don't have the key, sir."

"Well I do."

It was not a key, but a number-punching device, and I had already spoken with the museum's manager and obtained the code. The manager was as eager as any of us to get the matter sorted. I did not like to think what the theft would do for his insurance, but just for the sake of reputation it would be good to get someone behind bars.

I entered the code and there was a deep beep as it was accepted. I could actually hear the locking bolts move as the door unlocked. It was a powerful, satisfying sound indeed. Taking firm hold of the vault door, I tugged at it, and it slowly ground outwards. Shenna stepped forward to give me a hand and together we managed to get the thing open. I was amazed at how thick the door was and could not imagine even a barrage of grenades penetrating it. But then, I guess that was the idea.

I stepped inside, knowing sooner or later someone would follow. It was dark within, but I found a light switch to illuminate a fair portion of the area. It was vast inside the vault, far larger than I had expected, but for my purposes it was perfect. Rows of racking filled most of the space, upon which were stored boxes and sacks which without doubt contained priceless pieces of history. Items of greater size were stored towards the rear of the vault, and I could imagine if the shelving was cleared out there might well have been room for the Eiffel Tower. Well, perhaps if it was broken into pieces.

"This is some vault," Shenna said. I was not surprised she had been the first to follow me in. I turned to see the others were tentative about moving any farther, although of them all it was Shoreham who seemed to be debating on whether to follow us.

"Come on in," I called. "Trust me, in this vault I can prove who stole the diamond. Unless you're guilty, you have nothing to fear."

"Well," Payne said haughtily, "I certainly don't have anything to fear. And you didn't steal it, did you, Benjamin?"

Shoreham shook his head.

Payne strode into the room, Shoreham at her heels. That left only Watts and Harkett outside. Neither appeared happy at the prospect of undergoing whatever process I had in mind for them, although they both came in regardless. Which was a shame. If even one of my suspects had remained outside, I might have been able to work out just who the culprit was.

The only flaw in my plan was that I was still assuming the guilty party was one of my suspects and not someone else entirely. But I had a gut feeling it had to be one of them; which was a pleasant way of saying if it turned out to be someone else I hadn't a clue where to begin.

I watched them all enter. Behind them, the vault door fell closed and I adopted a look of horror.

"The door," Shoreham said, the first to notice. He ran for the exit, Payne only seconds behind, but was too late. With a dull thunk the door closed and we were sealed inside.

"Oh no," I said. "The door fell closed behind us. But don't worry. Someone will be along shortly to let us out."

"Be along?" Shenna asked. She did not seem worried in the slightest, although that was just her way. "Matthew, that door can't be opened from the inside and there won't be anyone by until morning."

"I'll get us out," Shoreham said, producing his phone. After a few seconds he looked deflated. "No signal."

"Vault's too think for that," Shenna said.

"Well, it looks like we'll have to spend the night here then," I said.

"It's worse than that, Matthew. The vault's airtight. By morning, we'll all be dead."

"Don't be ridiculous," Payne said. "This place is huge. There's enough air here to last weeks."

"Actually, no," Shenna said. "Trust me. I know a thing or three about vaults."

"You would."

"Ladies," I said, stepping between them once more. "The more we argue, the more air we use. Let's have a think about this. Mr Harkett, is there any way out of this vault?"

"Me, sir?" the old man asked. "What makes you think I know anything about vaults?"

"No," Shenna said. "There's no way out. If no one comes by, we're going to die here."

"No," Shoreham said, panic filling his face. He began hammering upon the door, screaming and cursing and crying.

"That's not going to do any good," Shenna said. "No one will hear you."

"Then we should get comfortable," I said, "while we have a think about what we're going to do."

"Do?" Shenna laughed. "Matthew, there's nothing we *can* do. Well, except die, obviously."

"Die?" Shoreham wailed.

"Oh, pipe down," Payne said. "Detective Blake, I demand you get us out of here this instant."

"Demand what?" Watts said in a half-strangled laugh. "Weren't you listening? There's no way out, Elizabeth. We're stuck in here until we die. Blake can't magic up an exit just by asking nicely."

"I was not talking to you," she replied acidly. "Kindly refrain from speaking to me again."

"Kindly give me back my diamond."

"What?"

"Well, you wouldn't be here if Blake didn't suspect you. And out of everyone here, you have the most to hate me for. Maybe you hired Tarin and got Bob in on it too, I don't know."

"Well, the nerve."

Miss Payne stormed off farther into the vault, which was good since I wanted everyone separated anyway. All the better to unroll my plans for them.

I would have to take each of my suspects in turn, and since Payne was already riled up I reasoned it would be an idea to begin with her. Knowing they would not be able to escape, I left the others to their own devices and followed Payne. She was walking aimlessly around the vault, searching for another exit. I was tempted to explain to her the purpose of a vault and that the great big door at the front would be useless if there happened to be a metal ladder leading to a fire escape, but she seemed to be doing fine all by herself in figuring that out. I stood back and watched her for several more moments, before stepping in to talk.

"Bad luck, that," I said. "The door closing behind us, I mean."

"You," she said, her eyes narrowing. If she could not batter down the walls with her venom, perhaps she thought she would have a better chance against me. "You've killed us all."

Finding a wall of racking to lean against, I offered an annoying chuckle. "We're not dead yet, Miss Payne. I'm sure we still have enough air left to us to get a few confessions off our chests."

"Confessions? I have nothing to confess."

"Everyone has something to confess."

"I did not steal the diamond."

"Nor did I. But I still have confessions." When she did not reply, I said, "When I was six I stole a bar of chocolate. I felt so bad I went into law-enforcement to atone for my sins. After all these years, I still don't feel I've done enough to make up for the crime I committed."

Payne lost some of her bluster as she tried to work through what I was saying. "Are you serious?"

I was surprised she was even considering that. "Yeah," I went with, seeing how far I could take this.

"Well," she said, a little mollified now, "that's a very sad story, Detective. But I still didn't steal the diamond."

"You're very adamant you didn't steal it, Miss Payne. No one else is denying it quite so vehemently."

"Then maybe everyone else isn't quite so suspected by you."

"To be fair, they are."

"Why would I want to steal it? Why would I want anything from that man? I have a new life, a new man in that life. Ralph can tie that diamond around his ankle and jump in the river for all I care. It's all he has left, so he might as well."

"You're acquainted with his finances then?"

She paused. "No."

"Yet you knew it was all he had left." Things were beginning to click. "You never got your revenge, did you? You dropped charges from where he hit you and it's been nagging you all this time. Stealing the diamond would have been your way to get him back. As you say, it's all he had left. You don't need the money, but taking it would remove the final thing he possesses. It would break him. You could steal it, toss it away, and be content to watch him flounder."

Her eyes hardened. "I did not steal it."

"Liz?" Shoreham called, walking in on us. "You back here. I … oh."

"Oh," I repeated. "Benny, I'm going to ask a blunt question. Did you steal the Teardrop?"

His eyes darted nervously to Payne. "No, sir."

"Why?"

"Why?"

"Why didn't you steal it? Miss Payne told you to get a job here so you could get close to the diamond. That much is obvious. She roped you in and put you in a position to take it. Why didn't you?"

"Did she say that, sir?"

Payne hissed and I smiled. That was a confession if ever I heard one.

"No," I said. "But she did anyway. You don't have the finesse to break into the display case the way the thief did. My guess is Miss Payne told you to make a smash and grab; then dump the diamond somewhere it wouldn't be found. Correct?" I asked either of them.

Neither replied.

"So," I asked again, "why didn't you steal it?"

"Because someone beat me to it," Shoreham said despondently. Payne hissed again, but Shoreham barked, "What? It's not as though we stole it. It's not illegal to plan to do something, then not do it. No, Detective, we didn't steal the diamond."

"What about the mention of Shenna Tarin?" I asked. "You both dropped the name."

"We were going to frame her," Shoreham said before Payne could stop him. "Sort of anyway. If we made it look as though Tarin and Watts had stolen the diamond, no one would be looking at us."

"Well," I said, "that's a nasty revenge for you."

"Aside from a full confession," Payne said tautly, "I'd like to see you prove it."

But the truth was I didn't much care for their manipulation and failed games of revenge. I knew they hadn't stolen the diamond. It was why Payne had been acting so odd when I had first spoken with her. I reckon at the time she hadn't been contacted by Shoreham and assumed he had indeed succeeded in stealing it. Only afterwards she would have spoken with him and discovered the truth, which was also why she had agreed to come meet me at the museum. Since she was innocent, she had nothing to lose. But she would still have been afraid I might have pieced together the circumstantial evidence of her connection to Benny Shoreham. Wielding that, I could have arrested her, albeit falsely, which would have perhaps destroyed her career and even her upcoming marriage.

But the truth was she and Shoreham were likely innocent.

"What happens now?" Payne asked warily.

"Now? That depends whether I entirely believe you, or whether further evidence just happens to rear its head. But for now, I go talk with someone else. For the moment, you're off the hook." I walked slowly away. "For the moment."

CHAPTER NINE

I had left it a few hours before speaking with anyone else. Payne and Shoreham kept to themselves during this time, with the occasional argument with Watts. Shenna meditated for the most part, by the looks of her, while Harkett wandered around as though still performing his rounds. Watts himself just grew angrier and angrier, argued with anyone he happened to meet, and looked as though he was verging on a heart attack. For my part, I wanted everyone to stew and sweat, so I found an empty section of racking and had a lie down. Other than that, I just followed people around and spied on them, which was good fun.

Eventually, I decided it was time I spoke with someone else and opted for Bob Harkett. He was still walking when I found him, and considering he was easily the eldest of us I was surprised to discover he was also the one with the greatest store of energy.

He had not even loosened the collar of his uniform.

"Mr Harkett," I said. "Got a minute?"

"By the taste of this air, I'd say we had at least several minutes, sir."

Humour in the face of death. I rather admired him for that.

"Just wanted to talk to you about your job. At least this way, they can't retire you."

"I'd not looked at it that way. Your idiocy in letting the door close has some benefit, you're saying?"

"Just looking on the bright side."

"I said I didn't want to retire, Detective, not that I wanted to die for it."

"Sorry. I just figured your work was your life."

"My work is important to me, yes. I take pride in what I do and always perform my duties to the best of my ability. That's what annoyed me when they told me they were getting rid of me. It's not about loving the job, sir, it's about them owing me more than just a by-your-leave and a boot out the door."

I had not heard him speak like this before and reasoned the vault might have introduced some panic to his brain.

"Is that why you considered stealing the diamond?" I asked.

"I considered stealing it?"

"I know you were looking into a buyer for it. Six months ago."

"Oh. That."

He did not sound particularly concerned that I'd found him out.

"Care to tell me about it?" I asked.

"I don't suppose it matters now."

"Now you've been sacked?"

"Now we're going to die." He looked at me strangely. "As I said, my work was never my whole life, Detective."

I waited for him to continue.

"Yes," he said, "I was angry how they were treating me. So I put out some adverts in newspapers. I was very discreet about it," he said proudly. "I wanted to see whether anyone would be willing to buy it."

"What did your advert say?"

"'R U looking 2 bye diamond?' You see, I used abbreviations and didn't mention the Teardrop by name."

He was right about it being discreet. I wondered how Shenna had managed to find him and once again began to suspect her of having something to do with the theft.

"I also attached a picture," Harkett said. "I didn't know how to crop the picture, but the background was a bit blurry anyway so it was difficult for people to see it was in a museum."

"I can't see how anyone found you out," I said dryly.

"Someone found me out?"

"Well I knew about it, didn't I? All right, so you put out an ad. Did you have any takers?"

"Not from the advert, no. But I did make some enquiries at a few jewellers, but no one was interested. After a week or so I realised how petty I was being so forgot all about it. When it was stolen, of course, I was a little pleased, even though it made me look bad. But I was already going by this point, so it didn't much matter how I looked."

"And I don't suppose you have any idea who stole it?"

"You asked me that this morning. I didn't know then and I don't know now."

"Shame."

The more I was talking to these people, the more they were convincing me it wasn't them. It was all well and good crossing people off my list, but if I ended up crossing them all off I wouldn't be making an arrest. But I couldn't think Harkett would be able to give me anything else to work on.

Leaving him to his rounds, I decided it was time to play some more mind games with someone else.

"Are you out of your mind?"

Water splashed the area before me and I started. It was a shame, since I had such a good little fire going. Shenna stood over me, bottle of water in hand, true anger to her eyes.

"Fire burns oxygen, you idiot," she said. "We don't have enough air as it is and you're burning it away."

"I was cold."

"Where did you even find the kindling?"

"Just papers lying around. They've been here so long, no one's going to miss them."

"No one's ... You're burning the museum's records?"

"Shen, you worry too much. If we're all going to be dead soon, what does it matter what I burn?"

She sank to the floor opposite me, keeping the final wisps of the fire between us. I was not surprised to learn she had brought a bottle of water in here. Shenna was a survivalist: there were likely many things she carried on her person at all times. Unless one of those was nitro-glycerine, however, they wouldn't do her much good in getting out.

"This is a mess, Matt. Isn't it?"

She looked tired, dishevelled. Nothing ever bothered Shenna, which was what I had always found attractive about her. I had never seen her so emotionally destroyed and I felt sorry for having put her through this.

"We'll survive," I told her.

She laughed sourly. "How?"

"Hold our breaths. A really long time."

For a moment she looked at me as though working out whether I was making a joke. Then she laughed, properly laughed, and the sound was the sweetest I had heard in a long time. "I've missed you, Matt."

"I don't think I'd miss me."

"You're not me."

"No. Shen, how are you? I mean, really, how are you? I get you're successful, I get you're on the straight and narrow now. But how is Shenna Tarin, the human being?"

"Shenna Tarin is miserable. If you want me to be completely honest, Shenna Tarin has been miserable ever since she was sent to prison. Once the trial was over, all the fun left her life and during her time inside she wised up. She decided she couldn't go through life pretending she was a teenager. So when she got out she cleaned up her act and to all her friends and family she was at last doing great."

"But she's not?" I said.

"My life's empty. I have so many things now, but none of it means anything. What's the point in money, Matt? You collect it, you invest it, you spend it on the things you like. I know I sound stuck-up because I'm someone who actually has money, but aside from paying the bills and having a little left over, what's the point in it?"

"Oddly enough, I've been asking myself that same question lately. My money goes to Gemma, to my bills and food. After that, all I do with money is gamble. I don't save, don't invest, don't spend it. So long as Gemma has a good life, I don't much care about it either."

"But you surely can't have a lot left over though."

"Depends how much I win."

"You still play poker?"

"Yep."

"Still good at it?"

I shrugged. "I played Watts last night. Now there's a bad player for you."

"I don't want to talk about Watts."

For one moment I'd entirely forgotten she knew him in her past life. "Sorry. I take it you didn't much like him."

"I think I just said I didn't want to talk about him."

"Sure."

Shenna stared into the remains of my dead fire and said, "I can see why Liz divorced him. You know he tried it on with me?"

"Watts?"

"Several times."

"Did he ever hit you?"

"If he did I would have gone to prison for aggravated assault. No, he was just a creep. And I don't think he's changed much. He was always watching me, you know? Everything I did, wherever I was working, he was there gazing at me with those ugly eyes of his." She shivered. "You heard enough about Watts yet?"

"Sorry."

"You apologise a lot lately, Matthew. It's not good."

I paused. "Sorry."

She looked at me dourly.

"Shen," I said, knowing I had no right to ask but deciding I had nothing to lose. "Shen, if we get out of this – when we get out of this, I mean. Let's show some optimism here."

"When have you ever been optimistic?"

"Fine. *If* we get out of this, you want to maybe think about picking up where we left off?"

"No."

"Oh."

"Picking up where we left off … It's been too long to do that, Matthew. It's been so long I think we've both changed. Well, I know I have anyway."

"I've grown less trusting."

"Is that possible?"

"I no longer trust my waistline to fit inside my trousers."

"You're a weird guy, Matthew."

"If we can't pick up where we left off, Shen, what say we start afresh?"

"Start afresh?"

"From scratch. Get to know each other all over again. It wasn't the most conventional of whirlwind romances we had before. This time we could do it properly."

I had no idea how she would react and tried not to think too much about it. My heart was pounding in anticipation of her response, but I refused to even hear it. As the silence stretched on, I became aware my blood was burning more fiercely than the sickly fire Shenna had already doused. I was all but praying she would not throw water on this fire as well, but I could not see why she wouldn't. We were both still young and neither of us had any idea what we wanted out of life. But Shenna Tarin was beautiful inside and out and I could not imagine her seeing anything in me now that the thrill of the chase was over.

"What we had," she said, "was of the moment. It's a part of who I used to be. I'm not going back to that. If you chased me all over again, would we end up in bed?"

"Probably."

"The only difference is I'm no longer a thief. I'm sorry, Matthew, but that life's gone."

"Then maybe I've changed as well. Maybe I'm a swell guy now."

She sighed sadly. "You were good for me, Matt. You were, and nothing can take that away. But do you know why I was crazy about you?"

"Because you loved playing dangerously?"

"Because you were clever, resourceful and brilliant. No one had ever come close to identifying me, let alone catching me. But there was something about you, something the other detectives lacked. I should have moved cities, like I'd done before. I should have moved cities as soon as you came along. But I didn't. And you were the end of me."

"I'm still clever, resourceful and brilliant."

"I don't doubt. But you don't surprise me any more, Matthew. Don't take that in a bad way; no one surprises me any more. But you've fallen into a rut and that's where you'll stay until you retire. I've no doubt you're a good detective, but look at us. You're jumping from suspect to suspect and still don't have a clue who stole the Teardrop. And to top it all off you've got us all locked in a vault and now we're all going to die. That's not good planning, Matthew, that's incompetence."

"And there's no room in your life for incompetence?"

"I know it doesn't matter what I say. I could promise you whatever you want to hear, but that wouldn't be me, Matthew. I can't lie to you. I wish I could, but I have to be honest with myself."

I rose. "Then I should get back to my investigation."

"Why? We're all dead, Matt. What does it matter?"

"Because I have to be true to myself as well. And I'd like to go to my grave having solved my final mystery."

"Matthew, I …"

"If I had time, Shen, I'd prove myself to you. I'm sorry I'm not the man you want me to be."

"And I'm sorry I'm not still crooked."

I left her to her memories and went to find Watts. I won't say I wasn't annoyed, nor that I wasn't upset. In truth, I was so badly torn apart inside I almost gave up on the entire case. But it gave me something to focus on, something other than Shenna's need to be entirely truthful with me.

I checked my watch. We had already been in the vault for several hours and the air was beginning to thin. My time with Watts would be short, but it would also bring to a close all my interrogations. After that, I was reasonably sure I would be able to name the thief. I could not help but feel it would be too little too late to save myself in Shenna's eyes.

That part of my life, it seemed, was gone forever.

CHAPTER TEN

"So, tell me about your day."

Ralph Watts looked over at me with an expression that could have soured holy water. He was flustering badly by this point but I did not regret my comment. Call me cruel, but I've never passed up the chance to see someone almost explode with indignation.

"Mr Blake," he said from where he was sitting on a crate. "I'll have you know I don't appreciate such glibness after everything that's happened."

I glanced around. There were many ways to define 'after everything that's happened' and none of them were good. Even the promise that we were all going to die of asphyxiation was not helping me sort out the entire mess the investigation was becoming. One of them was guilty, I knew it. Proving it, however, had become something of a challenge.

But I had to stay optimistic. If I allowed everything to get me down, the thief would walk away laughing. Feasibly, it still could have been any of them, but after everything Shenna had said to me only an hour earlier I was of a mind to start another fire and to hell with the air.

Forcing Shenna from my mind, I tried to concentrate on the man before me. When we had walked into this room, Ralph Watts had no idea what was going to happen, which made the torment I was putting him and the others through far sweeter.

"Tell me about the Teardrop," I said, sitting comfortably on a storage box. "After all, there's nothing much else we can do."

My words did not placate him, but nor were they meant to. I knew all about the Teardrop, obviously. But talking would take our minds off our impending deaths so it was hardly a bad idea. He said something about the Teardrop, but I wasn't really listening because I didn't much care. I probably even answered him, but whatever I said was hardly going to help us find it. In fact, it surprised me how passionately Watts could still talk about the jewel, especially since he was likely never going to see it again.

"Hey," someone called, not kindly. "Why are you two still going on about that stupid diamond?"

I eyed Shenna dispassionately. In the hour or so since I had last seen her, she had succumbed to the lack of oxygen, just as the rest of us had. Shenna Tarin, so cool and collected, was sweating with the thought we were all going to die. I felt guilty for having put her through any of this, but she was tough. She would get over it. Besides, she had hurt me and I wasn't that cut up about putting in a little hurt of my own.

"Because, Miss Tarin," I said, "I am a detective and I'm going to find out who stole it." I paused. "If it's the last thing I do."

"You did not just say that."

I grinned, taking obscene relish in seeing Shenna not in control of the situation. It was potentially the first time in her life she was in such a state – or possibly the second, if we're including the time I sent her down.

Shenna shook her head and walked off, allowing me to talk to Watts alone.

"I don't see how you put up with that woman," Watts said.

"She has her moments."

"None of them pretty."

I didn't like the way he spoke about Shenna, but then I didn't like Watts much anyway. At first I'd felt sorry for him because of his gambling addiction, but the more I learned about him the more I decided I didn't like him. I decided to ask him a very strange question, considering I was the detective.

"Who do you think stole your diamond?" I asked.

"Me? You're asking me?" He frowned. "Who do you think stole it?"

I set myself down on a crate opposite him and got comfortable. "Harkett had the motive, but not the skill. Also, he lost his desire since he took six months to calm down. Shoreham had the opportunity but not the skill. He was a puppet, but not a very good one. Payne had neither the opportunity nor the skill; but she did have the motive. Shenna had the skill but not the motivation. She makes her own opportunities."

"Why are you recapping for me?"

"Just laying things out as they are. Oh, and everyone but Shenna's already confessed to having an intention to steal the diamond, but they all claim they didn't do it."

Watts sputtered at that news. I'd thought he might.

"You forgot me," he said when he could find his voice.

"You?"

"You think I'm a suspect. So what do I have going for me? I don't have the motive, skill or opportunity."

"I'm not sure I'd go that far."

He did not seem pleased by my answer. "Go on."

"Motive? You have no money. If you wanted to sell the diamond, you couldn't break your contract with the museum, so stealing it would have been your best option."

"And I have the contacts to sell stolen goods?"

"You know where to buy and sell diamonds, yes."

"The Teardrop is distinctive. Even though I was the owner, news of its theft would have made my buyer turn me in."

That was an annoying truth, yes. "Opportunity, then," I said. "You own the diamond, so there's not much of a problem of you being left alone with it."

"And skill? I suppose I have the knowhow to have stolen the thing as well?"

He was sweating because of his fear over being asphyxiated and I had to admit the air was beginning to grow very thin by that point. But he wasn't just afraid of dying and I remembered something Shenna had said to me earlier.

"Tell me about your relationship with Shenna Tarin," I said.

"Relationship with her? I didn't have one."

"But you wanted one."

"She's told you I asked her out for a drink once, yes? So what? I was drunk at the time."

"I gather you were drunk a lot of the time."

"I used to have a problem with alcohol. Now I don't."

"What attracted you to Shenna?"

"I wasn't attracted to her. I told you, I was drunk. I would have asked out your grandmother if she was there at the time."

"Yet you were watching her."

He opened his mouth, closed it again.

"Shenna says you were watching her," I repeated. "A lot. She said she couldn't get her work done sometimes without you looking over her shoulder."

"She's a woman. They exaggerate."

"You weren't watching *her*, were you? You were watching what she did, how she did it. You were picking up tips and filing them away."

"I don't know what you're talking about."

I held up three fingers and pushed them down one by one. "Motive, opportunity, skill. You're the only suspect who had all three."

"Skill?" He laughed. "Watching someone work years ago is hardly any reason to accuse me of being able to cut out a diamond from underneath. No, for something like that you'd be best looking at your girlfriend Tarin."

"I didn't mention it was cut out from underneath."

"Then someone mentioned it to me," he said angrily. "Tarin did. She's behind all this."

"No, Watts, I happen to think you're behind all of this. You stole your own diamond, didn't you? You sold it to pay off your gambling debts. I was right about you all along."

"I haven't sold anything. I told you already, who would buy it?"

"I don't know that part."

"Then you don't know anything. Now stop asking me questions or if we get out of this I might have to go down to your station and tell them all about the cut Sally J takes from our poker games. That's illegal, Blake. That would look very bad for you."

Something hit me in that moment and I could not believe I had been so stupid. "That's it," I said. "I know where I recognised you from. Last night I said I knew your face. I know where I saw you."

"You haven't seen me before, don't be daft."

"You were at Sally J's a week before. I was there for a game and you came to see her. You didn't play, but you talked to her about something."

"That's not a crime, is it?"

"No, but you ..." I closed my eyes. "The lamp. The lamp at Sally J's. The one that sparkled like a rainbow. That was the Teardrop inside, wasn't it?"

"Of course not."

"But I don't get it. You sold it to ...? No, you didn't sell it to Sally J, did you?"

"No," Shenna said from behind Watts. I had not even seen her approach. She was eyeing him through narrowed slits and for all the world looked as though she wanted to tear off his head. "Sorry, I've been eavesdropping."

Watts looked about him. The others had gathered as well, looking upon him with faces varied from confusion to pity to outright anger. "It was my diamond," he said. "I could do with it what I wanted."

"Your addiction," I said. "You were feeding your addiction, Watts. You stole your own diamond so you could exchange it with Sally J to act as your buy-in fee."

"Hold on," Payne said. "This has all been about poker?"

"No," Shenna said. "This has all been about Ralph Watts being a despicable human being. And now we're all going to die for it."

"Is this true?" Harkett asked Watts. "Did you steal it?"

"No, I ... I can't steal what's already mine."

"But you did take it?" Shoreham asked.

"I ... Stop asking me all these questions."

"We're all dead anyway," Shenna said. "For once in your life, tell the truth, Watts. At the end of your life at least pretend you can be a decent human being."

With so many accusatory gazes upon him, Watts lowered his head. "All right, I stole it. You happy now?"

"Ecstatic," I said. Rising from my crate, I approached the vault door and tapped out shave and a haircut. We all waited for two snips. Instead the great door groaned, the metal bolts fell into place and it began to swing slowly open.

Fresh air blasted into the vault, along with a worried-looking Detective Jane Holbrook.

"Got it," I said, giving her a thumbs-up.

"Who was it?" she asked, looking me over with obvious concern to her eyes.

"Watts."

"Figures."

"It's your arrest, Holbrook," I said, stepping aside. "Not bad, considering my last acting performance was as a shepherd in my school nativity. The rest of you; sorry about that. But hey, from theft to arrest in under twenty-four hours? That's not bad."

CHAPTER ELEVEN

I hadn't been certain she was going to show but, as I sat there in the pub nursing my second pint, Shenna Tarin walked through the door. She went to the bar and bought two orange juices. I didn't have to ask her why. Addiction had ruined Watts and this was her somewhat less-than-subtle comment that she thought I drank too much.

"Thanks for meeting me," I said.

"I wanted to talk about what I said back in the vault the other day."

"About how our time together was special but we could never go back to it?"

"That was what I said, yes." She sipped her drink. "First tell me what happened with everyone else."

That had been an interesting experience. "Shoreham just wanted to bury his head and forget it ever happened. I get the impression he was terrified his old man would find out and put him away or something. Harkett just sort of gracefully sidled off. I hear he didn't go back to work: told them where to stick it. And Payne ... well, she was angry, full of abuse, but can't make a complaint when she admitted to me she'd planned to steal the thing herself. When I pointed out she was having an even better revenge against her ex than she ever dreamed, we parted company on good terms." I took a sip of my own juice.

"And Watts?"

"Called foul play on everything, but that's Holbrook's problem. With any luck, the judge he'll be put up against will be Anderson and Watts will be taken out of all our hair."

"And what about you?"

"What about me?"

"You continuing business as usual, Matthew?"

"Sure. But there's always something new with business as usual."

She smiled across the table at me. "So I'm learning."

It was a promising comment.

"You know the funny thing about all this?" she asked. "You spent the whole day searching for the diamond, and do you know who had it?"

"Sally J. She may have to give it back, actually, but that's nothing to do with me."

"No."

"No what?"

"No, that's not who I meant."

I was confused. "Who has it then?"

"You do. Watts used the diamond to buy into the game. Who won the game?"

"I did."

"So whatever money he got for it, minus Sally J's fee, went in your pocket. You were chasing around after that thing and it was in your pocket the whole time."

I'd not looked at it that way before and frowned. "I hope I don't have to give the money back then."

"Depends whether Watts makes the connection. He's far from stupid."

They were certainly thoughts for another time, for I had not asked her to meet me so we could discuss the diamond. "Shen, I don't want to talk about all the others. To be honest, I don't care about them. The best part of all this was seeing you, and I don't want that to end. I know you think I'm predictable and boring, but what can I do to show you I can still surprise you from time to time?"

"Oh, I don't know, Matt. Maybe lock me in a vault, deprive me of air, then reveal it was all part of your diabolical scheme to always get your man?"

"I …"

Her face broke into a huge smile. "Not every question needs an answer, Matthew." It faded somewhat as she continued. "I don't regret what I told you. I don't regret anything I said back there. But you're sneaky, and I like that. So maybe you're not as predictable as I thought. Maybe there's still some of the old Detective Blake that put me away all that time ago."

"Oh, I have years ahead of me for putting away sexy cat burglars, Shen. But I only ever target the pretty ones."

"Well then. We'll just have to see what happens, won't we?"

I tried not to let my hopes rise, but her demeanour was being extremely positive. "You mean we can go back to the way things were, Shen?"

"No. I mean we can do what we discussed. We can start over. A fresh beginning where we relearn one another. Where we put behind us who we used to be and discover who we are today." She extended her hand. "My name's Shenna Tarin. Pleased to meet you."

As I took her hand, I was grinning like a shark at a seal buffet. "Matthew Blake. Likewise."

She held my hand just a little too long for simple friendship. "I think I'm going to enjoy getting to know you, Matthew Blake. I think I'm going to enjoy it just as much as last time."

CHASING THE SHADOW MAN

CHAPTER ONE

Money had always been tight, but when he was laid off Mark Langley had known he was going to lose the house. It had taken him two weeks just to tell his wife that he had lost his job, and she had been as supportive as a paper girder during a fire. But he did not have to listen to her shouting at him to know he was letting down his children and that he needed to find another job as quickly as possible.

Six months on and he had found nothing. His money was gone and he couldn't slam the door in the face of the debt-collectors too many more times. Langley was desperate, lost and willing to do just about anything.

That was when Rob Stringer had approached him at the pub. He had known Stringer for several years, for they both played in the same darts team. Stringer had taken him to one side and asked him whether he wanted to help in some great venture which would get them both a shedload of money. Langley had not been naïve enough to think it was legit, but at that point he did not much care. If he had to put on a balaclava and knock over a bank, he would certainly have done so.

The girl whimpered and Langley suffered a pang of guilt, although knew he could not afford to feel such things. He could not feel anything: not until they were out of here anyway. Not until they had the money. It was all Langley could focus on, for dreaming of all that wealth was the only thing which could draw his mind away from his current situation. The situation he knew he would never have agreed to, but which he knew he would never have turned down.

"Stop that," Stringer said, coming back to join them. The three of them were holed up inside a jewellery shop, biding their time. It was late evening and they had been there for several hours now. The dark street outside was awash with red and blue lights, the crowds of people being kept back by a police cordon. Stringer had just been shouting through the door, making demands, and Langley was grateful to have been left in the back of the shop with the girl. He had never been good at public speaking and knew he would have just caved in moments.

"What's going on out there?" Langley asked.

"A lot of blustering, but they're not coming in here. They think we're armed."

"Why do they think we're armed?"

"Because I told them we were armed. Stop asking stupid questions. How's the girl?"

Langley tried not to glance across to her, and when he did he felt bad again. "Scared."

"Good. If we don't get what we want we may have to dangle her outside or something."

Langley did not reply. They had struck the jewellers right before closing time. There were only two people in there: a sales assistant and a girl of around twelve buying some earrings for her mother's birthday. There must have been a silent alarm or something because the police had been all over the place before they had even filled half their bags. That had been when Stringer had decided they needed a hostage and had kicked out the sales assistant so they didn't have two people to keep an eye on.

It left them with a terrified child. Thankfully she had not screamed or wailed, but that was only because she seemed too frightened to do much more than tremble.

Langley looked at her then, for the first time really looked at her. She was short and skinny, wearing jeans and a T-shirt. Her hair was formed of blonde curls, some of which were stuck to her forehead with sweat. Her eyes were downcast, and he knew she was afraid to even glance at the two of them. Langley felt sick even looking at her, for he had two daughters of his own and could only imagine what kind of monster could put them through such an ordeal.

"You all right?" he asked her. Stringer had moved back towards the front of the shop. The police had given him a radio and he was talking to them while leaning casually against the glass, knowing they wouldn't dare shoot him for fear of Langley doing something terrible to the hostage in retaliation. Suddenly Langley realised there may well have been armed police outside.

The girl glanced up to him and he offered a smile, although it was tight and far from reassuring.

"Pretty scary, huh?" Langley said, sitting opposite her. They were behind the counter, where Stringer had told them to be, but it did nothing to blot out the lights flashing against the wall. He noticed the girl had again not replied and said, "My name's Mark."

She glanced up at him again, but said nothing.

"It didn't mean to go down this way," Langley continued. "We were supposed to be in and out in fifteen minutes." He paused. "Sorry."

She looked up again, and this time her gaze lingered. "I thought I was lucky," she said tremulously, "getting in just before closing time."

"What's your name?"

"Sam."

"Nothing's going to happen to you, Sam. No one's going to hurt you. I promise."

"Then let me go."

She spoke with courage, although he could see the terror in her eyes. A part of him wanted to take her by the hand and lead her outside, but he knew what would happen then. He would be arrested and his own girls would be evicted. Nothing would happen to Sam, he would keep that promise, but he would not sacrifice his own girls for her.

"Stupid cops," Stringer said, peering over the counter and making Langley jump. "They're not playing the game, Mark. Seem to think we're not serious or something."

"Rob, we can't get out of this," Langley said, speaking slowly and carefully, not even knowing what he was suggesting.

"Of course we can get out. Here, give me the girl."

"Why?"

"Why? Because I want them to see we shouldn't be messed with here."

Langley stared in horror as Stringer pulled something from behind him. Tucked into his belt, Stringer had kept a revolver.

"You're armed?" Langley asked, his stomach sinking. This was armed robbery now, and he had watched enough TV to know that carried a deeper sentence than anything they had done thus far.

"Of course I'm armed. Now give me the girl."

"Why didn't you use it during the robbery?"

"You're asking stupid questions again, Mark." He reached over the counter and grabbed Sam by an arm. She shuddered, releasing a startled yelp, and Langley reached out instinctively for Stringer's arm, but he pulled back, releasing Sam in the process.

Langley could see anger and confusion in the other man's eyes. "This has gone too far," Langley said. "We need to give ourselves up."

"Are you out of your mind? We can get out of this. We can take the loot and the girl."

"And then what? If they don't know who we are, they'll figure it out eventually. I'm trying to save my house, Rob. I can't do that if I have to go on the run."

"Better on the run than in prison. We have enough here to put us away for a long time. Who's going to look after your daughters then, eh?"

Langley had not thought much of this through, but then he had not wanted to because he knew he would have only talked himself out of it. He wished now that he had thought more, because then Stringer would have been here alone. But Stringer alone with Sam ... That was an even worse situation. Langley felt at least he was around to help the girl. He could not honestly see he had any way out of this mess, but at least he could protect Sam against anything worse.

"We're giving ourselves up," Langley decided.

"Are we now?"

Langley rose, stepping between Stringer and the girl. "We're going out there together, Rob. Sam's going first, then the two of us." He spoke slowly, for he was terrified of doing this and terrified of not doing it.

For several moments Stringer seemed amused, but then he likely sensed Langley was serious. He raised the gun. "You're not going anywhere, Mark. Now sit down."

Langley clenched sweating fists at his side and fought for the response he wanted to give. "No," he finally managed.

"Really?"

"You can't shoot me, Rob. Why would you shoot me? Besides, if you start shooting, the police would bust through that door."

"That's true. All right, go then. I don't need you. Just tell the cops that I have the girl and that I'm armed."

"You do what you want, but Sam's coming with me."

Stringer laughed. "You're a desperate man, Mark. That's why I picked you. You're not a hero, so don't start fooling yourself."

Langley wanted to say something brave, something courageous. But he said nothing at all, for his body was still trembling and his brain was telling him he was going to prison.

Stringer opened his mouth to speak, but suddenly there was something in the room. The lights exploded as a form detached from the ceiling, hurtling towards them. Langley watched as a dark hand closed upon the gun in Stringer's grip, crushing the weapon as though it was tin. Langley heard the groan of twisting metal and the snap of yielding bone, and Stringer was screaming.

Langley took a step back, his eyes wide in horror as he saw the shadow move with the speed of lightning. An elbow shattered Stringer's nose, and the shadow dropped, spinning, its foot tripping Stringer to crash audibly upon the floor. Before he had even registered the attack, Stringer was consumed by the shadow creature, his body wrenched into the air to hurtle across the room, slamming into the wall and sinking to the floor an inert mess.

Taking another step back, Langley felt himself collide with Sam, who shivered in terror at the sight.

The shadow straightened and Langley could see now it was a man. He was tall, thin, with a deceptively powerful frame. He wore a long, expensive coat and walked with a straight cane topped with a dull jewel. The man gazed at Langley with hard, cold eyes set into an arrogant face. His hair was short and receding, while a thin, tidy moustache and beard framed his lips without touching his cheeks.

Langley could not imagine what he had been thinking, seeing the man as nothing more than a shadow.

"I'm here for the girl," the stranger said. "I would advise handing her over."

But Langley felt something within him stir. He had spent the past few minutes convincing himself he was no hero, yet the stranger emanated such a sense of wrongness that Langley would have preferred handing the girl over to Stringer than he would this man.

"You're not having her," Langley said.

"I'm not?" The man seemed to find such a statement amusing. "And what do you intend to do to stop me?"

Without thinking, Langley threw himself at the well-dressed man. The stranger caught his flailing fist with ease and Langley felt the sheer strength behind the grip. The stranger smiled but said nothing. Then he twisted sharply and Langley tumbled through the air, slamming his back upon the floor. Pain shot through him, but as he looked up he could see the stranger was no longer considering him. He was moving towards the girl. Langley did not know how, but he knew the situation was something he had to stop.

Light flooded the room and Langley turned his eyes briefly to the door, where police officers were piling inside. He could see two officers stopping beside where Stringer had been tossed, uncertainly creasing their features. Further officers came to Langley and hauled him to his feet. His body was writhing with pain, but he could feel no broken bones.

A plain clothes officer stopped before him, his jaw set firm, confusion flittering across his eyes.

"Where's the girl?" he demanded.

"Where? She's ..." And then Langley realised Sam was no longer in the room. In the second it had taken for the officers to storm the shop, the girl and the well-dressed stranger had vanished. "That's impossible," Langley said even as someone was cuffing his hands behind his back. "She was right there. I saw him walking towards her and ... She was right there."

"Saw who walking towards her?"

"There was this guy. I ... He was here."

The officer in charge sent people off to check out the back, but somehow Langley already knew what they would find. Whoever the well-dressed man was, he was good. And he was gone. And Mark Langley was going to prison.

CHAPTER TWO

Nothing made sense. Detective Inspector Jonathan Hope liked for his cases to have clear-cut answers. He was not averse to a bit of investigation, but usually there were enough clues so he could know where to begin looking. Crime, victim, suspect. They were the three main parts to any investigation, and each could be broken down into their own separate segments. They had a crime: attempted armed robbery and hostage-taking. They had a victim: Samantha Dickson. They even had suspects: Mark Langley and Robert Stringer. The only problem was that they no longer knew where the victim was, and neither of the suspects seemed to have had anything to do with her disappearance.

Hope had questioned Langley on the scene, but he hadn't heard anything that made any sense. Nor could his officers find any trace of the girl anywhere. It was as though she had simply disappeared.

There were two possibilities, so far as Hope could see things. One: the men had killed the girl and hidden her body somewhere in the building. Then they had beaten themselves up. Two: the girl had beaten up the two men herself and was now hiding. There was no way Sam could have got out of the building, yet she had been there when the police had arrived, for the sales assistant could vouch for her presence. He had had dogs sweep the entire building and they had turned up nothing.

Then there was this mysterious man Langley had raved on about. At first he had believed the story, but there was no trace of the man, and once Langley started going on about shadows detaching themselves from the ceiling Hope had realised it was all fabricated.

It was a mystery, and not one he felt he could solve.

At that moment, Hope was sitting behind his desk. The station was a busy place, and busy places always helped him think. Familiarity was good for his imagination, and imagination was the key to solving every mystery. He could never have imagined, however, that this would have brought back the woman presently walking through the door. She was another piece to a different puzzle and Hope was not sure whether it was a good thing, or whether it made everything even more confusing.

The woman was short, smartly dressed, flashing a smile as she approached his desk. She had a hard face for such a pleasant woman, and Hope had never had a bad word to say about her. He had lost contact with her some time ago, but knew her parents still lived in London's Chinatown and had meant to look them up in an effort to find her. He knew it was far from a coincidence that she was walking back into his life during such a confusing case.

"So you remembered your old DI at last then," Hope smirked.

Detective Sue Lin returned his smile, although there was something guarded to it, as though she was afraid to reveal too much before her old friend. Once upon a time, Lin had been the brightest young detective in Hope's team. Then she had transferred, pretty much overnight, and he had never seen her again.

"Sorry I haven't been in touch, boss," Lin said. "You know how it is."

"Your new DCI's keeping you busy, I understand that all right. You never got around to telling me where you transferred to."

"Nowhere special, boss. Doing the same job, just in a different department."

Hope did not raise the obvious question, mainly because he knew he would not receive an honest answer. Lin had left so suddenly there had to have been a reason for it. Even if that reason was because she had received a better offer, she still would have continued working for Hope long enough for him to find an adequate replacement. As it was, she had barely taken the time to say goodbye. It had been a great loss for Hope, but he didn't want her lying to his face about it.

Instead he said, "Why do I get the impression you're here on business?"

"You know me too well, boss."

"Your case or mine?"

"A little of both."

Hope nodded slowly, then pushed his notes towards her across the desk. "Jewellery heist. Two men in custody, one of those in the hospital. Man we have isn't talking much sense, and when the other wakes up I'm not sure we're going to get much out of him either."

Lin made a show of looking over the notes, but he could tell she already knew everything she needed to about this case. "Notes say there's a missing girl," she said as though she didn't already know that.

"Samantha Dickson. Vanished without a trace."

"And this other man your collar mentions?"

She was good, Hope had to admit. If she was talking to anyone else she would have fooled them by now. "There was no one else in the building, Lin. First Langley's talking about moving shadows, then a dapper gentleman with a cane. It's nonsense, of course." While he spoke, he eyed Lin carefully, but she betrayed no sign that she disagreed with him.

Finally she looked up at him. "I'd like to help. If you can use me."

"I can always use you, Lin, you know that. But I have resources of my own. Is your DCI going to mind you tagging along with me on this one?"

"He'll understand."

"Maybe I should call him." Hope reached for the receiver. "What's his number?"

Lin offered him a smile; half coy, half asking him not to treat her like an idiot. "You know I was sent here, Jon. Can we just agree not to ask me about it?"

Hope did not reply for several moments. He appreciated the honesty, especially from someone he had always regarded as a friend, yet it was still a lot to ask of him. "This is my operation, Lin. If something goes wrong, the blame falls on me. And we have a missing minor to consider. I'm going to need a little more than that to go on."

Lin considered his words, then said, "This man from the shadows. I'm after him."

"Why? He doesn't exist."

"Oh, he exists all right. But he shouldn't be out here, and he shouldn't be interfering in your case."

"Who is he?"

"I can't tell you that."

"But you've had dealings with him before?"

"Oh yes."

"Why'd he nab the girl?"

Lin's face fell and she looked away. Hope's heart caught in his throat and he suddenly regretted having asked so many questions of her. When she looked back to him she had regained some of her composure, although there was a fear to her eyes which he did not like at all. "I don't know," she replied. "My DCI thinks one thing, but I don't happen to agree with him. I'd like to find them both before I realise I'm really, really wrong."

Hope knew better than to ask further questions. Rising from the desk, he gathered his papers and said, "Then you're back on the team, Lin. You and me chasing the bad guys, like always."

She did not smile, and it was then that Hope knew something was terribly wrong. Whoever this man of the shadows was, he was certainly far worse than anything Detective Inspector Hope could ever dream.

His phone rang shrilly on his desk and as he picked up the receiver he noticed Lin's eyes narrow slightly, as though she was half afraid of what he was about to hear. She had secrets from him, and none of them were good, but he forced all of that from his mind and he listened to the voice on the other end. He made the appropriate responses before hanging up and looking into Lin's face. He did not know what he was searching for, or why he was stringing her along and making her afraid that he had discovered something. But he had a missing girl to find, and if Lin wanted to keep her secrets she was more than welcome to, so long as they did not interfere in the investigation.

"Uniform's found something," he told her. "Seems like our mystery man's out beating people up again. Not such a shadow after all, eh?"

Lin did not react and Hope wondered just what had happened to make her change so much.

CHAPTER THREE

There were officers taking statements from various shoppers, but DI Hope had heard all he needed to. He and Lin had arrived at the scene too late to do much, although from what Hope had heard the man that had been sighted had indeed been the same one from the jewellery shop. Hope wandered back to where Lin was waiting by the car. There had been a minor fight in the street, and one man had been hospitalised with a broken leg and a possible fractured skull.

"Your man was here," Hope told her, seeing she had bought them both coffee. "You didn't hang around to talk to the witnesses."

Lin shrugged. "He's not here now, and if we're chasing him we're not going to catch him."

"If you know anything we can do about getting one step ahead, fill me in."

Lin said nothing.

"He had the girl with him," Hope said, taking a sip of his coffee and watching her intently over the rim. He did not know whether to be pleased when he saw her start.

"Then she's still alive," Lin said.

"Witnesses say she was with him willingly."

"And what do you mean by that?"

"That she didn't make any move to run when he was laying into the guy. Then he grabbed her by the arm and they made a run for it, so maybe she was being coerced after all." He wanted to throw as many theories in the air as possible, just to see what kind of reaction he got from her. He felt if he dealt with the pure facts Lin would never reveal anything. It was bad enough trying to solve this case without Lin working against him.

"What do we know about the man who was attacked?" Lin asked.

"Not much. His ID says his name's Bill Yale."

"We need to see if he has a record."

"So our victim is now a suspect?"

"Everyone's a suspect, Jon."

"Why do I get the feeling the results are going to show the guy has form?"

"Let's just see what turns up first."

Hope looked at her calmly before opening the door to the car. "Let's get back to the station then and I'll phone through the name. Maybe we should drop by the hospital so we can fingerprint the guy in case he wakes up from his coma and does a runner."

She said nothing. A couple of years ago she would have berated him for being facetious. It was as though she was a different person now.

They did not talk as they drove back to the station and by the time they arrived there was a file waiting on Hope's desk. He flicked through it quickly before passing it to Lin. "Good instincts."

Lin studied the folder carefully and Hope leaned against the desk, watching her. Yale had form for GBH and burglary. He was hardly criminal of the century, but certainly not a nice man. Why a distinguished-looking gentleman would kidnap a girl and batter three criminals was not something Hope could understand at all.

"Care to share?" he asked.

"Share what?" She handed back the folder.

Hope looked at her in silence for several moments, then said, "I think we should get some lunch."

"Lunch?"

"My treat."

They left the station and went to a small café Hope knew well enough to own shares in. It was quiet, secluded and the staff there knew to mind their own business. Hope always used it if he needed quiet moments with people, and knew Lin would pick up on this within moments of their walking through the door. He ordered a fried breakfast simply because he knew it was bad for him, while Lin asked for a salad. They did not do salad so she ended up with a jacket potato and cheese.

Since sitting at the table, they had spoken of nothing more important than the menu, and as Hope tucked into his second of three sausages he felt it was more than time enough to bring up the reason for his wanting to talk to her away from the office.

"What's his name?"

Lin sipped her coffee. "Whose name?"

"You're such a kidder. The gentleman."

"What makes you ...?"

"Let's not insult each other, Sue," he said without looking up from his food. "You don't just drop into my lap after so long without so much as a phone call. You want something, or you wouldn't be talking to me at all."

"Jon, you really think I'd only talk to you if I wanted something?"

"It's been a year, Sue. Not even a phone call?"

She looked genuinely sorry. "I've been busy."

"Busy doing what?"

"Police work."

"I've been busy doing police work as well, but I still find time for my friends. We used to be friends once, Sue, you remember that?"

"We are."

"So what's his name?"

She looked away again. "My DCI wouldn't like me telling you."

"Why? Afraid I'm going to steal his collar? Whoever this guy is, we're bringing him in and putting him away. But I get the feeling there's more than a simple kidnapping involved here."

"I don't know. I didn't think so, but ... I don't know."

Now Hope really was confused. "Sue, what are you doing here?"

"Eating?"

"Cute."

She inhaled deeply and looked at him, really looked at him. He could see her struggling with what she wanted to say and what she was allowed to. Hope knew how difficult things could become if your DCI told you to lie to people, but there were things more important than your DCI.

"We used to be able to tell each other anything, Sue. What's changed?"

"Too much. The things I've seen, Jon, the things I've done. I ..." She toyed with the fork in her cheese. "His name's Jeremiah."

"Jeremiah what?"

"I ... don't know actually."

"Well it's a start. What does he want?"

"I don't know that either. I thought ... He disappeared last week. My DCI was going spare, wanted every officer looking for him. When I heard about the jewellery shop I knew it was him and figured he'd taken the girl and killed her. But she's alive, and I don't get it."

"Why would he kill a twelve-year-old girl?"

"He wouldn't. But the DCI thinks he would."

"Why would your DCI think he would?"

"He's a strange man. A little paranoid, I don't know."

Hope knew she was referring to her DCI, and also that she had not much more of an idea what was happening than any of them did. "If you know this Jeremiah you're our most valuable resource at the moment. We need a profile on him if we're going to find him."

"Finding him isn't an option. We need to figure out what he wants and get there ahead of him."

"But we don't know what he wants."

"No. We don't." A little of her former self returned to her face then as she smiled in a sign of dejection. "Never said it was going to be easy, boss."

"At least I have my old Sue Lin back." He started on his bacon. "What's say we don't have any more secrets between us now?"

"Sure. Jon, I'm sorry for being distant. When we realised Jeremiah was on your patch my DCI sent me in."

"It's a good call. Just a little obvious when you've disappeared for a year."

"That's my fault."

"Well it's not mine."

She looked at him with a wry expression. It made Hope glad for the first time since she had walked back into his life.

"We need to concentrate on Yale," Lin said, back to business already. "Jeremiah beat him up for a reason. I think we should take a look at Yale's known associates and try to figure out why Jeremiah did it."

"You know best."

"And put an officer at the hospital."

"You think Jeremiah's going to try to finish what he started?"

"No. If Jeremiah wanted Yale dead he would be dead already. I just don't want Yale disappearing on us."

It made no sense to Hope, but he had already decided to trust her so could not now deny such a reasonable request. "Finish your potato and we'll get back to work then. You sure there's nothing else you want to tell me, Sue?"

"Nothing else I can, boss."

It was an honest response, and one Hope knew he would have to respect, even if he didn't like it.

CHAPTER FOUR

The known associates of Bill Yale were short, but there was a connection to them; they had all disappeared. There were three people in whom Hope was especially interested, and none of them could be found anywhere. What had begun as a standard jewellery shop robbery was escalating into something Hope no longer understood. So far as he could determine, neither Yale nor his associates had anything to do with jewellery heists. They all had arrests for various violent crimes, and the most serious was premeditated assault. Hope supposed they could have moved up to armed robbery, but, even if he could believe that, there was no evidence they were in any way connected with the one the previous day. Hope even spoke with Langley again, but he knew nothing about the various people and Hope believed him. Besides, even if they were involved, it did not explain where they had all gone. It was possible Jeremiah had already attacked them all, but there was no trace of such a thing. It was as though the men had simply got up in the morning and vanished.

He asked Lin for her thoughts and she replied that she could never overestimate Jeremiah's abilities. She said she would make some calls and Hope knew she was phoning her office. It irked him that she was still working for them when she should have been working for him. When he had first seen her walk back into his station after so long he had wondered whether there was any chance he could get her to come back to work for him. The more time passed, however, the more he was coming to understand he had lost her the day she walked out that door a year ago.

While she was on the phone, some of Hope's other officers, Lin's former colleagues, had asked him about her. He wished he had something to tell them, but all he could say was that Lin was still one of the good guys and that he trusted her with his life. The latter was without doubt true, and he hoped she would not let him down with the former.

"Might have something," she said as she rejoined him. She seemed entirely oblivious of her former colleagues' curiosity, even the animosity from some of them, but she would have been a poor detective indeed not to have picked up on it. "One of my guys spotted Tom, Dick and Harry having a party. I think we should go gatecrash."

Hope raised his eyebrows. "And in English?"

"Huey, Dewey and Louie?"

He stared at her some more, glanced behind her to where two of his officers were trying not to make it obvious they were watching her. "Sue," Hope said quietly, "why are you acting like you're on TV?"

"Just having a joke."

"I have a twelve-year-old girl missing. I don't have time to joke."

"Sorry, boss. I guess I've learned to laugh at anything lately."

He could see there was a reason she was saying this, but could not imagine her job was too much different now to what it had always been. Yet she was acting as though she had the most depressing job ever assigned. He could accept she would be acting like this if she was tasked with spending every day telling parents their children had just been killed, but since there was no department which specialised in such a thing it was a ridiculous notion. Still, he had a vague idea of the work she did do, and could not fathom what depressed her so much about it.

"Do we have a location?" he asked.

Lin handed him a scribbled address. It was only a mile away and Hope knew even with a little planning involved he could get officers surrounding the building within the hour. "Does this guy carry a piece?" he asked.

"Jeremiah's hands are weapons enough, but no, he doesn't carry a gun."

Hope did not press for information he knew she would not provide. He had seen the evidence at the jewellers of Jeremiah's proficiency in hand-to-hand combat. He had likely been trained, was possibly army, and it was certainly enough of a logical explanation for Hope to work on.

Hope took Lin in his own car, arranging for backup to meet them at their destination. The address Lin had provided had at one time been a gymnasium, but it had closed down a year earlier and nothing had been done with it since. Hope recalled there had been a problem one time with squatters, but it had not been difficult to clear them out. Now it seemed as though some real villains had had the same idea. Aside from breaking and entering, however, there was nothing with which Hope could charge them. Suspicious gathering was not a crime either, although sometimes he wished it was. Still, he was confident by the end of this Lin would have helped him nab this Jeremiah, and he would at least have a body to put in a cell.

Having stopped off to collect the keys from the owner of the building, by the time Hope and Lin parked at the gymnasium he could see his officers were already moving into position to block the exits. Hope unlocked the door, careful to make no sound, and motioned for Lin and the rest of his officers to be ready. Lin's contacts had not told her precisely where in the building these men would be, or why they were even there, and to search the entire place would take time.

As soon as they stepped inside, however, they could hear the screaming.

"Move," Hope ordered, running towards the sound of the noise. Although the gym was closed down, much of the reception area remained intact, and he was forced to vault the pass-key operated metal barriers. He could hear sounds of a scuffle before him by this point and charged through the double door leading to one of the main gymnasia.

The room was large, able to contain at least twenty individuals working out at any given time. Some of the equipment was still lying around, although most had long since been removed. There were several people in the gym and Hope froze at the scene. A girl of around twelve sat tensely upon a bench, watching the scene unfold before her, while between her and the police four men brawled. Or at least Hope would have loosely called it brawling. One man was upon the floor, his nose split, bleeding onto a safety mat. Another stood nearby, terror flooding his eyes as he held onto some form of short metal pole which had likely been left over from the equipment. The third man was being held in the air by his throat by a tall, well-dressed gentleman.

Jeremiah turned a ferocious scowl upon Hope, his teeth bared as though he was a wolf. His eyes registered shock as he noticed Lin with him, and the man with the metal pole seized upon the momentary indecision and charged. But Jeremiah was swifter, dropping his burden and catching the metal pole even as it swung for his head. He twisted it from the grip of his assailant and tossed it to the side in one savage motion, slamming his palm into the man's forehead and sending him reeling.

"Hold it," Hope said, his officers pouring in and surrounding Jeremiah. "Place your hands on your head, Jeremiah."

"What?" Jeremiah asked, looking directly at Lin. "You told them my name?"

"I didn't have a choice." Lin sounded genuinely regretful, yet Hope could not deal with that right at that moment.

"This is Sanders isn't it?" Jeremiah sneered. "The old fool's finally given me up."

"Give yourself up," Hope told him. "You're not getting out of here."

"Who's this idiot?"

"Detective Inspector Hope," Lin said. "Your arresting officer. Come quietly, Jeremiah. The girl's all right, we can still work this out."

"Sam?" Jeremiah asked. "Of course she's all right." His expression hardened somewhat then and his eyes narrowed. "So that's it. I'm out killing children am I?"

"No one's killing anyone," Hope said. "Now put your hands on your head and get down on the floor."

Jeremiah snarled once more, and several officers took involuntary steps back. "You have no idea what's going on, Detective Inspector Hope. These men are just the beginning. Yale was a tool for bringing them together. And together they came, to discuss what had happened. But this is more than just a warning, it's a message. I need to get the message out, Hope. You'd do well to allow me to continue."

Hope felt something strange in the back of his mind. He understood something of what this man was saying, even though none of it made sense. He was on the verge of actually telling his people to back away when he suddenly remembered where he was and what he was doing there.

"On the floor," he said again.

"If only it were night," Jeremiah said, glancing back to the girl. "I'll come back for you. Say nothing if you want to live; I'll break you free when I can."

Hope had heard enough. "Take him."

The next few moments were a fiasco, and afterwards Hope spent many hours reflecting over just what had happened, for he knew it could not have been real. His officers lunged for Jeremiah, but the man leaped vertically, slamming his feet down upon two officers as they reached him and used them as a springboard to leap over the heads of the others. Hope shouted something, he did not afterwards remember what, and watched as Jeremiah landed with the grace of a medal-winning ballerina, launching himself in that same instant towards the exit. He collided with two officers, not even seeming to notice they were there, and before Hope could react at all he was out the door.

Shouting for his people to get up, Hope rushed to the door and kicked it open. The long corridor outside ended at the metal turnstiles, but there was no sign at all of Jeremiah.

It wasn't natural. No one could have done what Jeremiah had just done, no matter how long he spent in the gym. Yet it had happened, because Hope had seen it happen. It was the jewellery shop all over again, only this time he did not have to rely on the testimony of two villains.

Returning to the gym, he marched directly up to Lin and saw she was tending to the girl, who thankfully this time had not disappeared along with Jeremiah. He could see Lin was genuinely relieved to see the girl safe, but also that she was studiously evading Hope's eyes, knowing he would be coming to her for answers.

"She's safe, Jon," Lin said before he could say anything, "and that's the only thing which counts."

Hope did not agree with that statement, but he would not cause a scene before the frightened girl. Instead he cast his gaze about the room and tried to take in the scene of displaced police officers. No one seemed to have suffered any actual injuries, but the same could not be said for the three men Jeremiah had cornered here.

Then he noticed something on the ground and bent to retrieve it. It was a metal pipe, and he knew it was the one with which the hoodlum had attempted to strike Jeremiah. He recognised it now as a bar onto which would be attached weights for lifting. Due to its purpose, the metal bar had to be as strong as it could possibly be, else the weightlifter would suffer terrible injuries. The bar was now bent almost into a U shape.

And all because Jeremiah had caught the bar mid-swing and twisted it from his assailant's grasp.

Hope looked once more to Lin, who had draped her coat over the girl and was leading her away. There were so many questions now, but they would have to wait until they returned to the station. He had expected this to all be cleared up once he met Jeremiah face-to-face, but he found himself instead left with more questions; and he had a feeling Detective Lin knew the answers to them all.

CHAPTER FIVE

The securest place for Samantha Dickson would have been in one of the cells, but Hope did not like the idea of confining the girl too much. What he wanted most of all, however, were answers, and being nice about things was not getting him anywhere. Presently Lin had taken Sam to the station cafeteria. It was not a secure location and Hope still played with thoughts of the cell. If Jeremiah returned for her, he could only imagine the carnage the man would wreak before he got to the girl.

Having called the girl's parents, Hope knew he had a small window to talk to her before they took her away. Hope had advised them against such an action, for Jeremiah had said he would be back for her, and if he took her once more they would start the chase all over again.

Hope walked into the cafeteria and was pleased to see there was an officer with Lin. He trusted her, but he also knew if she spent too much time alone with the girl she would gain information she would not share. Lin had her own agenda, and Hope did not want this to all end without him having a clue what had happened.

He nodded to the officer, who departed as Hope sat beside Lin. She knew Hope's game but said nothing of it. They could not argue with Sam sitting in front of them. He could see Lin had bought her something to eat. It wasn't much, but then the officers had been complaining about their canteen for years and nothing had ever been done about it. The girl was demolishing her food as though she expected a famine, and Hope assessed her momentarily. She wasn't quite as afraid as she had been, although he could see by the tension in her body that she was wary.

"I called your parents," he said. "They won't be long."
"Did you catch Jeremiah?"
"No."
"He's too quick for you."
Hope had to admit she was right, but he said, "Did he hurt you?"

Sam's face clouded then and he realised it had been a bad question.

"I know he threatened you," Hope pressed, "but you're safe here."

"I'm not safe anywhere."

Hope frowned. A crash sounded behind him and he knew someone had dropped a tray. Sam all but bolted, and likely would have if her feet had not become entangled with the table legs. He could see now just how afraid she was, and wished he could protect her.

"It's all right," Hope said. "We can protect you. You couldn't be in a safer place than a police station."

"I was safe with Jeremiah."

It was the fear talking, and Sam's expression instantly changed as she realised she had said too much. It was, however, intriguing. Hope glanced to Lin, who was betraying nothing but clearly knew everything.

"Are you telling me," Hope asked slowly, "he was protecting you?"

Sam said nothing.

He tried to think about the situation, and saw he had been looking at the entire thing from the wrong angle. Langley and Stringer had robbed the shop and Jeremiah had interfered, saving Sam from being held as a hostage. From what the girl had said, Jeremiah could well have taken her from the scene to protect her. But protect her from what? Her captors were arrested. Why would Jeremiah take her along while he went out to beat up random ex-cons?

Another thought struck him and he looked across to Lin, wishing she would have kept her promise not to hold any more secrets. "Sam," he said, "did Jeremiah tell you who he was?"

Again she said nothing.

"He said if you talked," Hope continued, "you'd die. He meant there were people after you, didn't he? Who's after you, Sam? We can help."

"You don't need to help me," she said at last. "Jeremiah's helping me."

"I'm sure he's a swell guy, Sam, but Jeremiah's not a cop." He paused, closed his eyes as he realised what an idiot he was. "Jeremiah's a cop isn't he?"

Sam said nothing.

Lin said nothing.

"Jesus," Hope said, leaning back in his chair. "Sam, I'm going to get an officer to look after you until your parents get here." The girl offered no objections and Hope called someone over. Once they were gone he looked back to Lin, who sat tensely, staring out the window.

"With me," Hope said.

She followed in silence and they found an empty interrogation room. He had chosen it because it was out of earshot of anyone, but he could not escape the feeling of how apt the place was. She even sat on the opposite side of the table, as though she was being accused of something.

"Sorry," she said. "I know we said no more secrets, but that wasn't my secret to give."

"So Jeremiah's a secret cop now is he?"

"No. There's nothing secret about any cop, Jon. But my department doesn't like our names being put out there too much."

"Why not? What's so special about Operation WetFish that you don't want people to know about you?"

Lin started.

"What?" Hope asked with a frown. "Am I not supposed to know you work for WetFish? Your DCI's Edward Sanders; am I not supposed to know that either?"

"It's ... How do you know any of that?"

"I looked it up. When you transferred suddenly last year I looked up where you'd gone. Some care in the community scheme with a stupid name. What's so secret about a care in the community department? For that matter, what's so good about it that you left me for them?"

He knew he was angry, but he had been angry for a year. Since Lin had fallen back into his life he had been far too focused upon finding the kidnapped girl to consider much about Lin's life choices. But now the girl was safe, at least for the moment, and, while he had not meant to let his anger out, there were simply some things which could not be helped.

"They needed me," she said simply, having annoyingly relaxed slightly by this point.

"I needed you."

"I know. And I'm sorry."

Hope ran a hand through his hair, found himself walking towards one of the walls and turned around to walk back. "So this is what you people do then? Your idea of care in the community is some extreme form of witness protection programme?"

Lin's laugh was strangled. "Sorry," she said. "It's just that's so not what we do."

"Then what do you do?"

"We ... care for the community. Look, Jon, I'm sorry I didn't tell you about Jeremiah. Yes, he works with me. He's a decent guy, or at least I always thought he was. He's sweet and charming and will always do you a favour if you ask."

"God, you're sweet on him."

"I ... no."

But Hope could see something in her eyes as they turned from him. He had known her too long not to know what that look meant. "You're seeing him?"

"No."

"Just sleeping with him then?"

Lin straightened in her chair. "I don't see that's any of your business. Look, I was wrong about some of this, but so was my DCI. I like Jeremiah, he's a good guy to have your back."

"Because you really need people to watch your back with all that care in the community stuff."

Lin ignored him. "Jeremiah disappeared a couple of days ago. When the hit on the jewellery store went down and Jeremiah took the girl, my DCI panicked. He thought Jeremiah had abducted her to kill her or something. I couldn't see where he was coming from on that, but since you were my old DI he thought I should be the one to track him down. I couldn't understand why Sanders thought Jeremiah would have killed the girl, but it seems I was right all along. He's obviously stumbled onto something and is protecting the girl."

"*Was* protecting her. We have her now."

"But not for long. If Jeremiah wants her back, he'll just take her."

"I think I'm insulted."

"Don't be. I've seen Jeremiah do strange things. He's more powerful than you think."

"If he's uncovered something, he needs to share it with us. These people he's going around beating up. Who are they?"

"I don't know any more than you on that."

"But they're connected. They have to be. I get he's dragging Sam around with him because he thinks she's safer with him than anywhere else, but if he's a cop he needs to talk to us."

"Jeremiah's a great team player, Jon. When he wants to be."

"I have a few of them working for me." He sighed. "So what are we going to do about him? He's coming here, you reckon? Should we set a trap for him?"

"You still trust me?"

"I'll always trust you, Sue. At the moment what we need to do is talk with Jeremiah. You're my only chance of that happening. I trust you to do the right thing, and the right thing is to protect that girl the best way possible."

It put Lin in a quandary, but it was meant to. Hope was glad he at last understood some of what was going on, but he still had the horrible feeling as soon as she had what she wanted, Lin would flit out of his life once more, this time perhaps forever.

"Jeremiah would only have taken Sam for a reason," Lin said. "We need to figure out what he's thinking. What connects all the people he's been assaulting, and why would he stop at just beating them up?"

"Your man Jeremiah has a penchant for killing people then?"

"Now you're being ridiculous."

There was something about her tone he did not like. However, he had more important things to consider. "The obvious thing is that Stringer and Langley would have wanted to silence the girl for seeing them at the jewellers, but since we have both men in custody that makes no sense. What if they said something she wasn't supposed to hear? They could easily have connections to the other people Jeremiah went after. If there's some big boss at the head of all of this, maybe they said his name or something."

"Big boss?" Lin smiled. "Now who's talking TV?"

"Well what do you have?" He did not mean to snap, but the situation was infuriating.

"I think you're right."

"About the crime boss?"

"No. I think we have to talk to Jeremiah. Unfortunately he's not going to trust me now he thinks I've turned on him."

"He'll realise you're acting under orders from your DCI, surely."

"Jeremiah and DCI Sanders don't always see eye to eye."

"Have a few of those on my team as well." He checked his watch. "Sam's parents will be here any minute. If we want to get anything more from her we're going to have to move quickly."

"You know, of course, we're not allowed to interrogate a minor without her parents present."

"Who's interrogating? We're checking a victim of kidnapping is all right. That's what the police are for, right? Care in the community?"

He had intentionally said that to annoy Lin, yet she did not react at all. That had been the thing which had really got him this past year. Officers moved on all the time, especially the good ones, and Hope had always let them go with a smile and a celebratory knees-up. Lin had disappeared so quickly he had not even had the time to properly say goodbye. Being of an inquisitive mind, Hope had immediately done some digging and had eventually uncovered the name WetFish. It had not meant anything to him, and when he had discovered their remit he was only left more confused, slightly angry and feeling incredibly let down.

The pay, he had long ago decided, must have been colossal.

They headed out together to find Sam, although had not gone far before they happened upon the officer Hope had assigned to look after the girl.

"Where's Sam?" Hope asked.

"Sam?"

"The twelve-year-old girl I left in your care." Hope was already not liking where this was going.

The officer laughed. "I think I would have remembered that, sir."

Hope looked to Lin. "Another of your secrets?"

"Another of Jeremiah's," Lin said. "At least we know Sam's in safe hands."

"Do we?"

"Whatever Jeremiah wants, Jon, he's doing it to protect the girl. At least we've discovered that much."

"I'm not sure about anything any more, Sue. I guess this means I'm not going to get to talk this over with Jeremiah then."

"We'll find him. Maybe. If he lets us."

Somehow Hope did not find that especially encouraging.

"Sir," came a voice behind him, and Hope turned to find he was being introduced to a couple in their forties. Hope did not have to be a genius to realise who they were.

"Mr and Mrs Dickson," he said, trying not to sigh. "Won't you come this way?"

CHAPTER SIX

It had been difficult explaining to Mr and Mrs Dickson just where their daughter had gone, but DI Hope had told them the truth, or at least a certain aspect of it. He told them she was in the safe hands of one of his officers and that she had been taken into protective custody. It allowed him the opportunity to take the distraught parents into a room and ask them whether they could think of any reason a demented, exceptionally strong police officer would feel it necessary to take their daughter into protective custody. He did not, of course, phrase it in quite that fashion, but there was no way he would have been able to say it which would not cause them to panic and think him incompetent.

The impression the Dicksons made upon him was a simple one. They were ordinary middle-class people who dressed and spoke like ordinary middle-class people. Hope tried to reassure them as much as he could, but since he had himself no idea where Jeremiah had taken their daughter, or really even why, he could not offer them much in the way of comfort. It seemed they were having a spate of bad luck, for Mr Dickson told him of how they had been burgled only a few days earlier. Nothing of any real value had been taken, but their home had been ransacked and they were still trying to sort it all out. As such, their minds were already frazzled and having to deal with the possible kidnap of their daughter was pushing them over the edge.

It was when he passed them photographs of the various people Jeremiah had attacked that something interesting turned up.

"That's Bill Yale," said Mr Dickson.

"You know him?"

It was a stupid question. He'd just said the man's name: of course he knew him.

"Bill helped us with the money we got when my mother died."

"Helped you with ...? I don't follow."

"At the bank. Bill showed us which were the best savings accounts, that sort of thing."

Hope was beginning to get a headache from this case. Lin had gone off to report in to her DCI and he was beginning to wish he had insisted she stick around. Then something Mr Dickson had said suddenly sank in. "If you don't mind me asking," Hope said, "how much money did you get?"

"Mother wasn't well off, but she made some good investments in her time. Put a lot into property, which we sold off when she died. I'm an only child, you see, so all the money came to me."

"We're talking a lot aren't we?"

Dickson tried to sound modest about it, but failed miserably. "About half a million, why? What does any of this have to do with my daughter?"

At last things were beginning to make sense. He needed to get rid of these two and find Lin, so Hope gave them some answer he knew would not satisfy them before leaving them in the capable hands of the first person who happened to pass the room. He immediately went in search of Lin and found her outside in the afternoon air, just finishing up the call on her mobile.

"Reception's better out here," she told him. "I promise I wasn't trying to keep any more secrets."

But Hope did not at that moment care for any of that. "Bill Yale was part of a gang of hoods. They had an idea to kidnap Samantha Dickson so Yale asked his friend Stringer to nab her. Stringer roped in a buddy from his darts team, Langley, and together they hit the jewellers. Stringer wanted Langley to be caught and tell the police it was a heist, since that was all he knew, while Stringer made off with the girl. Once he got her back to Yale and the gang, they'd ransom her back to the Dicksons for half a million and the entire group would disappear to Spain or somewhere."

He stopped, a big grin on his face while he awaited Lin's reaction.

"Well?" he asked.

"You figure all that out by yourself?" she asked.

"Most of it while I was looking for you. You're not surprised by any of it though."

"I was. About five minutes ago. I was talking to my DCI. Apparently Jeremiah phoned the office and told him precisely what you've just told me."

Hope felt slightly deflated. "Well at least my detective's nose is still good for sniffing. What else did Jeremiah have to say for himself?"

"That he wants to be left alone."

"You think we should?"

"I think Jeremiah tends to know what he's doing. But I also think when people do stupid things like this they generally need more help than they expect."

"Did he say why he went around beating everyone up?"

"You tell me."

"Well he somehow found out about the kidnapping and got there before it could happen. He attacked Yale so all his accomplices would gather and discuss what they were going to do. He then went to deal with them and got them all in one go."

"Pretty much."

"So why come back for Sam? If we now have everyone either in custody or in the hospital, who's she in danger from now? Is he through assaulting people or is this just going to keep on escalating?"

"That's ... a good point." Lin frowned. "He clearly thinks there's someone else involved, someone higher than the goons we met at the gym."

Hope did not take it as a good sign that Lin was stumped.

"This is a nightmare," he said. "And here I thought WetFish was a reactive department."

"Oh, we can be proactive, boss. When we want to be."

"Have you tried phoning him?"

"He's either not carrying it or he's not picking up. He won't have time to assess my situation to work out whether I'm still against him. Not if he's concentrating on saving that girl."

"Which means we're just going to have to work out what he's trying to do. And just where he'll strike next."

It was not the way Hope liked to run his department, but he had a feeling he was lucky just to have learned as much as he had. He could not imagine what was so secretive about Lin's job, but he had things in his own department that he didn't want everyone to know about. Lin could keep her secrets, however. Hope had learned long ago there were things he simply did not need to know.

The rest of the day was spent without any progress at all. Hope had other cases to work on, and Lin offered to help where she could while they waited. Hope had feelers out, people actively looking for Jeremiah, although Lin assured him there was no way they would find him unless Jeremiah wanted to be found. They had been lucky enough to have met him at the gym, and that seemed to be the only stroke of luck Lin expected for them to have.

At ten o'clock, when Hope's shift was just about to end, Lin received a call on her mobile. From her face Hope could see it was important, and he assumed her DCI was giving her an earful about not having this wrapped up yet. He allowed her some distance to make the call privately, trying not to watch her from his desk, trying not to attempt to read her lips.

She was edgy when she approached him and he almost did not want to know what the call had been about.

"That was Jeremiah," she surprised him by saying. "He wants to meet."

"Why? He's realised you're not working against him?"

"I think he needs help."

"Of course he needs help. I just didn't see him as someone to admit it."

"He's given me a place he wants to meet."

Hope did not like the way this was going. "You're not meeting him alone, Sue. I don't care if he's your colleague, this crime is on my patch and I'm going to deal with it."

"That's pretty much what I told him. He wasn't happy about it, but agreed I could bring you along."

It was not quite the way Hope would have liked things phrased, but at least she had argued his case for him. "When does he want to meet?"

"Now."

"Then let's get on with it. I'm happy for you to take the lead on this one, but I want you to remember these collars are for my department. Whatever twisted game Jeremiah's playing, if there are crimes being committed here I'm dealing with them. Your Jeremiah will be lucky he doesn't get charged with kidnapping."

They headed out and Hope felt they were spending so much time in the car together Lin could well claim squatter's rights. Lin directed him towards a multi-storey car park. Hope knew at this time of night it would not be seeing too much activity, for in the main people used it for their weekly trips to the supermarkets. It was eerie in the dark, and as they travelled the spiralling levels he could see fewer and fewer cars. By the time they had reached the seventh level he could see but a scattering.

Hope parked away from any of them and the two officers emerged. There was a dankness to the air which made Hope shudder, and as he scanned the ceiling he could see the light-bulbs were placed too spaciously for his liking; plus most of them had blown. Shadows encroached upon them both and he wished he had brought a torch. He could only imagine this must have been what it was like for Langley when he had claimed to have been attacked by the shadow man.

"Your man Jeremiah picked a creepy location."

"I've been called worse," a male voice said.

Hope stumbled as he turned around. The tall figure of gentlemanly appearance stood barely a metre from him, wearing a long coat and leaning upon a cane. His face was stern, and while his lips were being tugged into a smile it was the eyes which denoted malevolence. They were old eyes: they had seen a lot of pain. Hope recalled the last time he had looked into those eyes and had almost let the man walk free. He did not understand it then and did not understand it now, but there was something about Jeremiah which wasn't normal.

"You wanted to meet," Hope said, "so here we are. Where's the girl?"

A face poked out from behind Jeremiah and Hope felt relief wash through him.

"What's going on?" Lin asked.

"That depends whose side you're on," Jeremiah said testily.

"All right, maybe I deserved that," Lin replied, "but I told Sanders you didn't go around killing girls."

"We know what's happened up to the point you took Sam back," Hope said. "You're in over your head now aren't you?"

Jeremiah glanced his way, looking over the two of them as though they were both his enemies, but each a necessity for his mission. "This goes a lot deeper than I expected," Jeremiah explained. "I thought it was simply a well-planned kidnap attempt. I thought Sam was just being targeted for ransom."

"You're saying she isn't?" Hope asked.

"Sam, tell Detective Inspector Hope about your grandmother."

"Grandma?" Sam still seemed afraid, but Hope noted she looked more at ease the closer she stayed to Jeremiah. He was starting to think it might not have been such a bad idea for Jeremiah to have done all he had, although was not about to admit that to him. "Grandma had a lot of friends. When she died, the friends went away."

"Went away?" Hope asked.

"Sam's grandmother," Jeremiah explained, "owned a lot of property."

"I know. We spoke to Sam's parents. The property was sold off for half a million."

"Do you know why she had so much property?"

"Because she was good at investing?"

Jeremiah's tight smile made Hope feel like a dog who had just leaped through a hoop of fire.

"They weren't empty," Jeremiah said. "She hired a man named Yale to deal with the financial side of things, to make it look like she was investing her money."

"They weren't empty?" Hope asked. "Who was living in them then?"

"No one. Lin, your old DI is dense."

Hope narrowed his eyes. He knew when he was being baited, and wished Jeremiah would just get on with telling him whatever it was he wanted to tell him.

"Sam's grandmother was running a series of brothels," Jeremiah explained. "She was never caught, never arrested. Two of her properties have been raided in the past, but her name was never linked to them. They needed her name entirely out of it because she was the actual owner."

"Who did?" Lin asked.

"I knew it," Hope said. "This is bigger than we thought isn't it? This is some crime cartel. When the old woman died, legal ownership of the properties went to her son, because she wouldn't have made a will leaving the houses to any of her criminal colleagues. If the will was ever pulled in as evidence against her she needed it to back up her cover story."

"Maybe not so dense after all," Jeremiah said.

"So she died," Hope said, "and the houses were sold, the money going to her son. What happened to the girls using the houses?"

"Moved around to other locations, it seems. Grandma Dickson wasn't the brains behind it all, not exclusively anyway. From what I can figure out, she didn't have anything to do with the day-to-day activities. She just owned the properties and raked in the money the cartel paid her."

"Right," said Hope. "So where's Sam fit into all this? If it wasn't kidnapping for ransom, what was it?"

"Oh, it was kidnap for ransom all right. But they didn't just want the money. They would have taken that, and then asked for more."

"But the Dicksons don't have any more."

"They do. They just don't know it. I have no idea why, but these people want Grandma's ashes."

Hope was certain he had heard that wrong. "You have to be kidding."

"These people are villains," Jeremiah said, "but they're not wacko. Whatever they want her ashes for, it has to be something important."

"You can't even get DNA from someone's ashes."

"Never said it made sense."

"Why not just burgle the house then?" Hope asked. "They could have stolen the ashes along with the TV and no one would have known what they were after."

"They tried that. They didn't find what they were looking for, so maybe the ashes weren't kept on the mantelpiece." He looked down to Sam. "You've been strong, girl. You want to go with the DI for now so I can get on with busting this thing wide open?"

"Hold on a moment," Hope said. "The only reason you called us was to give Sam back?"

"You don't want her back?"

"I don't want you running off on your own, kicking people around."

"I like being on my own, and I like kicking people around. It's relaxing."

"Lin, tell him."

Lin looked more than a little resigned, and Hope wondered how many other officers she had to work with who had this attitude. "He's right, Jeremiah. All you've managed to accomplish on your own is taking down the frontmen. The people you're after are wedged in tight and they're not going to give without a fight. You need backup."

"I need my colleagues trusting my judgement."

"I do trust your judgement, but you need to trust mine. I came to DI Hope because I wanted to help you, not because Sanders wanted me to bring you down. I trust you, Jeremiah: I always have done. But this thing is bigger than you, and if you get yourself killed who's going to look after Sam?"

She was good, Hope had to admit. She clearly knew this man better than anyone and he could see she was getting through to him. The one thing Jeremiah wanted out of all of this was Samantha to be safe, and for that Hope could not fault the man. There were so many other things for which to fault him, it seemed only fair to give him credit where he could.

"Fine," Jeremiah said, more than a little testily. "But Sam needs to be in a secure location. And I'm not leaving her with just any officer. If you two won't take her off my hands for a while, I'm going to have to take her back to Sanders."

"Good idea," Lin said. "Where shall we meet you?"

"Oh, we're not letting him out of our sight," said Hope. "Now that we have you here, I'm keeping you."

"And how do you plan on keeping me with you?" Jeremiah asked with a chuckle. His smile vanished when he heard the distinctive click of handcuffs. He raised his arm to find Hope had cuffed the two of them together. "Oh dear."

"Where you go," Hope told him, "I go."

"You really didn't want to do that."

"If you're so good, Jeremiah, break them."

"Keys."

Both men looked to Lin, who was holding out her hand.

"Car keys," she repeated, and Jeremiah fished a set from his pocket. Lin did not look pleased. "You two go have some boy time or something. I'll take Sam back to Sanders and meet you somewhere. Where are we meeting?"

Jeremiah's face had darkened and Hope oddly heard thunder rumbling outside. "There's an office block on Harlo Street. Floor twelve is owned by the people we're after. We'll meet you there."

"Floor twelve," Lin repeated as she took Sam gently by the arm. "Come on, honey. Let's get you somewhere safe."

Sam cast a final, desperate glance towards Jeremiah, whose face softened enough to offer her a reassuring nod. Hope did not like Jeremiah, did not like him at all in fact, but he cared for the welfare of the girl and that was really all that mattered.

"All right," Hope said, moving back to his car. "Get in."

"I'll drive."

"Like hell you will."

Jeremiah held up an arm. "You cuffed me on the wrong wrist then."

Hope realised he was right, but there was no way he was letting Jeremiah drive his car. "I'll manage."

"You'll manage. But I'll be bent over. My arm will be pretty much in your lap."

"I'll manage," Hope repeated sternly. But he wished he had thought through the cuffing a little better.

CHAPTER SEVEN

Lin was waiting for them when they pulled up before the office building. There was no sign of Sam, so Hope assumed Lin had somehow made it to her DCI and back already. He had no idea where Operation WetFish was based – it was something his research had never been able to uncover – but unless they were here, there and everywhere he could not see how she had been so speedy. Unless her DCI really didn't trust any of them and was himself hanging around in a car somewhere.

"What took you so long?" she asked.

"No need to be facetious, Sue."

"Who's being facetious?"

"Let's just get on with this shall we?" Jeremiah asked. "Since there's only the three of us we may as well go in together. We can't really bluff our way in, since no one should be entering this building this close to midnight. It's not a twenty-four hour building so there won't be any security here, which is a plus."

"I take it we're not using the lift," Hope said. "Twelve floors is going to be fun."

Jeremiah looked at him oddly. "You're complaining about twelve flights of stairs? How do you usually catch criminals? Ask them nicely to pop down the station so you can slap some cuffs on them?"

"Speaking of which," Lin said, "I'm glad you got over that silliness with the handcuffs. If we're going to get these guy we're going to need to work together."

"Handcuffs?" Hope asked, but Jeremiah cleared his throat loudly and started outlying his plan. Lin had meant something, but Hope could not fathom what she was talking about. Yet the more he thought about it, the more he was remembering something. Something to do with handcuffs. Whatever it was, he was sure it did not matter, and he focused on what Jeremiah was saying. Lin was right: they needed to work together on this.

Entering the building did not prove difficult. Jeremiah got the two of them to keep an eye out; then did something neither of them saw and the door was suddenly open. Hope was finding the man stranger and stranger the more time he spent with him, but if he could speed things along like that he wasn't going to complain. The door opened to a lobby, which was empty, and it was as they started on the stairs that Hope asked, "How much backup do we have coming?"

"Backup?" Jeremiah asked. "I thought you two were my backup?"

Hope stopped walking. "You mean it's just us? Are you nuts?"

Ahead of them, Lin had also stopped, and was frowning in horror at them both. "I thought you'd arranged reinforcements, Jon."

"I thought you had."

"We don't need any reinforcements," Jeremiah said in distaste. "Honestly, people, it's like you need help tying your shoes."

"Laces," Hope said. "You don't tie your shoes, you tie your laces."

"Is there a point to such pedantry?"

"Is there anyone who actually uses the word pedantry?"

Jeremiah shot him a look of stone.

"My point," Hope said, "is that even with the easiest tasks, one little mistake can trip you up. And when you're dealing with a floor filled with criminals one little mistake could get you killed."

"There is no way that's what you meant," Jeremiah said. "You've just made that up because you didn't think I'd call you a pedant."

"Sue, how do you put up with this guy?"

"At times like these, Jon, I'm wondering why I'm on this stairwell with either of you. Jeremiah," she said seriously, "what are we doing here? We can't take on these people by ourselves."

"I was quite happily going to take them on by myself before the two of you insisted on tagging along. I could have had the entire thing sown up by now and be handing Samantha back to her parents."

"Are you even armed?" Hope asked.

"No," Jeremiah said, holding up his hands, palms out. He clenched his fists. "But now I am."

Hope blinked, knowing one of them had gone insane in the last few minutes and not quite certain which it was. "Hold on, I'm calling this in."

Jeremiah seemed genuinely impatient. "Fine. The two of you stay here and wait for someone to bring you some mittens. I'll be upstairs beating in some heads."

"That's all this is to you, isn't it?" Hope asked. "An exercise in assaulting people. Because if you hit enough people someone sooner or later is going to tell you what you want to know."

"I am not a violent man, Detective Inspector Hope. But I'm not a pacifist either. The answers to all our problems lie twelve floors up. I'm going up. You can either come with me, or stay here and wait for your uniform and their loud sirens. Personally I would prefer that, but you do whatever you like."

"This is stupid," Hope said, but Jeremiah was already several steps ahead and turning the corner for the next flight of stairs. "Sue, tell him."

But Detective Lin looked resigned and he could tell she had suffered this often enough to know how it always played out. With a silent shrug she followed him up the stairs.

Knowing he could not abandon either of them, Hope called in his position, said he needed immediate backup, and continued upwards.

It did not take long to walk twelve flights of stairs. Hope was probably not as fit as he believed, for he was winded and his legs were aching with the effort. He knew it would pass in a couple of minutes and could see Lin was suffering similarly. Annoyingly, Jeremiah did not appear to have even noticed he wasn't standing on an escalator. The three of them had stopped at a wooden door sealed by an electronic reader. None of them had a card and, despite all his bizarre wizardry, he could not believe even Jeremiah could turn his fingers into magic security passes.

"Keep an eye on the stairs," Jeremiah said.

"No."

"Beg pardon?"

"I want to see what you do," Hope said. "You got us through the front door of the building, and I want to see what you did. Maybe I can pick up a thing or two from the mighty Lone Ranger."

"Lin, tell him."

Lin held up her hands. "I'm staying out of this. God didn't give me the right equipment to pee highest up the wall, so you two go for it."

It was not quite what Hope had wanted from her, but at least she hadn't immediately sided with her colleague.

Jeremiah looked more annoyed than angry, and Hope could tell he was never a man who liked to share anything. "Fine," he said testily. "Then we go the silly way."

Hope was about to ask what he meant when Jeremiah surprised him by knocking on the door.

"Pizza!"

Hope felt his stomach drop. "You have to be kidding me."

Shouts came from the other side of the door and Jeremiah pushed his two colleagues back into the stairwell. Neither offered any complaint and raced to the thirteenth floor. Hope took his eyes from Jeremiah for a single moment, and when he looked again the man simply was no longer there. He had to have gone down to the eleventh level, it was the only thing which made sense, yet Hope knew at once the man had gained what he wanted. Jeremiah had intended to fight this fight alone, and now it seemed no one could do anything to stop him.

"That man of yours," Hope hissed aside to Lin as the two of them crouched by the railing, "is going to be the death of us."

"He's not my man," she replied a little more savagely than she needed to.

The door opened then and someone poked his face out. He looked confused, as though he had expected either the police or a pizza guy. Opening the door fully, he stepped out and peered first down and then up the stairs, but could see no one. Hope knew Jeremiah was about to strike and let the man have his moment. He wanted to see what Jeremiah could do and now was a good time to ...

Something dropped from the ceiling and the hood collapsed with a mild shriek. Hope jumped, for even he had not expected for Jeremiah to have been pressed to the ceiling. Why the hood had not noticed him there was strange, but Hope had learned long ago not to question bizarre things and simply to accept them and move on. The facts of the matter were that Jeremiah had engaged the enemy and needed help.

With the grace of a panther, Jeremiah sprang through the door and roared a primal scream which chilled Hope to his marrow. On his way through, he also kicked the door closed.

"That ..." Hope and Lin raced back to the door, but there was nothing they could do to budge it. Hope pounded upon the barrier. He could hear shouts on the other side, screams in fact, and knew

Jeremiah was doing what Jeremiah did best. "Your friend has a lot of trust issues, Sue."

"This guy's out," Lin said, setting the captured hood to one side. "Jon, we need to get through that door."

"Then we're back to where we were before."

"Maybe not." Lin held up a pass and Hope realised she had been doing more than just checking the pulse of the downed goon. She pressed the key to the lock and Hope pushed the door, wishing he had some kind of weapon.

The door opened to a scene of chaos. The entire floor was set out like an office, although the desks did not appear to have much use and none of them were personalised with photographs or mugs. It was a front, Hope knew. The entire floor was rented by bad people who met here to discuss bad things. There were several bodies upon the floor before him, and he could not see how Jeremiah had managed to plough so easily through the squad of goons who had congregated at the door.

About thirty metres away Hope could see several figures being tossed around. Jeremiah was in the middle of them, fangs bared, his eyes feral. Hope watched from a distance, a part of him unwilling to wade into that fight without reason. Two men came at Jeremiah, from different directions. He grabbed the first by the collar and tossed him even as he raked the fingernails of his other hand across the face of the man at his back. Dropping into a crouch, Jeremiah momentarily disappeared from Hope's sight, and as he came up, two further men went flying. Hope saw someone pull a gun and went to shout a warning, but Jeremiah's hand found a desk and tugged upwards, tearing the heavy piece of furniture from where it was bolted to the floor, the entire thing colliding with the gunman and crushing him.

Hope could see why Jeremiah had not wanted any backup.

"I'm beginning to wonder who we should help," he said.

"How's that?" Lin had come in with him, but was not focusing on Jeremiah. He could see that instead she was disarming the downed men, dropping all the knives and firearms into an unused bin.

"Jeremiah," Hope said.

"You've found him?"

Hope looked back across the room, but Jeremiah was no longer there. He could hear noise of further fighting somewhere in the office and could imagine Jeremiah was having a jolly time.

"Don't worry about it," Hope said. "Any of these guys awake? I wouldn't mind talking to one of them."

"Wishful thinking. I'm heading out after Jeremiah."

Hope stopped her with a look. "You really think he needs any help?"

"What are you talking about? That's why we came with him."

"Look around you, Sue. The man's a walking arsenal. An unarmed walking arsenal."

"I ... What?"

"That man. He doesn't need any help with anything. Didn't you just see him? Didn't you see him at the gym?"

"You mean because he can fight?"

"Have you ever looked into the man's eyes, Sue? Have you ever stared deeply into his eyes to look for the real man inside?"

She looked away, a little colour rising to her cheeks. He realised it was probably a tad insensitive. He also realised something else. Jeremiah could do many things better than ordinary people, but perhaps his greatest ability was that of deflecting attention. Because Hope remembered the handcuffs now: he remembered handcuffing himself to Jeremiah earlier. But he didn't recall removing them.

Whatever else Jeremiah could do, he was a master of sleight of hand and hypnotism. He was a street illusionist on the payroll of the police. But ultimately it did not matter who he was or what he could do. So long as he was working for them his strange abilities could only benefit the force.

It was just upsetting to see someone as good as Sue Lin fallen victim to a man's deceit.

"Come on then," he said. "Let's get after him."

They ran together down the corridor, stumbling over the bodies Jeremiah had left in his wake. Blood spattered the walls, weapons were clattered all across the floor, and Hope could see several limbs turned in bad directions. But he could not see that any of the men was necessarily dead, and that was a good thing.

There was little noise by the time they found Jeremiah. In fact, the only sounds were from a frantic, whimpering female voice. They had come to a seating area beside a water cooler and a sink. Here they found Jeremiah, several more bodies, and a woman sitting in a chair and looking distraught.

Hope recognised her instantly.

"Mrs Dickson?"

"Thank you, thank you," she said, throwing herself at Hope when she saw him. Jeremiah stood off to one side, out of reach. "They grabbed me an hour ago. Kept saying they wanted something from me. They wanted something."

"Did you tell them where they were?"

"Where what were?"

"Your mother-in-law's ashes."

"My ... What?"

"That's what they're after. God knows why."

"Then it's a good job," Jeremiah said, "one of us used to be on speaking terms with God. Sam knew where the ashes were being kept. She was the one who hid them, you see."

"What?" Hope asked. "Sam hid them?"

"That's why no one could just ask Mr Dickson where they were, because he didn't know. It's why I kept Sam with me the whole time. It's also why I couldn't take being handcuffed to you, Hope." He smiled and Hope could see he knew Hope had remembered about the cuffs. "I needed to take a detour before coming here, you see. Sorry for keeping you, Lin, but I had to go fetch the ashes."

"*You* have them?" Hope almost accused.

"No. I gave them back to Mr Dickson."

"He has them back?" Mrs Dickson asked.

"Mmm. But no one wants the ashes, so it doesn't put him in any danger or anything."

"Hold on a moment," Hope said. "I thought this was all about the ashes."

"Oh, no," Jeremiah said with the air of an innocent child. "It was all about this." He held up a floppy disc. "It was hidden in Grandma's ashes. The idea was that no one would open the lid, so the disc could be collected later. On the disc, of course, is all the records Grandma kept as insurance. And whoever owns this disc holds all the information necessary for starting up the business again."

"I don't follow," Hope said. "Why put it in her ashes? I get that no one would root around inside, but surely it would be difficult for anyone to get to them without raising suspicion."

"Oh, there are a few people who could get to them easily," Jeremiah said, holding the disc between two fingers and pointing it accusingly. "Isn't that right, Mrs Dickson?"

Mrs Dickson opened her mouth, closed it, looked around in fear. "What's he talking about?"

"You can drop the act," Jeremiah said. "I've read what's on the disc."

"That stupid girl," Mrs Dickson spat. "Why couldn't she have just done what she was told?"

Hope was at last following some of this. "So Grandma asked you to carry on the family business. But you didn't count on your daughter's morality. What a wonderful family we have here."

"Where's Sam now?"

"Out of your reach," Hope said. "How could you hunt your own daughter?"

"I wouldn't have hurt her. I just needed her to tell me what she'd done with the disc."

Hope realised he had removed Sam from Jeremiah at the gym, only to almost deliver her straight into the hands of her mother. If Jeremiah had not returned to break her out, Hope could have ruined everything.

He caught Jeremiah looking at him and once more knew the strange man was reading his mind. He was man enough not to say anything out loud, however, and for that Hope had to respect him.

The sounds of a mob bursting into the office echoed eerily down the empty corridor and Hope knew uniform had arrived. He maintained his gaze with Jeremiah for several moments before nodding and going to deal with his own people. There were a lot of arrests to be made here today, but Hope was only confident of making a handful of them stick. Still, he was glad Lin had walked back into his department at last. Without her and WetFish he had no doubt this would have ended badly for the only person in this who mattered at all. The frightened girl buying some earrings for the mother she loved so much.

CHAPTER EIGHT

It was all over. Arrests had been made, Samantha Dickson was in temporary care, pending an enquiry, and Mr Dickson had been told the truth about his wife and his mother. It had been an especially terrible day for him, and he would now be faced with the truly awful task of trying to convince the world he really was dense enough not to have noticed what was going on around him. Detective Inspector Hope knew, however, that this was none of his business. His role had ended, and now it was all in the hands of people trained to deal in the softly-softly approach.

Care in the community.

He may not have agreed with Lin's decision to join such a department, but at least he had seen something of what she did. He may not have understood it any better now than he had before all of this madness happened, but he had caught a glimpse into her new life. And, in all honesty, it scared him.

He walked her to her car and knew he would not likely see her again for another year, perhaps never would again. Sue Lin had always been something of a mystery, even when she had worked beneath him, but she was a good woman, and that was all that mattered.

"So this is it," Hope said as he opened the car door for her. "You're walking out of my life all over again."

"Don't be silly. This time I'm driving."

He knew it was an attempt to lighten the mood, but they both knew this was the end. "Somehow, Sue, I'm thinking there's more to Operation WetFish than just making cups of tea and handing out tissues to bereaved relatives."

"Oh, I don't know. Jeremiah can work wonders with a teabag."

"Where is he anyway? Where'd he disappear to?"

"He's probably gone for some sleep, Jon. Or maybe he's still on a high and has gone to find out his next assignment."

"But this wasn't his assignment, was it? I mean, you'd tell me if it was, right? You said your DCI sent you after him because he thought Jeremiah was going to kill Sam. Why would your DCI think that?"

"Trust issues?"

It was more than that, but Hope knew he would not get anywhere through prying. He felt he should be overjoyed with what little he had gleaned from all of this, although it was the nature of detectives to want to push to find out everything. "And what is he?"

"What is he?" Lin asked. "I don't know what you mean."

"Yes you do. He's been trained to do all manner of weird things. Is that what your DCI does? He trains you all to be superhuman soldiers?"

Lin tried to laugh, but the sound came out strangled. "We're not soldiers, Jon. We're still police."

"Sounds like your DCI's waging a war on crime."

"Isn't that what we're supposed to do?"

"No. We're supposed to protect the civilians, defend people's rights and solve crimes." He could see his words were getting through to her, just as he could see she wasn't prepared to accept them.

"How many others are there at your department like Jeremiah? How many others can beat up a dozen men and not take a scratch? How many others know street magic?"

For a moment it looked as though Lin was going to leap into her car, slam the door and drive off without having to face answering that question. Then she looked him directly in the eyes and said, "Since joining WetFish I've seen a lot of horror, Jon. Things which don't give you nightmares only because they don't let you sleep at night. It used to amaze me how low humanity can go, Jon. When I used to work with you, I would investigate the crimes, piece together the train of events leading up to people even wanting to commit such atrocities. But with WetFish ... I don't know."

"Is the type of criminal you deal with so much worse?"

"It's not the type of criminal, Jon. It's the people hunting them. We're not human any more, none of us. Jeremiah's a sociopath who sometimes lapses enough for him to save girls like Sam Dickson. Sanders is so driven, so obsessed, that he'd be willing to sacrifice the world just to save his city. I just ... I think I'm headed down that route."

"Then come back. Come back to me, to your old job. Before you turn into a monster."

She laughed at this, although it was a sickly noise: the most beautiful sound soured by life. "It's too late for any of us, Jon. We're circling the drain trying to take as much filth with us as we can." She raised a hand, cupped his cheek and slowly she shook her head. "You're a good man, Jon Hope. Don't let the job change you. Work hard, retire, have a good life."

She removed the hand and got into her car, taking care to buckle her seat-belt. Hope used the delay to try to think of what he should say, what he *could* say. But nothing he could think of sounded less than trite.

"The door's always open," he told her. "If you want to come back, I'm a phone call away."

"And the master of cliché, I see."

"I'm serious, Sue. You want to leave this WetFish behind, you call me. I don't care how deep you think you've gone, you call me. And I'll dig you out."

She looked at him for several long, silent moments, then smiled a half-smile of self-defeat and closed the door. She drove off, out of his life, and Detective Inspector Hope knew he would never see her again. He had lost her to Operation WetFish. He had lost her to the monsters.

And he wasn't ever getting her back.

Printed in Great Britain
by Amazon